GIVER OF LIGHT

Kindred Book Four

NICOLA CLAIRE

Copyright © 2012, Nicola Claire
All Rights Reserved

The stunning artwork for the paperback covers in this series was created by Tithi Luadthong.

This book is a work of fiction. The names, characters, places and incidents are products of the writer's imagination or have been used fictitiously and are not to be construed as real. Any resemblance to persons, living or dead, actual events, locales or organisations is entirely coincidental.

All rights are reserved. No part of this book may be used or reproduced in any manner whatsoever without written permission from the author.

ISBN-13: 978-1482537109

ISBN-10: 1482537109

❦ Created with Vellum

ABOUT THE AUTHOR

Nicola Claire lives in beautiful Taupo, New Zealand with her husband and two young boys.

A bit of a romance junkie, she can be known to devour as many as half a dozen books a week if she drinks too much coffee. But her real passion is writing sexy, romantic suspense stories with strong female leads and alpha male protagonists who know how to love them.

So far, she's written well over 50 books. She might have caught the writing bug; here's hoping there's no cure!

For more information:
www.nicolaclairebooks.com
nicola@nicolaclairebooks.com

ALSO BY NICOLA CLAIRE

Kindred Series

Kindred

Blood Life Seeker

Forbidden Drink

Giver of Light

Dancing Dragon

Shadow's Light

Entwined With The Dark

Kiss Of The Dragon

Dreaming Of A Blood Red Christmas (Novella)

Mixed Blessing Mystery Series

Mixed Blessing

Dark Shadow

Rogue Vampire (Coming Soon)

Sweet Seduction Series

Sweet Seduction Sacrifice

Sweet Seduction Serenade

Sweet Seduction Shadow

Sweet Seduction Surrender

Sweet Seduction Shield

Sweet Seduction Sabotage
Sweet Seduction Stripped
Sweet Seduction Secrets
Sweet Seduction Sayonara

Elemental Awakening Series

The Tempting Touch Of Fire
The Soothing Scent Of Earth
The Chilling Change Of Air
The Tantalising Taste Of Water
The Eternal Edge Of Aether (Novella)

H.E.A.T. Series

A Flare Of Heat
A Touch Of Heat
A Twist Of Heat (Novella)
A Lick Of Heat

Citizen Saga

Elite
Cardinal
Citizen
Masked (Novella)
Wiped

Scarlet Suffragette Series

Fearless

Breathless

Heartless

Blood Enchanted Series

Blood Enchanted

Blood Entwined

Blood Enthralled

44 South Series

Southern Sunset

Southern Storm

Southern Strike (Coming Soon)

Lost Time Series

Losing Time

Making Time

Stitching Time (Coming Soon)

The Sector Fleet

Accelerating Universe

Apparent Brightness

Right Ascension

Zenith Point

The Summer O'Dare Mysteries

Chasing Summer

Sizzling Summer (Coming Soon)

For: Tony, Alex & Christian
My Light

DEFINITIONS

Accord – A blood binding agreement, often between two parties of equal power; cannot be broken.

Alliance – A word of honour agreement; has varying degrees of binding, some alliances cannot be broken.

Blood Bond – A binding connection between master and servant, requiring the exchange of blood to seal. It can only be broken by someone more powerful than the master who created it. A blood bond establishes a close relationship between the blood bonded. The master provides safety and protection, the servant offers obedience and loyalty.

Bond – The connection between joined kindred Nosferatu and Nosferatin; reflects the emotional and psychological relationship. Enables both parties to find each other over distance; to perform whatever is required to get to that person, overcoming any obstacle; to direct thoughts to each other; to feed off the life force of each other. It is always an equal exchange.

Command – A directive given by a Master vampire to one of his line. It requires *Sanguis Vitam* in order to enforce obedience. It cannot be ignored.

Dream Walk – A Nosferatin power, enabling the Nosferatin to appear in a different location. The Dream Walker is invisible, cannot be sensed or smelled, and only heard if they talk when in this realm. They can, however, interact and be harmed. The only exception to a Dream Walker's invisibility is another Nosferatin. Two Dream Walks in a 24 hour period results in prolonged unconsciousness once the Dream Walker returns to their body. A very rare power.

Final death – The true death of a Nosferatu. There can be no survival from the final death.

Glaze – The ability to influence another. It requires direct eye contact and *Sanguis Vitam* to insert the influence. Usually a Nosferatu skill, allowing a vampire to influence a human.

Herald – The Nosferatin who recognises the Prophecy. It is the Herald's responsibility to acknowledge the *Sanguis Vitam Cupitor* and thereby initiate the Prophecy.

Hapū – (Maori) Tribe; sub-tribe – e.g. the Westside Hapū of Taniwha is the local Auckland sub-tribe of New Zealand Taniwha.

Iunctio – (Latin). The Nosferatu connection and governing power. All vampires are connected to one another via this supernatural information exchange highway; enabling sharing of rules, locations of safe havens and hot spots to avoid. It is powered by both Nosferatu and Nosferatin *Sanguis Vitam*, but is operated by the Nosferatu in Paris. There are twelve members of the *Iunctio* council, headed by the Champion. The *Iunctio* is tasked with policing all supernaturals throughout the world.

Joining – The marriage of a kindred Nosferatu with a kindred Nosferatin. Upon joining the Nosferatu will double their *Sanguis Vitam* and the Nosferatin will come into their powers, but for the Nosferatin, their powers will only manifest after reaching maturity; the age of 25. The joining will also make the Nosferatin immortal. A symbiotic relationship, should one member of the joining die, the other will too. Without a joining, the Nosferatin would die one month past their 25th birthday. The joining also increases the power of the *Iunctio* and Nosferatu as a whole.

Kaitiaki – (Maori) New Zealand Shape Shifter (Taniwha) name for Nosferatin. Meaning protective guardian of people and places.

Kindred – A Nosferatu or Nosferatin sacred match, a suitable partner for a joining. To be a kindred there must exist a connection between the Nosferatu and Nosferatin; only those suitably compatible will be kindred to the other.

Line – The family of a Master Vampire, all members of which have been turned by the Master, or accepted via blood bond into the fold.

Lux Lucis Tribuo – (Latin) The Giver of Light. The third part of the Prophecy. The *Lux Lucis Tribuo* is charged with balancing out the Dark in Dark vampires, with their Light.

Master – A Nosferatu with the highest level of *Sanguis Vitam*. There are five levels of Master, from level five – the lowest on the *Sanguis Vitam* scale, to level one – the highest on the *Sanguis Vitam* scale. Only level one Masters can head a line of their own. Some Nosferatu may never become Masters.

Master of the City – A level one Master in control of a territory; a city.

Norm – A human unaware of the supernaturals who walk the Earth. They also do not have any supernatural abilities themselves.

Nosferatin – (*Nosferat-een*) - A vampire hunter by birth. Nosferatin were once of the same ilk as Nosferatu, descendants from the same ancestors, or God. The Nosferatin broke off and turned towards the Light. Their sole purpose is to bring the Nosferatu back from the Dark, this can include dispatching them, bringing them the final death, when they cannot be saved. They are now a mix of human and Nosferatin genetics.

Nosferatu – A vampire. The Nosferatu turned towards the Dark, when their kin, the Nosferatin turned towards the Light. They require blood to survive and can be harmed by UV exposure and silver. They do not need to breathe or have a heartbeat. They are considered the undead.

Prohibitum Bibere – (Latin) The Forbidden Drink. The second part of the Prophecy. The *Prohibitum Bibere* is a siren to the Dark vampires throughout the world, calling their Darkness towards the Light.

Pull – The Nosferatin sense of evil. Guides a hunter to a Dark vampire; sometimes, but not always a rogue, who is about to feed off an innocent.

Rākaunui – (Maori) Full Moon.

Rogue – A vampire no longer controlled by a master, full of evil and Darkness, feeding indiscriminately and uncontrolled.

Sanguis Vitam – (Latin) The Blood Life or life force of a Nosferatu. It represents the power they possess. There are varying degrees of *Sanguis Vitam*.

Sanguis Vitam Cupitor – (Latin) The Blood Life Seeker. The first part of the Prophecy. The *Sanguis Vitam Cupitor* can sense and find all Dark vampires throughout the world.

Sigillum – (Latin) A permanent mark of possession.

Taniwha – (Maori) New Zealand Shape Shifter. Dangerous, predatory beings. The Taniwha have an alliance with the Nosferatins.

Turned – The action of changing a human into a vampire.

Vampyre – Old term for vampire; used rarely in modern language.

*The Light will capture the Dark
and hold it dear.*
The Prophecy

1
IT'S ALL IN THE BLOOD

It was the drop of liquid on my eyelid that woke me. The warm wet pearl slowly working its way across my closed lid and out past the corner of my eye, then down my cheek, leaving a wet trail in its wake. I brushed it away without opening my eyes, I was tired, so tired and nowhere near ready to face the day.

The first drop was followed by a second. Same spot, same routine. Across my eyelid, out past the corner of my eye and then slowly, following the track of the previous drop, down my cheek. This time making it as far as my neck before I reached for it. As soon as it was wiped away another followed.

If this was Chinese water torture, it was doing a damn fine job. I gritted my teeth, but still didn't open my eyes. Choosing instead to pound my pillow into submission and roll over on to my side.

The next drop landed in my ear.

Bloody hell, can't a girl get some sleep around here? I swiped at the drop and then felt another and another and another, until I realised it must be raining in my bedroom. I opened my eyes in a rush, expecting to see the window open and a storm in full swing outside, but what met my gaze was far worse and deeply coloured.

Red.

Red everywhere.

I was drowning in red. Red drops so thick and sluggish I could watch them fall from the ceiling in slow motion. If I'd had the inclination, I could have rolled out of the way, missed their trajectory altogether, but I couldn't move, I couldn't breathe. I knew what this red liquid was. I could smell the metallic scent of it. It was as familiar to me as my own skin. My life was perpetually surrounded in, coated in, red liquid.

And now I felt the mattress shift, floating like a boat. I turned my head to the side and looked over my shoulder. Floating. Floating in a sea of red. I scrambled to the centre of the mattress, but it wouldn't help. I knew this as though I had been here before. First the red would start to seep into the mattress from the edges, closer and closer, reaching for me across the white expanse like spidery fingers, colouring everything in its path red.

And it did. Slow at first, I watched it inch its way closer and then all of a sudden, as though it had reached a critical mass, it accelerated and rushed towards me, wetting my knees and hands, making the mattress heavy, making it dip beneath the waves of red liquid as it washed against the side of my raft, the only thing between me and drowning in a sea of red.

I looked down at my nightdress, which once was white and now was a deep bright red, and watched as the red liquid lapped up my thighs, across my waist and then higher and higher. Quickly now, the mattress long gone beneath me to the deepest depths of the red, now just my legs kicking, trying to keep myself afloat, but feeling a pull downward that I knew I could not fight.

It was hard to move through the thick sludge that surrounded me, threatened to engulf me. I knew what this red was, but I didn't wanted to voice it. To say it, was to acknowledge this was real and to do that was to let it cover me completely, drown me forever, wash away all thought of clean and safe, replace it with death and destruction and the finality of *the end*.

As soon as I thought that it came to me unbidden. What this red liquid, splashing in my mouth, running down my throat, covering my head, filling my eyes, reeking in my nose and consuming my body, was.

Blood.

Nero's blood. There had been so much blood, so much. There was nothing I could do to stop the flow of blood. Just like now, it was going to win, to drown me. It took Nero, now it would take me too. There was no fighting the blood. My life was full of blood. Nero's death. Vampires' lives. It all needed blood to happen, blood to make the world go around. I lived in blood and it was now coming to finish me too.

I hated blood, but I could not escape it. I could not escape this.

I panicked and I thrashed. If I had just relaxed and let my body float it might have been OK. I think I could have floated in this thick sludgy blood. I think I could have been light enough, but I couldn't relax. I couldn't think straight. I wanted out of this nightmare, out of the blood. I wanted to be clean and fresh and covered in sea salt breezes.

As I struggled and flailed and thrashed around in the liquid, I smelt that sea salt breeze, so fresh and clean. I concentrated on it as hard as I could manage. If only I could reach the beach, pull myself up on the sand, let the fresh breeze wash away the metallic scent, all would be OK.

I reached out to the beautiful fresh sea breeze and the red world around me shattered. I took a crushingly deep breath in, realised my throat was raw and opened my eyes.

"*Ma douce, ma douce.* It is all right. I am here. It is merely a dream."

Michel's voice so strained, so tight, his warm strong arms wrapped around me, rocking me. A hand in my hair stroking me, his lips against my cheek, his breath hot, his body warm.

Thank God. It was just a nightmare. This was real. This was my life.

I let a shuddering breath out and collapsed back against his body.

Just a nightmare. But, I knew Nero was dead. Vampires would always need blood. And I was neck deep in the red stuff, in or out of my dreamscapes.

I sighed. "Sorry, I woke you."

"It is nothing." He paused. "How are you?"

Tired. Exhausted. Fed up with blood.

"You didn't drown this time. That is good, *non?*"

The fact that French had seeped into Michel's vocabulary said more than the words actually did. He was exhausted too. Worried even, I bet. This was about the sixteenth or seventeenth nightmare like this in the past three weeks. Each time he had woken me, reached me somehow through all that red, saved me. But I knew he felt as helpless as I did. These nightmares weren't going away and he had no way of controlling them. Just like me. And as he can read my mind when he wishes, a recent development which I am hoping will not be permanent, he often experiences the nightmares right along with me.

We were both tired.

He pulled me back down on the bed. I stiffened as my back came in contact with the mattress, expecting to find it wet, but it was just warm and dry and solid. I wasn't floating anymore. I was wrapped up in my kindred vampire's arms. I was OK.

Yeah, right.

"Have I told you about my time in Wallachia?"

I shook my head, unsure if my voice and throat had fully recovered yet. No doubt I had been screaming. Michel never said, but I always felt like my throat was raw after one of these dreams, like I'd been yelling at a rock concert, or screaming in terror.

He settled back against the pillows, making himself comfortable. This had become a routine for us. First the nightmare, then Michel distracting me with memories of his past. I couldn't complain. One, it worked, my heart rate returning to normal after only a few minutes of listening to his soft, steady voice re-tell stories of a life lived so long ago. And two, I always wanted to know more about Michel. I was fascinated by him. How could I not be?

"I decided it was time to educate myself in my new found life. It was not too long after I had been turned by Amicus and had accomplished my revenge on those who had killed my family and tried to kill me. There was a strong seat of the *Iunctio* in Wallachia. Not so much today, too many stories of Romanian vampyre princes have made that part of Europe undesirable to my kind. But, at the time, it was an outpost for Paris, where the *Iunctio*, as you know, has been based for millennia.

"Wallachia was then ruled by an extremely powerful and somewhat surprisingly well educated vampyre called Neagoe Basarab, part of the powerful Craiovesti family. He was a peaceful ruler, which in itself was unusual for the time and his race. Vampyres were not known for there cultural influences at the time, but Neagoe was different. Perhaps that is why I was attracted to his principality. Word had reached Paris that there was much to be enjoyed at the Craiovesti court.

"Neagoe was a lover of the Renaissance aspect of art and culture and had spent the first few decades of his reign enlightening those around him. I spent sixty years as a member of his court. It was perhaps the most influential of all the experiences of my life for the next few centuries. He was a mastermind politician, enabling his countrymen to expand their arts and crafts in order to pay their exorbitant tribute to the Ottoman Empire and also giving them employment and a sense of pride.

"He was also a consummate diplomat. He not only kept close ties with Wallachia's neighbour, the then powerful Hungary, but re-established connections with the Republic of Venice and the Papacy. He revolutionised religion in the area and made generous donations to various Orthodox Monasteries. He built fine buildings, emboldened his people and wrote works of art on philosophy, ethics, morals and diplomacy."

Michel kissed my forehead as he took a break from his memories. Then murmured against my skin. "I was fortunate to have called him a friend. He has influenced my life and I will always remember him, will always honour that friendship. Much of what I do today is as a result of his teachings. He was a fine vampyre. A fine man."

His hand brushed down my cheek, where only moments before I had felt the warm wet track of blood.

"He died the final death not five weeks after I moved on from his court. I have asked myself if things would have been different if I had remained behind, if I had been there when the Ottomans invaded. Perhaps. I can not say. But, I have learned to not dwell on what would have or could have been. He is dead, he would have died then or at another time, but I will not let his death detract from what he gave me."

He pulled me closer, lifting my body up on top of his. It was but a mere movement for him, as though I was a weightless piece of fabric and he simply picked me up and draped me over his body like a blanket. His hands reached up and cupped my face. His eyes, that beautiful rich blue with the odd indigo and violet swirls deep within, held my gaze.

"Do not forget what Nero has given you, honour his memory, cherish his lessons, but" - he kissed my forehead, my eyelids, each cheek - "do not let his death invade your soul. We each have our time on this earth and no one can alter that for us. Now, you must live yours, by honouring his memory, not his death."

He continued to stare at me for a moment, then slowly brushed his lips against mine. So soft and warm and beautiful. I craved his kisses, I longed for them. Sometimes he would tease me. He knew how much I adored his touch. Sometimes he would hover over my mouth, wait for me to bridge the gap, deny me that final perfect touch of his warm, soft lips, only to make me beg. It was a game for him. A way of taking back some of the control he had lost to either me or the claiming that we were still battling. His vampire inside of him had decided it needed to stake a claim on me, to let everybody and their dog know I was his. Michel found the claiming a force he could not control. His body responded to situations without the cool, methodical and thoughtful approach he normally has. It was because of that loss of control that he teased.

But not now. No teasing. He simply pulled me close, brushed his lips one more time across my face, my neck and then repositioned me in the crook of his arm. Cradling me, like you would a baby. Lovingly, carefully, innocently. It never failed to surprise me how lucky I was to have found this man. Granted, he had found me, but I still thanked my lucky stars he had. Right now, so full of memories of Nero's death, so full of my disgust for blood, I would not welcome an intimate coupling. I loved him and part of me always wanted him, but what I needed now, more than sex, more than making love, was to be held. To be cherished and not to be pushed.

Despite the claiming, despite the fact that he had established morning routines that involved saying *hello* to his marks when we woke, which never led to more. He was able to restrain himself, for me. He gave me comfort and love with the thought of nothing in return. He defied the claiming and his natural vampire instincts and gave me what I needed.

I smiled to myself, an amazing feat in itself considering the nightmare that had just woken us. But I couldn't help it. I had been so numb lately and I knew I was nowhere near out of those woods yet, but I took what little joys I could find to help me through. Michel helped me through. I honestly didn't know how I could face the hurdle of accepting Nero's death without Michel.

Even the routines we had established, him waking me, talking to me, distracting me. Even the way he was drawn to my marks each morning. They all held me firmly to this Earth, prevented me from floating away. It dawned on me that we had quite a few routines now. That we knew each other so well, that we had spent so much time together, that we had formed regular patterns in our life. He could still surprise me, but that familiarity was a blessing. When so much of my world was out of control, was one unexpected shock and then another and then another, that sense of belonging I had with Michel was a god send.

My life had changed when I moved from my parents' sleepy farm to Auckland two years ago, but it wasn't until just before I turned 25, about three months ago that it really took on the bizarre. I found out I was descended from a race similar, if not originally the same, as the Nosferatu. That I was a born vampire hunter, a Nosferatin and that in order to live, I would have to tie myself to a vampire and entrench myself in their world. Now, not only is my life in peril daily, I kill, I have had friends killed and I am surrounded by blood. Sometimes, I live it, breathe it, am consumed by it.

Is it no wonder I dream of drowning in blood?

But, Michel has always been there. At first, he was just another vampire in a scary, but slowly revealing, night time world. The Master of Auckland City. He knew who I was, but he didn't tell me at the beginning. I can hardly blame him. I would have run a mile, but he did manage to draw me in, far enough, so that when I was faced with what

I was, I didn't run, I listened and I chose. I chose life over death. I chose Light over Dark. I chose him.

Without doubt, the familiarity is a god send. I wouldn't want to wake up any other way.

He must have heard my thoughts, they are with him frequently nowadays, because he kissed my forehead softly and whispered against my ear. His arms, strong bands of warmth around me, his body blanketing me in his presence and unconditional love.

"Whatever you need, I will provide it. Whatever you want, it is yours. *I* am yours, *ma douce*. Forever"

2
PICK-UP LINES

I tried not to compare the liquid that washed over me in the shower to that which had woken me earlier. For starters, it was clear, not red and also it was scalding hot. The temperature difference was important, but it also meant I could only tolerate it for about five minutes, before I turned beetroot red and a little light headed from the after effects.

Michel had already left for *Sensations* as soon as the shutters had come up. We'd cross paths later, but things were starting to get busy again. Surprise, surprise. Vampire politics this time, not vampire Prophecy. His business interests both here and overseas were monopolising his time. He didn't go into too much detail, he kind of liked to protect me from that side of things. As he said, I had enough to worry about with the Prophecy, but still, I would have liked to know what made him stare off into the distance sometimes. What made that little frown line appear in between his eyebrows, when he thought no one was watching.

Erika seemed preoccupied too and as she was technically meant to be my guard, I knew when things were really heating up when she started heading into *Sensations* at the same time as Michel and not waiting for me. I couldn't shake the feeling that, although we had been through Hell recently, with things that had absolutely nothing to do with the Prophecy, we weren't out the other side yet.

But, as Michel had made it clear, he didn't want me to worry over non-essential vampire crap, I had to trust him. Not asking too many questions was killing me though. I am not the stand-on-the-sidelines-and-wait-patiently kind of girl.

So, in order to direct my attention elsewhere I was throwing myself into interpreting the Prophecy with my other room mate, Amisi. Besides, Amisi needed me right now. Hell, we both needed each other. If I was having dreams of blood and Nero's death, then I dread to think what Amisi was dreaming about. She and Nero had been very close. He'd practically raised her. Certainly for the past couple of years he had trained her. I think she had seen more of Nero in that time than she had done her parents. So yeah, her loss was great and initially I had thought perhaps too much for her to bear.

She had closed in on herself, lost that shine that she always seemed to have and buried herself in the Prophecy. For at least two weeks she had done little else but pour over scrolls, translate texts and cross reference paragraphs. It had proved useful, she now knew the Prophecy and anything else written about it by heart. Other than Nero, who tragically isn't reachable for questions relating to anything, let alone the Prophecy, Amisi is now the knowledge on all things Nosferatin/Nosferatu foretold.

But, luckily, some of Amisi was coming back. Just as well, because she's having to pick up my slack now. I thought that I was coping, but over the last few days my emotions have started to get the better of me. I just was finding everything too damn hard. Amisi though, had even started baking again, something she used in the past as a type of therapy. So, it was to the beautiful smell of freshly baked cookies that I came down the stairs, pink as a new born baby and feeling as tired as one too.

"Bats? Really? That's your cookie cutter of choice?" I had made it as far as the coffee machine in the corner of our large and extremely well appointed kitchen. Amisi was transferring little bat-shaped cookies from a baking tray to a wire rack for cooling. Maybe her sense of humour was also returning. I could live in hope.

"I couldn't find fangs, so bats it is." She was smiling, not something I had seen a lot of recently, but something I had sorely missed. Things were definitely looking up and I think I knew why.

"Don't let Erika see, she'll probably turn into one just to get back at you." Of course, turning into a bat is a myth. There's so many of them, sometimes its hard to keep up, but the most important fact is vampires drink human blood to survive and are fatally challenged by both sunlight and silver stakes through the heart. Quite frankly, there's not much else to know.

"She didn't seem to like the mug I got her." Amisi nodded in the direction of our kitsch corner. I've always had a penchant for novelty items. You know the sort, T-Shirts that read *Make my day, Punk* and the likes. Amisi has taken a shine to the mugs. A new addition to the collection I had started was sitting front and centre. Blood dripping red text on a solid black background saying *Fang-tastic! The drink of life – coffee!*

Of course it was right up my alley. Coffee was definitely the drink of life, to hell with blood. I nabbed the mug and got brewing my coffee. With cappuccino in a *Fang-tastic* mug in one hand and a bat cookie in the other I sat down at the bench and watched Amisi fuss in the kitchen. She was humming. I shook my head and smiled.

"So, had any phone calls lately? From, say... Wellington?"

She shot me a look that said *don't ask* and the smile faded. "He's still on my case to move down there. I'm not ready, Luce. Not until this Prophecy thing is over."

Part of me wondered if Amisi would ever be ready to take on the mantle of Gregor's Nosferatin. But, she had made a promise and in doing so released me from what could have been a lifelong battle of wills with the Master of Wellington City. Despite Gregor and I sharing *Sigillum*, we do not share a bed. Well, we did once and that was a *huge* mistake, which I will regret until the end of my days. Still, *he* was determined to repeat it and if it wasn't for Amisi agreeing to be Wellington's Nosferatin in due course, I would still be fighting off his advances.

As it was, he just flirted occasionally, but that was Gregor, he'd flirt with a tree branch if it got him out of the forest. Now, his sole bed-seeking attention was on Amisi. The problem was, she had a huge problem with his morals. But, that wasn't the crux of the issue. She was undeniably attracted to the guy. So, Amisi's current personal battle was ignoring the attraction and putting Gregor in his place. Gregor loved it. Challenges were always his big turn on and Amisi was proving a whopping great one at that.

She was old enough to hold her own with him though and as much as I would have liked to have protected her, Amisi did not need protection. She was nearly twenty years old, but had the experiences of someone twice her age. Amisi was an old soul in a young, beautiful, tall and athletic body. If I didn't know better, I'd say she had Gregor wrapped around her little finger. Shame she didn't plan on using that influence for romantic designs. Amisi was strictly business when it came to Gregor.

But the smile this evening said otherwise. Was our Amisi cracking?

"He knows that, Amisi, he's just pushing, you know what he's like."

She humphed in reply and started wiping down the bench and stacking the dishwasher.

"Perhaps you should start, at least, coming with me when I head down there. It's getting harder to persuade him you are busy with the Prophecy when nothing has really happened with it for the past three weeks." - Plus, I really did not think I could face being on my own right now - "He knows as well as us when a vampire comes knocking on my door. That bloody connection we still seem to have, it's easy for him to see through my lies when I tell him you're needed back here."

She stopped stacking the dishes and just stood there looking out the window over our back lawn.

"I have put you in a difficult position, haven't I?" She turned to me then, concern written all over her face.

I put my empty coffee mug down on the bench and held her gaze. "I'd do anything to make things easier on you, you know that." My voice cracked slightly at the end there. Amisi knew I held myself accountable for Nero's death. He had died protecting me after all, how could I not? That thought consumed me right now.

"Oh, Luce, you know that is not necessary." She looked infinitely sad then. "He would not want you to feel this way."

Amisi never said Nero's name, it was always *he*. I hoped one day she could voice it again, but I wasn't going to push her. Grief was a personal road you travelled down, how far and fast you travelled was up to you and no one else.

"So, come with me tomorrow night, we'll paint Wellington red." I cringed at my tactless terminology. Amisi just laughed. Black humour, go figure, Amisi likes it.

"OK." She nodded, fortifying her resolve, I think. "OK. Tomorrow we'll go to Wellington together. Maybe an adventure into the lion's den is just what I need."

"Amen sister. If there's another lion's den full of as much adventure as Gregor's I'll eat my stake."

She really laughed at that one. No one could be as much of an adventure as Gregor and we both knew it.

We polished off a few more cookies, then tidied up and headed into town. Thankfully, Amisi grabbed the keys, assuming rightfully, that I wasn't quite up to controlling a car just now. As it was a Friday, town would be busy and I only hoped we'd actually get some hunting under our belts. The past three weeks of practically no evil-lurks-in-my-city pull or the Prophecy type pull either, was making me antsy. Surely tonight would be the night we could try out my new power and see if it did the deed. That is to say, see if it managed to turn a vampire towards the Light and not crispy critter it.

I knew this last power was the one we had all been waiting for. It was one big Energiser Bunny of a Light boost. Michel had been there when I received it, but since that wattage filled moment nothing miraculous had happened. I was already in possession of several Nosferatin powers as well as two other Prophecy related ones. I am the *Sanguis Vitam Cupitor*, or Blood Life Seeker, as well as the *Prohibitum Bibere*, or Forbidden Drink. Those make up two of the Prophecy components. The last, the *Lux Lucis Tribuo*, or Giver of Light, was all that was needed to seal the deal. It made sense that what I had received, when all the bright light engulfed me and half the universe, was indeed the final key to the Prophecy. But, what to do with it?

I had tried practising using my Light. I could already shape it, mould it and fire it any which way as a weapon. I could also flood vampires with it, usually leaving them in a state of post coital bliss, but also capable of rendering them excruciating pain. Aaaand, it had a habit, every now and then, of taking over completely and simply frying a vampire to dust. That one was a bit scary, to say the least. I had worked very hard to be able to control my Light and not let *that* ever happen again, but still, I had no idea what this new power could actually do. No bloody vampire had appeared who would call forth the magic.

There had been the odd evil-lurks-in-my-city one, but no truly Dark vampire and I couldn't help feeling that the Prophecy was only concerned with the dregs of vampire society, those vampires truly lost to the Dark. The Prophecy was all about good versus evil, after all. I mean, *the Light will capture the Dark and will hold it dear* screams Good banishing Evil, doesn't it?

So, after three weeks I was still no closer to solving the mystery of my latest power boost. Tonight, though, might just be the night. Let's just hope I am up to it.

Summer had come early, thankfully, so we had the top down on my BMW Series 1 convertible as we cruised along Tamaki Drive towards the city. Lights on the water sparkled and danced, sending their orangey glow in reflections back towards us. Auckland at night was stunning. I was seeing more and more of night time Auckland, although officially, still employed by the BNZ Bank in Queen Street, I hadn't spent too many hours there recently. Life, my nocturnal one, had taken up a tad too much time and as much as it crushed me, I'd had to take extended leave. I just didn't feel right about all the glazing Michel's vamps were having to do on my work colleagues. Covering my ever more frequent absences, wiping their memories of crazed supernatural hostage situations and making them think I had been there, when in fact I had been out cold due to some injury or another. I hated glazing, even though I was quite capable of glazing vampires when needed, I tried not to. It just wasn't right having that sort of influence over someone else.

So, no work right now, which also meant no income. I did have a little saved and my insurance had come through for my trashed possessions, courtesy of the Taniwhas and my former best friend, but money was tight. Michel however had insisted I live rent free in his house and I'd had to cave on that one. I mean, truthfully, it was the lesser of two evils. Either take free board or take money from Michel. Free board won.

He of course was cock-a-hoop. Plus, no matter what I did, the pantry and fridge were always stocked to the brim. I hadn't had to spend a cent on groceries or household necessities since I moved in permanently. I blamed Michel, but he steadfastly refused to discuss it. Amisi just shrugged it off as par for the course and Erika just laughed at me.

Was I ever going to feel independent again?

I chose to roll with it for now. There was just too much on my plate and I wasn't in the right headspace to be able to combat a smothering boyfriend. Plus, I was trying to let my loved ones help me when needed. Not bottling so much up inside, admitting when I needed a shoulder to cry on. The new me. It was taking some getting used to. The new me was a mess.

Amisi parked at *Sensations* in the underground car park, in my usual spot over by the door. It wasn't that we particularly wanted to start out at the club, but the parking was safe and free, so that's where we always headed. And besides, as far as bars go, *Sensations* is one cool club. OK, it was filled to the brim with vampires, but even the Norms, who know absolutely nothing about our world, congregate here. The club just has that right mix of exotic, extravagant and elite. It's dark and inviting and altogether a little sinful. Plus, vampires are gorgeous and if you're heading out on the town, then no doubt about it, you want to look at gorgeous.

At least, that's what I tell myself when I look at the poor innocent humans that flock to Michel's club every night of the week. I know Michel's vampires are just as capable as the next to influence humans, but they are more on the side of good than evil, so I just have to hope that nothing untoward goes on in the shadows I can't quite see into. It goes against the vampire hunter in me, but I am also very much part of this world now and as such, I have to trust that they aren't all bad. If I didn't, I'd definitely be drowning in those dreams filled with blood each night. I just know it.

The club was pumping as we entered, lots of regulars to be seen. I spotted Jett and Shane, off to the side animatedly talking. Shane seemed to have made an impression on Jett, which was surprising. One is meek and mild, the other tough as nails, but somehow they got along. Shane could do that to you though, he somehow knew exactly how much innocence and guile to play to reel you in. I guess his fish at the moment was vampire, not human. Playing it up to the second in command to Michel was not a bad move, politically. I had hopes Shane would live a long and happy second life, it looks like he did too.

Erika was missing, as was Michel, but I could sense both in Michel's office. I had no intention of interrupting, business being the way it was right now, I knew I'd only be a distraction. I couldn't even send him a thought to say hello, surrounded by so many memories. Nero had saved my life in this bar. So, Amisi and I just took a seat quietly over by the bar and let Doug ply us with alcohol. Always a good place to start a Friday night.

"Good to see you, Luce," Doug said as he slid my drink across the bar top to me and likewise did the same for Amisi. Doug is a man, or vampire, of little words, but I like him. I know he'd have my back if the need arose. I've seen him fight, like most of Michel's line he knew how to hold his own in a battle, but what you saw on any ordinary night was just a bartender with a pleasant smile and a few kind words. His greeting tonight would be genuine though. Doug was my guy, through and through.

I smiled and waved him off to his paying customers. I'd just taken a sip of my drink and turned to talk to Amisi, when a couple of human guys approached. One on either side of us, so I was guessing they were tag teaming it tonight. It's not that I have stopped noticing other guys, now that I'm with Michel. I still do, you can't help it, especially if they're dressed to impress like these two were and flashing handsome smiles and come hither looks. But really, one vampire is quite a handful, I couldn't even contemplate adding anything else to the mix. And why would I? I mean, come on, Michel is gorgeous and he is all mine. Humans just don't have a chance any more, I'm afraid.

Still, I thought I'd humour them, it might just get me out of my blue funk. I did notice, though, a few of the vamps coming in for a closer look and it wasn't for the scenery, they were definitely not liking the *Master's* Nosferatin being disturbed by mere mortals. I took pity on the guys and smiled back.

Big mistake.

Blonde and handsome slid into the seat next to me and devoted his whole world to dazzling with those pearly whites, while rugged and brunette did just the same to Amisi. We were trapped, both men deciding to set up home at the bar and win us over. The vamps began to circle.

"So, do you come here often?" Jeez, where have I heard that one before?

"Is that the best you can do?" I said willing myself to concentrate. I hadn't meant to encourage him. Of course, he had planned it all. Maybe I'm just out of practice on the whole picking up someone in a bar routine.

"It got a response from you, so it must have worked. Still, I see your point, I'll just have to try a little harder." He rolled his R's like they do down in Gore, it's kind of nice, quaint even. "How about this? What's a pretty girl like you doing in a place like this?"

OK, pathetic, but it did help to make me focus. Sometimes, even a brief moment out of reality can be a balm. My world had been so Dark lately, talking to a human, albeit a bad one-liner human, was kind of refreshing.

"I kind of like it here. It think it has a nice feel to it, don't you?"

He looked around as though seeing it for the first time and nodded slowly. "I see your point, I hadn't really noticed it before, you kind of stole the view as soon as I walked in." He flashed that smile again.

"Now that was pretty pathetic," I said, taking another sip from my drink.

"Damn. You're one tough customer, I'll have to pull out the big guns." He tapped his chin in mock thought. "Got it!" He straightened himself up, put on a faux sober face then looked me in the eye. "Do you have a map? Because I keep getting lost in your eyes."

If it weren't for the dozen or so vamps on hot approach I would have laughed out loud, but this had gone on long enough. "Look, you're entertaining, but I'm waiting for someone. The guy who owns the bar actually. So, maybe you should try your beautifully cheesy pick up lines on another girl. They really shouldn't be wasted." I forced a smiled, hoping he wouldn't be offended and would just walk off.

"That would be Michel Durand." He was all serious now, his voice low and quiet so only I could hear. And it's not that humans don't know who Michel is, hell Michel even has groupies, but it was the way this guy said it, that had my head spinning.

"Yes. It would. He's my boyfriend." I said it slowly, unsure if admitting it would be helpful here or not, but feeling perhaps the line needed to be drawn in the sand anyway.

"Then I'm in the right place and talking to the right girl." He picked up my drink and sniffed it, shrugged and downed the rest of the glass. Looking me back in the eyes, I noticed his had a strange glow to them, the blue taking on a hint of pink, like the sunset on a hot summer's day. Sky-blue-pink my childhood friend used to call it. This guy had sky-blue-pink eyes.

"Lucinda Monk, you're going to want to call off the hounds, let them know everything is OK and for them to go back to their blood bags."

I froze. "Why?" It wasn't the best comeback, but I couldn't think straight. In fact, the room had started spinning and all clear thought had slipped away.

"Because my friend here will hurt your girl, that's why."

I glanced over my shoulder and saw Amisi's face was very grim. The brunette looked relaxed and was talking away as though they were having a great conversation, but it was all one sided. Amisi's eyes shot down to her lap then quickly back up to mine. I looked where she had and I could see something protruding under her blouse. I followed the shape to its origin and wasn't surprised to see it started by brunette.

"What is he holding against her?" My voice was even and low. This could *not* be happening, right in Michel's bar, right in front of Michel's vamps. Of course, they may not like a human chatting me up, but they'd never think for an instant that a human could get the slip on me or Amisi. They're human, not even worth considering as a threat. But right now I felt threatened.

"That doesn't matter, Lucinda, call the vamps off or your friend will be sporting the latest fashion accessory from Muggers-R-Us."

I glanced at his eyes and knew he meant it. This was no idle threat. To have entered into Michel's club and come against us in such a fashion, could only mean one thing. These guys were professionals, they knew who the vamps were, they knew who I was, they knew how to play the game.

I looked over at one of Michel's vampires and caught his eye. "It's OK." I mouthed. "Stand down." And followed it up with one of my pissed-off glares, the ones I usually reserve for Michel's vamps when I'm about to blast them with a nice dollop of Light. The vampire in question cringed and quickly ordered his cohorts to retreat.

The human next to me waited until they had all slithered back into the shadows and then winked. "Atta girl. I knew you'd do the right thing. You've just got goodie-two-shoes written all over you."

I ground my teeth together. I'd sure as hell like to show him exactly how wrong he was on that score.

"Right," he said, clapping his hands and rubbing them against each other. "You and I are going to walk out the door together. Fred here will keep your girl entertained for a bit longer. Don't worry, he's as gentle as a lamb, aren't you, Fred?" Fred, if that was his real name - and who calls their kids Fred now days? - just grunted, not exactly reassuring the gentle as a lamb persona at all.

"They'll follow," I said not moving from my spot. "I don't normally walk out of here with humans."

"Then glaze one to keep the others occupied."

My breath left me in a rush. Yes, I could glaze vampires, but there was no way anyone should know about it. Especially a friggin' human. What the fuck?

He just laughed at the expression on my face and leaned in to whisper in my ear. I could smell his expensive cologne, not unappealing under normal circumstances. But this was not normal.

"We know all about you, Lucinda, so come on, let's boogie. I'm really starting to lose my patience."

At that Amisi let out a little whimper and I shot her another glance. The guy had his arm about her chair back, gripping her shoulder. At a quick look it would have just seemed like he was leaning in to say something quiet in her ear, but his other hand, hidden from anyone else but me, was clearly pushing home whatever was under her shirt. And I was picking it was sharp.

A tear spilled out from her eye and trailed down her cheek. And didn't that just do it for me. It may have been clear, but all I could see was red. Blood red. Images of Nero dying, to save me, flooded through my already numb mind, making logical thought an impossibility.

She shook her head at me as I abruptly stood up. "Don't do it, Luce. Don't go with him."

Doug sensed something was up at that stage. I'm not surprised, even with a bar packed to the brim, he kept an eye on me. As he was the vampire to approach first, he got the glaze. A simple command - I almost didn't realise I had done it, through the fog enveloping my mind - that all was OK and he was to make sure none of Michel's vampires followed me. He nodded, like any good glazed vampire does and proceeded to round up the vamps in the room, allowing cheesy-one-liner to walk me out the front doors unhindered.

A quick robot-like glaze to the vampire bouncing on the front steps and we were free.

Or at least, he was. I was betting it was going to be a long time before I could get free. How could I? Amisi was being held hostage in the bar, what else could I do but walk willingly with one-liner away from the safety of *Sensations*.

I didn't even send a thought out to Michel.

Almost in a mechanical stupor, I just simply walked away.

We walked a fair distance from the bar without saying a word. I was using every Nosferatin skill I had to lower my heart rate and slow my breathing, trying my best to ascertain if there were any other threats nearby. It was all but useless, I couldn't really think straight.

There weren't any other supernatural threats in the vicinity, at least I didn't think so. So I concentrated on the man next to me. What the hell did he want with me? I flicked a glance his way and took in his relaxed demeanour, thick blonde, spiky short hair, sky-blue-pink round eyes, with thick blonde lashes which swept down his cheeks when he blinked. He had a strong jaw line and square facial features, with a wide neck and broad shoulders. I was sure he could hold his own against any human that came his way, but a Nosferatin? I doubted he'd have much of chance against me normally despite his powerful human presence, but I wasn't firing on all cylinders right now. He hadn't even disarmed me, I still had two silver stakes, a silver knife and a Svante sword sheathed down my back.

Still, do I try? Amisi was no doubt back at the bar under constant knife threat even as we walked along the street lamp lit pavement, further and further away from *Sensations*. And of course, this guy knew that, that's why he hadn't even bothered to disarm me yet. He knew I wouldn't risk Amisi. Not when she had a knife already piercing her skin, even she couldn't magic her way out of that one. A knife at close quarters like that was impossibly stiff odds and the brunette, Fred, didn't seem like the sort to lack quick reflexes. Any move she made could be fatal, as could any I made now.

Shit. What now? We just kept walking, the blonde next to me kept whistling and I felt like an utterly useless piece of crap. Being in positions of complete impotence does not make me happy. I had to take control of this situation, but physical attack was not the answer.

"So, what is this all about? What do you want with me?"

He flicked me a glance and smiled, flashing those impossibly white teeth. "It's not what I want, Lucinda. It's not what anyone else but they want. They ask, they receive. It's just a shame your *boyfriend* didn't cotton on to that sooner."

"That doesn't tell me much. Who are they and what has it got to do with Michel?"

He stopped walking, we were outside the BNZ Bank, my workplace, of all places. I tried not to look at it too longingly. Oh, to be back in familiar coin counting territory.

"All will be revealed in good time. Or not."

I heard a soft footfall then and spun round to face the noise. Another male human, just as well presented, just as strong as my unwanted companion, but he wasn't trying to attack me. No, his job was pure distraction, because as soon as I turned toward him and away from the blonde, I felt a sharp sting on the side of my neck. Not unlike the sharp piercing prick of a vampire bite, but this was just one spot, very fine, very small. But rather than a sucking sensation, I felt like something was being pumped in.

By the time I got my hand up to the spot, Blondie had removed the object of sharpness and the sensation of something entering my bloodstream had disappeared. Only to be replaced with a slight blurring to the scene before me, a sudden onset of nausea and then the whole world went black.

3
NOT A VICTIM

I woke slowly to the hum of an engine and a pain pulsing through my head. I groaned and rubbed my temples, feeling both light headed and cotton wool padded inside. Nothing seemed to be working. My eyes blinked in the surroundings, taking nothing in, my ears only produced a thudding noise, in time with the pulsing in my head. And my hands, other than rubbing my temples, felt like they belonged to someone else. Actually, my whole body felt like it belonged to someone else, I was just along for the ride.

Slowly the room around me coalesced and I was able to comprehend my location. On a plane, a private jet it looked like, sitting in a well padded caramel coloured leather armchair with a blanket over my legs and half way up my body. The blanket was cream mohair, so soft and delicate. I ran my fingers along it and realised I was able to feel a lot more than a few minutes ago. Sensation was coming back to me, which was a relief, but memories of how I got here were not.

That thought woke me up completely and was immediately followed with others. Who were the people on board with me, where were we going and where had we been? And then, the most frightening, who the hell am I? I started to feel clammy and hot, but a deep seated coldness began to churn in the centre of my stomach. Something was so very wrong about this situation, so very wrong indeed. But, I had no idea what it was, or what I should be feeling. That alone was enough to terrify me though. I suddenly felt very alone and very, very scared.

My eyes flicked around the cabin of the plane. Everything was top notch. These people had money to either hire a jet like this or maybe even own it. It had half a dozen comfortable caramel coloured leather armchairs, like the one I was seated in, polished mahogany tables and a side dresser, covered in bottles of top shelf liquor. A 50 inch plasma TV screen, which was showing a movie of some sort. And about half a dozen vampires littering the space.

I knew this, I'm not sure how, but I knew they were vampires without a doubt and I also felt very much at home with that thought. Instinctively I knew Vampires exist and that I am part of their world. This was such a basic idea it actually calmed me. The fact that not all vampires are created equal was also thrumming in my head, but the familiarity of vampires overcame that fear completely. Still, a sense of wariness stole over me. Vampires could be lethal, I had to watch my back.

One of the vampires turned then and looked at me. He was tall, although sitting in an armchair, his strong long legs were stretched out in front of him, taking up the small space of open carpet in the cabin. His broad shoulders and muscled arms made him appear bigger than all the rest and that was saying something, they were all pretty big on the muscle front. He had unruly shoulder length blonde hair, but it didn't look windblown or bed tousled, it looked a little staged, but it also made him seem carefree and handsome. That, and his piercing azure coloured eyes.

He was gorgeous, with golden brown coloured skin as though he had been tanning it at a beach resort. Of course, I knew that was not possible, vampires can't survive the sun. How I knew this I couldn't say, but I just knew it as a fact.

He smiled and it lit up his face, his long body unfurling as he came over to crouch down next to me. I didn't pull away in fear, I didn't brace myself for an attack, I just didn't feel anything.

"Who are you?" My voice was steady and my throat not dry. So, I hadn't been out for that long then.

"How's my girl?" His accent was American, mine wasn't. He reached up and brushed a strand of my hair behind my ear. A movement so familiar and laced with care, I wondered if I was meant to know this man intimately. I tried to rack my brain for any memories of him, but came up blank. In fact, when I tried to think of something from the past, anything at all, it was all blank.

"I don't know you." I wanted to say more than that, like I don't know where we've been, where we're going, who I am, what's happening, but I chose to push those thoughts aside because I could feel they would only lead to hysteria. I was on the edge of a cliff already, I needed to stay in control of my emotions or all would be lost.

He smiled sadly. "It's all right, Lucinda, you don't need to remember, I can do that for both of us."

I shook my head at him, I couldn't form any more words. He looked so sad, so heartbroken, but also so sincere. I must know this man, he must know me. I wanted to reach up and brush his face, to reassure him, but I felt nothing for him, other than what pity I felt at the look on his face right now. I kept my hands clasped in my lap.

"You've had an accident, which has taken your memories. We're bringing you home and hoping our doctors can help you to remember. If you like, I can tell you a bit about us. Would you like that?"

I just nodded, what else could I do? My head still felt as though it was stuffed with cotton wool. It must have been a result of the accident.

He settled himself down in the seat next to mine and took one of my hands in his, rubbing the back of it with his thumb. The motion felt familiar, I couldn't take my eyes off what he was doing. This felt familiar. I looked back up at him and found he was watching me intensely.

"I remember this." He seemed momentarily surprised, but then happy.

"Good, that's good. We always hold hands."

"We're friends?" I think I knew what his answer would be, but I wanted to get it out in the open. Everything felt so foreign, but his thumb on the back of my hand did not. I was confused, scared and wanted some answers, even if they would create more questions in their wake.

"We're more than just friends, but it's OK," - he saw the look of outright fear and utter confusion gracing my face - "we'll just take it slowly, until your memories come back, or until you're comfortable. Either way, you're in charge."

The way he said it made me think perhaps he wasn't sure my memories would come back at all. I felt a little detached at that thought, as though not having my memories back would be a good thing, part of me thinking that remembering would only make this so much worse.

"Where are we going?" Maybe getting some facts would help.

"Home. Colorado, the United States. We've been there for a while, I'm hoping seeing it again will bring back some memories."

Huh, Colorado. It absolutely did not bring back some memories. In fact, I had absolutely no idea where, in the United States of America, Colorado was. How was that possible if I had lived there before?

I sighed, he just kept rubbing the back of my hand, a soothing motion that did make my blood pressure lower and my heart rate steady. I decided I liked him holding my hand.

"What's your name?" My voice was small, I didn't like admitting I couldn't remember him. I wanted to remember him, I wanted to make him smile.

"Jonathan."

That twigged a memory, or something, I couldn't quite grasp. But it felt familiar, not quite as much as the thumb rubbing on the back of my hand, but still, it was something, wasn't it?

"I remember your name, I think, I'm not sure, but I know I've heard it before."

He smiled, but I picked up a sense of tension in his body that hadn't been there before. I'm not quite sure how I managed to do that, it seemed like the signals he was giving off were minute, but somehow I could pick up the nuances as though this was just a natural part of who I am. Reading people. That made me wonder what I did for a living.

"What do I do in Colorado?"

He pulled himself together, although I'm sure to anyone else they wouldn't have even picked up that something was wrong.

"You're my wife, you don't need to work, your place is by my side."

I had a sudden sense that was wrong, that there was more to me than someone's other half. I hid my reaction with a shift of my hand in his, now taking hold of his instead of letting him hold mine. I smiled up at his surprised face and said, "Good. I like that." And prayed he bought it, because I knew now he was lying. I had no way of knowing what the truth was, but I knew this was not it. Jonathan was not my friend, let alone my husband and I knew this with such conviction it rocked my soul.

The rest of the flight was much the same. The other vampires, who Jonathan introduced to me as his work colleagues and friends, sat watching the movie, while Jonathan tended to me. Getting me food and drinks and telling me about our supposed life together. I let my mind wander, still taking in what he was saying, but allowing myself the luxury of self analysis. Who was I? Why was Jonathan going to such extremes to make me believe I was part of his world? And where had we just come from?

Because the further we were getting from where ever this plane had taken off from, the more I felt like a part of me was being left behind. I clung to that part as it felt more real than the vampire sitting by my side, but no matter how much I tried to identify it, I couldn't. It was lost to me and that sense of loss almost made me cry.

Just before we were due to land, Jonathan came back from the galley with some tablets and a small cup of water.

"Take these, sweetheart, they're your medicine." Then seeing the slightly sceptical look on my face, he added, "Without them you tend to have seizures. We don't want that, do we?"

I wanted to argue. I wanted to ask what they were. But, I knew when my back was against a wall. We were on board a plane, I was surrounded by vampires, I could not have fought back or escaped, this was not the time to rock the boat. So, I took them and I swallowed them. He was watching me too closely, to play with fire and pretend. My time would come, I told myself, because as sure as I knew that I was more than just some trophy wife, that there was more to me than meets the eye, I knew I would escape these vampires.

I knew it and I grabbed hold of that thought, held it close and settled in my armchair waiting for whatever the drugs would do to me to happen, knowing in my heart that it wasn't about seizures at all.

It took a good ten minutes before I realised I was tired and perhaps another ten before I could fight the fatigue no more. I let it wash over me, I stopped fighting it, but I promised myself, I would fight it again tomorrow.

The next time I woke I was in bed, in a big bed, the size of a truck, in a nicely decorated airy room. Pale duck-egg blue walls, delicate furniture, gauzy curtains on the windows, the moon in full glory hanging outside. I watched that moon and thought it didn't look familiar. Shouldn't it, if I am home? The shapes to the shadows, the contours across its surface. All looked out of kilter. This was not my moon, I told myself. Then this was not my bed.

I got up and walked over to the window and took in my surroundings. The building I was in was surrounded, at least on this side, by a large expanse of green grass, rolling away to wooded leafy trees in the distance, some twenty or thirty metres away. In this light it was difficult to tell the shade of the leaves, but they looked pretty and abundant. Lots and lots of leafy trees bordering the edge of the large green grassed area. I couldn't see any neighbouring houses, we weren't in a city, that was for sure and I knew that vampires liked cities. So, why the expanse?

I opened the window - which surprised me as it wasn't locked - and was met by cold, frigid, clean, fresh air. We were high up, I could tell, this air was thinner than I was used to and much colder. Perhaps we were in some mountains, Colorado is mountainous, isn't it? Damn, I wished I'd paid more attention to geography in school. I wasn't sure of my surroundings, I knew damn near nothing about Colorado, or even if this was in fact Colorado as Jonathan had suggested. As far as sussing out my surroundings go and formulating a plan of escape, this sucked.

I tried to settle my breathing and decided to explore. There was absolutely no point in succumbing to fear. Fear wouldn't help solve this mystery, fear wouldn't get me out of a potentially dangerous situation.

Fear was not my friend. So I bottled it up as best I could, grabbed hold of the thought that home was back where we had come from and headed towards my door. I expected it to be locked, but like the window, it simply opened with ease.

I walked out onto the landing and looked around. The house I was in was well decorated, lovely pale colours and pale, distressed, wooden furniture. Very un-vampire like, but charming and quaint. This had the feel of a holiday home perhaps, a place in the country to get away from the stresses of urban life. Maybe that was it, maybe the vampires I could sense downstairs didn't normally live here, but came here to unwind. It sounded like it could be possible.

I started towards the stairs that I could spot over to the right, which I knew would take me closer to the vampires below. I began scratching at the bend in my elbow distractedly as I tip-toed towards them, then realised I could feel raised bumps where my finger tips were brushing. A quick look told me everything I needed to know. Needle marks. I had been drugged with more than just the tablets on the plane.

A shudder ran through me and for a moment the fear almost succeeded in taking over all rational thought, but I rallied, I dug deep, because this could not be my life, it just could not.

I never went for playing the victim, I wasn't about to start now.

That thought and that thought alone, made me rejoice, because I was more than what I saw and felt right now.

I was not a victim. I never had been.

So, all I had to do was remember exactly what I was and all would be OK.

4
THE BEST LAID PLANS

The vampires were all in what was obviously the lounge, a large open-plan space with light coloured furniture and pastel coloured furnishings, all very cottagey in fact. So *not* American or vampire, but kind of nice. Relaxing even. I sort of had the feeling it should have been a house at the beach though, not something nestled in a tree rimmed, grass expanse, land-locked piece of property high up in the mountains.

They all looked up when I came in the room, but it was Jonathan who came rushing over, concern written all over his face. A face that still felt very unfamiliar to me.

"You're awake, sweetheart. Can I get you anything."

He seemed genuine, but his affection only made me cringe. Not from fear, but something else, something I couldn't name, no matter how hard I tried to home in on the feeling.

"Where are we?"

He came and clasped my hand, immediately rubbing his thumb across the back of it. My heart rate started lowering straight away and the strange feeling from moments before evaporated. This was familiar, but that thought only left me feeling a little disoriented now, as though my world was spinning out of control.

"You're at home. Everything is going to be OK."

Jonathan pulled me towards a two seater sofa and sat us both down side by side. His leg brushed up against mine, I could feel the warmth emanating from the long length of his body. His thumb continued its hypnotic swirls against the back of my hand, I watched it for a while, trying to piece my tumbling emotions back together. To make sense of everything and nothing that seemed to engulf me right now, but it didn't work. Even though the room was full of six or so vampires and one was holding my hand affectionately, sitting right next to me, I felt so alone.

I looked up into his bright azure blue eyes. They were captivating, but I felt not a thing as I stared across the short space between us.

"What is it, sweetheart? Can you still not remember us?"

I shook my head, unable to form any coherent words. He looked sad, but resigned, as though he had expected that answer all along.

"It is all right, Lucinda. I have already told you, I will remember for both of us. Trust me, can you do that?"

My mind and heart shouted no, my head nodded yes. I could only put the reaction down to survival instincts, because make no mistake, I was fighting for my life and I knew it.

We sat silently for a while, him still stroking my hand, me trying to take in as much of my surroundings as I could manage. I felt a little tired and fuzzy, but you always do after a long flight and although I had slept most of it, my body was still remembering the trip. Plus, I was sure whatever drugs they had been injecting were also partly to blame.

What the hell was I going to do? I needed to formulate a plan. I have always been practical in all that I approach, so breaking down the task ahead into smaller manageable parts made sense. I smiled slightly to myself at that thought, the more I remembered who I was at my core, the better. Jonathan didn't notice my smile, he just seemed happy to sit with me while I glanced around the room. Maybe he thought I was trying to jog my memory, maybe that thought made him happy too.

I knew there would be nothing here for me to remember. I just knew it, just as I knew at sunrise the vampires would not be able to go outdoors and that was when I would need to make my escape.

So, practical part number one. Escape. It covers a lot more than just physically getting myself away from these vampires. It also means I'd stop being injected with whatever drug they were using on me. Two birds with one stone. That I could handle.

How to escape, of course, was the next hurdle. I needed to get myself armed for starters and just as I knew sunlight was detrimental to a vampire, I also knew silver was too. Stakes were best, but I doubted I'd find one anywhere near here, so a knife would have to do. Arm myself and then escape. Things were looking up on the planning front.

Next, I would need to have an understanding of the layout of the land. Which direction to head in. Obviously away from here as fast as I could, but if I didn't find a road and just wandered for the duration of daylight hours, the vampires would pick up my scent and come after me by nightfall. I was picking I would only have one shot at this, I had to make it work.

OK. Arm myself, escape, know the way out. Getting better, but still not perfect. How far was I from civilisation and what would I do once I got there? I had no money, I had no idea where to go or to whom to go to, I had no memories of who I was.

Part of me hoped the drugs were responsible for this and once away from here, away from the medication, my memories would return. I could take myself to the human police, but what would they do? They'd make a fuss about an amnesiac and that would call attention to me. I would need to hide out until I could remember enough to find help.

I didn't for a second think it would be easy, but I was resolved to start at least, to put my plans in motion. First up. Layout of the land.

"I looked out my window before. It looks lovely outside. Can we go for a walk?"

Jonathan perked up at that, his lovely blue eyes sparkling in the lights of the room.

"A splendid idea, sweetheart. We always liked to walk in the evenings around the property."

He suggested I get changed, as I was in a nightdress still. I hadn't even noticed, which shocked the hell out of me. Who had put me in it?

Only one answer, as the other vampires all kept their distance and there was no one else in the house that I could sense. The thought that Jonathan had undressed me and put me to bed made me sick to the stomach, but I pushed it aside. I couldn't allow the luxury of a response to anything right now. As with his comments, I had to stay focused and strong. And not show my fear or give an inch. I had to stay on guard.

I almost tripped over the step I was about to climb onto, when those thoughts ran through my head. Holy shit. They were familiar. They were rooted deep down inside me and felt so right I wanted to laugh out loud at finding them again.

Never show fear. Never give an inch. Always stay on guard.

What the hell was I before this happened to make me have a mantra such as that? Because, that's what it felt like, something I had repeated to myself again and again and again in the past. Something that was part of who I am.

I walked into the dressing room attached to the bedroom I had woken in and was confronted with a huge display of clothes, all in my size, all never been worn before, all in colours I couldn't imagine I would usually wear. Whites and reds and blues and pinks and greens. Not a dark colour in sight. I wanted something dark, something I could hide in. Hiding felt natural to me, not standing out like a Christmas cracker.

I chose fitted blue jeans and a white T-Shirt and popped a blue sweater on top. I figured it would be chilly out. When I came downstairs again, Jonathan had grabbed some coats for us to put on and showed me where the boots were, all the while asking if I remembered anything. Once again, the more he did it, the more a little doubt crept into my mind. Why would he act like this if it were not true? I tried to push it away again, to concentrate on all the little things, like the needle marks, the sense that home was where we had flown from, the fact that my heart felt heavy and I was constantly rubbing over it and not even noticing I was. It was as though a hole had opened up in my chest and was slowly getting bigger, the more time I stayed in this house.

I was stupid. I knew people could lose their memories and feel like an imposter in their own lives, but I couldn't shake the feeling that this was more. So, I kept pushing those moments of uncertainty aside and forged on with *the plan.*

We walked around the perimeter of the property, well at least the grass lawn part, right up next to the lovely leafy trees, which on closer inspection showed all green colours, but in amongst the leafy evergreens were a few bare deciduous trees, leaving me in no doubt that winter was in full swing here in Colorado. That was not good news. It was unbelievably cold right now, but I could only hope, during daylight hours when I intended to escape, the Colorado sunshine would prevail. Escaping in the dead of winter on foot seemed an insurmountable challenge, but escaping at all costs was essential. There were several out buildings, one was obviously the garage and a well equipped one at that. I momentarily thought stealing a vehicle might be the way to go, but when we walked past it was obvious the security system on that building was exceptional. Cameras everywhere, automatic sensor lights, a huge box on the side that looked like it could make a lot of noise if needed.

I didn't need further complications to an already paper thin plan, so taking a vehicle was out. I'd have to go on foot.

The other building was guest accommodation, Jonathan said. It looked substantial, almost as big as the main house itself, so I guessed that was where the other vampires slept. How many more, than the six back in the lounge, were there? As long as I made my escape during daylight hours, then surely that wouldn't matter at all.

The only accessway or indication of where a road might be, was the very long driveway. It was so long that I couldn't see the gate from the edge of the trees. The only saving grace? Once I reached the trees, I wouldn't be visible from the house. So thirty metres and home free. Yeah, right.

By the time we made it back to the main house I was exhausted. It hadn't been that long a walk, but I felt so frail I was having to rely on Jonathan to steady my gait. Initially, he just offered a hand when I tripped, or to aid me up the steps to the front entrance area. By the time we reached the front door, his arm was around my waist. I didn't like it, but I had no choice. Once we got inside, it was clear I needed to get to bed, so rather than dine in the dining area downstairs as he had planned, he helped me back to the bedroom and said he'd return with my supper.

I stripped off my clothes and dressed again in my nightdress. I could feel dawn approaching, so I knew any more reconnaissance around the property would have to be resumed tomorrow and I certainly didn't feel up to just winging it and trying to escape today. I stretched out on the bed and waited for my food to arrive. I didn't feel particularly hungry, but I knew I would need sustenance to carry out my plan. So, no matter what it was, I told myself sternly that I would eat every last bit of it.

As it happens, I only managed half before feeling so nauseous I thought I'd bring it all back up again. I was asleep within twenty minutes of eating, only to wake up several hours later aware that someone was in my room. The shutters were down on the windows, so it was still daytime, but the light was dim in the room. I didn't want to switch the bedside lamp on, so lay there for a while and just tried to listen. I could hear breathing, slow and steady as though someone was asleep, off to the side and I knew instinctively that it was a vampire. Jonathan, asleep on the couch which was over by the windows.

Great. Just great. I had no doubt that this would be a regular pattern. I would not be alone in my room, no quick and easy escape with a vampire right beside me. I fought the tears, but they silently came anyway, they had a mind all of their own. I felt so helpless, so lost and alone. This could not be my life. I didn't know this man and I was sure I wasn't his *wife*. I didn't know this house and I was sure it wasn't my *home*. All I knew was I had to get away from here, but doing that would be damn near impossible. I rolled over as quietly as I could manage and held my sobs inside.

When the shutters rose again for a new night I'd already refortified my goals. While I had been feigning sleep for the past few hours I had discovered more needle marks on my other arm. So, dinner put me to sleep and the injections came afterwards. Whatever was in the injections was blocking my memories because the later in the day, the more of me I could remember, whereas now, I just wasn't sure anymore of anything.

Jonathan rose from his couch and came over to sit on the side of the bed. I decided I'd play along for a bit, the more compliant I was, perhaps the more information I could gather. Maybe even spot a weakness I could exploit.

"Did you sleep OK on the couch?" I asked softly.

He smiled sweetly at me and brushed a strand of my hair off my face.

"As long as I am near you, I am happy."

I swallowed, pretending to be all buddy-buddy was not easy, could I be convincing enough? I had to try.

"What happened to me? How did I lose my memories?" I knew pretending I could remember something was reckless, but not asking what happened to me would seem remiss as well.

"It was relatively simple, we were on holiday and you fell down some stairs and banged your head. That's all. You were out for several days, the doctors said you didn't have a bleed, so no operation was necessary, but when you woke up, you couldn't remember a thing. I am sorry, Lucinda. I wish I could make this easier on you."

He seemed so genuine, but then he always did, didn't he? If this was all a lie, then Jonathan was a consummate actor, if it wasn't a lie... I couldn't finish that sentence, I just couldn't. This was not my life. This was not my life. This was not my life.

Arming myself that day was not an option, nothing suitable came to hand. Delaying my escape seemed like the only reasonable thing to do.

So, our daily routines started that night. We'd take turns showering and dressing, he never stepped over the mark, but when we went to leave the room, he withdrew a key from around his neck and unlocked the door. Escape while he showered was not an option. And escape while he was in the room just took on a whole new meaning.

He would prepare breakfast for me, read bits and pieces from the newspaper while I ate, then we would go for a walk around the property. Every day I seemed to be able to manage less and less distance. This did alarm me, but not nearly as much as it did Jonathan. His concern was palpable.

No matter what I tried over the next few days, I couldn't find anything silver, I couldn't find any weakness to take advantage of and I simply couldn't escape without either. I spent the nights exploring the house, which Jonathan and the other vampires had no issue with. I made out I needed to get my memories of the property back and perhaps exploring would help. They could hardly argue if this life of mine now was true and I soon became aware that there was nothing in the house that could aid me in my endeavours. Hence, no objection from my jailers to my night time pursuits.

The rest of the time I spent pretending to be interested in Jonathan, asking questions about what he did for a living, what we used to do together, what our plans for the future were. All of his answers were given with enthusiasm and without hesitation. He doted on me, anticipating my every need, spending every moment with me, trying to make me laugh, to smile even. His care and attention were limitless.

I began to have serious doubts the longer I was there. Not only had I not discovered a weakness, nor found a weapon to aid in my escape, I was beginning to actually like Jonathan, even if I couldn't remember being married to him.

"When will you go back to work?" We were playing a game of chess in the corner of the large open plan lounge, Jonathan's vampire mates were here and there throughout the lounge and maybe back in their own quarters, as only two were present with us now. Jonathan was sipping a wine, I had a glass of water. Wine only seemed to make me more light headed than usual.

"I've taken extended leave for a while. I am hoping having my company will help you regain your memory. You enjoy my company, don't you?" He flashed his devilishly handsome smile at me, it really was quite remarkable. Initially I had tried to ignore it, now it was something I wanted to see.

I smiled back and received a mock sigh in return. "You stun me whenever you smile, sweetheart, it takes my breath away."

He had started getting more flirtatious in the past 48 hours or so, which had really only taken him less than a week since we had arrived. I, on the other hand, had been smiling more, despite previous reservations and doubts, he was winning me over.

Maybe, I had been wrong, maybe this was my life after all and sooner or later my memories would return.

"I have a surprise for you," he added as he moved his Queen into position, checkmating my King. A not unusual completion to our games, he was far better at them than I.

I raised my eyebrows at him as I tipped my King over in defeat. "I like surprises." Or at least, I thought I did.

"Yes," he said, sounding quite pleased with himself. "Grab your coat and meet me out the front of the house. We're going for a drive."

The thought of getting out of the house, which had felt like a prison for the past week, was astounding. As he took hold of my hand to help me stand up I was beaming, I knew it, I knew my smile would have stretched the length of my face and some.

He paused momentarily to look at me, his face awash with affection, the lights of the room dancing in his blue eyes, which had started to swirl with cyan and turquoise. For a second I couldn't breathe, they were just so stunning. He cocked his head to the side and held my gaze for a minute.

Finally, he cleared his throat and leaned forward to kiss me on the forehead, this was the most intimate he had dared to be.

"I would move Heaven and Earth for you, Lucinda. You have stolen my heart."

I felt it then, I'm not sure why I hadn't felt it before, but something opened up inside of me and it felt like sunshine, liquid gold and the promise of so much more.

Maybe, this was right after all.

5

LIES & MORE LIES

When I came out of the front door he was already standing beside a white convertible car, which on closer inspection turned out to be a Chevrolet Camaro. It looked like it was built for speed. My eyes must have bugged out a bit because he laughed as he approached to help me down the stairs.

"Does it go fast?" I asked quietly, unable to pull my eyes away.

"It can do. Would you like it to?"

Hell yes. A little speed felt about right just now. I just nodded as he settled me in the passenger seat. In a second he was seated beside me and the thrum of the engine starting made me smile some more. He didn't put the vehicle in drive straight away and I glanced over at him to see what the hold up was. He was just staring at me, with another look of affection on his face, this time laced with astonishment.

"You have been kept inside long enough, my love. You are simply alive this night and you have only just made it to the car. I cannot imagine how you will be when I show you my surprise."

"This isn't the surprise?"

He shook his head and smiled. "Hardly, but had I known a car could have this effect on you I would have had you in here a lot sooner. I can think of plenty of things that we could do in a parked car." This was said in a very low, sexy voice which had me blushing even though I knew he was just teasing. He had been nothing but a gentleman. He hadn't pushed me in any way, always happy to just be with me. He rarely touched me, only to assist when I was tired, he never hinted at any past intimacies. He'd been just so damn polite and chivalrous.

I suddenly felt that perhaps I didn't want that anymore.

He must have sensed my change of mind, because his eyes dropped to my lips and he swallowed. I watched his Adam's apple bob up and down and couldn't pull my gaze away.

I expected him to do something, to lean forward and kiss me perhaps, but he just shook his head, as though to clear his mind and put the car in gear. He navigated the driveway and took us smoothly out onto the road. It didn't seem like a very busy road, certainly not at this time of night and I suddenly realised this was my opportunity to see how close neighbours were or whether it would be plausible for me to find help if I escaped.

Rather than get excited at that prospect, I pushed the thoughts away. I didn't need to escape, I was quite fine right where I was. I reached over and took hold of Jonathan's hand as it rested on his thigh. I could tell I had surprised him, the car slowed slightly as soon as I made contact. His head whipping round to look at me.

"Lucinda." He didn't say anything else and it wasn't a question.

"Well, are you going to show me how fast it can go?"

He smiled again. "With pleasure, my lady."

It turns out that a Camaro can go very fast. He didn't lower the top, I think we would have frozen had he done that, but the thinness of the cover made it feel like we were so much closer to the environment around us as it sped past. There hadn't been any houses near us, as it turns out, I only vaguely registered when the first neighbour sped past. The speed of the car, the beautiful lush scenery out the window even in full dark and the warmth of Jonathan's hand as he held mine, made me feel safe and happy. I just sat back and enjoyed the thrumming engine and sense of escape the drive provided.

After about half an hour we entered a well lit area, with a rather large car park and more and more buildings the closer we came. Jonathan parked the car and came around to help me out of my side.

The air was crisp and fresh, but not too cold, still I wrapped my coat a little closer around me. Jonathan's arm came about my shoulder and added to the warmth. I could see tall, rock like mountain peaks, on either side of a well lit area and hear the sounds of voices from what must be a crowd of people. It was hard to believe he was letting me near other humans. I had been isolated for a week, with only Jonathan and his vampires. If I had wanted to escape, now would have been the time.

Instead I walked happily toward the entrance and took in my surroundings. The sign above the gateway read *Red Rocks Amphitheatre* and the show tonight was *Diana Krall*. I had never seen her in concert before, but I knew her music. I was definitely into a little light Jazz.

"You like?" Jonathan whispered in my ear as we walked through the entrance without anyone stopping us to see our tickets.

"Yeah, I do." I couldn't keep the smile off my face, I felt free. Finally free.

He knew his way around the venue and led us directly to a private viewing area above all the many people already in attendance, but off to the side. It was enclosed and I had the thought that it might have been why he had taken the risk of bringing me here. I wasn't going to be anywhere near the humans who had flocked to see Diana. They were all seated on long curved bench seats, which made up the amphitheatre, leading down towards the stage. The lights that lit up Diana's grand piano and the beautiful red rock walls on either side making it look like a Christmas scene, sparkling and vibrant and alive.

If it wasn't for the fact that I was out and about, the bright lights alone would have made my heart soar. For some reason the lights sang to me and I knew this would probably be more true than the music itself. I had been in a house surrounded by darkness and now I had found light. I decided I needed more light in my life. Maybe I could ask Jonathan for flood lights on the gardens back at the house. Light felt very important to me, I couldn't say why, but I just knew it was so.

We sat down and waited for the show to start. Our timing couldn't have been better. Diana came on stage and began her set. I found myself moving forward in my seat and kind of dancing where I sat, the music was great. The performance brilliant. I particularly liked the drummer and the acoustic guitar player, but watching Diana's fingers fly over the keyboard was also a thrill.

It was towards the end of the performance that I realised Jonathan hadn't been watching the show at all, but had instead been watching me. I felt a little self conscious when I turned towards him. He just smiled a small shy smile, one I hadn't seen on his face before.

"Do you know when I first fell in love with you?"

I shook my head, unable to remember when that might have been, unable to form any words at that moment anyway.

"We met in a bar." He laughed at that. "You walked in on a private function without realising it. We haven't talked much about what I am, but I know you know. It was a vampire function and those humans present were either there as our meals or for entertainment. I thought perhaps you were a late comer to the event and all my dreams had been answered at once. You wouldn't have a bar of it, or me." Something flickered across his face, something alien and frightening, but it was gone before I could recognise it. Replaced with a soft look of longing. "Without a doubt I lost my heart to you that night." He lifted my hand, which he had been holding, to his lips, flashing his fangs while he went in to kiss the back of it.

I hadn't seen his fangs before and yes, I knew what he and the others were, I'd always known. Plus, I had seen cars arrive to the out building, delivering humans for their meal and then leaving again. But no fangs had ever been on display. But it wasn't that fangs made me draw in a sudden sharp breath, it was the story of where we met, because it rang true. For the first time I felt we actually shared a memory. For the first time I truly believed him.

He saw the look on my face and smiled again, his eyes now dancing the most wonderful shades of vivid blue. "You remember," he whispered and when I nodded slowly, he said, "Do you remember what else happened that night?"

I shook my head and he breathed a long breath out, one he had obviously been holding, but I hadn't noticed. "We kissed."

"Did we?" I whispered back. "I don't remember that."

His eyes trailed down to my mouth and stayed there. "Shall I remind you?" His voice was husky and low, I couldn't help it, I licked my lips.

He groaned and didn't wait for a reply, pulling me into his chest, wrapping his arms around me and kissing me with such passion and need and hunger it stole my breath. It also didn't feel in the slightest bit familiar, but it did feel OK. I thought distractedly, that it should feel better than this if we had been in love, which he so obviously indicated, but the thought was soon gone as his lips trailed down my chin and jaw, over my neck and then without any warning at all, his fangs entered my skin above my pulse and he began to drink my blood.

Part of me realised this was something he had little control over, maybe it was something we had done regularly when we kissed. Maybe he had missed it so much that when faced with such an intimate chance again, he simply could not stop himself. But the stinging sensation of his fangs biting did not feel unfamiliar, just the fact that it was *him* doing the biting that did.

He didn't waste time changing the bite to a more pleasurable experience, making my legs tremble and my body arch and a whimper of need escape my mouth. My hands found their way into his hair and as I began running my fingers through the strands he responded with a quick change of my position, making me end up in his lap. His own hands roaming over my body, down my back, up my arms, across my chest until he found my breast and started rubbing my nipples.

I was immediately on fire, my body responding even though my brain was still trying to catch up. I hadn't felt attracted to Jonathan before tonight, I had begun to like him, to enjoy our conversations, the time spent together, I had even started to want to make him smile. All of this could have led to an attraction for sure, but this response right now was not my own.

I realised this with a sudden rush of clarity and started to push back against his chest. He was of course, very strong, he's a vampire, but I think both of us were surprised at how strong in fact I was too. Because I managed to make him retract his fangs and release his grip on me to the point where I slid off his lap and landed on the floor.

"Damn it!" he exclaimed as he knelt down beside me and reached for my neck. I scurried back from him as fast as I could until my back rested against the wall.

"Lucinda. You're still bleeding, let me stop it for you. I'm sorry, I scared you, I got carried away, but I have to stop that bleeding. Now."

I reached my own hand up jerkily to my neck and pulled it away when I felt warm liquid run down my fingers. I stared at the red blood as it tracked its way down my hand, over my wrist and under the sleeve of my jacket. So red, so much of it. I felt a little dizzy at the sight of it and it had nothing to do with the fact it was mine. I knew I hated blood, all blood, but I couldn't remember why. I had a sudden flashback to a man lying covered in blood at my feet, then it was gone. The abruptness of the memory shocked me, but in its wake all I felt was a deep seated fear and sudden sense of pure loss.

I looked up at Jonathan and he paled at the look on my face. "Let me make this right." He spoke softly and slowly, so as not to frighten me. I just nodded, still dazed and stunned and hollow.

He crawled toward me and carefully reached out to hold the back of my neck. "I will need to bring my face in against you. I have retracted my fangs." He smiled to show me they were gone. "I promise you, no harm will come to you. I will merely seal the puncture wounds. OK?"

I nodded again, unable to voice any concerns, unable to see anything other than blood.

He leaned his head in slowly, but the actual licking over the wounds was fast. He moved right away and sat across from me, just watching my face.

From moments before to now, seemed like an eternity. I had felt like I had come so far and that things were getting better. I still didn't have my memories, but I was beginning to feel a sense of calm at where I was and who I was with. Now, it all felt like a storm tossed sea and I was once again so lost.

Jonathan was very quiet on the trip back to the property and for the next few days. He began to return to more of his normal self some time later, but we never had another trip away and he never tried to kiss me, let alone bite me, again. A line had been crossed and we both knew it. For me, it had been a revelation, it had woken me up from a dream. I was no longer accepting of my surroundings, I was questioning absolutely everything all over again. I could only presume Jonathan didn't want to rush me, as he returned to his attentive, caring, but distant self.

I was happy with that, but having had a taste of freedom I craved for more.

However, my mind might have wanted another road trip, but my body could not have agreed. Three weeks after I arrived I was fading. Not only had a depressive cloud stolen any light I may have had, I was tired only hours after waking and my appetite was getting less and less.

On the fourth week, almost one month after the start of my new life, things changed. By this stage I had stopped eating almost completely. Jonathan tried liquid foods, bland foods, cold, raw, fresh, organic, anything he could think of to make me eat, but I just couldn't keep much down. And with the lack of food came an even greater sense of exhaustion, although the exhaustion had started well before the inability to eat began. I was so frail, so weak and had lost so much weight that even my renewed plans of escape seemed like climbing Mount Everest.

Finally, Jonathan called a doctor in to assess me. He was a vampire - I knew this as soon as he entered the room - and he was short. Really short, like shorter than me and that's saying something. I'm only 5'4" tall, so this guy was practically a midget.

He had done his doctorly thing and they were standing out on the landing. I had fallen asleep by the end of the exam, so maybe Jonathan thought I was still out cold and that's why he hadn't moved further away before confronting the doctor. He looked tired and ragged, as though the thought of me being ill was hurting him too. I felt a little sad then, that I wasn't better. Not for me and my once again fervent plans of escape, but to make Jonathan happy. I knew it was wrong, he was holding me, still drugging me, against my will. And after the kissing and biting episode, he just didn't feel right, but he had also been so caring, so loving and had done nothing else untoward to me since that fateful *Red Rocks* concert night.

Drugs and imprisonment were more than enough though, weren't they?

As I listened to them talk over the results of the examination my head lolled to the side and before I could close my eyes again I spotted it. A slim, shiny, sharp knife on the tray the doctor had been using. He had used it to open something when he had examined me and had placed it to the side and then forgot it when he packed up to leave. It wasn't silver, stainless steel, but it was long enough and sharp enough to do damage. I grabbed it quietly and slipped it beneath my pillow. I was armed.

Jonathan's strained voice floated in from the hall. "She is exhausted. She won't eat or sleep properly. She is fading away. Have we made a mistake with the medications?"

"No sire. It is not the medication. Her body is pining for her kindred. The longer they are apart the worse it will get."

"Why didn't we..." I didn't hear the rest of what Jonathan was saying, as soon as the short vampire had uttered that word *kindred*, my world had sharpened and also conversely collapsed.

Kindred.

Michel.

6

NO MORE MR NICE GUY

I tried not to sit bolt upright and did manage to stop myself from making any sudden movements that would give me away. I could do nothing for my rapidly beating heart however. It was trying vainly to escape my rib cage. At the thought of Michel so many memories came flooding back in. Not all of them, I was sure, but the main one, the one that kept dancing before my eyes, kept making my heart skip a beat, was of Michel. My Michel.

I knew he was my vampire and no one else came close.

Oh dear God, what the hell had happened?

Putting it all together was a little harder than picturing my kindred's face now seemed to be. Obviously, Michel was where ever we had come from on the plane. It had been a long flight, but how long, I could not know, as I had slept most of it. The fact that I had been so stiff towards the end, just before I received my last sleeping tablet dose, confirmed that. Secondly, Jonathan was not, nor had he ever been, my husband. We shared nothing together that I could see, so he had abducted me, but why?

I was still having trouble remembering what I used to do, who I used to be, where I used to live. But, I did know I was meant to be with Michel, so that was where I had to go. I shifted in the bed to test my limbs. Everything felt sluggish, terribly unresponsive. I was in bad shape, but I hadn't felt this invigorated since arriving here in these mountains. I had no other plans, other than my original one. Arm myself, done. Escape and get the hell outta here before the vampires can follow.

I sensed it was almost dawn and as I had been awake on and off for the past night, restless and nauseous most of the time. Despite being so tired, I hadn't received my end of night sleeping tablets crushed in my meal, nor my injection. I knew it was a long shot, but if I was going to make a break for it, it had to be today. I could only imagine things were going to get worse from here on out and surprisingly, the thought alone of my kindred seemed to give me not only renewed hope, but a renewed strength, almost as though I was getting a boost from somewhere, as though someone above had decided to lend a hand.

The shutters whirred down not long afterwards and some ten minutes later, when I knew the sun had well and truly risen, Jonathan came back in the room. I had not sat myself up, although I felt I could have managed it now, but I had shifted the knife into my hand and held it concealed under my bed covers.

"You're still awake, sweetheart. Can I get you anything?"

"You know, I think I could try another herbal tea. I feel a little thirsty."

He smiled and came over to the bedside. "That's good news." He sat down on the edge, right next to the knife in my hand. I willed myself not to stiffen and forced one even breath in after another. Show no fear.

His hand came up and brushed my hair out of my eyes. He still looked like he cared so much. I was sure that wasn't an act. Everything else might have been lies, but what he felt for me was the truth. Why? Just because he had been charged with looking after me? It didn't make sense, but then it didn't need to. I needed to get away, not solve any god-damn mystery.

"I am sorry you have been unwell, sweetheart. We overlooked something." He shook his head and looked down at the bed covers. For a moment I thought he could see the shape of the knife through the material and I actually held my breath.

"We're working on a solution, we'll have you fighting fit again before you know it. I promise." His eyes came up to my face and there was such a look of intensity there, it made me blink. It also made me breathe again, thankfully.

I forced a smile on my face and let him kiss me on my forehead, hopefully he hadn't noticed the thin film of sweat which had started coating my skin, or maybe he just put it down to my illness.

He got up then and turned to the door. "I'll grab you that tea."

He closed the door behind him and I waited to hear the lock click. It didn't and my heart thumped loudly in relief. I waited a full two minutes then got up gingerly from the bed. When the world didn't tilt, I rushed to the dressing room, threw on jeans and a sweater, socks and sneakers and went back to try the door. The thought of testing it first had crossed my mind, but the need to get dressed had prevailed.

I reached out a shaking hand, the other clasping my knife so tightly that my knuckles had turned white. I took a deep breath in and turned the knob. It moved cleanly and quietly. I exhaled slowly and pulled the door open a fraction, straining to hear any noises. I couldn't even make out Jonathan downstairs. I waited for a few seconds and then took the first step towards freedom.

The landing was clear, so I wasted little time and headed toward the front of the house and the stairs. Trying to escape out of a window would have been great, but all the shutters were automatically controlled, no individual one could be manoeuvred without setting off alarms. I had made it half way down the stairs when I heard him. He was still in the kitchen, the noise of the kettle coming off the boil and the movement of china against granite rang out. It was now or never.

I crossed the expanse of tiled floor to the front door on tip toes and had just put my hand on the door knob when I sensed him behind me. I spun around and was met with a quizzical tilt of the head.

"Do you think you would get far, sweetheart?" His voice was even, calm and showed no emotion whatsoever.

I moved back against the door and tested the knob behind me. It didn't shift.

Jonathan casually held up the key to the lock in his right hand.

"I think you forgot something. Now we shall pretend this never happened and I'll help you back to bed." He took a step toward me, no doubt expecting me to cringe, cry out, to run, hell who knows. He seemed so different from his usual caring persona, that I knew this was the real Jonathan and the rest had all been part of the lie.

"Do you really care for me, Jonathan, or is that all an act too?"

He stopped half way between the stairs and me and slowly smiled. "Have I not treated you well, Hunter?"

Hunter?

When I didn't answer and thankfully showed none of my surprise at what he had called me but my neutral mask, he went on.

"I have been patient and kind. I have been caring and attentive. I thought, the night of the concert, we had finally made progress, but when you baulked at my advances, I retreated. And this is how you repay me?"

He lowered his face and shook his head and when his eyes raised to meet mine again the azure blue had been eclipsed by cyan and turquoise and a dazzling display of colours in a symphony of swirls. They were vivid and bright, so amazing, yet also so terrifying. Because I knew he wasn't holding back.

"I will not tolerate your escape from me for a second time," he said, whisper quiet. "I have played the nice little vampire for too long, but because I would prefer you to participate with enthusiasm rather than not, I will give you one last chance." He held his hand out to me, palm up and open in an invitation. "Come to me willingly and I won't punish you for your pathetic attempt to flee."

At least, we were being honest. Finally, I knew where I stood. The sense of relief at knowing my desire to escape was not just an unfounded dream, an illusion of reality, but the only course of action now left available to me, felt entirely liberating. I had been right. This was wrong. And I had to get away.

"Go fuck yourself, Jonathan," I said it as evenly and neutrally as he had been speaking to me.

He just smiled and let me see his fangs extend slowly.

"Fucking isn't exactly what I had in mind, sweetheart, but teaching you a lesson certainly is."

He launched at me before he had even finished talking. I don't know how, but somehow I simply danced out of the way. I say *dance*, rather than jumped, or fell, or scampered, because that's exactly what it felt like. One minute I had been standing with my hands behind my back, one holding the knife, the other the door knob to the front door. The next I was crouched down some five feet away to the side, having executed the most lovely spin in the air. Holy shit.

Jonathan seemed as surprised as me, but recovered far quicker, coming back for another try, this time managing to clip me with his arm as I danced again to the side. Rather than land in a well balanced crouch, I ended up sprawling across the tiles and banging my head into the wall opposite the stairs. The next thing I knew he had me by the throat.

Looming over me, his fangs glinting in the light of the room, I had no idea how to stop the inevitable, he was going to bite me and then do much, much more to cause me pain. My heart was well and truly hammering by now, I couldn't breathe, even if he hadn't been cutting off my oxygen I don't think I would have been able to draw a breath anyway. Spots had begun to appear in front of my eyes and all I could think was *no*. This could not be happening.

I reached up with my right hand, the one holding the knife and sliced his cheek, not holding anything back, but going for maximum damage with minimum fuss. I don't know how I was able to do it, it seemed such a brutal move, but my body simply acted of its own accord and the knife slit his skin exactly where I had intended it to. Fuck. What was I before all of this happened?

He howled in rage and released my neck, dropping the key to the front door, he had been holding. It bounced and landed by a potted miniature palm tree off to the side of the door to the lounge. Both his hands were now on his face, assessing the damage, but it hadn't been silver, so it wouldn't slow him down for long. I took advantage of his distraction to crawl out from under him and sprint across the foyer.

He slammed into my back before I had managed three steps. The air leaving my lungs was only partially annoying, the crack to my head as it hit the unforgiving tiles was much more of a problem. The spots I had seen before turned to stars. Just as well I hadn't eaten in a while, because nothing would have stayed down when the room began to swim.

I felt Jonathan grab my hair and yank my head back. His snarl as he came in to bite me went right through my body, making me freeze, when perhaps I could have thought of something to get me the fuck out of his hold. As it was, I was blank with fear. Once he bit me, I knew I'd be done for. Nothing could stop his influence then.

I didn't have time to think of anything else, because his hands began to rip at my sweater to gain better access at my neck and the blood vessel there and his fangs pierced my skin. There'd be no softening the sting and pain of the bite, this was all about control and discipline. My punishment for attempting to escape him. Suddenly his fangs left my neck and I thought he had changed his mind, only to have him flip me over onto my back and for his mouth to resume the same spot above my pulse and his fangs to slide in once again. This time he had the front of my body pinned beneath him and his intent was perfectly clear: pain. He tore at my flesh with his fingernails, scraping and scarring my skin. His movements lightning fast. So many gouges, so many tears to flesh. So much blood. He alternated between creating gashes and then creating bruises. His fists pummelling at my sides. But, all I could feel was the terrible pain of his sucking my blood at my neck and the shock that this was actually happening.

I felt a tear run down my cheek as I fought the desire to give up. To just let this happen, to not fight and then it would all be over. As the tear drop tracked its way down past my cheek and over my jaw, then onto my neck, I remembered. Blood, dripping, falling, sliding over the same track. Someone's blood, someone important. I had to honour that person, so their blood was not shed in vain. My breath left me in a rush and I tightened my hands into fists, preparing to pound against the marauding vampire on top of me. As soon as my right hand tightened, I realised I still held my little knife.

I settled my grip more accurately and raised it over his back. It wasn't silver, it wouldn't hold him for long, but nobody, vampire or human, likes to have their heart stabbed with a knife. He'd shed it within seconds, but seconds may just be long enough. Just as I felt his pounding of fists against my ribs switch up a notch in speed and force,

I sent the knife home, knowing exactly what angle to use, how much force would be required and what spot to enter at.

It went in right up to the hilt and he stopped. I pushed against his chest with all my might and rolled him off me. Panting and scurrying away like a crab. I didn't take my eyes off him until I reached the pot plant with the miniature palm and had to look for the key. It took three precious seconds to find it, another four to stumble to the door and an awful, excruciatingly painful, five seconds to get the key in the lock and turn it. The door releasing and opening back towards me, making me take a staggering, imbalanced step back into the room, before it swung wide open.

I took one last glance over my shoulder and screamed. Jonathan was behind me, reaching forward, a look of utter desperation on his face, combined with a feral look of murder in his eyes. His fingers brushed down my front as I fell backwards through the door, still under cover from the sun on the porch. He followed, landing on top of me again, pushing what little air was left in my lungs out and slamming me back hard against the wooden planks of the stoop.

I kicked and punched and writhed and screamed. I gave everything I had, but not enough. I was so close, so close to the sun, I couldn't believe how cruel fate could be. My renewed energy was waning, he was still so determined to cause pain and so strong. I also knew I was still bleeding from his bite, he hadn't licked it when I stabbed him, just pulled cleanly free. And the scrapes and scratches were seeping into the torn material of my jumper and shirt. How much blood I had lost I was unsure, just thinking about it made me feel dizzy.

"You are incredible, Hunter. I had heard, but this is truly remarkable. So ill, so frail, still you are able to fight off an attack. I shall enjoy taming you, my love. I shall enjoy breaking that beautiful spirit you hold so dear. I shall enjoy exacting my revenge for you spurning me at *Sensations* so long ago."

I was numb hearing the utter anger and spite in his voice. I simply lay there, trapped by his body and words of vengeance. I don't know who was watching over me though, I don't know how miracles happen, because I can't remember ever seeing one before, not that I can remember much right now, but still, by their natures, miracles should be rare. So, how I warranted a miracle that day is beyond me. But, before Jonathan could effect his plans for crushing my soul, the sun shifted. Whether clouds had hidden it and then dispersed, or the sun simply moved a fraction in the sky, either way that's all it took for the porch awning to not be enough cover for us and a beam of pure sunlight to cross his face.

He reacted instinctively. Vampires' number one rule is to survive at all costs. Luckily, it didn't include grab your hostage and drag her back with you to the shade, because he leapt off me and sprang so very gracefully back into the shadows at the door. Some three feet away.

I sat stunned for a second, no more and then rolled feet over head away and skidded down the front steps on my stomach. I was left breathless and aching from head to toe staring up at the very angry vivid blue eyes of my captor. We looked at each other for a few seconds more, then I calmly ripped off a strip from my ragged sweatshirt, thanking the gods it wasn't a knitted one, but a material that could actually be used as a bandage and wrapped it around my neck, wadding up a piece to use as a pressure point against my bite wounds. Once done, I assessed the state of the rest of the top and discarded it. Jonathan had done quite a number on it.

I stood gingerly and glanced back at the vampire, knowing I was now safe in the sun, too bright and strong on this crisply fresh winter day high up in the mountains.

"I don't suppose you'd lend me your jersey?" I asked, only wanting to rub it in a little and not expecting an answer at all.

Surprisingly, I got one, unsurprisingly it was just a low growl.

"OK, then. See ya."

I turned and used every ounce of strength I had not to hobble, or limp, or stagger away. And walked at a brisk pace directly towards the gate. It took me eight minutes, I'd guess, to reach the trees. I turned one last time and could see the front door still open, a shadow outlined by the lights behind in the darkened interior of the house.

I'd never seen the house in daylight. It was actually quite attractive, somewhere you could imagine having a romantic interlude. I shuddered and knew this wasn't over yet. Not by a long shot.

Turning my back on my prison, hoping against hope it was for the last time, I stepped into the camouflage of the trees and began running.

I lasted five minutes before I collapsed to the ground in pain and exhaustion. And the world turned grey.

Then black.

Then nothing else at all.

7
LODO

I don't know how long I had been out, but the sun was high in the sky by the time I came to. After midday then. Thankfully, the sun had prevented me from freezing, but being in a somewhat ripped and torn T-Shirt at this altitude was not the best scenario. that was for sure. I was covered in goose bumps and was shivering, my teeth actually rattling slightly as I pushed myself into a sitting position. My body ached.

I had to keep going. I couldn't afford to be anywhere near this place when the sun set. The vampires would find me in a instant. Not just my scent, I realised, but my blood. The makeshift bandage at my neck was soaked. I didn't leave a pool of red on the ground when I sat up, but I knew I had lost a shit-load of blood to the slightly loose fibres of the material at my bite marks.

I shook off a rising sense of nausea, braced myself and got to my feet. The world turned black immediately, but not enough to take me down. I held my stance, closed my eyes, lowered my head slightly and let it wash over me. When it finally moved on I took the first of many painful and slow steps forward.

I had stopped counting them at 300 and was just simply telling myself *one foot in front of the next, in front of the next, in front of the next.*

This must have gone on for at least two hours. I was thirsty, barely able to lift my feet off the ground, instead dragging one foot along the road after the other. I must have looked like a zombie, the living dead. That just made me laugh. And the more I tried to stop myself the more I just kept laughing. I had actually stopped walking, or dragging my feet as the case may be and had both hands on my knees and my head down, racked with laughter when a farmer's truck pulled over to the side of the road next to me. I hadn't even heard it approach, it was only when the loose stones on the side of the road crunched beneath its tires that I stilled and braced for a fight. My fists came up beside my chest, one foot forward, the other back, slightly crouched, ready to defend or fight.

An old guy got out of the cab, grizzled features, grey unruly hair, a tooth missing in the front. He was human and his smile was kind.

"Are y'all right there, Missy?" he asked, his accent strong, but not daring to step any closer when he saw the look on my face and the fighting stance I had adopted.

I swallowed. I had a choice, tell him to move on or accept help. I glanced down at what I was wearing and then looked up at the sun. I was running out of time.

"Are you heading into town?"

"I'm on my way to the city. Ya need a ride. Climb in there, lass, I'll take ya as far as I can. Ya need away from here. I can tell."

I eyed him suspiciously, what did he know of this neighbourhood? What did he know of where I had come from?

He hadn't moved since he told me to climb in his truck, he just stood there, relaxed, open and friendly. Was I trading one captor for another? Was he friends with the vampires?

Shit. I had no choice. Civilisation was near the *Red Rocks Amphitheatre*, that I was sure of and that was a good half hour away by a very fast Camaro car. On foot, I was screwed.

I dropped my fists and nodded, then walked around to the passenger side of the truck and climbed in. No way was I showing how weak I was.

The old guy didn't say anything, just slipped back in his seat and started the truck back up. As he slid it off the shoulder I held my breath, but he didn't drive back towards the vampires, he headed off down the road the same way Jonathan and I had driven to get to the concert. After about three miles I let out a long breath. I wasn't safe, not by a long shot, but I was a step closer to being so.

The old chap reached down under his seat and pulled out a first aid kit, he placed it silently next to me on the seat between us.

"My name's Gus. I live just back down the road a few miles from where I picked ya up from. I seen a lot of things in my time here. Ya need not worry I won't tell a soul of where ya been, or where ya goin'."

I didn't say anything, just picked up the kit and started to rifle through it. Some ten minutes later I had stemmed the blood flow at my neck completely and patched it up with clean gauze and dressings. I couldn't do much for the scrapes, scratches and bruises. There were too many, there was no point trying to cover them all, so I just let them be. I tilted my head back on the seat and closed my eyes. I wasn't going to sleep, I just needed to think.

What now? There was obviously a large town nearby, a city, Gus had said. What would I do when I got there?

"What's the name of the city?" I think I surprised Gus, he jumped slightly. Maybe he thought I had been asleep, or maybe he had expected me to know where I was. Even asking it, I was risking giving too much away. I should have just kept my mouth shut, surely there would be something to give the location away when I got there.

"Denver. Ya're in Denver, Colorado. Ya have somewhere to go?"

"I think it's best if you don't know Gus. Safer. For you, maybe for me."

He nodded, as though that made complete and utter sense.

"How 'bout warm clothes, money?"

I chanced a glance at him. I must have looked a wreck. My T-Shirt was blood stained, I had definitely experienced something nasty at my neck, I was covered in bruises and scratches. And I was no doubt pale, gaunt and pathetic looking. I needed help, but the more I took from Gus, the more danger he would have been in. Deep down inside me I knew it was people, humans like him, I was meant to protect.

"I'll be fine, Gus. Thanks anyway."

He humphed, but didn't push any further.

I was scared the vampires would track me, that they would somehow be able to pick up my scent, lose it at where the truck had pulled over, but somehow be able to determine what truck it was, who it belonged to and track old Gus down. It wasn't out of the realm of possibilities. Maybe, they'd had a run in with Gus before. He seemed to know more than he was letting on. I couldn't chance that any more interaction with him would be safe. As soon as we got to Denver I would be on my own.

That thought terrified me almost as much as being back at that house did.

The rest of the trip passed in silence and then I recognised the suburb, somewhere near *Red Rocks* and some twenty minutes later we were in downtown Denver right outside a mall filled to the brim with people.

"This is the 16th Street Pedestrian Mall, it's busy and will be all day. Lots of people, lots of cover, lots of food. There's a visitor centre here too."

He had pulled over to the side of the road after saying that, near a crossing to the mall. The truck was still running and he hadn't turned towards me. I decided to make myself scarce, even though the thought of what I could possibly do now sent a shiver down my spine.

Just as I was about to slip out of the cab Gus added, "Take this. It's all I got on me, but ya need it more than I do."

I turned back to him and saw he was holding a fifty dollar note out to me. I looked up into his eyes and shook my head. "I can't take your money, Gus."

"Ya're a long way from home, Missy and I wager y'ain't got no idea where to head to next. I got me a grand-daughter your age, I would like to think someone would help her out when she needed it too."

He slipped the note into the top pocket of my jeans and then looked back out the front of his windscreen. I didn't know what to say, a lump had appeared in my throat. I swallowed hard past it and blinked away the tears. I wanted to tell him to move, shift house, stay away from that neighbourhood. I wanted to tell him to lock his doors and stay inside when it's dark. I wanted to tell him to always carry silver, preferably a stake. But I didn't. The less I said the better.

I thanked him and got out of the cab and watched as my good Samaritan drove off down the busy street in a puff of exhaust fumes, his ratty old farm truck bouncing along over non-existent pot holes.

I wasn't hungry, I still couldn't stomach food, but I needed warm clothes, I needed a map and I needed somewhere to hide. Fifty bucks wasn't much to accomplish all of those, but it was a start.

I entered the throng of people and wandered the shops, feeling for the first time in quite a while that I wasn't alone. Finding something to wear was actually harder than I thought it would be. There were restaurants and cafés galore and clothes shops, but they were all incredibly expensive. So I opted out of clothes hunting and just went to the closest bathrooms I could find. Turning my T-Shirt inside out, I hoped I'd avoid too many looks. I washed the blood and dirt off my face and arms and then ventured back into the throng towards the information centre.

The visitor centre had a wealth of information and I was soon set with a map, a cheap *Discover Denver* sweatshirt to keep me warm and an idea of where to hide out at least until the wee hours. I headed out to catch a cab. The LoDo District - the Lower Downtown Historic District - was a mishmash of old brick buildings, historical Denver sights and a whole lot of pubs and clubs. I suddenly felt at ease.

I knew the pedestrian mall I had started at would wind down at 5pm, but LoDo would keep going well after dark. Once the pubs and clubs all closed, I was going to have to think of another plan of attack. But for now, a club was the best place to be. The sun was getting low by the time my cab deposited me at my destination and I did a quick scan of the area, sussing out any dark alleys, dead ends, potential traps. The more time I spent away from the house, the more sure I was of how to look after myself. But still, I felt so weak. I'd been riding a high since I had escaped Jonathan, I knew any moment now I'd be hitting that low.

I scanned the area for something loud, busy and pumping, something that wouldn't quit too early in the game. I wasn't after a good time, just a well hidden time for as long as I could get away with it. An Irish Pub was the best I could come up with, large enough to accommodate a good number or patrons and not likely to turf out a tourist with a Denver sweatshirt and crumpled jeans.

O'Hagan's was in full swing. Irish music wafting out of the front doors onto the street, the smells of beer and hot potato chips and the sounds of laughter and merriment calling to me. I had no idea if I was a regular pub goer in my previous life, but *O'Hagan's* just seemed to be perfect right about now. Maybe I could even stomach a salted chip or two. A girl could only dream.

I wended my way through the already busy throng of pub crawlers and made it to the bar. Ordering a Guinness - which I had no intention of drinking - and a plate of hot chips, I found a spot in a dark corner to hide and watch the front door. I knew instinctively that I was close to the kitchens and a possible back entrance would be available if needed. I was also up against a wall, nothing could surprise me here. I sat and picked at my plate of crispy spud slivers, even managing to eat one or two and spent the next hour just watching. No one approached me, maybe I really did look pretty pathetic, but also no vampire crossed the threshold either. The stars had appeared not long after I arrived, so I knew they would be out and about for sure.

I could only hope by moving from where Gus had dropped me, having a different coloured top on and redoing my hair so it looked short from the front, would help to conceal me. But deep down inside I knew it was all futile. Vampires had ways of tracking you, a network available to find you, supernatural powers that only us humans could dream of. They were nothing if not efficient hunters and I didn't for a second think I would be difficult prey to find.

That thought just made me more and more nervous as the night wore on. Finally, after being eyed a few times too many by the bartender, I thought it was time to move on.

I snuck out with a loud group of revellers and walked at the back of their group for a while. My eyes darting from shadow to shadow, my senses on high alert, my fingers tingling with anticipation and downright fear.

The group I was tagging along with actually ended up passing Union Station, which even at this time of night was lit up like all good historical buildings should be from the outside, but also bustling with human activity on the inside too. I ducked in through the main entrance before my group had finished passing the front doors and hid behind a flower stand to survey my next refuge. Train stations stayed open all night, didn't they? I could only hope so and looking at the number of people purposefully marching across the great expanse, heading towards platforms and waiting trains, or off towards buses and taxis out to one side, I felt my hopes rise.

I waited for another group of commuters to walk past heading in the right direction then tagged on to their group. As they passed the public toilets I slipped inside. It was well appointed and big. Also relatively clean for such a busy and public place.

I was beyond exhausted now. The low had finally arrived and with no other safe options available I resigned myself to a night in a toilet stall. Images of Will Smith's *The Pursuit of Happyness* movie came to mind. If Chris Gardener could sleep in a loo with his little boy, then so could I.

I found the farthest toilet stall possible, thanking my lucky stars that there were some ten or so others readily usable for any foot traffic that came my way and locked the door behind me. OK, so no back door out of here, no window either. If a vampire were to track me here, I'd be trapped. But, the thought of sleeping on a bench out in the main area didn't sound much safer either. Maybe I'd just catch an hour's sleep here, no more. Then shift on. Surely one hour would be OK.

Besides, I was dead on my feet. No sooner had I put the lid down on the toilet seat and slumped down to rest, than my head was against the narrow side wall and I was sound asleep. If I'd stopped to think about how surprising that was, considering my heightened level of fear and anxiety right now, I would have realised how sick I actually was, but I didn't, I just slept.

Until I woke up inside someone's apartment and I immediately knew I was in trouble. My first thoughts? *How had they found me*, which were quickly followed by, *don't be ridiculous they're vampires*, only to be chased by, *I know this place, I've been here before.*

I turned around slowly, noting the shuttered large expanse of windows to the side, the expensive furniture and fine art and then registering the smell of cherry trees and chocolate ice cream in the air.

"Lucinda. My God. It worked."

I just stared at the vampire in front of me, unable to say a thing. I knew, somehow, that he meant me no harm, but I still couldn't shake the sense of danger. Hell, there would be nothing but danger for some time to come, at least until I could remember who the hell I was.

The man in front of me was tall, over six feet tall, dressed casually in fine black trousers and an open neck black shirt. He had shoulder length black hair, tied back at the base of his neck, he also had a prominent scar running down from his eye, across his cheek, but that wasn't what I recognised.

I recognised his eyes. They were a beautiful grey, with flecks of silver and platinum, surrounded by a bright multicoloured mark, that when I looked at it, made me want to go to him. Made me want to throw myself directly into his arms.

I wrapped my own arms around my waist and bit my lip.

"Who are you?" I managed to say quietly.

He looked utterly shocked for a moment, then infinitely sad.

"What have they done to you, my little Hunter?" he whispered.

I shook my head and took a step backward. He ran a hand through his hair and turned to sit in an armchair behind him. He clearly wasn't going to rush at me then. I relaxed my stance marginally.

"Do you know who you are?" he asked not looking at me, maybe he thought I would scare more easily if he looked me in the eye. I appreciated the sentiment, I didn't trust it though.

So, I didn't trust him, but I also felt he wouldn't harm me and more to the point, I needed some help. I was lost, alone, no doubt being hunted and without means or memory to help me. Could I take the risk?

I looked around the room for inspiration and spotted a mirror over a bookcase on one wall. It was directly opposite me, but I wasn't reflected in it at all. I spun around behind me, taking in the lamp and chair at my back, then returned to look at the mirror. The lamp and chair sat proudly front and centre in the mirror, but no me.

What the fuck?

The vampires eyes flicked up to me and he sighed. "You're wondering why you have no reflection?" I flicked my own glance at him, but didn't say anything. "You are Dream Walking, I called you to me in your sleep. Where are you sleeping, Lucinda? Is it safe?"

"Who are you?" So many questions coursing through my mind and all I could come up with was *who are you?* Go figure.

"My name is Gregor. I am a friend. We know each other, quite well actually, but we are what I consider to be very good friends. You trust me, well to a certain extent, but I unflinchingly trust you. I am in Wellington, New Zealand and we have no idea where you are, or where you have been for the past month. We have been desperately trying to find you, but you have been cut off to us. This is the first time I have managed to call you to me in a Dream Walk and believe me, I have been trying daily to do so. Michel is in no fit state to reach you, we all hoped that I could. Where are you, Lucinda? Let us come and bring you home. Please."

So, the moment of truth. He knew me, he seemed familiar, if not remembered, but I'd been fooled before in the past. Still, I'm asleep in a toilet stall in a train station in Denver, Colorado and I have no money, no memories and absolutely no strength to go on anymore. Sooner or later Jonathan and his vampires would catch up with me. I needed help of the divine kind, maybe this was it.

"What train station?" he asked.

I sat straight down in the chair behind me in complete surprise.

"You can read my mind."

"We share a connection, I can read your thoughts when they are strong, or you are weak. I am guessing it is the latter right now."

I just nodded, what else could I do?

"What train station in Denver, Lucinda? We can have someone there within the hour."

Within the hour. Holy shit. Who were these people? Vampires? Whatever.

"We are your family. Or at least, Michel is and it would be one of his vampires, his acquaintance who would come for you. Enrique is in New Mexico, he could be with you in an instant. His speed is unparalleled."

"Who is Enrique?"

"A vampire aligned with your kindred. He can be trusted."

There was that word again, *kindred*. Michel. I knew it was right, but I couldn't put all the pieces together, none of it fitted. No memories to back up the feelings, just hunches and a gut feeling that seemed so very right. What if this was a trap though? What if this vampire was one of Jonathan's, he was prone to elaborate plans wasn't he? Pretending I was his wife to exact revenge was one hell of an elaborate plan.

Gregor was on his feet as soon as those thoughts crossed my mind. His fangs down and a low growl emitting from deep within his throat.

"Did he... did he harm you?" His voice was rough, uneven and low. I knew what he was asking, but I couldn't answer him. Jonathan *had* certainly hurt me, but I had no voice to say those words. He had also drugged me, lied to me and held me captive for over a month.

Gregor let another long breath out and yet another hand went through his hair. I was picking he was having trouble not coming to me. I got the impression he wanted very much to make sure I was OK and not harmed. If he was a friend, we must have been close.

"We were. Once." His voice cracked slightly and he had to clear it.

"Where are you, Lucinda, let us help you. I swear to your goddess Nut, that I mean you no harm." He fisted his hand over his heart and bowed low. Whether it was to me or my supposed goddess, I'm not sure, but I got the real sense he was being truthful.

"In a toilet stall at Union Station, LoDo." I said it in a rush.

"Enrique will find you. Stay where you are, he will come to you." He smiled a small smile. "Go back to your body, it's unsafe to Dream Walk for long. Try to rest. I'll see you soon, *ma petite chasseuse*."

I wasn't sure how to go back to my body, but it didn't matter, because just then there was a loud bang on my toilet stall door that woke me up with a start and sent my Dream Walking self hurtling back to my body in a mad rush.

I woke to a persistent angry thumping against the metal stall door, making it shake and rattle and almost come off its hinges from the abuse.

My heart in my throat I prepared for battle again.

8

THE ROCKY ROAD TO ESCAPE

"We know you're in there! Come on out! You can't stay here any longer."

It was a human male, not vampire and from the shoes I could see at the bottom of the toilet stall door, he looked like military, police or security. I heard the crackle of a radio, a walkie-talkie, I think.

"We saw you come in here on the security cameras. It's been an hour, get your ass outta here. This is not a hostel." Another loud bang on the door.

I sighed in relief. Security then. I opened the door to the stall and looked up at the brown eyes of the guard. He blinked slowly at me, probably picking up on how fragile, battered and sick I looked.

"Sorry," I mumbled as I moved past him. "I didn't realise I'd been in here that long. I'll go."

"Are you all right? Do you need the paramedics, ma'am?"

I shook my head and walked out of the toilets. I knew he was following. I knew he wouldn't just let me walk off and hide somewhere else. Union Station was no longer an option for cover. I was going to have to brave the night outside and hope that this Enrique, that Gregor had talked of, would be able to find me just the same. But also know that I would have to hide myself well, if I didn't want any other vampires to find me either.

Crap. The night was still young. At least well past midnight, but I could tell we still had maybe three, possibly four hours until dawn. How the hell would I stay invisible until then? I rubbed at my face and moved awkwardly and stiffly to the exit.

"You got somewhere to go?" The guard was still with me, I had stopped paying attention to my surroundings. I cursed myself silently and took a quick look around. The station was just as busy as before, people milling around waiting for their trains. Denver was pretty busy after dark it would seem, but if it had a strong vampire holding, then that didn't surprise me. Vampires tended to spice up the night life and make it more desirable to humans. It was an unfortunate side effect to their inhabiting a location, one that played into their hands, not the humans.

"Yeah. I'll be fine."

He just looked at me, still rigidly militant, but also a hint of compassion there too. I was continually being bowled over by the humanity of people in this area. First Gus, now this guy. They all seemed to really care about their fellow man. Even in a vampire stronghold such as this, humans instinctively knew to band together. Maybe this was how we had survived the vampires for centuries. Maybe it was evolution, survival of the fittest, those willing to help each other making it through the night.

I smiled at up at him, willing him to believe. He didn't need any complications and helping me would only place him in immediate danger. I knew without a doubt that Jonathan's vampires would have made the assumption I had made it to Denver and would be trawling the streets right this second. I wasn't going to drag an innocent into my misery.

"You know, there's a crop of trees across the courtyard. It's a warmish night, maybe with the cover you'll be all right." He didn't smile when he said it, just opened the front door to the station and held it ajar for me. I nodded and walked through heading towards the trees he had recommended, then when I heard the station doors close behind me, took off in an entirely different direction. It wasn't easy to find somewhere safe to hide. Out in the open, it was even colder than I had thought possible. I wrapped my arms around my body trying to keep the warmth in.

I knew I needed cover, but I also needed somewhere I could watch the front door to the Station from. Somewhere with a wall at my back, but also possibilities for escape. I no longer had a weapon, but I did have my wits. The short sleep I'd had - and for some reason visiting with Gregor in his apartment - had revitalised me a bit. As cold as I was, I was also on full alert again, able to take in my surroundings in a glance, know where potential traps were hidden and actually sense where danger may be lurking. Even the frigid air was waking me up more so than I had been for a while. I warned myself that it would only last so long before the cold seeped in to my bones and stole what fortitude I had again.

How long I would have to wait for this speedy vampire to *rescue* me, I didn't know, but I could only guess it was going to take longer than what will power I had left. I straightened my back, determined to fight to the end, even if that only meant staying alert and focused and hidden.

I chose some buildings across from Union Station's entrance. Elaborate brickwork, Romanesque arches and sandstone trim made the behemoths stand out even in the dark. This really was a lovely district and under differing circumstances, I might have enjoyed the architecture. Now though, I was more interested in the deep wide entranceway, dark stoops and perfect vantage point, that the potential hiding spots provided.

I quickly snuck into one, pushing myself well back out of the lights of the streets, using the shadows to cover me as best as I could. I crouched down and folded my body in on itself for warmth and an illusion of protection and waited, alert and focussed on my surroundings, both immediate and across the courtyard, back towards the still bustling station.

At least there was a lot to keep me busy. Many more people out on the streets at this early hour than I had expected. I let myself sink into a semi trance, still keeping my eyes open and still making sure I was prepared. I shifted my legs and arms frequently, just enough to keep the circulation going and trust that my body would instantly respond to a threat without seizing should it be needed.

It was a long time before I realised I was sending my senses further and further out, that I was sending my senses out at all. I hadn't done anything like that since I had been with Jonathan, once again a reminder that I hadn't had my latest lot of injections for over 24 hours. I had actually missed two by now and that was having an effect on me. I knew instinctively that was why Gregor had reached me, I also knew it was why I could send my senses out right now. It made me feel more confident in my ability to look after myself, but I wasn't naïve, I was still unarmed and although I couldn't sense any vampires nearby, I knew my luck wouldn't hold forever.

Sure enough, some forty minutes after leaving the station, I felt them. A group of four, approaching from the west. I shifted again, checking the use of my limbs, they were stiffer than when I had first crouched down here, sluggish and achy all over, I was also more tired than when I started this vigilant game. The cold was making my teeth chatter, the breath in front of my face condensing the air in little puffs of steam. I lowered my breathing, only letting a small amount of air to circulate through me, trying to diminish any signs that I was even here.

The vampires would sense me, they could either smell my fear, my blood, although dried, or hear my heartbeat, which was unfortunately climbing. But I willed every fibre in my body to relax, hoping I could convince them I was simply a homeless person hunkered down for the night. The fact that I *was* a homeless person was just a coincidence.

The vampires kept to the shadows moving in formation. One in the lead, two on either side of him a step back, the fourth coming up the rear, but keeping a healthy lookout over his shoulder for approaching threats from behind. I recognised none of them, but they were definitely on the hunt. Was it a hunt for me or for dinner? Any old human would do. I couldn't tell, but I knew my body was trying to determine the answer to that question anyway, it just wasn't able to do it. I had the sense that it certainly felt like it should be able to, just couldn't yet make everything function the way it was meant to. Those damn drugs were still in my system.

I knew this, not only because of my body's fervent desires to ascertain what threat these vampires were, but also because none of my memories had resurfaced yet. A pure bolt of terror ran through me at the thought that perhaps they never would. That Jonathan had done permanent damage and I would be alone and lost in this world forever.

That jolt of fear must have done it, because one of the vampires paused mid-stride and glanced towards where I was hidden. I knew he couldn't see me in the shadows, their eyesight is keen, but not that keen, they did need some form of ambient light to discern shapes. But he could sense me, smell me, feel me. I held my breath and willed the fear to recede. It didn't.

He said something to his companions and they all looked my way. The rest of the courtyard vanished, my world shrunk to just me and them. My heart rate climbed, not just out of fear, but because it knew I needed the boost in oxygen to choose to either fight or run. Adrenaline shot through me, making my limbs dance alive, my brain clearly focus and my body ready for action.

This was it. They may not have been Jonathan's vampires, I couldn't be sure, but I doubted they wouldn't know who I was and once they had me in their hands, they'd soon put two and two together and get Jonathan involved. Either way, Jonathan's or not, this was it.

I couldn't stay where I was hidden, I was just dinner waiting to be served. I knew I couldn't outrun them and part of me reluctantly acknowledged that, unarmed and so weak, I couldn't fight them either. There were four of them and only one of me. But, I could hope to keep them in the open and maybe, just maybe, one of the many humans still walking around the station courtyard would come to my aid or frighten them off. It was the only course of action left available to me. I was both out of luck and out of time.

I stood up, a little unsteadily and walked down the steps towards them. My whole body wanted to run, my mind kept repeating over and over and over again, *run!* But, my heart knew it was futile. To run would be to offer a chase to the hunters who faced me and that would lead to where? Somewhere dark and unlit, somewhere away from humans, somewhere fatal. I chose to face my death head on with the smallest of hopes that the venue I had chosen would save me.

Never show fear. Never give an inch. Always stay on guard.

I stopped right in the centre of the courtyard, bathed in light from lamps around the edge of the clearing, conscious of the human lives that surrounded me and the undead ones that faced off with me some six feet in front of where I stood. And I waited.

They weren't sure what to do. I could see them quickly assess the situation, taking in the light level, the humans and the fact that I obviously knew what they were. They seemed unsure, but hungry. Their eyes taking on hints of red, a glow that only softly gave their heritage away. No one walking past recognised them for the danger that they were, no one even glanced at the red they now sported in their eyes. Whether they were expending a little power to cloak us, I didn't know, but they were weighing up their options as if they had a choice.

They didn't, as far as I could see, too many humans, too many people to glaze if they gave themselves away, their only choice would be to move on and leave me. I was certain they would, I'd called their bluff and other than cause a major disclosure of their kind, they had no choice.

So, that's why I wasn't fully prepared. One of them sprang towards me, while another began to circle to my rear and the two remaining began to gather humans, capturing them in their glaze and misting the whole area from sight. It all happened so quickly, but not fast enough for me not to realise they knew who I was and I was worth the effort and risk of exposure to capture.

My body reacted intuitively, without thought or reason, I danced out of the way, spinning in the air and landing some few feet out of the approaching vampire's grasp. I didn't pause for breath, conscious of the vampire behind me readying for assault, I danced again and sprang through the air like a gazelle, landing gracefully apart from both. I took a breath in and braced for the next move.

I knew I had about two more dancing steps in me, before I'd falter and make a mistake. I knew this, as surely as I knew how to breathe. It was natural, a part of who I was, it was me. I didn't question that knowledge, I just went with it, hoping it would be enough for them to give up the chase, for the effort to not be worth it and for the mist that covered us to disperse and the human police to arrive. It was all wishful thinking, but I didn't allow myself a moment to out guess it. I just danced as soon as one vampire sprang, fangs down, red glow now obvious in the low misty light filtering through to us where we danced.

I made it past him with ease and just managed a dance step out of the reach of the second vampire, only to land in front of the one creating the mist. He simply struck a hand out and punched me in the face. I went sprawling backwards and landed in a heap on the concrete pavers, blood pouring down my face, my head thumping, my body aching from excruciating, mind numbing pain.

One of the original attacking vampires landed on me in an instant, making any breath I was attempting useless. His body weight crushed me into the concrete, his arm across my throat cutting off all further thought of breathing, but made me at least think a bite to my neck was going to be slightly delayed. Of course, there are other veins to target and the second vampire grabbed hold of my wrist and sank his fangs in there, not making any attempt to soften the sting. I screamed, unable to stop the noise escaping and number one vampire clamped a hand across my mouth and growled.

I felt another vampire take my other wrist, his fangs causing unbelievable pain as he ruptured my vein there and the pull of blood doubling from both points on either side of my prone body. I was pinned above, held down at the wrists, unable to move. If they had wanted to return me to Jonathan, they were making sure I would be barely capable of conscious thought or movement when it happened. Or perhaps, now that they had a taste for my blood, they couldn't stop drinking, because I knew the two sucking were starting to lose themselves to bloodlust. Their sucking becoming urgent, no longer content to just suckle at my vein, they had started worrying there instead. The pull of my blood now coupled with the pull, from side to side, of their fangs in my flesh. I whimpered, still unable to scream, but the vampire above me just held his forearm against my throat firmer, making it impossible to swallow and soon all sound was out of my reach.

"Are you going to get on and feed from her?" A voice over the shoulder of the vampire crushing my throat said quietly. I was guessing it was the vampire controlling the mist and keeping the humans at bay. He had obviously drawn the short straw tonight.

The vampire above me grunted in reply, nodded to himself and then swiftly removed his throat-crushing arm and struck with his fangs in my neck, on the opposite side of the gauze and dressing from Jonathan's earlier munch. Pain shot down through the puncture site, coursed red-hot through my veins, snaked out along my nerve endings and made the world around me turn red. Sweat began to grace my skin, trickling down my neck and between my shoulder blades. My heart leapt inside my chest, as though the sudden increase in beat was enough to escape the pain. I felt hot tears run down my cheeks, but they didn't register. I knew they were there, because I knew I was crying. But I couldn't feel them. All I could feel was pain.

So great, so consuming, so complete. My entire body was one ball of blazing fire and pain. These vampires didn't care for glazing their meal. They didn't care to alter their bites from a mild sting to something more pleasant. They wanted to feed the lust for blood that had consumed them, that had made them rogue. They wanted little else but to consume all of me and if, in the process, they made it painful, so much the better. Darkness lurked within their souls. A Darkness I recognised but couldn't name. It was familiar and frightening and yet, at the same time, it felt like home.

I shuddered at that realisation, that I could be so in tune with a Dark soul. That it would feel, not exactly welcome, but at least accepted. I struggled through the haze of pain to determine why I was kin to Dark, but the answer was tantalisingly just out of my reach. What on Earth had I been before this, to be so accepting of Dark? I didn't want to be that person. These vampires were evil and although I knew not all vampires were the same, these ones, these rogues, were part of what I was.

The tears increased, my silent sobs of pain morphed into despair. How could I be this close, this familiar with such evil, such Dark? How could I feel connected to it in such a way? Lack of blood had made me dizzy, but it was the thoughts of Dark's familiarity that made my stomach clench and nausea roll through me. I hated that I felt an affinity towards these vampires who were now intent to drain me dry, to take my blood as though it was their right, to harm me, to kill me, without a second's pause.

I hated them, I hated this and those thoughts alone allowed me to find myself again. I didn't know why the Dark inside these vampires felt familiar, but I did know I didn't condone it, like it. Even if a part of me accepted it, I knew a bigger part of me detested it.

I held onto that thought and fought the threatening blackness that engulfed me. I breathed through the pain that racked my body from head to toe, not a single inch of my flesh was free from that pain. But my mind, my thoughts, were. I was good, these vampires were bad. And if I had to die tonight, I would reach Heaven, my soul pure and light. I may not be able to stop what was happening and although the futility of my situation depressed me beyond words could convey, I clung to the fact that I was Light and these vampires were Dark and somehow that would set my soul free.

This scene was so surreal, but pain the only thing I could feel or sense and my thoughts of Light the only thing I could hear. Suddenly, the vampire at my neck burst into dust and I woke up, pain no longer so intimate, but still clinging to my body like a glove.

It was a minute or two before I noticed just one vampire at my side, his hand brushing the hair on my face aside, his voice unable to reach me. The fact that he was licking all my wounds closed and the small amount of release from pain that provided, just a tickle on the edge of my consciousness.

When he simply lifted me in his arms, I let him, my own going around his neck, clinging to what I saw as my salvation from pain and the Dark. He cupped my face with his free hand and stared into my eyes as he ran us away from from the scene at such speed I couldn't see anything other than flashes of light and dark shadows passing by alternately.

His voice reached me this time, his dark brown, almost black eyes dancing with flecks of amber and ochre holding me captive.

"Be still and sleep." His accent thick and rich, maybe Spanish, but so beautiful, so warm, so full of concern.

Within a second, maybe two, blissful, languid sleep engulfed me and I allowed myself the luxury of thinking I was finally safe.

9

HOMEWARD BOUND

I woke lying on a leather couch and immediately recognised my surroundings. I sat upright and caught the glint of something shiny on a small table to my side. I snatched the stake up and held it reverently before taking in the scene before me.

A jet plane, not too dissimilar to the one Jonathan had spirited me away in and across from me sitting in a leather armchair sat the vampire who had rescued me from the Union Station courtyard. His gaze watched me intently, but he didn't move or speak.

I fingered the stake in my hand and felt a familiarity with it that shot through to my core. I don't think he could have gifted me anything that would have accomplished the sense of peace this bit of sharpened and honed silver did. He was either confident he could hold off any attack with it from me, or confident I wouldn't attack him at all. Either way, he was letting me take some control of my surroundings back and I reluctantly appreciated it.

"Enrique?" I asked uncertainly.

"*Si, Señorita.*" He nodded his head slowly towards me, but didn't shift any further in his seat. "I am sorry, I was not quick enough. I let you down." His eyes darted away, but the mention of his rescue just reminded me of all that familiar Dark. A shudder rushed over my body and I swallowed back a little bile.

His eyes shot back to my face taking my response in. He smiled a sad smile, that made him seem so much more human than I thought a vampire should be.

"Well," I said, then cleared my throat. "I'm alive, so you must have done something right."

He cocked his head to the side, no doubt sensing my need to change the subject, but all I could see in his deep brown eyes was compassion, mixed with a hint of concern. He was trying to hide the concern and the thought that he could fool me, with a vampire's skill at schooling their features to show only what they wanted shown, made me a little uneasy. But, I wasn't scared of this vampire. I knew somewhere in my returning memories that I knew him and I could trust him, at least to some degree.

"There is a bathroom on board." He indicated where it was with his elegantly dressed arm. "Also a change of clothes, more suited to your normal attire." He kept his gaze resolutely on my face. I knew he was trying to appear as non-threatening as possible. I did appreciate it, but also felt a little like a victim right now and *that* did not sit well at all.

I glanced down at what I was wearing and cringed, there was blood and dirt all over my sleeves and top. Not nice. But, the thought of what attire would constitute something more suited to me had me curious, so I stood, a little unsteadily, stake still clasped in my hand. He didn't move to offer assistance, just watched me with those slightly concerned eyes.

I was relieved to find the door had a lock, although nothing would really stop a vampire from breaking in if he really wanted to, save from silver lined titanium of course. I found a pile of black clothes neatly folded on the bench and hesitantly picked them up. A short, almost mini, skirt, a tight fitting black T-Shirt and a fitted jacket with a pocket ideally suited to fit the stake. Also a change of underwear and tights. I stared at the clothes spread out on the bench before me and willed myself to remember wearing something similar in the past.

I glanced up at the mirror and blinked in shock at what I saw. This was me? I looked so pale, so gaunt, so fragile, as if a breeze could blow me over and snap me in half. My cheeks were hollow, my collar bones jutting out vividly, dark smudges under my eyes. And those eyes, the hazel seeming flat and dull, no sparkle, not very much life. I had been to hell and back, but I was alive. I took solace in that thought - a little of the victim leaving - and ran a hand through my thin long and limp hair, feeling how brittle it was, how full of muck and gunk it had become, just like my body, polluted with chemicals, not of my doing.

I suddenly felt nauseous and only just made it to the toilet before I dry retched into the porcelain bowl. I coughed and spluttered through another couple of waves of nausea and dry retching, then collapsed on the tiled floor and hugged the loo.

"Lucinda. Do you need help?" Enrique, just on the other side of the door. I flushed the toilet even though I hadn't managed anything else other than a spit or two and wiped my face with my filthy sweatshirt.

"I'm fine," I whispered, then stronger, louder, "I'm fine."

I could tell he hadn't moved from the door, but he didn't say anything, didn't open it up and come storming in. I heard him slowly slide down the partition between us and come to rest on the floor on the other side.

"I am sorry." His slightly muffled, accented, voice managed to penetrate the thin door wall. "I was too late to save you from those rogues." He said the word *rogues* with what sounded like bitter contempt. "I should have been faster. I am sorry." His voice had gone whisper quiet, full of remorse and perhaps a little shame at not having rescued me sooner.

I didn't know what to say. But I did know, that him being supposedly late to rescue me was not what had made me sick just now, neither was the fact that the rogues had fed from me to such a degree. Although that memory was going to be etched in my mind forever and the thought of another vampire feeding from me right now did make me feel a little ill. No, the dry retching into the toilet bowl had all been about Jonathan and what he had injected me with.

"It wasn't you," I finally answered. "I wasn't sick because of you or them."

I heard him sigh on the other side of the door. Followed by the soft thump of something coming to rest against the wall between us. His head? His hand?

"We have been searching for you for weeks. Michel has been beside himself. You have no idea how many people are thrilled at the news you are safe and coming home."

He paused, the silence stretching out between us. It was me who broke it first.

"I don't remember any of them." Even to me it sounded hollow, defeated.

"It is all right, you will. I tasted Benzodiazepines and other substances in your system when I closed your wounds, all of which have an amnesic effect, blocking short term memories, but they will return. You will remember."

I reached up and touched my neck, noting not only had the most recent wounds been healed, but the dressing over Jonathan's also removed and the wound there healed too. That was the extent of what Enrique had done to me it would seem, I was still dressed in my original clothing, I was still covered in dirt and blood, bruises and cuts and grazes still graced my skin. Only the vampire marks were gone, but what they represented wouldn't be cleared away so easily.

"Have your shower, little Hunter, you will be with your kindred soon."

I heard him get to his feet swiftly and smoothly and then nothing more, just the sound of the plane's engines thrumming through the fuselage, droning away in the background. I stood carefully and turned the shower on. Once the water came up to temperature I couldn't get in there fast enough. Under the hot sharp spray I scrubbed and rubbed and scoured my skin, despite the pain it caused on the injuries blooming all over me. I washed my hair four times, then conditioned it twice. I covered myself in soaps and body washes and repeated it again and again and again. And I cried. I cried for the ordeal I had endured. I cried for the memories still so lost. And I cried for the vampire who had been *beside himself* at the loss of me. My kindred. Michel.

I could picture him. I knew how handsome he was. But I couldn't really remember much more than that. Which only made me cry more.

By the time I came out of the shower and dried myself off, dressing in robotic movements, I was all cried out. Empty on the inside. Blank. The clothes fitted well, although slightly loose and did feel familiar, a small spark of memory igniting within. Not enough to make me dance a jig, but enough to make me feel a little warmer inside, to make me feel lighter somehow.

I crept out of the bathroom and tried not to shuffle to the couch. The silver stake was quietly resting inside my jacket. I smelt of lavender and vanilla in abundance, my hair now lank, but clean, running part way down my back, my breath minty fresh.

"Are you hungry?"

I shook my head. I hadn't eaten in days, those two hot chips at the Irish pub in LoDo the last morsel of food I'd consumed and hardly sustaining food at that, but I wasn't hungry. I couldn't stomach food. I rested my head back on the couch and forced myself not to go to sleep.

"You can sleep if you wish. No harm will come to you."

I was sure he hadn't read my thoughts, just my body language, but I shot him a glance anyway. He was in the same armchair as before, his legs crossed at the knee, a glass of dark liquid in his hands. Something strong, I was betting.

"How long until we land?" I might as well keep myself awake with conversation. And besides, I needed the distraction from my thoughts and memories of the past few hours.

"Two hours, or there about." He took a sip of his drink, his eyes never leaving me. I tipped my head to the side and held his gaze.

"How do I know you?"

He smiled, a genuine smile, his eyes lighting up and displaying a beautiful combination of browns. Even without trying, this vampire made me feel safe.

"I am a friend to your kindred's line. Michel and I share an accord. Do you remember the first time we met, in his office?"

When I shook my head, he continued. "You pulled a stake on me." He smiled affectionately at the memory, one I couldn't yet share. "You were captivating, enchanting, but clearly lost to anyone else but Michel." He laughed then, at the memory no doubt, although how me pulling a stake could make him laugh, I didn't know. "I have lamented every day since, fate's cruel hand, I had wished you were mine." I wasn't sure I believed him, he seemed to be trying to lighten the mood, more than make a statement that he had once coveted me. His words more flippant than weighty. He took another sip of his drink. "And since that day, you have grown more and more powerful, no longer simply a beautiful, adorable prize, but a strong and commanding one too. You are set to change the world, Lucinda, the very fabric that has defined our kind for millennia. I may not hold your heart, but I am more than happy to hold your hand and aid in your fight."

What fight? Holy shit, what fight? Why can't I remember? I started absently scratching at my arms, through my jacket sleeves at the crease in my elbows. A damp sweat had broken out on my skin and my knee was starting to jump up and down in small jerks. None of this even registered to me, but Enrique shifted immediately.

"What are you feeling?" He leaned forward in his chair, still holding his drink, but almost as though he had forgotten it.

I was beginning to feel like something was crawling under my skin, but I couldn't answer him, too busy shifting in my seat and scratching more places on my body. Through clenched teeth I did manage to say, "What's happening to me?" Before slipping off the edge of the sofa and curling in a ball as pain shot through my stomach.

He was beside me in an instant. I had no idea where his glass had gone to, but he was stroking my back, brushing my hair and trying to calm me with both hands, so no drink then.

"You are going into withdrawal," he said, helping me out of my jacket, then throwing it over to a seat nearby. "There is nothing I can do to remove it, but I will try to ease your suffering. Until Michel can heal you, unfortunately you will have to ride the pain to some extent, I am sorry. The drugs you have been inflicted with are powerful and your body now craves them regardless of the danger. Lower your shields and I will try to distract you from the pain."

I wasn't sure how to lower my shields. What shields? Enrique had lifted me off the floor into his lap, cradling me again in his arms protectively, holding both my hands at the wrists with one strong hand of his own, to stop me from scratching myself raw. I writhed and moaned against the restraint, pain coursing through me, hot and cold and cold and hot. Sweat beginning to track down my temples, down my chest, every sensation making a fine line of hot sharp pain follow its path across my skin, searing me, burning me, sinking deep down inside me, making me cry out and whimper in distress.

"Lower your shields, Lucinda."

I didn't know how, but was vaguely aware of something against my mind, something soft and warm and full of light, something nudging and encouraging and pushing in a constant pressure. I homed in on that feeling, that warmth and light and the more I focused the more I became aware of a wall like structure visible in my mind. I grabbed hold of that wall and instinctively knew it was my shields. Pushing back at first against Enrique's light didn't do a thing, so I simply tried to imagine the wall no longer existed at all.

It shattered in an instant, leaving me completely open and bare. Enrique's power forged forward, no longer being blocked at all and completely engulfed my mind. He cried out in surprise, trying to pull his power back a little, but it was too late. His warmth and light washed over me like a tsunami, totally wiping any sense of pain away, bathing me in comfort and peace to the point of being unable to feel my skin, my body, my limbs at all. And only recognising a deep seated sense of calm before I blacked out entirely and was swept away to sleep.

I woke still in Enrique's arms, still being cradled, stroked, whispered to in Spanish, words I had no way of understanding. When he noticed I was awake again, he switched to English.

"Damn, Lucinda. I had no idea you'd drop them completely. I am sorry."

"How long have I been out?" It felt like I'd been asleep for a week. I was so relaxed, so peaceful, so calm. I stretched my body in his arms like a well fed cat. He growled low, then cleared his throat and looked away abruptly.

"No more than five minutes." His voice was stiff and formal, as though he was trying to distance himself from me. I tried to move from his cradling arms, but he held me firm against his chest, without making eye contact at all.

"Enrique," I said quietly.

"Stay still. I can't... I can't let you go yet, just a minute more." He still wasn't looking me in the eyes, but I had the impression that if I moved he would chase me. I shifted uncomfortably and he growled, holding me almost painfully tight. "Do. Not. Move."

His eyes when he glanced at me were a maelstrom of browns; amber, ochre, deep redwood, bronze.

"Jesus, Enrique. What's wrong?"

"I have delved too far in your mind." Every word was forced out through clenched teeth, he was fighting to stay in control. "I..." He licked his lips. "I need to hold you a little longer." He finished rather lamely, then looked away.

I resigned myself to sitting still, very still and just listened to his ragged breathing and then concentrated on the feel of his hand stroking my back in slow, slow circles. It didn't feel intimate, but it did feel soothing. Me or him? All I knew was, what I sensed from Enrique right now was a fierce desire to protect me. To keep me safe. His vampire within had woken up and decided I wasn't in the category of prey, but instead protection. I was infinitely grateful for that fact.

I cringed at the unwelcome thought of prey and being fed upon by vampires, lots of vampires and Enrique stiffened.

"Please do not think of them, Lucinda. Please." Shit, he was reading my mind and it was upsetting him, or at least upsetting his vampire-within. But, it was the way he begged that kept me from my memories, those recent memories of vampires attacking me. I concentrated instead on his plea, he was determined to protect me - even protect me from my memories - and although he was unable to release me right now, he meant me no harm. He didn't want to feed from me, to satisfy a hunger in any way, shape, or form. He was using every muscle he had to keep me safe. Not that there was anything in this cabin to threaten my safety, other than him, but his vampire-within was determined I'd stay safe regardless.

"Just a moment more, Lucinda. Just one more moment." He rested his head down on my chest, his thick dark hair brushing against my chin, his hot breath coming in quick succession against my skin.

I didn't say anything, just held my breath and tried to think of something calming, waiting his vampire out. A picture of a farm came to mind, little lambs in the distance wagging their tails, a slight breeze gently breaching the hill behind me, making the thin film of my dress sway around my legs, baring my naked skin underneath.

"I can read your mind because your shields are not yet up and I have already traversed so deeply within. Because of that depth of mental connection my vampire feels inordinately protective of you. I cannot dissuade him, until he is ready to let go." He pulled back slightly and smiled. I could see he had, in fact, got himself and his vampire more or less under control again, the colours in his eyes still swirling, but much more languidly, much more muted than before.

He picked me up effortlessly and placed me back on the couch then took the few steps he needed to collapse in his own chair again. The drink was to his lips in a second of parking himself firmly in the chair and downed completely in one single gulp.

I watched him closely, wondering just how far his vampire-within would go to protect me now and how permanent such a connection would remain. It was, at least, a safer and more positive response than most vampires would have and it's not that I wasn't grateful that his vampire had chosen to cherish me over something less invited. But still, any vampire connected to me right now was more than a little unnerving. I couldn't help it. Lacking knowledge of who and what I was, incomplete memories of where I came from and who was important to me, coupled with recent images of aggressive vampires and near-death experiences, just didn't make accepting a vampire I felt I barely knew as my guardian angel. Something told me I already had one of those, one that would be more welcome than this vampire. Despite him being so caring, protective and having saved me from certain death.

"How close were we before?"

He had refilled his glass and was halfway through it already.

"We were acquaintances. I am your kindred vampire's ally. Nothing more."

So, having him as my permanent guardian angel was something altogether new in our relationship dynamics. I really didn't have the strength to politely decline his offer of chaperoning me everywhere I went.

He laughed at my thoughts, a delightful chuckle from the back of his throat. When he saw the response to him hearing my thoughts again on my face, he added, "Have you considered replacing your shields? The effect of my influence over the drugs you have been subjected to should last until you reach Michel, at which stage he can heal you completely, I am sure."

I was surprised his new status as my self-appointed protector would allow that suggestion. Surely keeping tabs on my thoughts would allow his vampire to know when I needed its aid?

He smiled slightly and shrugged his shoulders in an elegant roll of muscles. "Somehow, I don't think we will ever be simple acquaintances again, Lucinda. I will always feel as though I should look out for you. Like a brother does a sister. But, yes, please raise them, before my vampire insists otherwise."

I worked on imagining strong brick walls around my mind and within minutes felt they were complete. I watched as Enrique visibly relaxed. So, he didn't like hearing my thoughts? My regard for him increased ten fold.

"That's a nifty trick, you know, getting so far inside someone's head," I said conversationally. "Somewhat more direct than talking." Cuts out the misunderstandings, anyway.

He laughed again. "It is usually reserved for the most intimate of relationships, one built on trust and love. When taken out of that context it is an abuse. I would never abuse you."

Just then the fasten seatbelt sign pinged on and Enrique sighed.

"It has been a pleasure, *Señorita* and I am glad to have successfully distracted your mind, but your kindred awaits and no doubt when your memories return you will remember this gift you have shared with me and perhaps bestow it on someone more worthy, such as him."

I thought about that for a moment, unable to picture wanting that emotional connection with anyone, unable to envisage letting myself be laid so bare, so open, so vulnerable again. Enrique had caught me at the most weakest of moments, entirely unintentionally and with no further desire than to protect, but still not given as free will.

Was I really that close to my kindred that I would feel able to give him this *gift*, as Enrique had called it?

I guessed I was about to find out. Auckland City spread out below my window, the lights calling to me and welcoming me home.

It was only as the wheels of the plane touched down on the tarmac that I realised, I had recognised it. Enrique had never told me where we were heading, but I knew it was Auckland.

And I had finally come home.

10

HOME SWEET HOME

Waiting at the hangar our plane taxied to was a Land Rover Discovery, all shiny sleek black, tinted windows, large alloy wheels. The plane stopped just in front of it and Enrique opened the door, lowering the stairs.

"Are you staying?" I asked as I went to walk past him.

He smiled, that genuine smile of his and nodded slowly. "I will be staying at *Sensations,* but I believe I will not be travelling in your car. Mine is no doubt due here momentarily, I shall bid you farewell from here. I am sure we will be speaking again soon."

I suddenly felt reluctant to leave him. I had felt safe with Enrique, he had rescued me, found me in Denver and brought me home. For a brief moment I wondered why it wasn't Michel who had saved me. Why hadn't my *kindred* moved Heaven and Earth to get to me too?

"It will be OK, Lucinda. Your memories should return within the next day, two at the most. With it, so much more will make sense. Trust me." He took my hand in his and kissed it briefly on the back, then released it again. No lingering kiss or touch, very impersonal, yet respectful.

"Your guard awaits." He nodded towards the car and sure enough, a female vampire was standing next to it waiting. I didn't recognise her.

"Do they know I can't remember?" I whispered, still unable to walk away from him.

"Yes." His voice was soft. "They know everything I know."

I looked at his face then and clearly he saw fear on mine. He reached up and cupped my chin. "It will be OK, little Hunter, they are your kin."

"I want you to come with me." My voice sounded pathetic and I was trembling slightly. In my mind Enrique was safe now, any other vampires most definitely were not.

He looked pained, but after a quick glance at the vampire waiting he reluctantly shook his head. "I am not family, Lucinda. I would not be welcome, not until they have had a chance to embrace you themselves. To ensure you are safe. I am merely the messenger, if I over step my place, we may not see each other ever again. I should like very much to see you again."

I nodded slowly and took a deep breath in. I could do this. I have survived so much more recently, I could face this last hurdle. I felt inside my jacket for my stake, immediately feeling my heartbeat settle at the touch of the cool silver against my finger tips. Enrique smiled at the action.

"Always the Hunter."

I wanted to ask him what he meant, what was a Hunter? But, I knew I would only be stalling and if what he said was true, I would find out soon enough. Two days. Just two more days and it will all make sense.

He better be bloody well right.

I turned without saying goodbye and got halfway down the steps before stopping. Looking back at him I whispered, "Thank you." He heard me, smiled and fisted his hand over his heart and bowed low at the waist. Then retreated into the cabin, making my only course of action to return to the vampire waiting beside the car.

I walked slowly and a little stiffly towards the woman. She looked about my age, long blonde hair, my height too, which was kind of nice. And she was beautiful in a cute, but tough, kind of way. She looked like she could eat vampires for breakfast, but still look appealing while she skinned them alive. She smiled genuinely at me and took a step forward. I stopped immediately, noticing she had risen her arms, as if to hold me in an embrace. She lowered them slowly, but kept smiling.

"Welcome home," she said softly in an American accent that made me cringe in fear. But she didn't acknowledge my response, just opened the front passenger door to the car.

I took the cue and slid in. She shut it and was around the driver's side in an instant, the engine started and we were off. I buckled my seatbelt as I watched the plane disappear behind us, Enrique still on board.

It was a little awkward, travelling in silence, just the lights of passing cars and Auckland city to break the monotony. I thought she'd just let the still air sit silent, but she began talking after we had left the immediate airport grounds. Slowly at first and then faster, almost a rush to fill the gap left by my stillness and silence. But, I had the sense that it was all planned, all methodical. Nothing this woman did was not thought out.

"Amisi has baked your favourite. She's been baking non-stop since we heard Gregor had found you. There's bat cookies and hot cakes, blueberry muffins and something she called pavlova. It was a trial, being Egyptian I don't think she had made it before. I still don't know if it was a success, she covered it in a whole shit-load of cream and then chopped up kiwi, so it's now this crispy creamy white mountain covered in green. Kind of impressive in a lump of goop kind of way."

I listened as she kept talking, enjoying her mannerisms even though her accent was American, like Jonathan's, but she seemed more relaxed, more normal somehow. I wondered if that was the Kiwi influence, whether she had been here long.

"You haven't missed much, *chica*, things have been pretty much rolling along in your absence. Amisi has picked up the slack, she's been hunting here and can you believe it? Wellington. Gregor's no doubt cock a hoop, finally he's had Amisi all to himself, shame she's dissed him at every turn. I think he thought she'd be all friendly and nice since you were missing and all, they'd have the loss of you in common, but she's been calling him out on every little thing. Bombarding him with *Iunctio* rules and how he is frequently breaking them. It's damned amusing, Gregor the Enforcer kowtowing it to an immature Nosferatin, but he's besotted. A bit like how he was with you. Still, you'll be relieved he's looking at Amisi all doe eyed now and not you. And Amisi can handle him. Totally."

I don't know if it was the fact that she had called me *chica* or the fact that she had just continued to talk about familiar every day things, or the fact that the drugs were finally wearing off, but as she kept talking, almost nonsense, but familiar nonsense none-the-less, I started seeing flickering images, memories I realised, flashing before my eyes. A dark skinned girl with long black hair, tall athletic build and a beautiful smile cooking in a kitchen, I knew instantly that it was Amisi. This vampire sparring with me, our swords glinting in the moonlight, her name coming to me without even trying, Erika. A club, all rich dark colours and solid wooden furniture, a friendly smiling bartender, fangs flashing, but I knew he was a friend. Doug. More and more images of people I knew, places I had been. Some of it easy to recognise, others just flashes, there one second gone the next, no chance to decipher them at all.

And Michel. Michel smiling at me, Michel laughing with me, Michel embracing me, holding me, loving me and as those beautiful memories came pouring back in I felt my love for him in return, my yearning for him, the hole in the heart was all for him. It frightened me. It enthralled me. It excited me. It made me suck in a sharp breath and Erika to stop mid sentence and cast a worried glance my way.

"Too much?" she asked, worry dripping off her words.

I shook my head and looked at her fully for the first time. "I... I can remember some things." I was sure it wasn't everything, I still couldn't remember what it was I did for a living, what a Hunter was, who I really was, but it was a start. And suddenly I wanted to get to Michel, I wanted to face him, to see that he was OK too.

Erika drove on in silence, clearly unsure if she should push her luck. As we approached a familiar suburb she shifted uncomfortably in her seat. I flicked her a glance.

"What is it?"

She sighed and rolled her shoulders. "You should be prepared. Michel is not well. I don't want you to be shocked when you see him. The time apart from you has taken its toll and I think..." She swallowed noticeably. "I think he has been sending as much of his power through the Bond to you as he could manage. I think he has been sacrificing his strength in order to feed your need." She looked at me quickly then and added, "Don't get me wrong, you look like shit too. You're skinny-as and pale, and you could pack up a family of four in those bags under your eyes, but Luce, he's worse. OK?"

I nodded, unable to say anything right then.

A few minutes later we pulled up outside a well lit house on top of a cliff. I could hear the ocean wash against the beach at its base. Erika hadn't parked in the attached garage, but out on the driveway. I stood holding on to the door of the car looking up at the warm lights shining through the large expanse of windows along the front of the property. I recognised the place, the word *home* floating through my mind, but even as my mind said it, it still felt a little disconnected from what I was feeling.

Erika stopped next to me and looked at the house too. "Do you remember it?" she asked softly.

"Kind of," I whispered.

She nodded and offered me her arm, I didn't hesitate, I knew I couldn't mount those steps on my own. One, I was shit scared all of a sudden and two, my legs had turned to jelly, I was feeling so damn weak. We walked slowly up the stairs and the front door opened as soon as we made the top step. Amisi stood on the other side, a big smile on her face, a tea towel in her hands. She went to take a step forward, but I caught Erika shaking her head at my side. Amisi paled slightly, but continued to hold her smile.

"I'm sorry," I muttered as I shuffled past her. I could see the shock on her face, but I couldn't help it. All these people knew me, obviously cared for me, but I couldn't muster the response they all craved. I just couldn't. That left me feeling sad and an apology was all I could muster.

In the foyer of the house I sensed vampires everywhere. In the lounge off to the left, in the kitchen towards the back, in the back yard, downstairs in the cellar.

"There's a lot of vampires here," I said quietly, beginning to shake.

Amisi came around and stood in front of me, her face calm and friendly, concern clearly written all over it. "They are all family, Lucinda. They won't hurt you. They are here for Michel's protection. And now yours."

I stared at her eyes, so deeply brown, so round and big and tried to see the truth there. My fear was ratcheting up, I couldn't help it, it was threatening to consume me and all rational thought was swiftly disappearing.

The vampires seemed to disappear while I held her gaze, all of them, save one upstairs and Erika at my back, flowing out of the house and retreating some distance away.

"Michel has asked them to pull back for now, *chica*. They are no longer here."

I flicked a glance back at Erika and she smiled. I swallowed convulsively and couldn't still my heart or stop the shakes. She took my hand and squeezed it.

"Would you like to sit in the lounge and just get your bearings for a moment?"

It was a kind offer, I knew she was trying not to rush me or push me, but something was pulling me upstairs. Like a fish caught on a tight line I felt the pull, I took a step towards the stairs and stopped, forcing myself to breathe.

"He's up there, isn't he?"

"Yes." Erika again, at my side. "He needs you, Lucinda. He needs his kindred."

I pulled my hand out of hers and began wringing them. If I was going to do this, I wanted to do it alone. I barely remembered Erika or Amisi, I felt OK with them, but not entirely safe. I did know that I had to climb those stairs. That I had absolutely no choice, that if I didn't do it now, I would soon collapse and have to be carried up there. I did not want that to happen. I had survived kidnapping, drugging, physical assault and several hours in a foreign city on my own when weak and impossibly outnumbered. I could do this.

"I go alone. I don't want either of you there." It sounded harsh, but if they noticed they didn't show it. Erika quietly closed the door behind us and Amisi walked off into the lounge. I looked back at Erika standing statue still at the door.

"I'll not follow, but I will watch you climb those stairs. If you fall, I can catch you before you hit the bottom." She crossed her arms across her chest and stared straight ahead. She wouldn't be budged. I sighed and took the first step towards that pull.

I made it to the top without falling, but I was breathless and so weak. I had to hold on to the banister rail for a moment to catch my breath and in case the world did continue to fall away to the side as it had been threatening. I had no idea how long it took me, possible only a minute, maybe ten. I was pretty drained and covered in sweat.

Finally, my heart rate slowed and the blurriness at the sides of my vision faded. I took a tentative step away from the safety of the rail and rejoiced when I didn't topple over. Tough Hunter, that's me. I smiled despite myself and kept heading towards the now undeniable and fierce pull, almost making me run, even though I had my heart in my throat and could barely draw a breath.

The door to the room was ajar, not fully closed and I could feel him on the other side. I placed my hand on the door and just stood there, unable to push it open, unable to pull away. What was on the other side was important to me, I knew this, but I was also so, so very scared. What if I couldn't remember him properly? What if what I remembered was false? Another lie, another trick to make me feel safe. What if I felt nothing when faced with him?

I felt a tear slowly track its way down my cheek and I angrily swiped it aside. I could do this. I had to do this. I *was* doing this.

Still my feet stayed rooted to the spot and my hand didn't push that damn door. Fuck!

Come to me, ma douce.

If I thought my world was tilting before, it was nothing to what I felt now. An onslaught of memories slammed into me and made me crumple to my knees on the floor. I held on to my head and stifled a cry, tears coursing down my face as I rocked back and forth. So much love, so much care, so much emotion. It filled me up and threatened to split me apart. I couldn't take it, I knew it would knock me out cold before too much longer. How could someone love another so much?

I barely noticed the door opening, or the vampire who knelt down in front of me, slightly swaying, as if he couldn't quite get his balance. I barely noticed his hands on my arms, his soft voice in my ear as he pulled me to him. I didn't resist, I just went with the pull; his arms, this connection, whatever it was, it didn't matter, I just let it happen. When his lips brushed my cheek and his arms crushed around me, my body sighed, it damn near gave up the battle there and then. I relaxed against him, struggled to stop the white noise in my head, the images flashing like strobe lights in front of my eyes, but they were winning.

Before I could register what was happening he lifted me in his arms and took me back in the room, the door closing quietly behind us unaided. I felt the mattress dip beneath us, he almost lost his balance then, tipping sideways, but putting a hand out on the bed head in time to stop the fall. He lay me down gently and slid on to the bed next to me, wrapping me up in his arms again, making the duvet at the bottom of the bed fly up and drape over us somehow.

I felt his power brush my shields and for some reason it didn't scare me, it felt so familiar, so normal, I just lowered them enough for him to slip in. His healing touch washed over me, wiping away the pain and ache and lingering sluggish response of the drug and replacing it with warmth and happiness and love. It was as normal as existing, as familiar as the back of my hand, I didn't even realise I was doing it, until I felt the light flow around us, wrapping us, coating us, in a vibrantly bright glow.

Ah, ma douce, you have found your Light again. Ma petite lumière. Welcome home.

I fell asleep in my kindred's arms, my head on his chest, his heartbeat in my ears, his arms holding me so tenderly and I knew I was indeed home.

I wasn't sure if I could remember everything, but I could remember this, remember him. I held on tightly as sleep pulled me under and thanked my goddess Nut for bringing me back in one piece.

For bringing me back to Michel.

11

NEW MEMORIES

I woke up in exactly the same position I had fallen asleep in. Michel's arms wrapped around me, our bodies pressed close together, my head on his chest. He was breathing deeply and evenly, still sound asleep. I allowed myself a moment to take in the sensations of having him so close, letting the warmth wash through me, the smells embrace me, the feel of his big, strong, safe arms around me. It all felt so right, but there was still big gaps in my mind.

Not about him, I think. I had no urge to flee from his hold, but the gaps were there and they kept gnawing away at my psyche. I wanted to remember. I wanted to be me again, but all that kept going through my head was the past month. Those memories were the most vivid. They were the ones that occupied my mind, no matter how I tried to direct my thoughts to Michel, they kept going back to that house, to Jonathan, to those vampires outside Union Station and if I was honest, to Enrique, my saviour.

I didn't want to think of Enrique as my saviour, I wanted Michel to have that role, that's what felt right. Somehow thinking of Enrique seemed like I was cheating on my kindred, but as much as I tried to chastise myself for those thoughts, they still prevailed. Enrique pulled those vampires off me, he rescued me from a grim and painful death.

He brought me home, he made me feel safe when all was lost, he delivered me to my kindred's arms alive.

No, I couldn't stop thinking about Enrique. I shifted slightly against Michel, trying to turn away and lie on a different side of my body. I wasn't sure how long we'd been asleep, but the shutters were down so daylight had come and it must have been a while, because the arm I was lying on had gone to sleep and now as I moved slightly, pins and needles had shot through the length of it making me cringe. But, as I tried to turn my body, Michel's arms tightened their hold. He didn't wake and I got the impression that this may have happened again and again while we had slept. Me shifting slightly, him tightening his hold and not letting me move away.

I paused and waited for him to relax then shifted a bit more. His arms tightened immediately and I actually realised I was smiling at his reaction. It was cute. He didn't want to let me go. I think I kind of liked that idea, but my arm was aching, I needed to roll over. So with small incremental movements, interspersed with him tightening his hold and then relaxing, I finally managed to turn right over, so he was now spooning me, his face in my hair at the back of my neck, his arms tightly wound around my stomach, pulling me close.

I think I could have fallen asleep again like that, I was still quite exhausted, but suddenly I realised Michel was awake. He stiffened slightly, realised maybe who he was holding, how close we were and then the inevitable early morning response kicked in and I felt him harden against the back of me. I held my breath waiting to see what he would do. Part of me wanted him to pull away, it was too soon, too much after what I had been through. But part of me longed for that connection again with him, someone I knew, without a doubt, was important to me.

I think he was having a hard time deciding what to do too, because it was a good minute before he shifted against me, allowing his hard length rub between my thighs, his face began to nuzzle my neck and although I had thought it was too soon, I rubbed myself back against him anyway, encouraging him further, making his breath come out in a short hot shot against my skin, sending a shiver down my spine. Perhaps if we had just continued like that for a while longer it would have been OK, I wasn't thinking of anything other than the feel of him against me, the warmth radiating out from between my legs to my finger tips, to my toes, but, Michel - maybe because he couldn't help it, maybe because it was just a normal thing to do when with me - took it one step further and burst my bubble.

His fangs came down and I felt them scrape against the sensitive skin at the side of my neck, pausing above my pulse point, pressing ever so slightly, denting the skin. And making me scream in fright in my head and shoot right out of the bed and slam into the wall between the shuttered windows, panting and crouched down, my arms around my body and my eyes never leaving him in the bed.

It took a moment for me to realise how bad he looked. Not only terrified at what he had done, but also so pale, so gaunt, so weak. Shit. Erika had been right and I hadn't even noticed last night, but now in the dim glow of the room I could see how very, very sick Michel must have become. If nothing else, that made me forget about what had just happened and returned me to me.

"You don't look well." It was all I could think of to say.

He smiled slightly, still a little petrified at scaring me I think. "I have been better, *ma douce*, but with you here, I can already tell I am returning to my former self." His smile turned a little bitter then. "I am so sorry."

Those four words were said with such emotion, such clear regret, that it was enough for me to go to him. He wouldn't hurt me, no matter what, he wouldn't hurt me.

I crawled back onto the bed, his eyes going a little wide and stopped just in front of him. He was sitting half up resting on his arm, I don't think he was capable of moving anywhere, he was trapped staring at me, unable to look away. His breath was coming in short rapid bursts, his eyes, so very familiar, were swirling an indigo, violet and amethyst maelstrom of colours, it took my breath away just to look at them.

I knew he wouldn't make a move towards me. I knew if anything were to happen, it would be entirely started from my end. He was almost a statue, save for his uneven breathing, he wasn't even blinking.

I think for him, time had stopped, it felt a little that way for me too, but I was in control, in complete control of what happened next.

Maybe it was that thought, the fact that I was in control again, that made me do it. I could have just sat there and talked. I could have just sat there and looked at him. I could have even just got up off the bed and had a shower, he wouldn't have stopped me, but the thought that I was in control made me feel more like me than I had ever felt before. I suddenly didn't want my recent memories to be what kept my mind so active. I suddenly wanted something of my doing, something beautiful for me and I wanted it to be with Michel.

I lay myself down in the crook of his body, resting my head on his upper arm, where it had been holding his own head up. It meant he was practically above me, looking down at me now. His lips were slightly parted and he had a puzzled look on his face.

I wanted to say something witty, something to lighten the mood, it felt so very heavy, filled with monumental importance, maybe that was because it was. Instead I just reached up and traced the lines of his face, allowing myself to remember each curve, the sensation of his perfect skin beneath my fingers. He had an obvious stubble on his jaw, a little thicker than he would normally allow. I liked it and my attention seemed to be caught there for quite a while. He smiled slowly, but didn't make a move to touch me, just let me find my own way.

After a while I moved on to his eyes and just let myself get drawn into their depths. Michel can't glaze me any more, not since we joined and even if he could, I knew instinctively that he wouldn't, not now, not in this moment. They were the most beautiful eyes I had ever seen, so deeply blue, so big and round, infinitely wonderful. Magical even. I shook my head at the sight of them. His smile widened a fraction more.

Then I found his hair. I'd always had a little thing for his hair. It's down past his shoulders, dark brown, almost black and so thick and luxurious, absolutely stunning and when you run your fingers through it, it's like running strands of silk through your hands. I must have laid there and run my fingers through his hair about a dozen times, maybe more, before I realised what I was doing. All the time he had just let me, not moving, not making a sound, just watching me with a look of wonder on his face, so open, so innocent, so pure.

I swallowed slowly at that look, but kept going with my discovery of the man before me. My hands made their way down to his neck, across his broad shoulders and then back to his pulse point, so obvious with the blood pumping through it rapidly now, also so sensitive to my touch. His eyes did close when I stopped there, his mouth parting slightly, his breathing hitched and now uneven. I licked my lips, watching his response, feeling a demanding one course through me. But, I couldn't get past his pulse.

Before I even realised what I was saying, it was out.

"Who have you been feeding from?" Michel only ever fed from me, well since we had become a solid item that is. And the thought that he'd had to feed elsewhere while I was gone froze me. I tried not to think of him feeding from Amisi, she seemed the most obvious choice, here in the house, convenient, well known, a Nosferatin. Our blood is stronger than a human's, it has more *Vita Vis*.

All these thoughts were rushing through my mind while I waited for his answer, I hadn't even realised I had called myself a Nosferatin, that I had recognised our powerful blood. That more of my memories had returned, without me even noticing. All I could see was Michel's eyes as he studied me and his reluctance to answer the question.

"Anonymous donors." His voice was quiet, soft, downright scared, I should think, of my reaction to them. No doubt he thought I wouldn't have wanted to hear that, but in fact, it was the only answer that would have been acceptable to me. Humans he didn't know, plural. Not one, which could get attached to his bite.

"Why not Amisi, she would have made you stronger?"

He did look a little shocked at that. "She did not offer and I would never have considered it anyway."

I smiled then and he visibly relaxed. Without realising it his eyes slid to my throat, to my pulse point, he licked his lips. As much as I wanted to offer him my vein, knowing it would strengthen him beyond measure, I couldn't. Not yet. What I could offer, was what I needed, my body. I needed him to claim me, to give me a memory that was true and right and us.

I took hold of his chin and brought his eyes back to me, registering the appalled look on his face at what he had been staring at.

"Soon," I promised. He nodded slowly. "But first, you need to do something for me."

His eyes widened. "Anything," he whispered.

"Make love to me. Claim me. Give me a memory that I want."

I don't think I could have shocked him more than if I had pulled a stake and thrust it through his heart.

"It is too soon, *ma douce*. I can wait."

I shook my head. "Do you want the only memories I keep replaying in my head to be those of the last month? I can't stop them cycling through, even though I am remembering more and more of who I am, it's those memories that keep resurfacing. They're the strongest, they're the ones I can't banish. I need something new, something good. I need you."

I stroked his face, all the while willing him to understand my need, to not say no.

"I am scared of hurting you," he whispered.

"I'm not," I breathed in return, then lifted my head off his arm and kissed him, putting as much of my need and hunger into that kiss as I could manage.

He only hesitated for a moment, then allowed himself to sink into the kiss, to deepen it even more, his hands beginning to find my body beneath him, a deep moan escaping the back of his throat. The sound so primal, so desperate, it made me arch against him, begging for more.

"Oh dear God, Lucinda," he husked against me, his kisses interspersing his words, trailing a path down my cheek, trying his damnedest to stay away from my pulse point, instead heading down my throat. "I have missed you, my love."

I wished I could offer the same sort of encouragement, but really, it would have been a lie. I hadn't remembered him until recently, I had felt something missing, something so very sacred and special to me. I even felt like there had been a hole in my heart, which was only now beginning to fill, but I couldn't say I had missed him too.

He must have realised and wanted to distract me, because his lips were back on mine making it impossible to utter a word at all, let alone the ones I wanted to say, but couldn't. His tongue began darting in and out, in and out. And that just did it for me. I grabbed hold of his shoulders and pulled him the rest of the way on top of my body, my only thoughts of the wonderful sensation of Michel on me, his hard, long body, his soft warm lips, his arousal pressed between us.

"Take me," I managed to breath out between tongue thrusts. "Make me yours. Please. Now."

He groaned and shifted his body weight, pulling himself into a kneeling position and moving a hand between us, in an instant his boxers were gone - I don't think I had even noticed he was wearing them - and so had my knickers. He pulled me slowly down the bed on my back towards him, taking one of my legs tenderly and lifting it high above his shoulder, the other leg he pressed gently wide, opening me up for his inspection, but he didn't pause long to take me in, he lifted my hips up off the bed and plunged so slowly, so reverently inside in one hard long thrust. A groan of ecstasy escaping his lips, a murmur of surprise from mine, which quickly turned into demands for *more* as his thrusts remained so controlled, so slow and gentle. Still scared of scaring me, hurting me, frightening me away.

I knew he was trying not to think it, trying not to let the words spill from him to me. I knew he wanted so desperately to utter them, but didn't want to alarm me. He was trying to keep things slow, to love my body and show me that love through his soft touch on my flesh. But, I could tell the claiming was still in full effect and as he had lost me and only just found me again, his vampire's need to claim would have been tremendous. Yet still he fought that urge to utter the words and more surprisingly he fought his body's response at not uttering them. His body wanting to claim me in ever more fervent ways, even if his words did not. But still he loved me so tenderly, so softly, so slowly. So beautifully. This was not a claiming, even though a part of me wanted it to be. This was a rediscovery, a delicious reminder of what we actually meant to one another.

We both needed it, this reconnection, this closeness again. We both wanted to feel this. So familiar, so right. But, I also wanted to hear that I was still his. I needed to hear the words. That he still wanted me to be his, despite where I had been, how long I had been away, how much had happened in my absence.

"God, Lucinda," he breathed. "I want you so much. I need you." And then just as we both came, him in a slow, languid stroke inside me he murmured them, the words I wanted to hear, with such depth of feeling it rocked my soul. "You. Are. Mine."

He collapsed on top of me utterly breathless and totally spent. For a moment I was worried. I had pushed him too soon, he hadn't been well enough. But, it was only a minute before he moved again and I could breathe properly, his weight no longer pressing into me. His arms wrapped around me protectively, securely and it was with a sudden knowledge that I realised Michel was everything I needed in a saviour. He may not have been able to rescue me himself, but no one could compare to him in my eyes.

The road would not be easy, I was making new memories now to dull those of the past few weeks, but I knew now, without a doubt, that Michel would get me through any hurdles that would arrive in the wake of my time spent in America. Michel would be my guardian angel from this day forward. Michel was all that I needed.

"*Je t'aime, ma douce. Je t'aimerai toujours.*"

Now, this memory would be the one I could replay again and again. I smiled and whispered, "I will love you forever too."

His arms crushed me to him and we stayed like that for quite some time, both luxuriating in the afterglow of sex, in the warmth of the embrace, in being so close to each other after so long apart. But, we weren't done, not yet.

I shifted against him after a few minutes and turned to look him in the face, both of us now on our sides, facing each other.

"You still look like shit, Michel."

He laughed at my phrasing, his chest rising and falling with each chuckle. His hand came out to touch my face, resting there as he rubbed a thumb along my jaw. "Being close to you heals me, *ma douce*. Although, too much of the kind of vigorous activity such as just now, may be beyond me for a while longer." His smile was full of the promise that he wanted more, but tinged with the regret he was not up to performing the task too often.

"Well," I said, taking his hand and moving it to my neck, just above my pulse, "we can't have that."

He watched where his hand was being placed and licked his lips, his eyes flicking back up to mine. I saw the hesitation there, but also the desperate hunger for my blood. His body was craving it, but his mind was saying no. His fangs came down automatically and he tried to pull away, closing his mouth to hide his reaction from me. I held him firmly in place and ran my thumb from my free hand across his lips.

"Show me them," I ordered, my voice suddenly lower than usual.

He shook his head, but I clasped his chin in a strong hold to stop the motion.

"Show me them." My voice was stronger, I was enjoying this control over him, this position he had placed me in. His reluctance made me stronger, made me realise how much control I actually had of the situation right now. I was the one in charge, not him. I needed that control, but I also knew, he needed my blood.

He opened his mouth and pulled his lips back slightly, just enough to show the tips of his now very long fangs, but not enough to make him grimace. He was still so very attractive, so very sexy and the fact that his fangs were longer than I had ever seen before just turned me on completely. I had done this to him. I had made his fangs come out and lengthen to such a degree. He wanted me, but he wouldn't make a move until I said so. The power of that was intoxicating.

"You're going to do exactly as I say," I commanded, he just smiled slightly and nodded, his eyebrows rising up just a hint. I think he was enjoying this as much as I was, if the glint of magenta in amongst the amethyst and indigo was anything to go by.

"Kiss me here," I said, pointing to my cheek. He held my gaze and came in slowly, following my command to the letter, a soft, feather-light touch of his lips against my cheek where I had been pointing.

"And here." I pointed to my eyelid. He smiled, his lazy sexy smile, obviously getting into the swing of things quite nicely now and touched his lips to my eyelid, so softly, so slowly, then pulled away awaiting his next command.

I licked my lips, his eyes tracked the movement, unable to stop staring at my mouth.

"Here," I whispered, pointing to my forehead. I saw the flash of regret wash over him, he'd obviously wanted my lips. This had promise. But, he dipped his face down obediently again to kiss my forehead, just as softly and slowly as before, returning to his position and staring at my mouth.

Ah ah, I thought. Not yet. "Here." I pointed to my ear. He swallowed and slowly leaned in, kissing my ear and daring to follow through with a small nibble on the lobe.

I smiled at his audacity and whispered, "and here," pointing to my throat, purposely avoiding my pulse point.

He obeyed, kissing a line down my throat, not just one light brush of the lips, but several, laying a track all the way from my chin to the dip at the base of my throat, before pulling away and cocking his head as if to dare me to tell him off for giving more than he was commanded.

I just frowned at him and received a wicked smile in return.

"Here," I said pointing to the crease between my breasts. I was still wearing my T-Shirt, so he would have to kiss me through the material, but he had definitely decided he would take a few liberties now, because he ducked down and lifted the base of my T-Shirt up and burrowed underneath, laying long, hot, wet kisses up between my breasts and making me start to writhe against his touch.

Damn. This wasn't meant to happen, I was meant to be in control here. He pulled out and sat back watching me, I could see he was having trouble not laughing out loud at my reaction. He purposefully reschooled his features into a blank mask and waited for my next command, quite prepared to go with the flow for eternity.

I pointed to my pulse at my neck. "Here." I held his gaze and saw I had him. He'd expected me to continue with the game, everywhere but there. His breath came out in a rush and his own pulse began to jump at his neck, his eyes swirling a delightful dance of violets, faster and faster and faster.

He held my gaze and moved in so very slowly, making it take as long as possible before he found my neck and could no longer look at me. He hesitated, unable to cover the final few millimetres from his lips to my neck, then when I thought he'd give up and pull back his lips crushed against my skin, he licked and then began to suck my skin back into this mouth, his tongue pulsing against what was captured of me inside of him. The sensation was mind blowing. My hands grabbed at his hair pulling him closer, making sure he wouldn't pull back, pull away, stop the magic he was making at my neck.

He didn't, he kept at it, his hands going around behind my shoulders, lifting me off the bed, cradling me as he sucked and licked above my pulse, a strange sound coming from the back of his throat, almost a purr, so beautiful and hypnotic, rolling in time to his sucking.

Finally I found my voice and commanded extremely huskily, "Bite me."

His fangs entered immediately, his body jerking at the first taste of my blood, his arms going rigid around me, holding me in place as his tongue lapped at my precious blood in his mouth and then the pulls began in earnest. He'd tempered the spike of pain of his fangs entering my flesh immediately with wave after wave of his love, his gratitude, his thanks, his relief at my return to him, his desire for my body, not just my blood.

I floated in his arms as though I was on a cloud, I let his emotions wash over me, filling me up with so much more than what they were on their own. I closed my eyes and went with the feelings, the sensations, I didn't fight, I didn't strain, I wasn't scared. I was in love with the man, the vampire, who held me so tenderly and gratefully took what I offered expecting nothing in return.

This memory I decided, I would savour for eternity.

12
BACK TO NORMAL... ALMOST

We spent the next few hours just lying naked in each others arms, talking softly about everything and nothing, just relishing the warmth of the other, allowing the familiarity to return. Not really talking about the past month, skirting it, not wanting to ruin the moment. Both of us aware it would have to be covered in due course, but not yet.

By about 5pm my stomach had started rumbling, hunger returning at last and I knew if I were to eat now, I would no longer suffer any nausea. Michel had healed me, not just with his *Sanguis Vitam* but with his nearness, his body against mine. The joining and Bond we shared needed this to stay strong, both of us having suffered considerably with our separation. Together again at last, we were finally getting better.

Even Michel had more colour in his face, the gaunt look disappearing, the shadows under eyes no longer so noticeable. Of course, as a vampire, he would always physically heal faster than me, I on the other hand, would need food.

"I'm hungry," I murmured against his hair, his head bending to lay kisses across my chest for the umpteenth time that day.

"Mm. So am I," he purred as his face began to nuzzle its way back up to my neck.

I laughed. "Already? Haven't you had your fill?" Vampires tend to only need to feed once a night, no more.

"Never." He kissed above my pulse point then pulled back to look at me. "However, if you do not eat, I cannot eat. There simply will be nothing left of you to share. So, food."

He jumped off the bed as though he had all the energy in the world. I just stared at him in wonder as he grabbed a robe from behind the door and slid it on. He slowed his movements as he caught me watching him, slowly tying the sash around his waist, our eyes locked.

"You're definitely looking better," I grumbled as I slowly got up off the bed. I didn't ache any more, but I was certainly feeling pretty weak still.

He laughed as he came around with another robe for me. "The joys of being vampyre, my dear. For a half human you will recover fairly quickly, but you cannot expect to match my recovery rate."

I half heartedly glared at him and let him help me into the robe, once on, he pulled it closed and knotted the sash securely.

"No one but me gets past these," he said quietly, while he double knotted to make sure.

"I think you might regret that later." It felt right to be teasing Michel again.

"That is what fangs were made for, *ma douce*," he said pulling me into his arms and kissing me soundly.

It didn't surprise me, that once I got past the memory block to Michel I would want to keep touching him as much as he did me, but I was still left breathless by the deep desire the joining forced upon us to constantly touch. Before I went to America - my new term for that horrid month - I had got used to both the effects of the joining and the effects of the claiming, now having not experienced it for four weeks, it was again a bit of a shock. Still, it didn't frighten, just made me catch my breath at every moment.

"Mm," Michel murmured against my lips. "Are you sure you are hungry, *ma belle*?"

I pushed against his chest and smiled at him. "It's always all about you, isn't it?" I teased.

"Actually," he said straightening up and putting on one of his most haughty vampire looks, "I was thinking of ways to distract *you*, my dear. Your pleasure is my only concern." He bowed low, his hand across his chest.

"Yeah right, Casanova," I retorted and headed out the door.

"You don't believe me? I can prove it, if you would only return to our boudoir. "

"Uh-uh," I said shaking my head as I started down the stairs. "Only in your dreams, Romeo."

I heard him chuckle behind me. "If you only knew what I dreamt about, *ma douce*, you would not be so cruel as to deny me now." His voice was light, thrumming with happiness.

"I can imagine what you dream about, Michel, aaand how long those dreams would be."

"Then why fight it? You know you would like it." The last was said whisper quiet in my ear, his arms having gone around my waist just as we entered the lounge.

Maybe it was the fact that they hadn't seen me in a while, maybe it was the fact that Michel had also been so ill and now look his chirpy self again, but the stunned look on the many vampires sitting in the room we had just entered made me stop in my tracks, my heart leap to my throat and my breath become all but non-existent.

Immediately we were surrounded by extremely happy, relieved, over joyed and excited vampires. All of them clamouring to touch us, to say how pleased they were to see us, to even try to embrace us. I wasn't exactly scared, I mean Michel was holding me, he'd make sure nothing happened, but so many of them in one room, so many coming towards me all at once, did make me freak.

In an instant I was cowering behind Michel and then I was just plain mad. Dammit, he had not only taken me and my memories from me, but Jonathan had taken my courage too. Something I valued above all else, something that was so a part of me. I burst into tears at the injustice of it all.

"Get out," Michel murmured quietly to the vampires, making sure to shield me from seeing them move. It was only a second and they were all outside the room, but not the house, the sun *was* still up. He turned slowly, taking me in his arms, but unable to stop me crumpling to the floor. He just went with it, until we were both on the carpet, him rocking me backward and forward, stroking my back, whispering it would be all right, I was safe, over and over again in my ear.

I don't know how long he held me for, but eventually I stopped crying and rubbed at my puffy eyes. "Sorry," I said meekly.

"There is nothing to apologise for. I should have anticipated this. I should have made sure you were not overwhelmed." His voice was soft, full of compassion, it just made me angrier. Not at him, but at Jonathan, for doing this to us.

"I want him dead," I whispered.

"It shall be done," he promised, not needing an explanation of who I was referring to.

We sat there for a while longer, then Michel asked, "Has your appetite returned, *ma douce?*"

I could smell something delicious wafting out of the kitchen as soon as he mentioned my appetite. I had forgotten all about eating, too consumed in my own dark thoughts of revenge, but as soon as I smelled what was surely going to be a roast of some sort, my stomach rumbled loudly.

"I will take that as a yes." He helped me to my feet and didn't let go of my hand as we entered the kitchen.

Amisi was in her favourite spot at the kitchen bench, slicing up a roasted leg of lamb and serving it up onto a plate.

"Oh. Great." She smiled and turned to grab an extra plate. "Perfect timing." I doubted it, she would have been advised we were coming down for food, Michel would have told Erika telepathically, Erika would have passed it on. I knew how it all worked and that only made me smile. The more I could remember, the stronger I would become and when I was strong enough, I would go after Jonathan.

Roast vegetables followed the lamb, then a thick gravy over the top.

"Is this standard Egyptian fare, Amisi?" I asked as Michel ushered me into a seat at the table. I wouldn't let his hand go though, choosing to pick up my fork with my left and use that to stab what I wanted off the plate. He didn't say anything, nor act as though it was strange, he just held it and started rubbing his thumb across the back of my hand in a slow swirl.

My fork clattered to the plate loudly. "Shit," I muttered. "Sorry." It had been the thumb on the back of the hand which had done it. Damn, I had known that movement was familiar and when I had mentioned that to Jonathan, he had used it in his act, as though it was something he had always done, not my kindred.

Michel stiffened slightly next to me, only a moment, then continued swirling his thumb lightly over the back of my hand. It was so quick a pause, that I actually wondered whether he had paused at all.

I felt a tear slide down my face at the thought of what Jonathan had done. Amisi had stopped eating, not answering my question, but watching in shock the tear streak down my cheek. When I picked the fork up again and began to nibble on a piece of lamb she relaxed slightly. Michel just continued to stroke my hand, I refused to pull away and deny him that movement, it had been *his* first, not Jonathan's. I was done giving Jonathan anything else.

"I thought I'd educate myself," Amisi said as though nothing had happened. "Your mum gave me the recipe when I asked her what you would like best."

Holy shit. Amisi had talked to my mum? "When did you talk to her?" I asked, shovelling another succulent piece of lamb in my mouth and almost groaning with approval. Michel had started laughing quietly beside me, I shot him a look and he just shrugged. He'd always found my reaction to food amusing.

"I've been deflecting her calls. They never knew you were missing, just on various bank courses, then a holiday to Vanautu and finally a camping trip with your boyfriend. That one got her attention. I may have mentioned you'd been seeing him for a while. She'll expect an update."

My parents, actually my Aunt and Uncle who have raised me since I was a little baby, didn't know about me being a Nosferatin, let alone me being practically married to a Nosferatu. It would not be something I could bring up over the dinner table if I ever visited the farm again. But, I guess I could pull off a story about a *boyfriend*.

"Any characteristics this boyfriend have I need to know about?" I asked, moving on to the peas and potatoes, the latter cutting up nicely with the fork on its side.

"He's sitting right beside you. I described him to perfection, I think your mum thinks you're dating a god. She definitely wants details. I wasn't going to go there, sorry." She didn't sound sorry.

I just scoffed. A god, indeed.

"That's not what you were thinking a few hours ago, *ma douce*," Michel teased.

OK I may have choked a little then, Michel's free hand came out to pat me delicately on the back. He wasn't really concerned, I'm sure he knew how I would react to him reading my mind. I had totally forgotten that he was able to that, I guess the connection had clicked back on.

"When? I mean, since when have you been able to read my mind again." I chanced a glance at him, his eyes were watching me intently.

"Since you woke earlier today." His voice was soft.

I wondered when he was going to let me know that was happening and then I wondered if I had thought anything that I would regret.

I cleared my throat. "Since I woke, or you woke?" It seemed a silly question, surely he couldn't read my mind when still asleep, but then had he been? Maybe it was all an act.

He glanced at Amisi, but she was looking at her plate and studiously concentrating on her lamb, pretending either we weren't there or she wasn't.

"The first conscious thought I received of yours was your terror when my fangs scraped your neck and you jumped from the bed."

Amisi abruptly stood up and mumbled something about washing needing to be folded and practically ran from the room.

Michel went on, ignoring Amisi's exit. "You had enough to worry about without that complication, I wanted to spare you a little longer, but I had not intended it to be as long as it was. One thing led to another and before I knew it we were downstairs and again my vampyres set you back and..."

I put my free hand up to his lips to stop him, I could tell he was frantic to explain, to make it right. I wanted to be angry at him, hell I was pretty much filled with anger right now, a good thing as it kept me focused on Jonathan, but that was where I wanted my anger to go, not at Michel. "It's OK Michel. It's OK. There *is* a lot to take in, my memories are still coming back at odd times, I get sensations which were normal before, but feel so foreign initially now, but... I need you. Near me, with me, maybe even reading me right now. Some of what I feel and what I went through, I don't know if I will ever be able to say it all aloud." I paused, thinking it over. "You have my permission to listen in, OK?" I smiled up at him, he visibly relaxed, took my hand he had been holding and softly kissed the back of it with his lips.

"I would do anything to make this better, anything." His eyes flashed amethyst and indigo, bright purples across the blue.

"You already are."

He smiled and shifted his seat closer to mine, wrapping an arm around my shoulders he kissed my temple and then rested his head against me. "Use both hands, *ma douce*. Eat properly and as much as you can, I want you back resting in our bed."

I laughed as I let him cuddle me and began eating my beautiful dinner in earnest. "Can you get Amisi back in, she needs to eat too. She looks like she's lost weight."

"Both my girls have," he said, squeezing my shoulder. I kind of liked that he thought of Amisi as one of his girls too. I knew at that moment, that she was so very important to me too. "It is done, Erika will also join us."

Amisi slid into her seat a few seconds later, followed by Erika.

"This is beautiful, Amisi, just like Mum's." I had almost finished the entire plate and still felt hungry. "Is there more?" I asked hopefully. Amisi beamed at me from across the table, but it was Michel who stood and took my plate, piling it high with food and returning it to me.

As soon as I started eating again, his arm draped back around me casually and he settled in to watch me eat. It felt familiar, comfortable and very right. Little by little, I felt myself coming back. Not all of my memories, not yet, but enough to make me know with a certainty, that Michel was mine and I was his. And there was nowhere else I'd rather be.

I seemed just as hungry as when Amisi had piled that first plate high. I knew I shouldn't be eating too much, after having such a long period of time with so little in my stomach, but I couldn't help it. It tasted so good. It tasted of home. Images of my parents' farm flashed through my mind. I embraced them. These were deep seated memories. Hidden away due to the drugs and a part of me wondered, if also due to self preservation. I always felt refreshed when I visited my parents farm, recharged, ready to face the world again. Whether it was in person or in my mind. Or in the dreams Michel created. I smiled to myself as the memories, the make-up of my mind, of me, kept tumbling back in.

All through these magical flashes of my past, my life, the girls chatted away merrily and Michel simply watched me, a look of utter contentment on his face. A man full of relief and happiness. And just for a moment, the worries of revenge and the politics of vampiredom were absent from his features. In their place was a young man, full of life. In that second of seeing such natural beauty in the man that I loved, I realised Michel was so much closer to the Light than he had ever been. Despite what we had been through, despite what lay ahead. I helped Michel toward the Light. Just as he helped me back from the Dark.

His fingers started playing softly with my hair on the collar of my robe. I don't think he even realised what he was doing. It wasn't sexual, it was full of comfort and love, but Erika's eyes fixed on the movement and a smirk graced her porcelain face.

"Oh pur-lease. We don't need to see all of your sordid moves from the bedroom at the dining room table."

Playing along with what she thought was just a joke, a moment of lightening the day from the recent memories of such Dark, Amisi added, "She's not been back 24 hours and already we have to deal with them unable to keep their hands off each other. Just wait another day and the heavy petting will have moved to the couch. Again." I had a sudden memory flash before my eyes which made me blush furiously and caused Michel to enter the banter.

I think he chose to humour Amisi, but the look he cast Erika, so very quickly it was almost missed, let her know she had overstepped the mark. "Girls, girls, please. You are just jealous that you do not have a kindred as irresistible as mine." Michel leant over and took my chin in his hand then proceeded to kiss me with a slow, languid brush of his lips.

"Oh for God's sake, Michel, you're as bad as a teenager, control yourself," Erika chastised, ignoring the look he had flashed her before. I could remember Erika teasing Michel in the past. I knew she, more than any other vampire in his line, was game enough to push his buttons. I couldn't remember specifics, but maybe this was always how it was.

"Not likely," Amisi added. "He's on a roll."

I listened to the teasing banter go back and forth for a while between the three of them. The more it continued and the more Michel entertained it, the calmer I got. The calmer Michel became as well. The only other sound in the house was the whir of the shutters retracting for the night. It turned into gentle ribbing and mock teasing and all of a sudden felt very familiar indeed. This *is* what they always did. I had misinterpreted Erika's initial remark. It was all a tease and Michel just played along, helping to lighten the moment. He gave as good as he got, if not more. The man had no shame and clearly loved anyone at all knowing how much he loved me. It made me smile, despite the embarrassment of being the centre of everyone's attention. This felt right, it felt like home. Michel relaxed even further next to me, probably receiving all of my thoughts. Even that didn't feel wrong anymore. I felt like I was back to normal, almost. Maybe it would all be OK in the end. Surely there were only a few more memories to come back, nothing too monumental. I could do this. With these guys around me, I could do anything.

Just then Amisi pushed her plate away and sighed. "Duty calls," she said, getting up from the table. "You want to come along, Erika?"

"Sure thing, *chica*, wouldn't miss it for the world."

"What duty?" I asked sitting up straighter in my chair.

Amisi shot a surprised look at Michel, I didn't catch his response, I was too busy looking at her.

"The, ah... the pull. I feel it. Don't you?"

The pull. The evil-lurks-in-my-city pull, the one I was born to feel, born to respond to.

And I couldn't feel a thing.

13
24 HOURS

"24 hours, *ma douce*. That is all." Michel was consoling me at the dining table. Erika and Amisi had just headed out the door towards that pull. The pull I couldn't feel.

"The drugs are almost out of your system, I could only taste a trace before, by tomorrow you will remember more. I am sure."

He was sure. I wasn't. The pull was part of my make-up, a gift from Nut. It wasn't just a skill I had learnt or acquired, it was in me, a part of me since birth. There should have been no way I wasn't connected to it. Never before had I failed to recognise when an innocent was being threatened by the Dark. Part of me knew the logical explanation was the drugs, or what was still left of them inside me, but a more petulant part, a more angry and disillusioned part, thought perhaps Nut had forsaken me. Perhaps this was not reversible, correctable, or fix-able.

I stood up and started pacing across the tiled floor of the kitchen, thankfully it's fairly large, so I got a good three or four paces in before having to turn around and go back the way I came. A round trip lasted about four seconds, I was pacing pretty quickly. Michel just leaned back against the wall, arms crossed over his chest, legs crossed at the ankles, watching me. He didn't say anything else, he could hear my thoughts just fine.

If I didn't get a handle on this anger I thought I might just explode. It felt as though my skin was stretched tight all over me and that everything inside was expanding and expanding and soon there would be nowhere left for the anger and hurt and fear and disillusionment to go, but out. I clenched my fists and kept on pacing. I needed a plan. I was good at plans. A plan had got me out of that house. OK, it had got derailed along the way, but when I was ready to come back to it, it was there and it got me out. So, I just needed to think of a way to end this constant tightness in my chest, tightness in my head, tightness in my heart. Everything was so tight I could hardly breathe. I was smothering myself, I was going to drown in all this negative emotion. Drown in all the blood.

"*Ma douce*, you are glowing. Take a breath." Michel's soft voice sounded so far away, although he was just standing not six feet across the room from me.

I looked down at my body and noticed it was indeed glowing, a bright, stunning white light. Shit. I couldn't even control my Light, another example of how fucked up I was.

Michel walked over to where I had stopped pacing, slap bang in the middle of the kitchen, which now was bathed in an ever increasing bright, white light. We didn't need the overheads on, I was providing enough illumination for the whole friggin' house. His arms wrapped around me, pulling me against his chest. At first I resisted, I was too wound up to relax in his hold, but he was strong and persistent, he wasn't going to take no for an answer.

We struggled together for a moment, him trying to pull me closer, but also not hurt me in the process, me trying to pull away and remain rigid in my anger and fear. Michel won. As soon as I capitulated and collapsed against his chest my glow slowly began to ebb away. It took several seconds, Michel constantly stroking my back, rubbing circles in a slow methodical manner, almost in time to his heartbeat, which hadn't risen at all, unlike mine.

After a while the room returned to its normal night time light levels; halogen assisted, not Nosferatin.

"You do not have to do this alone, Lucinda. I can help, if you will let me."

I didn't say anything, I felt so tired again. I may have recovered remarkably well in such a short amount of time, no more bruises or scratches on the outside, but on the inside I was still so run down. One meal, albeit an extremely large one and several hours with my kindred, was not enough to fully replenish my energy levels. I needed rest, even though all I really wanted to do was chase that bastard vampire down and run my stake right through his heart.

Michel sighed. "We have not been able to locate the house, although I have my and Enrique's men searching. From your description," - I hadn't actually given a description, but I was guessing Michel had managed to get one from my thoughts - "it should have been relatively easy to find, but it must be warded significantly and beyond our detection. We will find it, or he will make a move to come here. Sooner or later, he will suspect that we have you back with us. I cannot imagine he will give you up so easily. He will retaliate. And we are ready."

We are ready. I'd like to think I was too, but until I had full use of my powers, all my memories back where they should be, I was more a liability than an asset. And didn't I just love that thought?

"There is time. By tomorrow, you may well be... whole again." I was guessing he was having trouble picking his words, even the use of *whole* made me cringe. "In the meantime, there is nothing to be done, even I am not meeting with my kin today. One more day and we will plan and then execute our revenge."

He spoke so calmly of revenge and I had the feeling that previously I may not have been so comfortable with the notion, but now, I needed to hear his resolve, his determination to do just that. Avenge the wrong against me. I didn't want karmic discussions on how Jonathan would get his comeuppance eventually, I wanted Michel to use his formidable strength and power to back me on this, without question, without pause.

I thought again, *what have I become? Who am I?* If there was a way to talk to Nut I would have, a little divine guidance right now wouldn't go astray. But, I was on my own, well, not entirely, I had a very pissed off and powerful kindred vampire on my side. Things could be worse.

I pulled back and managed a small smile at Michel. He leaned down and kissed my forehead softly, then rested his head against the same spot. The feeling of familiarity washed over me again, this was one of Michel's favourite positions, arms wrapped around me, forehead to forehead, his warm breath washing over my face. He inhaled deeply and I knew he was taking in my scent, savouring the candied apples, sunshine, honey and spring that is my signature. To a vampire there can be nothing more personal than someone's scent.

"I have missed you so much, *ma douce*." There was an ache so deep within his voice it broke my heart to hear.

I reached up and stroked his face, pulling back to look him in the eyes. That beautiful mix of violet, amethyst and indigo had taken up residence again, I didn't think I could ever get enough of seeing that colour combination. I stood up on the tip of my toes and kissed him lightly on the lips, just once, then pulled away. His mouth had opened slightly, his eyelids becoming heavy, I couldn't help it, I had to kiss him again. This time I didn't stop, letting my tongue slide in between his open teeth, working it around his own tongue and receiving a satisfying groan in response.

He responded, for a moment, maybe two, then pulled the kiss back from the brink and made it more delicate, more gentle, no hint of what else could occur if we let our bodies take over. Part of me was surprised and a little annoyed. I couldn't help feeling attracted to this man. But a bigger part of me was just so relieved. I was tired, exhausted, and right now what I needed was his support and care and love, with no pressure of having to give anything else in return.

It was selfish and normally I wouldn't have tolerated it, I think. But right now I allowed myself the luxury of thinking of only me. My needs, my road to recovery. Michel had said he would get stronger simply by being near me, that was true also for me. Sure, he would need to feed off me again and probably sooner rather than later. But already he was looking almost healed, whole. Me, not so much. I needed his arms around my body, his face resting against my hair and neck, his breath coating me in warmth and love. I needed him this way.

And although Michel was still in the throes of battling his vampire's need to claim me, he was winning, because his arms gently enfolded me, his face nestled into my neck and he sighed, a contented sound, hot against my flesh.

His strength at being able to battle his vampire-within astounded me. Right now when he was not at his best physically, emotionally and psychologically, he was still able to control the claiming. There were times when I was so very glad to see him lose control and succumb to the claiming, but now was not one of them. And once again, Michel was showing me how very much he was in tune with me, with my needs and wants and desires.

Michel was perfect. There was no other word for it. He completed me in every possible way.

He started chuckling softly against me, his chest rising and falling beneath my own.

"Hey!" I protested. "Are you laughing at me?"

"I have *never* been called perfect before, *ma douce*. If only you knew what was going through my mind right now, having you back in my arms. You would not think me so perfect."

Oh, but he was wrong. The thought that he still wanted me, still fantasied about being with me, but was still able to fight the claiming his vampire had subjected him to, proved beyond a doubt in my mind that he was perfect. I was sure, once I was physically well again, that I would gladly welcome back his vampire's urge to claim me. But right now, what I needed was comfort and sleep.

"Very well, my love." He swung me up in his arms and carried me from the room. As he lay me gently down on the bed, he whispered against my neck, "Sleep, *ma douce*. And know that I love you, need you and will always desire you. Sleep."

I didn't need to be told twice, I was asleep before he'd managed to pull the duvet over us, the sound of his steady heartbeat thrumming through his chest and into my ears, so very comforting.

I dreamt of Jonathan, not a wanted dream, not a happy dream at all. I could see his face when he was trying to punish me, his anger and determination to make me pay for trying to escape. I could feel his need to taste my blood again. His face broke into a grin as he held me down on the floor, his fangs obvious as they peeked out past his curved lips. He ran his tongue over one fang slowly, growling in pleasure when I shuddered beneath him in fear.

I tried to fight back, but my arms wouldn't do what I asked them to do, my legs felt like dead weights, unresponsive, as though they weren't even there. He felt so heavy, so hard against me, I couldn't breathe, I couldn't scream, I couldn't move. I was useless, I was pathetic. I knew he would start hitting me, scratching me, hurting me and I was just going to let him do this, it was all my fault. His eyes sprang open and he held me in his glaze. I knew it was a glaze, the amber and ochre in them turning to a more malevolent maroon and bitter-sweet burgundy, showing the red that vampires need when they glaze.

"You are mine, Lucinda. I will have you again. You cannot escape me and you will pay for your disrespect." His hands held my arms above my head rigidly still. "Say it," he purred, as the maroon and burgundy swirled in his eyes, still holding me captive. "Say you are mine."

I fought it, I really did. I have a certain amount of natural resistance to a vampire glaze, but he is strong and I was still so weak.

"Say it!" he ordered, his voice wrapping around me and pulling me towards him. I felt my head leave the floor, my body strain against his hold on my arms, trying to lift my face to whisper the words against his ear. "Say it!" he ordered again, banging my hands back against the floor, making the bones in my wrists rub against each other as he held them so tightly, shooting stabs of pain down my arms. "Say it," he whispered against my lips.

"I am yours." The words were uttered by me, but they didn't sound at all like my voice. My mind was screaming *no*, the words said otherwise. His lips peeled back triumphantly in a mockery of a smile and I just felt sick, sick to my stomach. And then I froze, as hot breath from his mouth trailed across my cheek, over my jaw and down my neck, until his fangs bit into my pulse and my blood poured down his throat.

It was the bathroom door slamming open against the wall of the bedroom that woke me and broke the spell. Michel's weight as he landed on the bed beside me, his wet arms and body lifting me up off the sweat soaked sheets and his words - full of curses spilling out his mouth, as he cradled me - filling the night air and waking me up fully.

"That fucking bastard! I am going to take great pleasure in killing him slowly and very painfully," Michel managed to get out between clenched teeth.

"Get in line," I muttered and then promptly threw up two courses of roast lamb and vegetables all over my kindred and the bed. "Ah, crap."

Once the vomiting stopped and the world steadied again, Michel carried me to the bathroom and stepped under the still running shower with me in his arms. I could barely stand, but he held me firmly, letting the water wash all the regurgitated gunk off of us both and then starting to soap my body up with the utmost care. His jaw was rigid, his lips in a thin line, his eyes flashing magenta - and only magenta. Man, he was fuming.

I couldn't blame him, not only was he pissed off at Jonathan invading and manipulating my dreams, but I was betting he was pissed off at himself for leaving my side, even briefly to shower. No doubt thinking had he been with me in bed, he would have picked up on the dream sooner and stopped it. Of course, I didn't blame him, at all. All blame was going squarely on Jonathan's shoulders and no one else's.

I reached up and touched my neck where Jonathan had bit me in the dream, Michel noticed and forcefully relaxed his unyielding stance. "There is no mark. It was only a dream, not a visit." I'd had *visits* in dreams before where a vampire had abused my neck, almost biting me. Michel could also visit me in a dream. But, that other vampire, Max, had left me with bruises after his visit, so the fact that Jonathan had not managed to *visit* but only influence the direction of my dream, had me collapsing in relief against Michel. That meant the glaze Jonathan had attempted in the dream was not legitimate. Thank God.

"My guess is he is trying to disorientate you, confuse you. In your current state he is hoping you would not know the difference and would perhaps believe the glaze was true." Michel's voice was soft and careful as he held me under the warm spray. I got the feeling he was thinking how possible that scenario could actually be.

He'd heard my thoughts, of course. "Dreams can be very influential. Under certain circumstances they can be as destructive as a vampyre's glaze."

"Can I do anything to stop him invading my dreams again?"

"Get better. The stronger you are, the more resilient you will be to invasions in your sleep."

Get better. I glanced at the clock on the bathroom wall, it was only 11pm, my 24 hours were not yet up. I sent my senses out into the night and quickly found Michel's vampires dotted around the property and then vampires further afield through the city, the country and with a sense of pure joy, throughout the world.

It was still a little sluggish and I was picking I was still missing something else in the scenario, but it was a definite improvement.

24 hours, I was beginning to believe Michel was right. I would have *me* back again and it would be soon. I lay my head against his chest, my arms wrapped around his waist and let the water run over us.

After a few moments of just luxuriating in the feel of him and the warm water that surrounded us, I said, "I don't want to go back to sleep, will you sit with me, keep me awake."

I felt his chest rise and fall in silent laughter. "I will try my best to keep you distracted, ."

"Awake and resting Michel, emphasis on resting."

He was truly laughing now. "I am sure I can find a way to let you relax *and* still adequately distract you, my dear."

Yeah. I bet he could. I bet he bloody well could too.

14
HAUNTED

True to his word, Michel kept me relaxed and distracted, but never overstepped the mark. His restraint and careful attention left me reeling. The more time I spent in his arms, comforted but not coveted, the more I wanted of him. Eventually he caved, lavishing my body with his. But it was so beautiful. So intimate, so special. I knew without a doubt, he loved me and I loved him and making love was the ultimate way to express how we felt towards each other. Several times he washed my body with his *Sanguis Vitam*. It was instinctive to let him in, even allowing him egress as deeply as Enrique had accidentally had on the plane. It *was* a gift, as Enrique had said, it was so pure and intimate and private. Something for only us. Every time his warm *Sanguis Vitam* flowed through me, I felt a little better. A little more of me settling into my bones. Michel has always been able to heal me physically, now I wondered if he was in fact healing more than that. Maybe even healing a part of my mind.

By the time the shutters whirred up again, signalling the third night home in New Zealand for me, he was grinning like the cat that had got the cream. I wasn't quite sure who was more satisfied, me or him.

More and more memories had come flooding to the surface throughout the day as well. My Light had made an appearance a couple of times, especially right at the moments when Michel was working his hardest to distract. That always got an extremely triumphant look on Michel's face when that happened. I'm sure he made it his main mission to get me to light up like a firecracker as often as possible throughout those daylight hours.

The first evidence that I was really getting *me* back was when memories of the Prophecy, Nero and Nut came rushing back in. I had accepted Nut was my goddess, but it was only when I remembered how I had met her, visited her and heard the children laughing around her, that everything fell into place. The memories of Nero however, were the hardest. Not only had Jonathan taken my memories, leaving me feeling lost and adrift, but by doing so, he had made me relive them all over again when the memories returned.

The good memories did outweigh the bad and as pleasant as it was to relive them, their effect paled in comparison to the bad. I couldn't help crying all over again at the loss of Nero. Michel just held me, feeling my emotions along with me, stoically standing by me and sharing each wave of grief, despair and loss. And then successfully distracting me again afterwards, saving me from experiencing the replays in my head for hours and hours.

But, the memories of the Prophecy had the most lasting effect on me. The knowledge of who or what I am. The devastating weight of what it all meant. The only thing making it easier was the fact that I had come to accept my fate before my trip to America, I had accepted my role in the battle to come. And as scared and frightened as I was at what that may entail, I had accepted my part in all of it. I kept telling myself this when it threatened to consume me again now.

With the knowledge of the Prophecy came my powers. First the *Sanguis Vitam Cupitor,* or Blood Life Seeker powers. I played with them for a while, sending my senses out and feeling the Dark vampires throughout the world. Plotting their positions on my mental globe, spinning it around and around and watching their flashing red lights blink as the map rotated.

Next was the *Prohibitum Bibere*, or Forbidden Drink powers. Likewise I played with that one, opening and closing the door in my mind that let the Dark vampires see me, sense me, And as uncomfortable as the sensation was to watch them long for me and begin to seek me again, I forced myself to keep the door open, knowing they needed to come to me and even if I wasn't quite ready, I needed to let them. I felt strong enough to do that, despite the final Prophecy power and its continued weak link.

The *Lux Lucis Tribuo*, or Giver of Light. I could feel it within me, but no matter what I did, I couldn't figure out how to use it. I played with my Light, moulded it, sent it out around the room and even took Michel by surprise and washed him in it when he hadn't been expecting anything of the sort. It was pure power to watch him writhe in uncontrolled pleasure due to my Light. I'm not sure how Nut would have felt about my use of it, but I was hoping she'd allow me one session of non-Prophecy related usage to satisfy my kindred. And satisfy him it certainly did. It was some ten minutes before he could move or utter a single word and as soon as he could he paid me back, murmuring something like, *payback's a bitch,* as he threatened me with images in my mind of every conceivable way he would seek his revenge when I least expected it most. I hoped it would be soon.

So, it was unsurprising that I finally felt my pull, the evil-lurks-in-my-city pull. I wanted to rush right out and face it, I was itching to get a stake in my hand and get my butt back in the metaphorical saddle, but Michel would have none of it. Forcibly holding me down on the bed until Amisi dealt with the threat and the pull evaporated.

I wasn't too happy about that.

"You can get off me now, she's staked him," I growled, staring up into his impassive, but determined face.

Michel just glared at me a moment longer, obviously unsure if I was telling the truth. Even though he could read my mind and emotions, I'd given him a run for his money just now. He was wearing a few decent bruises and his breathing was still a little out of control.

"It has been a while since we have sparred. You need practice." He followed up this statement with a rough thrust of his hands holding my arms above my head on the mattress of our bed, just in case I planned to disagree. Not that I had, he had been able to hold me down successfully after all, his body now securely pressing me into the padded bed below us, but I wouldn't let him get away with taunting me.

"Then why haven't you released me yet?"

"Maybe I intend to teach you a lesson," he growled leaning his face down to run his fangs across my jaw and around to my ear, gently biting with one of his sharp incisors, drawing blood and making me gasp. His tongue quickly lapping up the drop of red at his puncture site.

"Is that..." I swallowed, trying to get myself under control. "Is that the best you can do? I mean it's hardly a challenge, is it? I'm not even armed."

Oh he liked that, his growl was deep and long. "What weapon would you choose?" His fangs going across my jaw on the other side of my face and finishing up at my other ear with another nip and suck.

Oh boy, he wasn't playing fair, but I was also amping for a fight. I needed it, I craved it. I would so damn well have it.

What was I thinking? Oh yeah. "Svante," I managed to get out in one quick breath, his fangs now dancing along my neck, past my throat and back around the other side on my neck to find my pulse. He didn't answer straight away, he was too busy sucking on my pulse, his fangs scraping either side but not entering. I arched off the bed, my body begging for him to bite. Shit. I was addicted to his touch, his fangs, his drinking of my blood. Humans can quickly become addicted to a vampire's bite, but as I am joined to Michel, that's not actually the case. The joining does not allow one member to hold that sort of influence over another, that's why Michel can no longer glaze me or influence me with his *Sanguis Vitam*, only when I let him by lowering my shields. Maybe I was letting him have this addictive control right now. Maybe it was all my choice. Shit.

"You were saying?" he asked, moving down past my collar bone and to the dip between my breasts.

Before he could distract me further, I replied. "Svante. I already said it, you're not paying attention."

He laughed against me. "I assure you, that you have my undivided attention right now." His mouth going around a nipple, his fangs scraping almost painfully against the sensitive skin on either side.

I thought he'd only tease, that's what he had been doing, but with a primal moan he bit hard and started pulling my blood into his mouth.

His hands left my arms and circled around me, lifting me off the bed and holding me up as he drank me down. My body almost bent back in half as I draped over his arms, my breast trapped in his mouth, my arms unable to move for the lust he poured through me right then. And it was right, so very right. No other thoughts than those of my kindred, intimately feeding from my vein, entered my mind. I almost wept with joy at feeling so whole again.

I realised he'd moved one of his arms from around me, strong enough to continue to hold me draped over just one, while the other slipped between my legs and began playing. I welcomed him. It didn't take long for him to get me writhing, so close to coming, what with his mouth around my breast, his tongue lapping at my blood, his fangs holding me firmly in place. But as soon as he sensed I was about to crest the wave of heat that was washing through me, he shifted his fingers and plunged them deep inside, taking away the orgasm and making me cry out in protest and then quickly moan as I rode his fingers. His movements making them plunge in and out and in and out, then back to stroking me to an impossible high, then only deny me all over again with deep thrusts.

This went on for some time – the to-ing and fro-ing – and all the while he continued to drink me down, a low purr-come-growl came from the back of his throat. Finally, he must have decided he had taken enough blood, because he allowed me to follow through with that blissful wave of lust until I crashed down the other side in jerky movements against his arm and chest, his fingers again inside me as I clenched them again and again in my wet, wet folds. He slowly withdrew his fangs, licking my breast and then his lips and at the same time removed his fingers, bringing them to his mouth and licking them clean too.

"Mm. Svante, you say. I think that can be arranged." His voice was so low and husky, his eyes, when I managed to lift my head and look at them, were shot with magenta, in amongst vibrant violets and amethysts.

"You sure you can handle it?" I asked, trying to keep a straight face and knowing I was failing miserably.

He smiled a sinful smile and lowered me to the bed. "I will make a deal with you. If you can get yourself off this bed and dressed within five minutes, I will spar with you and your weapon of choice." He had a decidedly cocky look on his face. One which I had every intention of wiping off in the next five minutes.

OK, so it was close and I wasn't entirely sure if I had dressed as well as I normally do. I'm sure I forgot underwear, but that was because I couldn't find any and time was running out. It had taken three minutes to roll over onto my stomach, all the while Michel just sat there watching with an enormous grin on his face, but I did make it. I got up, stumbled, got to the dressing room and managed some yoga pants and a T-Shirt, which on closer inspection once I was back in the room, was inside out. But hey! I was dressed and standing and four minutes fifty-three seconds had passed.

The look on Michel's face was a mix of incredulity, amazement and respect. He really hadn't thought I'd make it. Sucker!

He chuckled and shook his head, sleekly shifting off the bed with all the grace of a panther, proving how much more in control of himself he was and how stupid I was to even consider sparring with him right now. I spent the few moments it took for him to dress to limber up, shake off the last of the post coital bliss and focus on my need to fight. My hand was itching to hold a Svante again, itching to swipe at a target. If Michel was prepared to be that target, then so be it. Bring it on.

He came out of the dressing room in casual black trousers and a black shirt, open at the neck and sleeves rolled up, his usual fighting wear. There was a small smile playing on his lips, he'd obviously heard my thoughts and was finding it amusing. Damn he was so confident.

"Erika has swords out in the backyard. I hope you do not mind, but we will have an audience."

I paused on the way to the door and looked at him. An audience. I wasn't sure I could handle an audience. Michel just cocked his head at me and smiled that infuriatingly knowing smile of his.

"Having second thoughts?"

Yeah, I bet he'd like me to back down. "No, not at all. The more the merrier."

He laughed out loud and nodded toward the door. "Ladies before gentlemen," he murmured, unable to stop the grin on his face broadening.

I was quite sure he was doing it all to egg me on, to make me rise to the occasion and not think about what I was doing, to just do it. Michel's whole purpose the past 48 hours had been to help me get back *me*. I didn't think for a moment that he had stopped, but part of me also riled at his attitude, his teasing, his confidence that he would prevail. I may not have held a Svante sword for a while, but I had been through a hell of a lot and if there is one thing I have always managed to do, it was to use what experiences I'd had to bolster me, to fortify my resolve.

So, life had been shitty lately, but now I was back and no amount of taunting or distracting would save Michel now. As I picked up one of the practice Svante swords from the outdoor table where they rested, I centred myself with the feel of its weight in my hand and told myself this was all practice. Practice for when I was faced with Jonathan and could slice the blade into his flesh and heart.

Michel watched me closely for a moment, no doubt registering my thoughts, the strength of them, the decidedly dark nature to them. Maybe he feared for himself, but I doubted it, Michel could take me in an instant. I knew he was only entertaining this idea to allow me to release some frustration and limber up, but maybe he was a little worried for me, for where my thoughts were taking me. I had never been an overtly Dark person, I have too much Light, but as someone had once told me, *where there is Light there is always Dark and where there is Dark there is always Light.* The universe is based on balance, I was just evening myself out.

He nodded slowly as I stepped into the circle of light on our back lawn. I could sense vampires all around us, but they were holding back, unseen in the shadows. I worked hard to ignore them, blocking their signals out, ignoring their *Sanguis Vitam* pulsing in the air. I rolled my shoulders and bowed when Michel did, never taking my eyes off his. When we stood up straight again, he winked.

I stifled a smile and fell into a fighting stance. When I had learned to wield a sword Erika had made me repeatedly practice Weapon Dance moves again and again and again, until they were instinctive, requiring no thought, just an extension of who I was. She had damn near made me collapse with those moves and how far she had pushed me, but now I just thanked her silently in my mind because they all came crashing back into me and settled over my skin like a well made glove.

Michel was the first to move, he always is. I don't think he lacks patience, I just think he likes to show his aggressive side and advance before his hand is forced. I know his moves pretty well by now and I'd forgotten how good it was to fence with him. My arms had lost conditioning over the past month, so the sword did feel a little heavier than usual, but the moves were all pure joy. I danced through strike after strike, unable to land much more than a glancing blow or defensive parry, but it was fun. Hell, it was magical. To be fighting again, even if it was just Michel whom I had no intention of hurting.

He must have heard that thought or perhaps he decided I'd had enough of a warm up, because his next strike landed, slicing my top down the front and grazing my flesh. Adrenaline shot through me and suddenly the fight took on a whole different meaning. His eyes flashed amethyst and his fangs dropped down. I bit my lip and renewed my efforts.

Of course, he didn't let me get near enough to threaten a slice of his skin which only made me more and more angry, the longer the fight went on. I had managed to hold off any further contact from his sword, which looked like it was beginning to frustrate him slightly, but it was still not the reward I was looking for. If I was going to face Jonathan, holding off his strikes was not going to be enough. Not nearly enough.

After about ten minutes of beautiful swordsmanship on both sides, I'd had enough. I was tiring, sweating, my T-Shirt's rip was widening and as I didn't have a bra on underneath, I was conscious I was flashing the odd vampire in the backyard. They had all come out in the open after I had started sparring for real, sensing when my head was well and truly in the game. They no longer concerned me, not scaring me, nor threatening to send me down a slippery slide of memories, they just existed on the sidelines, firmly in the category of Michel's vampires and no hazard for my mind to negotiate at all.

Michel still looked picture perfect and I think that was what did it for me. I've always felt I look a little clumsy when I fight, not that I stumble or lose my balance too often, but I don't have that suave appearance and devil-may-care display that vampires often do, especially vampires like Michel. He was, however, no longer looking smug. I think he had expected me to have given up by now, not necessarily by choice, but because of exhaustion and he was still unable to land another blow, so I took what advantage I could. He'd settled into a routine of just countering my every move, no longer attempting to strike, I think he had decided to just wait me out until I collapsed. It was a good strategy, I was starting to see double, but I made myself continue with the same moves over and over and over again, lulling him further into a sense of monotony before I used the last of my reserves, all the while playing the repetitive Weapon Dance motions over and over and over again in my mind - and nothing else.

So, he hadn't heard my thoughts, he didn't know my plans, until I sprung them and even then I feinted a spin dance to the side, allowing him to hastily change position to counter it - he's fast and he knows how I can dance my spins in a fight - but it wasn't what I was going for, not really. The moment his stride was altered to counter my feinted spin, I struck him fair and square in the chest with a bolt of my Light and as soon as he landed on the grass I had the Svante's sharp tip at his throat and my foot on his chest holding him prone.

"Do you concede, vampire?" I asked casually.

He swallowed, no doubt trying to get the after effects of the Light blast under control and use the time to determine possible escape paths. I pressed the sword a little firmer into his skin, not breaking it and all the while smiling at him. He licked his lips then, his eyes flashing violet, indigo and then amethyst, the only hint that he was going to try something, the magenta that followed in their wake. Before I even registered the colour change, he had grabbed my ankle, the one attached to the foot on his chest and flipped it out, then used his sword to brush mine away. The clang of metal on metal distracting everyone from the fact that I had sliced his skin at the throat because of his stupidly idiotic attempt at escape.

It was only a nick, enough to draw blood, but not really damage.

But it was all it took for me to hesitate. The blood running down his neck, not just dripping, but looking like there was way more blood than there actually was. For a moment all I could see was blood, so much blood, but it wasn't on Michel, it was on Nero and that's all he needed to spin me around, disarm me with one hand and hold the length of his Svante sword at my throat with the other.

"Never," he whispered in my ear.

I registered the shouts of his vampires in support of their master. I felt his hard body encasing mine at my back. I even smelt his sweat mingling with his scent of fresh sea breezes and clean cut grass, but all I could see was blood.

He must have seen and heard my thoughts a moment later, maybe he had not been paying attention to what was playing through my mind, too involved in his escape from my blade. But he stiffened now, a split second before I elbowed him hard in the stomach, making his grip loosen and sword lower and then I ran Nosferatin-fast down the side of the house and to freedom.

All I heard in my head was the pounding of my feet on the pavement and my heartbeat thumping in my chest and Michel's desperate cry after me...

"Lucinda!"

But all I could see, was blood.

15

OUR MOTHER OF PERPETUAL HELP

Michel found me not long after, sitting in the front garden of a church a few blocks away, squashed between a statue of the Virgin Mary and a sign that read: *"For the life of the flesh is in the blood... for it is the blood that makes atonement for the soul. Leviticus 17:11*

He walked up to me silently, hands in his pockets, then slowly lowered himself in a graceful move to the ground next to where I sat. His eyes taking in the statue and the sign with a slow measuring gaze.

"Coincidence?" he asked, eyebrows raised as he looked at me properly for the first time, no doubt taking in the streaks of dried tears on my cheeks. Fucking tears.

I didn't answer him. Our Mother of Perpetual Help had this sign up longer than I had been living in the neighbourhood. I'd memorised it as I drove past on the way back from various hunts. So, no, not a coincidence.

Michel sighed next to me, but didn't add anything else. We sat in silence, just the night time sounds of a suburban neighbourhood swilling around us. I was guessing he was quite happy to wait me out, let me be the first to talk, but I had nothing to say. Nothing at all.

Finally, he cracked first. "I am sorry. I thought you were ready."

"Don't you dare apologise," I said through gritted teeth, my hands bunched in fists at my side. "Don't you dare."

He took a slow breath in, held it for a moment - like he was counting to ten or something - and then let it out, his whole body relaxing incrementally.

Silence slipped back between us like a possessive pet, unable to share its owner with their loved one.

It wasn't so much the apology, as the excuse for what happened. I couldn't face the fact that I wasn't fully healed, that I was still a fucking mess not only from the loss of memories, from what Jonathan had done, from the vampires' attack in Denver, but also from losing Nero. Would I never be able to just be strong again on my own?

"You may not wish to hear this, but I will say it anyway. You are the strongest person I have ever known."

It wasn't the first time I had heard him say that.

"Is it enough?" I asked quietly. "I'm not some average human battling average nightmares. I'm supposed to be the *Sanguis Vitam Cupitor,* the friggin' *Prohibitum Bibere* and the *Lux Lucis* fucking *Tribuo!*" My voice had risen towards the end of that little lot, but I brought it back under control and managed to quietly add, "It's not enough."

Michel's lips were twitching slightly at the edges, but he didn't laugh, his voice was earnest when he spoke again. "It is, if you choose for it to be."

"What the fuck does that mean?" I asked incredulously. "Some bloody yin and yang philosophy? Get a grip, Michel. Nut chose the wrong girl."

"You can be incredibly infuriating, you know that, Lucinda!" he burst out. "And self absorbed." I cringed at that one. "So, you've been burdened with a Prophecy and there is absolutely fuck all you can do about it, yet you still battle it at every turn. Life is not easy." His words were laced with bitterness. "It is a constant challenge, but you have been given the chance to make it better, not just for yourself, but for others of your kind, for others in this world. You have been given gifts and powers beyond any mortal's imagination. And you scoff at them, disregard them, ignore them." He stood up swiftly then, in one smooth motion, the old vampire puppet-on-a-string fall back. He ran a hand through his hair, still obviously frustrated with me then and turned back to look at me. "I love you. Do you know that? I absolutely adore you. And I want to protect you, to take care of you, to save you from everything and anything that may harm you." He paused and took a deep breath in, his words so much softer when they finally came. "But, I am beginning to think it is not someone else I need to save you from at all. And no matter how I try, you won't let me save you from *you*."

He took a few steps away and then turned back, reaching inside his back pocket and pulling out a dark object. He threw it towards me, my reflexes making me catch it with ease. "You shouldn't be unarmed when you're out and about." And then he turned and disappeared. Poof. Gone. And all I was holding was a silver stake wrapped tightly in black felt.

Fuck! Arrogant, demanding, know-it-all vampire! Haven't I been through enough shit lately to warrant a get-out-of-jail-free card? Does he have to ride my arse too? And like he's so perfect. He's egotistical, self-absorbed and power hungry. Not to mention a fucking exhibitionist too. The guy is definitely not perfect. Sexy, dangerous, maybe even a little hot. Shit, who am I kidding, he's super hot. But, he's not fucking perfect.

Neither are you. That is my point.

"Come back here and say that!" I shouted into the eerie silence outside of my head.

I didn't get a reply.

Coward! I barked inside my mind. Add to the list coward, self-righteous and pompous.

Pompous! Ha! His voice echoed in my head.

"Are you going to leave me alone to contemplate my many failings, Michel, or continually interrupt my train of thought?" I answered aloud.

"I seem to be unable to walk away from you." His resigned voice came from just a few feet away.

"Does that mean I win this argument?" I asked as he stepped out from behind a tree.

"No, not at all. You *are* incredibly infuriating, there is no argument to that." He sighed loudly and reluctantly added, "I, however, am nothing without you. I couldn't even run my line while you were gone, Jett has been handling everything."

Holy shit. I flicked an apologetic glance at the Virgin Mary towering over me and then looked back at Michel.

"I'm sorry. I didn't know."

He tried not to laugh. "And you expect me not to baulk at your apology? It is my failing, not yours."

I stood up stiffly and walked towards him. "It's not a failing to be fucked in the head, Michel, because of circumstances."

He did laugh at that. "Shouldn't you take your own advice?" His arms came out and wrapped around me, his head resting on my forehead. I sighed against him. He was right. Of course he was right, he's always fucking right.

"Once I thought I was wrong, but I was just mistaken," he whispered. I punched him playfully in the stomach receiving a grunt in return.

We stood like that for a while, just enjoying the closeness of each other. It was me who spoke first.

"What am I going to do, Michel? I can't fight this battle if every time I see blood I think of... Nero. I relive that moment."

"What do humans do when faced with a mental block?"

I thought about that for a moment. "I guess they see a therapist."

"A therapist." He rolled the word around his mouth as though he was tasting it. "Maybe you should see a therapist."

I started laughing. "Yeah, I can really picture how that would go. Hey Doc, my vampire hunter trainer got killed by a goddess who wants to kick my butt because I'm the Prophesied and I'm having trouble getting over it. Can you help? Yeah, that'll work."

"We do not have therapists in the vampyre world."

"No I guess not, your little sojourn into La La Land while I was gone is a prime example of not needing therapy."

"Sarcasm is the lowest form of wit, my dear." But, he wasn't being serious, his lips kissing softly on my forehead told me so. "Is there someone you could talk with?" he asked, his lips sliding across to my temple, his nose nuzzling into my hair.

I thought about that. Was there? Erika and Amisi were good for girl chats, but I needed someone a little removed from my day to day life, but also someone I felt wouldn't bullshit me, wouldn't indulge me I suppose. I could think of only one person in our world who fitted that bill.

"Oh no. Definitely not." Michel had stopped kissing and nuzzling and stood before me with a scowl on his face. "I will not let you go to him."

"He'd put me in my place, Michel, you know that, he'd also know where I'm coming from. I can't explain it, but Gregor understands about the Nosferatin thing, he just gets it."

"I will not let you anywhere near your former lover and that is final."

Former lover. I slept with him once and only because I was pissed off with the world and Michel and had let the Dark too far into my soul. I regretted it immediately and have never had the urge to repeat that mistake ever again.

"I need him, Michel. I can't put it into words exactly, but Gregor would help me." It's not that I wanted to cause Michel pain and I knew what Gregor meant to him, but I couldn't explain it, Gregor just understood the Nosferatin side of me. Maybe it had something to do with the fact that our blood calls to him, I don't know, but Gregor does have a connection with Nosferatin, not just me, but all Nosferatin. I knew he could help me, I just knew it.

"I... I can't let you go to Wellington again. I just can't."

"Then invite him here. Better still, lets have a party."

"A party?" he asked a little incredulously, eyebrows raised, head tilted - sexily I might add - to the side. "We are in the midst of war, your abductor no doubt about to make an appearance and you want to party?"

Well, when you put it like that...

"Your line has not see you for a while, have they? And they certainly haven't seen me. Don't they need to get all touchy-touchy, feely-feely with us to reinforce the love, or something?"

He laughed. "Reinforce the love." But that's all he could get out, he was laughing too hard to form any more words right then.

I pushed on regardless, a party felt bloody good to me, there'd been too much death and heartache and God awful crap lately, I wanted light hearted and loving and full of fun.

"The crew need a bit of bolstering. No better time than right before a battle to lift the spirits and get them eager."

Michel brought himself back under control. "Granted, but I would prefer to just have family for that, Gregor is not family."

"Neither is Enrique and I'm guessing you've got him hanging around for the same reason. The impending battle."

"Well yes, but..."

"You could show me off." That made him stop mid sentence. "You know, let everyone know I'm..." I paused and took a deep breath in. "That I'm yours."

"Are you mine?" His voice was very quiet, hopeful.

I swallowed picking up on the colour change in his eyes. "Yes." My voice was more quiet than I had intended.

He looked at me intently then, just stared for a moment, as though he was looking for an answer. I don't know if he found it, he didn't smile or whoop for joy or kiss me passionately, he just stared at me for a bit and then nodded. One short nod, almost to himself.

He cleared his throat before he spoke again. "And you would let me show you off?"

"Yes." I answered too quickly on that one.

"Be careful how you answer that, little Hunter." Michel never called me little Hunter. It was usually *ma douce* or *ma belle* or Lucinda or even my dear, but not little Hunter. That made me pause for breath.

"What is your interpretation of showing me off?" Best to get this straight first methinks.

He did smile at that, then reached up and took hold of a few strands of my hair, wrapping them around his fingers. "It would involve me picking your outfit out for you." His eyes flashed amethyst. "I would insist on certain privileges." His eyes moved to violet. "It would definitely involve some public display of affection." And there was the magenta.

"I'm..." I licked my lips and swallowed. "I'm not having sex with you in front of the team, Michel."

"Of course not, I wouldn't dream of taking it that far."

I scoffed. He lowered his face to kiss behind my ear, his hands running the length of my body - just to push my buttons even more, I was thinking.

"Are your guards here? Watching this now?"

"Of course." I could hear the smile in his voice. He was just loving this. "I am not at full strength yet."

I pushed against him and looked in his eyes. "How much PDA?"

His smile was wicked. "Some things are better left as a surprise, *ma belle*. If you wish for your Gregor and a party, then concede to my demands."

Well, there you go. Vampire wheeling and dealing at its best. Michel was a consummate politician, able to exact precisely what he wanted out of a situation and make you think you still held all the cards. I did want a party, I wanted to feel happy and have all my friends around me and also, I admit, flick a middle finger at the Queen of Darkness and Jonathan the Prick. A party, in the face of everything that had happened, was one big *fuck you*.

"All right," I said carefully. "You can show me off."

Michel's arms came around me in an instant, picking me up and holding me tight, then he spun me around and around in the Church's front yard, finally allowing the world to slow down after a dozen or so revolutions and his mouth to claim mine.

When he was done eating my tongue he pulled back and whispered, "Mine." A hint of surprise in amongst the letters that formed that word. "You are mine, aren't you?"

He sounded like a little boy, seeking reassurance from an adult that he'd performed a certain task well. It wasn't a tone I heard from Michel often and it reminded me how affected he had been by my absence.

I placed my hand against his cheek and looked him in the eye and said, "Michel Durand, I am yours and you know it."

He smiled then, but it was still a little sad, just around the edges. He noticed me frowning at him and he pulled me close, his mouth again beside my ear when he spoke.

"It is all right, *ma douce*. Hearing you say it, is enough for now."

I wasn't sure what he meant by that. I really wasn't sure at all, but I decided I'd trust him. Besides, he was going to throw me a party. I had more pressing things to think of.

Like, what would he make me wear?

16

MAKING HAPPY

It wasn't as bad as I thought it would be. I mean, I should have known he wouldn't go for a butt-cheek-high slinky number, it's just not Michel's style. Whenever he has visited me in my dreams he has dressed me in long flowing dresses, intricately decorated and beautifully designed, but he always said it was the hint of what lay beneath that was the enticement, he liked to let his imagination run wild. My short-short fighting skirts had always been a reluctantly accepted part of my wardrobe. He never complained when they provided such easy access, but he did bemoan the longer dresses of yesteryears.

So, the length of the exquisite piece of shiny and thin slinky fabric before me wasn't a surprise, the fact that it could be so long and consist of so little material, did.

It was in a deep emerald green, a colour I had not ever considered wearing before. I have brown hair and usually well tanned skin - but at the moment my tan had taken a hiding and I was more a cream colour - and brown eyes. None of that screams green, but at least it didn't clash. It also had extremely thin spaghetti straps, a plunging neckline and slits either side of the skirt that went from my ankles right up to the top of my thighs. Considering how short I am, that's not a long stretch, but the effect of all that long line of flesh did make me seem taller than I actually was. And I reluctantly admitted, along with my now paler complexion, the green looked stunning.

I was standing in front of the floor length mirror in our dressing room admiring the colour on me and trying to figure out how to move without flashing way more skin than I was comfortable with, when Michel walked back in the room. He was dressed in one of his many uber-expensive Armani suit trousers, dancing dragon gold cuff links at the ends of his crisp white Pierre Cardin shirt sleeves and a gorgeous deep, deep blue, shot with emerald green tie, loose around his neck. He stopped at the door as soon as he saw me and let his eyes lazily roam from head to foot, a small smile playing on his lips.

"You are stunning, *ma douce*."

I raised my eyebrows at him and flicked a leg out slightly, displaying how much flesh, didn't so much as peek through the split in the divine fabric, but more like shouted to the world *look at me*. The contrast between my cream skin and the deep colour was striking though.

His smile broadened. "The effect I was going for."

"When you choose to show something off, you really like to show as much of it as possible, don't you?"

He stepped up behind me, the mirror still at my front and ran his hands down the sides of the dress, resting them on the slight curve of my hips, his fingers digging into my naked skin at the top of my thighs possessively, his lips kissing softly along my bare shoulder up to my neck.

"Can you blame me?" he whispered against my skin, his eyes holding my own in the mirror.

I shook my head and leaned back into him, wrapping my arms up around his head behind me, his hands shifted slightly on my legs, his fingers almost whispering against my skin on one side, sliding tantalisingly under the fabric at the split.

"We'll be late," I breathed as he teased me.

"Mm and you'll be flushed." He turned me around in his arms and proceeded to lay kisses up my neck, over my jaw, until he finally claimed my mouth with his.

"Is this one of the privileges you spoke of?" I managed, when we broke to allow me some air.

"Absolutely."

I shifted against him, deciding a little kissing could be tolerated after all.

Within seconds he had me weak at the knees, my insides warm and abuzz with butterflies. My face flushed and my body tingling. All from a simple kiss. Finally, when he was convinced I'd had enough, he pulled away. An extremely satisfied look on his face as he leaned back against the door jam and watched me steady myself against the mirror.

"That was uncalled for," I breathed and glared at him, knowing damn well I was very flushed now. "And now we're late."

He laughed, a low sexy chuckle. "Yes and now you are flushed."

"You bastard!" I shot at him, but I was smiling. I had Michel back. I had me back. Every time he teased, every time he pushed me further out of myself, I felt like I had made it home. I knew half the reason for his constant teasing was to bring me back to me. And I was grateful. He never seemed to go too far, just the right mix of pressure and pleasure. Somehow still keeping his claiming vampire in its little box inside of him. But, I was beginning to wonder if it was time for the vampire-within to come out.

He laughed at my thought, his eyes flashing magenta. I always thought that when magenta entered his beautiful blue eyes, it was his vampire peeking out from within. Maybe his vampire had heard my thoughts. Maybe it liked them too.

He glided over to me and let his hands drift up my arms to my shoulders, one settling behind my neck, up into my hair. He tipped my head back and slowly lowered his face to mine. I stopped being angry with him making me flush as quickly as the emotion had hit me, but I wanted to tease back. I shifted my face to the side, denying him my lips, but that only made him growl playfully and firmly turn my face back towards him, his other hand on my chin.

"Every single little thing you do turns me on, *ma douce*. Fight with me, don't fight me, whatever you chose, I will only want you more and more. You are my drug and I take great delight in tasting you in every guise you present." He'd taken my tease and was running with it.

His mouth crushed into mine and he pulled me hard against his body, taking his time kissing me, making me sink into the moment unable to think a clear thought at all. Letting me know his vampire was coming back. Sometimes, Michel could kiss like he wanted to exist inside my body, all lips and teeth and tongue and the entire length of him along for the ride. By the time he pulled back to let me breathe, I was lost.

"Good," he purred, looking at the effect he'd had over me. "But, there is still something missing." He looked me up and down, holding me out at arms length, I'm glad he hadn't released me yet, my legs were all but jelly right now. He reached over with one hand and opened the top drawer of his tallboy dresser, pulling out a shiny pendant on a long platinum chain. My dancing dragon.

I'd been wearing it when I was kidnapped and forgotten all about the beautiful piece of jewellery Michel had gifted me not long before I had been taken. The sight of it made me expand with happiness, I had thought it had been lost. Suddenly I could stand on my own two feet again and almost jumped up and down with unbridled joy.

Michel laughed at my reaction and unclasped the chain, reaching forward to place it around my neck. I held my hair up, out of his way, so he wouldn't get it caught. The pendant settled down between the crease in my breasts, just above where the material of the dress began, precisely positioned for maximum effect, drawing the eye to the dip between my creamy mounds.

"Perfect," he whispered, eyes flashing amethyst and magenta again.

"How did you find it?"

Michel swallowed, his eyes still on either the pendant or my breasts either side of it, he reluctantly pulled his gaze away and looked at me.

"It was discarded on the pavement outside your bank, along with your stakes and Svante, when you were taken." There was a brief haunted look in his eyes, which he banished with a quick look down at my breasts again. He licked his lips and took a step back.

His eyes roamed over me one last longing time and then he reached for his jacket and slipped it on. Turning to the mirror to quickly do up his tie and then button the jacket closed. I watched for a while, mesmerised by his swift and sure movements and then walked up behind him and slipped my arms around his waist, resting my face against his back. I felt his hands come up and cover mine in front of him.

"Who found them?" I asked, but I think I already knew the answer.

"I did."

"You came after me." It wasn't a question.

"Of course," he replied quietly. "Your glaze was effective on Douglas, none of my line prevented you from leaving, but I sensed you go and by the time I came out of the office, you had left. It took a few minutes to ascertain that you weren't on a hunt and Amisi was being held. Erika dealt with Amisi's captor and I gave chase, Douglas still holding my line from pursuing. By the time I found your discarded items, you had been placed in a vehicle and fled the scene at great speed. I followed our Bond connection as far as Mt Albert and then you were lost to me. The drugs already taking hold."

I squeezed him more tightly aware of what he must have gone through and how much worse it must have got for him as the days passed. There were no words to offer to dull that pain, nothing could take those memories from him and make them better. He had his own reasons to want to land the killing blow to Jonathan. Maybe we could tag team it together.

He laughed quietly in my arms. "Deal," he said and turned to face me. "Enough of that, we have tonight to forget. *Sensations* has been well warded and Enrique's men are providing cover around the building. Not that I believe anything will happen tonight, it is too soon, but if it does we are prepared. And in the meantime, *ma douce*, we will party, *d'accord?*"

I nodded in agreement, Jonathan was not getting this night. Tonight was all about making happy, for us, for our line. It may be our last chance to do this for a while, I intended to make good use of what time we had left.

Two of Michel's personal guards rode with us in the Land Rover, both in the front seats, another two cars full of guards followed behind. It almost felt like overkill, but although Michel looked to be back at full strength, I knew he wasn't entirely and somehow I was sure he was doing it for me too. I hated that he thought I couldn't take care of myself, but I hated more, that he questioned he could protect me too. That was not Michel's style, he was almost omnipotent in my eyes, the battering to his ego and confidence from losing me must have been significant.

He slipped an arm around my shoulders and pulled me against his chest, his lips running a line down from my temple over my jaw and down my neck. I wasn't sure if he was doing it to distract me from my thoughts or not, but it worked. I stopped thinking about my time away and the effect it had on everyone I cared about and I started thinking sinful thoughts of Michel naked in his chamber at *Sensations,* completely lost under my careful ministrations.

"I do hope that is a promise, *ma douce,*" he whispered in my ear. "And not just a tease." He'd seen my thoughts, the pictures playing through my mind. My hand resting on his thigh slowly tracked higher, making his already half hard erection jump in response.

He laughed, quite sure I wouldn't try anything in the back seat of the Land Rover with two of his vamps sitting quietly, but knowledgeably in the front. He was right, of course. I wasn't quite at his level of exhibitionist behaviour, but I did manage a slow stroke, followed by a firm grip through his trousers, making sure he closed his eyes before shifting away.

His eyes languidly slid open again and he smiled, a cheeky smile and said loud enough for the two goons in the front to hear. "A tease then." I blushed, which I could only hope was hidden in the dark of the vehicle. He just laughed some more.

Sensations was in full swing when we arrived. It was still early in the evening, only just past 9pm, but Michel's line had started well before we arrived. No doubt quite used to our later arrivals and the fact that we got easily sidetracked on a regular basis. The club was, of course, closed to the public, just Michel's vampires, Amisi, Enrique and one or two of his line, the rest outside on watch.

My eyes found Enrique's as soon as we entered the room. Michel had his arm around my shoulders and was busy greeting some of his line, his grip casual but firm. I watched as Enrique smiled slowly, his eyes running the length of my dress, resting momentarily on my dancing dragon and then finally making their way back to my face. Men, honestly, they can never control themselves.

Michel squeezed me tightly for a second and then whispered in my ear, "Go to him, *ma douce*. I know you want to."

I was surprised Michel would let me, I had the feeling he wouldn't have wanted me out of his sight tonight. I turned to look him in the face and he just smiled, one of his lazy knowing smiles. "It will be that much more enjoyable when I whisk you effortlessly away from his side."

I couldn't help it, I smiled back at him. I knew him letting me go was showing his line he was back in control, holding me too close would have been a crutch, he now had to walk the fine line of balance between showing little concern when I wandered away, but bringing me back before the claiming reared its ugly head. I thought I'd make it a little easier on him, it was the least I could do.

"Is that a promise or a tease?" I asked innocently and enjoyed the wonderful smile that graced his face in return.

He growled low, only those vampires nearby would have appreciated his response. His lips brushed mine and he whispered, "You have my word I shall come for you, *ma douce*." He kissed me lingeringly, then said, "Always."

I watched the amethyst and violet swirl in his eyes for a moment and then took my leave, walking across the club room floor towards my saviour. I tried not to think too much about how grateful I was to Enrique, about how I did feel like he was my saviour, the one to rescue me in the end, because I knew Michel would still be in my head, but it was hard. Enrique was all of those things to me and Michel was just going to have to accept them.

My heart, my body and my soul belonged to Michel and although I was now aware that he physically couldn't have come after me himself, Enrique was the one who now held my gratitude. I also knew, however, that Michel had done everything in his power to get someone he trusted to me when I needed it. It just so happened that it was Enrique and not one of Michel's line.

Enrique watched me walk towards him with a surprising amount of hunger on his face, he didn't try to hide it, he didn't try to temper it. I couldn't reconcile the protector from on the plane with the vampire before me. I was left a little confused. I stopped just in front of him and smiled, then when he made no move but to smile languidly in return, I stepped forward and wrapped my arms around him in an embrace. He did hesitate then, maybe lusting after me from a distance was acceptable in his eyes, but actually following through with physical contact was a no-no. That settled my suddenly rapid heartbeat. Maybe Enrique wasn't looking at me the way I had suspected at all. Maybe I had got it wrong. Eventually though, even he couldn't resist the opportunity presented and his arms wrapped around me in return, one hand sliding lower to cop a feel. I jumped in alarm and further surprise. Just what was he playing at, this was not the Enrique I had come to know.

I pushed back from him and swatted his hand away. "What's the matter with you?" I said in a low but steady voice. He just smiled winningly back.

"How are you, little Hunter? You look... well." I could tell there was a lot more he wanted to say there, but *well* worked.

"I am. Thank you." I picked up a glass of champagne as it floated past on a waiter's tray and took a sip, trying to ignore the gnawing feeling that Enrique was simply not himself tonight. "Thank you for everything," I added quietly, returning the moment to something a little less dangerous, but equally as emotional.

His smile dimmed a fraction, a more serious look coming over his features. "It was my pleasure, *Señorita*. Entirely my pleasure." I relaxed a little at his words.

We stood in silence for a few seconds and then he took my arm and directed me to some comfortable seats in the corner, helping me sit beside him, so we could face the room and also talk more privately than in the middle of the dance floor.

"Have you received all of your memories?" He was drinking champagne too, although his was already almost all gone. He casually placed an arm along the back of the bench seat we were on as well and crossed his legs, giving the picture of utter ease and contentment.

"Yes. I think I'm all back to normal." Well, except for visions of blood and recurring images of Nero's death that is.

"Excellent, I am so glad. We cannot have our *Sanguis Vitam Cupitor* unprepared." Many of the vamps only ever referred to me as my first prophesied title, not bothering with the rest. I guess it's the one I've held longest.

"I didn't know you were a supporter of the Prophecy, Enrique?"

"Of course, it is why I approached Michel to form an alliance. You do not think he was the only one to recognise you for what you are, do you?"

I hadn't really thought about it. Michel had known what I was, or what I could potentially become, even before I moved to Auckland. He had sensed my power from afar and arranged for my successful transfer to the city and once I came here, he made sure it was him I came to know first and foremost. You'd almost say he engineered our getting together. Hell, that's exactly what you could say. He did.

But, I'd long gotten over that, he'd proved again and again that despite the planned meeting, he had well and truly lost his heart to me too. It used to piss me off, the how of our getting together, but sometimes even fate makes us believe someone else had a hand in it, who's to say Nut didn't organise Michel into this role as well.

So, although I was aware of Michel's interest in me from the start, I hadn't really thought too much about anyone else's. Enrique's knowledge wasn't that much of a jump in understanding though, was it? I wondered briefly how many other vampires had wanted to seek me out as well. I shuddered a little at that thought. Michel was enough of a handful.

Enrique had received a refill to his glass and was having another sip, he obviously wasn't concerned that I hadn't answered his question, his other hand across the back of the seat had started playing with my hair. I got the distinct impression he may have had quite a few drinks and was a little bit tipsy. Maybe that was why he was acting so strangely. Although he had mentioned on the plane that we would, no doubt, be more than just acquaintances from now on, I was sure he had meant we would be like brother and sister. Care for each other, wish to only protect. From the feel of his hand on the back of my neck and the way he had manoeuvred himself snug against my thigh, I wasn't so sure about that right now though.

He shifted slightly to turn towards me, his leg making the material of my dress move apart at the split, he lowered his hand holding the champagne glass down to my thigh and ran a finger along the flesh displayed there, the wine almost tipping over the top of the glass. "I like your dress, little Hunter. It suits your luscious skin."

"I think you're drunk, Enrique." I had started shaking, I wasn't happy with where this was going, but I was still trying desperately to figure out a reason why. This was not the Enrique I had come to know on that plane.

"Vampires don't really get drunk, not on alcohol any way."

"What do they get drunk on?" I moved slightly to put some space between us.

"Power. Blood." His hand holding his glass came back to rest on my thigh. "Sex."

Holy hell, where was the Enrique who saved me? This was definitely a whole other vampire, that was for sure.

"You need to back off, Enrique, Michel would castrate you if you tried a move." It was the only thing I could think of to say. And as soon as the words were out, Michel was in my mind.

Ma douce, do you need me?

I swallowed. This wasn't Enrique, something was wrong and Michel coming to my rescue now could be disastrous. I needed to figure this out and I needed to be able to do it on my own. Michel must have heard my thoughts and although I could tell it was reluctant, he withdrew from my mind with a simple caress that whispered his faith in my ability to handle the situation on my own. I couldn't believe the sense of power his actions caused in me. A power of belief in myself.

Enrique smiled up at me, unaware of what had transpired in my head and shifted away, his arm from behind my seat also returning to his side. "You are correct, little Hunter. I am acting completely and utterly inappropriately. My mind is clearly distracted. Forgive me."

"What's got into you?" I said with relief. "This is not the Enrique I know and trust."

He looked a little pained at that and I think he would have answered me, given the chance. But he didn't get the chance, because a tall blonde haired, buxom Italian came to stand in front of us, her blood red slinky dress defying gravity and making my splits look like small tears in the fabric.

"Drowning your sorrows, *mio caro*? I told you, I value strength not weakness and this is... weak."

Enrique looked up at our newcomer and smiled bitterly. "And I told you, Alessandra, that I would no longer play your games."

She laughed out loud, a clear sound like tinkling crystals ringing through the room. "But you play them so well, my love. How can I not be addicted to your jealousies, but" - she flashed a look of disgust at me, the first time she had even acknowledged my existence - "you could have chosen a better rival for my affection, *mio caro*. This one has already been used and abused."

Several things happened at once then. Enrique abruptly stood, no doubt to defend my honour, Erika appeared with a Svante sword drawn and pointed at Alessandra's throat and I leapt to my feet and punched the female vampire at the top of my most hated list. My fist connecting squarely on the nose making her shriek and splutter and blood pour down her body to mingle with the colour of her dress.

Who said I couldn't take care of myself?

17
LET'S GET THIS PARTY STARTED

"**T**ake a breath, *chica*," Erika said to me. Svante sword still drawn and held at Alessandra's throat as she bent over trying to stem the flow of blood from her now fractured nose.

I hadn't realised I had been holding my breath, but I let a long rush of air out at her command and tried to unclench my fists. Fucking Alessandra, I hated this bitch.

"What are you doing here, Alessandra?" I asked through clenched teeth. I sure as hell wouldn't have invited her. Although she had an accord with Michel, like Enrique did, she had long been after my kindred for more personal reasons, much to my chagrin. And then to top it off she had betrayed Michel, when Gregor came to New Zealand trying to seduce me away from him. Just where she stood in the whole political minefield that was Michel and Gregor I wasn't sure, but she definitely wasn't on my ally list.

"Why, Michel invited me of course, *bambina*. He had to have some form of company while you were away."

OK, red flag to a bull moment. If Michel's arms hadn't come around my waist right at that moment I would have launched myself at her and gouged out her eyes. She did not deserve to look at my kindred in that way.

"Let go of me!" I cried. "I won't hurt her. Much."

Michel just laughed as he held me still firmer in his arms.

"And you're laughing at me?" I asked incredulously, trying to wriggle my body round to glare at him.

"You are amusing, *ma douce*," he murmured against my ear, then in my head, *She is teasing you, she wants you to fight because she knows you are not at full strength.*

Then let me prove her wrong, I shot back.

You are unarmed.

I reached out and broke my champagne flute in half against the table to the side, leaving a nice jagged weapon at my disposal. *Not anymore.*

He didn't reply nor release his rigid hold, instead he turned to Alessandra and said icily cold, "You are abusing my hospitality and pushing my kindred too far. You will make amends immediately or leave."

She just smiled sexily and shifted her hips into what she no doubt thought was an alluring position. She had forgotten the blood streaking down her front, it kind of spoiled the moment.

"Michel," she purred. "I am only here to be of aid, you need my support in the coming battles. I think dismissing me would be detrimental, *mio caro*, no?"

In an instant Michel had released me. I thought briefly, *great, now I can stab the bitch*, only to have the strong arms of Jett slip around my waist and lift me off the floor and back from the scene in front of me. Which, when I managed to get my shock and anger under control again, was Michel's hand around Alessandra's throat and her body shoved against the wall with her feet no longer touching ground.

"You forget, *dolce*, who I am." I had heard Michel use this tone before and I had certainly seen Michel exert this kind of *Sanguis Vitam* before as well, but it always took my breath away regardless of how often I saw him wield his power and strength. If he wasn't at full strength yet, you would not have known it, he glowed with thrumming and menacing power, the room practically hummed with it as it danced around our bodies. The hair on the back of my arms was standing straight up, my breath was stolen from my throat and my heart rate was rocketing. It's not that I was scared of Michel, at least my mind wasn't, but my body sure as hell was. It was a natural fight or flight response and my body wanted to run the fuck away. Quickly.

I glanced around the club and noticed all of Michel's vampires were on high alert, leaking their own *Sanguis Vitam* all over the show. Enrique was well and truly sober again and looking terrified of the power display Michel was putting on, but not daring to move in case he noticed him as well.

Nobody said anything for a while and I really had no idea which way this would go, but shit! The woman had disturbed my party, I'd had enough of stroppy vampires ruining my vibe.

"If you hold her still, I'll stake her," I said evenly.

Michel slowly glanced over his shoulder at me and I winked. He started laughing quietly and shook his head in disbelief. After a full minute of chuckling he lowered Alessandra to the ground, but didn't let go of her throat.

"It pains me, but we have an accord. You have already pushed the boundaries of said accord to the very limit, I suggest you not try my patience any further. This is your last warning, next time I let her stake you. *Capito?*"

She nodded awkwardly against his hold. Then with a bored shift of his shoulders, Michel thrust Alessandra toward Enrique.

"Enrique, take your lover in hand and leave. We will discuss strategy tomorrow, but you both are no longer welcome in my home this night."

Lover? Well that explained a lot. What a fucking idiot Enrique is to take on that wench. It was clearly having an effect on the man's behaviour. And not in a good way at all.

As Enrique gripped Alessandra's arm firmly, no doubt leaving bruises in his wake and dragged her out of the club, Michel turned to me and smiled, a small twinkle in his eye.

"Now," he said sauntering over to me, then ran a hand down my face and around the back of my neck. "Have I left you alone long enough, *ma douce*? May I now have the pleasure of your company for a while?"

"I don't think it would be wise to leave me to my own devices, I tend to pick fights with your allies."

He chuckled, that delightful sound rumbling though his chest and making me melt in his hold. "Oh, but the effect it has on my libido." He rubbed his hips against me sinfully, placing his other hand in the small of my back and crushing me against him.

PDA moment number one, but this I could combat. If he wanted a handful, he could have one. I moved against him with a small smile on my lips as well, then snaked my arms up and around his neck, pulling his head down towards me. His eyes shot amethyst and violet just before my lips softly brushed against his mouth, then continued around his cheek, across his jaw and down his neck. I bit the skin over his pulse playfully and received a stiffening of his arms around my waist in response. I think I had successfully taken him by surprise, he hadn't expected me to play the game so well, let alone so openly. This was his arena, where he usually had me at a disadvantage. I'm not sure if it was the fact that Alessandra - and Enrique to a certain extent - had pissed me off, by placing a dampener on my evening, but I was all for getting a bit of a party spirit back in the room.

"You want to party, *ma belle?*" Michel asked huskily in my ear, my mouth still playfully sucking over his pulse.

"Ah-huh," I said, too busy having fun.

Music started thumping through the speakers in the room and Michel manoeuvred me onto the dance floor with practised ease, somehow managing to shift us both without me having to stop nuzzling his neck.

"You are driving me crazy, *ma douce*. Stop, before I ravish you right here," he husked.

"If you can't stand the heat, vampire...." But I just kept nibbling his ear, his neck, anywhere I could get my teeth to.

"Oh, I can play with fire, Lucinda, but can you?"

I just laughed against him, swaying to the music, nibbling his body, inhaling his scent, swimming in all of him. I had no intention of backing down, to hell with the vampires who danced around us, to hell with anyone else, I finally felt like this was a party.

Michel shifted me in his arms and returned the favour, his mouth going to my ear and down my neck, nuzzling against my hair, finding my pulse and sucking gently on it. His hands had gone down my back, one resting on my hip, the other slipping through the slit perfectly placed there, to rest on my bare skin under the slinky material of the dress.

Oh, dear God I want you, ma douce. Right now, right this second. I want to bury myself deep inside your wet folds, I want to feel you convulse beneath me, I want to drink you down while you come for me again and again and again. And I don't ever want to stop.

I was already on board with all of that and thankfully he must have decided that sort of entertainment was better carried out in the privacy of his chamber - even exhibitionists have their limits - because he started working us towards the door marked private. I didn't fight, I just moulded my body to the length of his and let him lead me over there. Just before we made off the edge of the dance floor however, he received a firm tap on the shoulder.

Michel's head shot up, magenta flashed in his eyes as he snarled in annoyance at the cause of the interruption.

"May I cut in? I was invited by the lady after all, it is only fair I receive a dance before you retire altogether."

"Your timing as always, Gregor, leaves a lot to be desired," Michel hissed in return.

Gregor just smiled openly at Michel, not in the least bit concerned that he was being washed in the angry *Sanguis Vitam* of a joined Master Vampire.

"Michel," he said with what appeared to be genuine affection. "I know how distracted you can get, *mon ami*. You would not return to the party until it was well and truly over. I have only one night in your fair city and I believe Lucinda needs me."

I was sure Gregor was enjoying himself. Michel must have given him an idea of why he had been invited to the party, he was clearly under the impression that it was at my request and because I needed him. He held all the cards and he was loving ruining Michel's plans, and no doubt quite happy to deny him an intimate moment with me. Gregor had always taken every opportunity to put a wedge between my kindred and myself.

He saw it as his job to educate me, making sure I was aware that I did not necessarily have to fall into bed with Michel just because I was joined to him. Of course, Gregor's solution, was for me to fall into bed with him instead, but that was just a technicality as far as he was concerned.

Michel was practically vibrating with anger, I knew this could escalate quickly, so I stepped between them and gave Gregor a quick glare. "Give us a moment please, Gregor, I'll be with you shortly."

He bowed low and when he came back up a wicked smile played over his lips only managing to elicit a terrifyingly low growl from Michel, but he did back off and walk to a booth a few feet away, getting the attention of a waiter and no doubt ordering his first of many stiff drinks.

I grabbed hold of Michel by his jacket lapels before he could storm off after Gregor and rip him to pieces and propelled him through the private door letting it shut quietly behind us. The hallway was dark, no lights were on, but the magenta in Michel's eyes was enough to illuminate the space.

I leant back against the door and watched him, trying to decide how best to bring him down from the brink. I knew he'd be battling the claiming in full force right now. A threat to his possession of me, such as Gregor had just pulled, was big news for the claiming genie inside his vampire, but I also was no longer in the mood to be seduced. Somehow the confrontation and the talk of how much I needed Gregor had brought images of Nero's death back to the front of my mind. The whole idea of getting Gregor here was to be able to talk to him about how to deal with this recurring nightmare, how to reconcile my role as the Prophesied with my loss of my friend and Prophecy confidant. I had no idea if Gregor could give me what I needed, but something about the whole Nosferatin thing made me think of Gregor. There was no rhyme or reason, I even wondered if Nut was directing me, but I knew I needed to talk to Gregor and time was not on our side.

With the door open in my mind again, the Dark vampires throughout the world had started paying attention. They'd had a month of no pull and now I was back, they wouldn't take too much longer before answering my siren's call. I needed to get a handle on myself and I saw Gregor as the only road available to achieve that.

So, sex was definitely not on my mind, even though I'd started contemplating it more and more lately, I couldn't simply offer myself up on a platter right now. But, I could offer up my blood.

"Come here," I said into the darkened space between us.

He didn't hesitate, he'd been no doubt holding himself back with every last bit of strength he possessed. His lips crushed into mine in brutal possession, but before he could get too carried away I shifted against him and using my hands on either side of his head, moved his face and lips across to my neck, right above where his mark was and held him there.

I expected him to bite immediately, but he must have had more control than I had imagined, because he simply continued to kiss me above the mark, rough and hard and with raw need, but no fangs. I was about to ask what was he waiting for, when he pulled back, tipped my head over and returned to Gregor's mark on my neck. His fangs entering now without further delay, his arms gripping around my back and crushing me against his chest. His tongue lapping at my blood and mouth sucking at his puncture mark, a low growl coming from his mouth.

It took me a second to register what he was doing, I was too wrapped up in the primal need he was displaying. The not so sensual, as explosive, desire he was pumping through my body, but finally his words reached me through the blissful haze he had created, *mine, mine, mine, mine*. They didn't surprise me, I'd certainly heard them enough times recently, but the *Sanguis Vitam* that accompanied them did. When you mark someone, it requires a little power of your own to send it home, but that's not all, the person being marked has to accept it as well. Gregor had tricked me into giving him my mark and into accepting his in return, I had no idea what I was doing or how personal and permanent that was. Michel has marked me twice and made no bones about the fact that he would continue to mark me many times over until I got the message that I was his. It sounds very Neanderthal, possessive to the extreme, but is also so very precious in the vampyre world. To be claimed as belonging to someone is a big deal, an honour, a privilege. It is not viewed as oppressive or controlling, the mark merely tells the world that you have accepted that person to be your advocate, your ambassador, your spouse.

I had decided after Gregor, that I would not share my mark with anyone ever again unless I really, truly meant it. It was permanent, it was personal and it was not given easily.

So, the fact that Michel was trying to mark me for the third time was kind of a surprise, but then again, not. He had warned me he would keep trying and if the position of where he had chosen to try to place this mark meant anything, he was trying to remove Gregor's completely from my skin. Normally, I would have denied Michel this right, he's marked me enough, he's proved his point adequately I think, but two things changed my mind right then.

One, I loved him, undeniably, unequivocally and although I wasn't sure I could mark him just yet and open myself up that far and let the world see how much he had me; mind, body, and soul, I did want him to know I was his and no one else's. And two, I so wanted Gregor's mark gone once and for all. I had no idea if it would work, but I lowered my shields and sent a bit of my power out to meet Michel's, hoping together they could eradicate Gregor's mark from my neck once and for all.

Michel's eyes already so brightly magenta flashed an even more vibrant colour, making the small hallway we were in dance in an amazing display of violets and purples and mauves. He kept drinking for a few moments longer, his power wrapped closely with mine, wending in and out around each other, brushing along the sides of our bodies, curving between our legs and wrapping back around heads until they burst apart in a shower of purple sparks raining down all around us.

His fangs retracted and he gently licked his puncture marks and pulled back slightly to see what he had created. He didn't say anything for a moment and I wondered whether we'd really stuffed things up and I now had a hideous combination of marks on my neck more obvious than they had ever been before.

"Well," he said, licking his lips and then clearing his throat. "I don't think we need to worry about Gregor's mark any more."

I reached up and felt where Michel had bitten me, it felt no different from any other bite. It shouldn't anyway, a normal bite and a mark look the same, it's just that a bite will disappear pretty quickly and a mark, or *Sigillum,* will stay for good.

Michel watched me with a little smile playing on his lips.

"What is it? Is it OK?"

"It's beautiful," he whispered and pulled me towards his chamber and through to his bathroom, switching on lights with a flick of his wrist.

He stood me in front of him and kissed my forehead and then slowly turned me back towards the mirror. I expected something else, he had called it beautiful, but I hadn't really believed him. Michel's bite is unique, but it's just a bite. Vampires can recognise who's bite belongs to whom, but they all look pretty much the same to me. This bite however was not. I could see Michel's mark, his two tiny points, evenly spaced, a certain shape and size and distance from each other that all means him. But around them, interwoven through them, covering any other mark that may have hidden below was a beautiful colourful spectrum of colours, a geometrical design, laced with flourishes and swirls, similar to a light and pretty tattoo, that is unique to me. My Light. My *Sigillum*. Shit. Had I just marked myself?

"That's a bit kinky isn't it?" I asked Michel, thinking marking yourself was just a bit too narcissistic.

He laughed and shook his head. "It is beautiful. It shows everyone who sees it, that you not only accepted my mark, but welcomed it as your own. And" - he said, lowering his lips to kiss above the spot - "it lets Gregor know he is completely out of luck. His mark is no more."

Wow, he was right. I looked closer and there was only one bite mark evident under the iridescent swirls. Not two and my brightly bizarre tattoo-like mark. Gregor's mark had simply vanished. Exactly what I wanted.

But how the hell was I going to go to work at the bank with *that* on my neck?

Ah shit.

18

GREGOR

"I guess this well and truly covers any privileges you wanted to take this evening."

We were still standing in the bathroom of Michel's chamber, neither of us able to stop looking at what was most definitely the prettiest mark I had ever seen. I mean, Gregor wears my mark, but it was given under duress and kind of when I was angry, so it's colourful, but a bit gaudy in an amazing sort of way. And also in an in-your-face literally kind of way, as he wears it around his eyes. His eyes had caught my attention at the time and I guess that's where my *Sigillum* decided to go.

Michel wound his arms about me and began nuzzling my neck, laying kiss upon kiss above the new mark. He simply couldn't get enough of it.

"Do you have any idea how happy I am right now, *ma douce?*" His voice was muffled against my skin. I couldn't help but smile.

I'd honestly never meant to hurt Michel when I came back from Dream Walking to Gregor with his mark on my neck. I'd had no idea what I had done, let alone the pain it would have caused my kindred. But, now, finally, I felt like I had made amends for that mistake. I was thrilled Michel was happy.

"I love you," I said simply. His eyes came up to look at me in the mirror.

"*Je t'aime trop, ma douce.*"

We looked at each other for a moment longer and then he straightened and popped one of his austere vampire looks on his face.

"So, now I have shouted to all and sundry that you are mine and no one else's, you can go talk with Gregor. I shall allow it." He winked as he said the last, I just gave him a quick shove back and placed my hands on my hips.

"Don't get any ideas of grandeur, lover boy. Just because you have three marks on my body does not mean you own me." I joked in return, but really, I meant it.

"Lucinda. Would I ever think anything like that?" he asked in mock shock, offering me his arm to escort me back to the party.

I just sighed and took what was offered allowing him to gloat all the way back down the hall. Once we came through the door and took in the party scene before us he spun me back towards him and kissed me hard and long. His hands possessively roaming all over my body in full view of the room.

"There's not been enough public displays of affection, *ma douce*. Just in case you forgot the other part of our deal."

I shook my head and went to step away, only to receive a short slap to my rear that made me jump and glare at him. He just smiled and shrugged, that elegant shoulder movement he makes seem so sexy. He really was in a jovial mood though, wasn't he?

I ignored all the delighted faces of his vamps who not only took in the kiss and affectionate butt slap, but also were well and truly glowing at the new mark on my neck and headed over to Gregor's booth. As I slid in next to him Doug pushed a *Bacardi and Coke* along the table to me and after taking in my mark, smiled and walked away.

I took a sip, registering that it was a 50/50 mix, Doug obviously felt I needed bolstering and then finally met Gregor's eyes.

I knew I'd get a reaction, but I wasn't expecting this.

"What have you done, *ma cherie?*" His hand was over his heart and I don't think he was play acting.

I watched him for a moment unable to think of what to say, sorry?

I wasn't, not really, he'd tricked me into his mark in the beginning and I really wanted it gone, so I wasn't sorry it was no longer there. Still, I hated seeing him hurt, even Gregor held a place in my heart.

"Can you forgive me, my friend?" I asked quietly.

His eyes lifted from the new mark to meet mine and he sighed, a weighted sigh.

"You were always his, Lucinda. Even when you slept with me, you were still his." He ran a hand through his hair, making the glorious black strands come loose at his clip. He roughly grabbed the clip and tossed it down on the table, ignoring where it landed. "The great Gregor Morel finally lost a prize." His voice was a little bitter. I wanted to interrupt, but I felt he needed to get this off his chest and nothing I would say would make it better. The next time he spoke it was quiet, reflective even. "You know? This is the first time in centuries that I have felt remotely human." His eyes returned to me. "I always thought you would be my saviour." He laughed briefly. "I had just assumed it would be that you would bring me the final death, but maybe that was wrong."

I had forgotten how suicidal Gregor was when I first met him, how Dark and desperate for release he had been. He had hated himself, he said he hated what he had become, but as far as I could see, he was just like any other vampire. He had a choice to let that Dark in or let the Light prevail, he'd just chosen the wrong team.

"You have already brought the Light back. I thought it had long forsaken me, but no, I feel it again, because of you. And now, I wonder, if you have made me more human too. And is that not a type of saving?" He took a long drink from his glass and shuddered slightly. I was thinking that was more to do with the conversation than the alcohol, Gregor wasn't one unable to handle his drink.

"You have always appeared human to me, Gregor." Well, human laced with a very cunning, devious and delectable vampire thrown into the mix.

He smiled. "You are unique, to most I am the epitome of vampyre."

He took another long sip of his drink and waved the empty glass in the air. Within seconds it was replaced with a full one. At least no one could complain about the service at *Sensations*.

"I told you once that one day I would divulge my past to you, perhaps now is as good as ever. You seem a little lost, *ma petite chasseuse*, perhaps this is my chance to give you something in return."

I really had no idea where this was heading. Gregor had always been a troubled soul, but he seemed like he was on the brink of destruction here and it worried me. He seemed even more screwed up than me. Maybe talking about it would help him and when that was done, we could talk about what bothered me.

"Why do you think Nosferatin blood calls to me?"

Whoa. I hadn't expected that question. "I don't know."

"Hazard a guess."

"I'm no good at guessing," I replied automatically.

"Humour me, Lucinda. What could it possibly be about Nosferatins that attracts me so?"

"Their power?"

He nodded. "A good assumption. Compared to a human, Nosferatins do have stronger blood, more powerful and those of your calibre are quite delicious, but no. That would mean all vampires would be attracted to your blood. It is good when tasted, don't get me wrong, but it is not addictive."

"Then why?"

"I was once Nosferatin."

Four simple words, so quietly spoken, so softly whispered, no one but me would have heard them. The room disappeared as I contemplated those four simple words. It was just me and Gregor. And two now forgotten glasses of booze.

"How is that possible?"

He smiled. "Yes. It is unusual."

"Unusual? Gregor, Nosferatins can't be turned." It was something Michel had told me at the beginning, when he had first disclosed what I was. Nosferatin and Nosferatu were of the same ilk, but had separated centuries ago. One into the night, one into the day, evil versus good, Dark versus Light. We could never be brought back as one again. You can't reverse evolution, not intentionally nor by accident, the rift, the break, was final. The only way we could be together again was side by side, as Michel and I are now.

"Yes, you are right, but I am the exception."

I wondered then if Gregor had lost it, I was suddenly a little scared. A crazy vampire is an unpredictable vampire. I didn't like where this was going.

Are you all right, ma douce? Do you need me?

Michel had obviously picked up on my sudden emotional shift. I tamped down my fear and decided I needed to see this through to the end, for me, for Gregor. Maybe for all Nosferatin.

I'm OK, Gregor just said something I wasn't prepared to hear.

I felt him brush my mind in support and disappear. I looked back at Gregor. "Explain."

"I was a mature unjoined Nosferatin in Paris in the late 16th century. My 25th birthday had already passed and I had barely days until my demise, but I had found a suitable vampire to join with. On the day of my joining however, his court was ransacked, totally destroyed, while they all lay in their day time beds. By the time I made it there at night fall, they were all dust and she was waiting for me. Crying, so desperately sad at the loss.

"She was beautiful, surrounded in bright white light. Dark skin and fine features, high cheek bones and long black hair. But it's her eyes I remember the most. Big, round pools of lava, a bright, bright gold. She was so sad, so very sad at the loss of so many Nosferatu"

He paused to take another gulp of his drink, but I didn't need the break in his monologue to mull over the description, because I had met her too. Nut. Gregor had met Nut. But, why was Nut at the scene of massacred Nosferatu and why was she so distraught?

"Paris was not the haven of sophistication and awareness of which we see today," he went on. "It was a cesspit of degradation. Vampires flocked there for easy prey, it was full of the Dark. She told me I would not find another Nosferatu to join with who was worthy, that time was not on my side, so she raised one of those who had not yet turned to dust but was moments from it and made him change me. She said she could not do it alone and once it was done my sire burst into dust and was no more.

"I was alone in the cesspit and I did not know why she had done it."

"She never told you?" I asked incredulously. Surely Nut had a plan.

"She vanished during my turning and was not there when I awoke."

"You know who it was, don't you?" I asked carefully. I wasn't sure he knew at all.

He looked at me with a far away cast to his eyes. "It was Nut," he answered simply. "My goddess had forsaken me, I was now a creature that I despised and she had made it so."

I didn't know what to say. To be turned into a vampire, when we are made to hunt them and kill them, would have been horrific. Talk about your culture shocks. It's one thing for a human to turn, but they're not going against everything they are born to be. Not that all vampires fall into the category of stake fodder, take Michel, I could no further consider staking him, or having to hunt him, than grow fangs myself. OK, maybe that wasn't a good analogy considering the former Nosferatin sitting opposite me now sporting a nice set of long sharp incisors, but you get the picture. This was big and it didn't make complete sense.

Some of it did though. "She was saving you, you would have died without a Nosferatu to join with."

"Then why didn't she let me? I would rather have died an innocent than become what I did."

It's hard to argue that train of thought and even suggesting to Gregor that he'd had a choice, to be a nice vampire or a nasty one, wouldn't have helped. Vampires are all nasty at their core, it's their strength of will which allows them to fight that Dark within. Gregor had lost his the moment he had been turned. It's not easy to stay perky when you've become the thing you fear the most.

But, there must have been a reason why Nut did this. Not just to save a life. If that were the case, then hundreds of my kind would not have died needlessly over the centuries when we pulled away from the Nosferatu, denying them our power. So why?

"Did she never tell you why? Give you a hint or anything?"

Gregor smiled at me, it was so full of sadness. Memories of a life lived against his will, of a trust broken by something which should never have let him down.

"She did return once, in a dream, about a century later. I had accumulated all of my power by then and had a line of my own. I'm not sure if she returned to tell me off, to get me to return to the Light, I had strayed a fair way by that stage, but she did come back. Most of what she said went over my head, made little sense at all, but one thing did remain. She said, we all have our paths laid out for us prior to our birth and that those paths are crossed by others, choices are always made; which branch to take, left or right. But no matter how we get there, we always end up where we are meant to be. The destination was determined before we were even conceived. Fatalistic, no?"

He took another sip of his drink and stared off into the distance, not even taking in the room around us. I played his words over in my head, if Nut had said them, then they meant something. So, Gregor was not meant to have died at that massacre, that's why she intervened and he is here now, with me. Why? If she had not had him turned, he would not be sitting opposite me telling me about his past, helping me to see a way through my pain to reach my end goal. And that's it, isn't it? I've been so hung up on Nero's death, so deep within my own grief, that I've been endangering myself, endangering the path I am on, maybe even changing my future because of that weakness. And really, why grieve? Sure, he is dead and I miss him, but if Nut is right, he had reached the end of his path anyway. If he hadn't, wouldn't she have stepped in? She didn't, he died saving me. No matter how he got there, he was meant to be there at the end, he was meant to save me.

Shit, it puts a whole new meaning on the word fate, doesn't it?

I didn't know if I would stop dreaming of blood, would stop seeing Nero's death in my head. I'd like to think I was finally letting him go, a part of me certainly felt more calmed from the knowledge of why he left me and the fact that I could not have done a thing to change that destiny for him. But, I knew it wouldn't be easy, I'd have to work at it, remind myself of the bigger picture, a term I have never been particularly fond of before. But it did make a sort of sense now that settled in my soul.

As for Gregor, I wasn't sure if I could help him like he had helped me. His demons were still so very present and even though he had said those words of Nut's, that our destinies are preordained no matter what path we choose to take, I don't think he actually heard them. I wanted to help him, but I wasn't sure if I was the one to do it.

"Thanks, Gregor, for telling me. You don't know how much it's helped."

His eyebrows raised and a little of the old Gregor returned, a small smirk on those soft lips. "I have, *ma cherie*? What brilliant luck." I knew then he wouldn't entertain any words of wisdom from me, his path may be crossing mine, but I wasn't his end goal. I looked around the room and spotted Amisi, drink in hand surrounded by Michel's vampires. All of which were behaving themselves, but definitely trying to reel her in.

"Would you like another damsel to rescue?" I asked innocently.

"I'm always up for a rescue mission, little Hunter. Who did you have in mind?"

I nodded towards Amisi and watched the light return to Gregor's eyes. "Ah," he said. "A difficult damsel indeed. I'm not entirely sure she would welcome my assistance. Quite independent that one, even more so than you."

I laughed, he could say that again. "Yes, but haven't you always said you enjoyed a challenge."

His eyes returned to me with sharp assessment. "Are you trying to get rid of me or perhaps you'd like to see me crash and burn? You are wicked, I would expect nothing less."

I laughed even harder. "I don't think you'll crash and burn, Gregor, maybe have to dodge a few bullets, but not explode in a shower of body pieces. And, I believe her current round of suitors are simply not up to the task. She's practically eating them all for dinner."

He laughed then, a full throaty laugh, a welcomed sound that chased away the memories and wrapped me up with sunshine.

"So be it. I will have to just take one for my kin," he said, standing in a smooth glide. If we hadn't have just had the conversation we had, I would have missed it, but it was there. A slight bitter resentment at the fact that he had to class himself among the vampires, as one of them. My heart ached a little for him, but if anyone could make him snap out of it and have a reason to live, it would be Amisi. And did I for a moment worry that I was setting my Amisi up with a wounded vampire? No, not at all, Amisi was lost to Gregor the moment she met him.

Just as I was to Michel.

Speaking of Michel, I wasn't alone for long. No sooner had Gregor left my side than a very happy, very content, very amorous vampire slid into the bench seat beside me.

His arm went around my shoulder and his lips found my new mark, a reverent kiss was gently placed upon it.

"How is my kindred?"

"Good. Really good." And I think I meant it, for the first time in over a month I felt whole: me, purpose returned, world levelled. Well sort of, I still wanted that slime-ball Jonathan killed, but otherwise I knew where I was heading, what I had lost, but how to move on without it. "Yeah, I'm feeling pretty damn good actually."

"Excellent," he whispered, voice low against my skin. "Would you care to share some of your goodwill with your kindred? I am open to small gifts, nothing monumental. Maybe," - his free hand came to take mine from my lap and place it on his groin where I was rewarded with an already rock hard arousal beneath the thin material of his trousers - "this could give you inspiration."

"Oh," I said. "I am feeling rather inspired."

He chuckled and shifted himself closer, turning his body from the dance floor, providing us with a small measure of privacy. Oh shit, he wanted me to do something right here? Crap.

As it happens, my morals were saved by Jett, who came up so quietly I hadn't even heard his approach. Michel no doubt knew he was there, but was choosing to ignore him. But, once Jett blocked the light out, throwing us both into shadow, I'd lost any nerve I'd had at all.

Michel sighed when my hand returned to my lap and turned to face Jett, not bothering to hide his erection tenting his trousers in the slightest.

"This had better be interesting, Jethro."

Jethro? Go figure.

"We have received a call to arms from America." You gotta hand it to the big guy, he didn't beat about the bush.

Michel stiffened considerably and turned more to face his second in command.

"Why?"

"They wish to honour their King's reputation," Jett replied with a growl.

"America has a King?" I piped up.

Michel answered, almost distractedly. "They have a Council of Families, the head of one is elected as their chosen King."

"Who is their King?" I asked, but I was already drawing my own conclusion.

"Obviously not who I thought it was this morning," Michel said in a low voice looking at Jett.

Jett returned his look with one of pure disgust.

I didn't need him to say it, it was written all over his face, the disgust that this vampire had risen to a position where he could threaten us with the might of all the American families behind him, when he was simply considered lower than dirt on the bottom of Jett's shoes.

Jonathan.

The slime-ball had been organising a coup since I escaped. He had been a busy boy, hadn't he?

19
THE CALL TO ARMS

"Six families, spread across the continent, some as big as 120 vampires per family, but we would not expect every vampire to be involved. Just a core number of their elite fighters from each branch, backing up the King. They wouldn't want to leave their own backyards undefended. Not only from us, but from each other, infighting is rampant among them."

Erika had joined Jett at our table and our intimate party setting had immediately turned into a make-shift war room. A map of the USA spread out in front of us, areas highlighted in different colours, depicting different families who ran that particular city and surrounding land. It was colourful and most of the land mass that makes up America was covered, making the task ahead seem so very daunting indeed.

I stared at the map, trying to take it all in. Differing colours from green in Seattle, Washington, down to blue in Las Vegas, Nevada. Across to yellow in Dallas, Texas and then round to brown in Atlanta, Georgia. Up to orange in New York, New York and of course, slap bang almost in the middle, red in Denver, Colorado. A kaleidoscope of colours, butting up against each other almost engulfing the entire map. They pretty much had the whole country covered, a small section up in Montana was left blank, uncoloured. I guess there just wasn't the population density to warrant a vampire stronghold there. Or maybe they were saving it for expansion at a later date.

"The previous King was based in Atlanta," Erika continued, thrusting a finger on the map in the vague direction of Georgia. "Samuel was a tyrant, he'd been in charge of the Council for at least five decades, a pretty significant time for America. They're staunch rule followers, but they also are devious sons of bitches. Any opportunity to get up the ladder would be taken and damn the consequences. Punishments were harsh if you were caught, however, so only those who really thought they had a chance, be it strength wise or suitable numbers in support, would challenge the King. But, lower down the ladder, loyalties change quickly and so do positions upon that ladder.

"From what I last knew, Jonathan was about a third or fourth on the ladder in Denver. I know for a fact that the head of that family, Tomas, had a powerful second by the name of Manuel, who was unbelievably protective of his family's head. For Jonathan to have passed him to claim head of the family is impressive, but not impossible. He may have managed some sort of manoeuvre after I left, he's had time to climb since then and I wouldn't know. Even though I wasn't based in Denver, my exit was noted, all of my contacts have gone to ground. I'm *persona non grata* now."

She didn't seem too fazed by that. When Erika was first called back to Michel's line she made it quite clear she was happy to be out of the American fold. Erika is tough, but even she shuddered whenever she talked of the punishments meted out by the yanks.

"So, political manoeuvring into head of his family is not altogether unbelievable, but to have moved on to the position of King, is. I couldn't even offer up a possible scenario on how he has managed that. Samuel was well protected and although an utter maniac, he was well respected across all families. In the past fifty years he has brought wealth and order to what was an absolute hodge podge of vampire debauchery. He's been given the sole credit for saving the American Families from self destruction. Jonathan having usurped him is nothing short of miraculous."

"Perhaps the hows and whys are not so important, the fact is, he is

King now and as such commands a formidable army." Michel's voice was fairly unemotional, just stating facts. Even the way he was sitting didn't give anything away, he was casually leaning back in our booth, legs crossed at the knees, arm resting easily across the table top playing with the edge of the map. But his other hand, resting on my thigh, was firm, unyielding, as though the contact with me made it impossible to hide his true feelings. He covered it well on the outside, throughout the rest of his body, but through that touch on my leg I could tell he was concerned. Very concerned.

"How many can we expect in his army?" Jett asked Erika.

"They've not called anyone to arms for several decades. Although their everyday lifestyle is harsh and unforgiving, peace has actually reigned in America for some time. I could only guess what their tactics would be from minor skirmishes they have had, here and there, over the past decade, that I have witnessed."

"Then guess." It was said without preamble, either Jett was as concerned as Michel, or he and Erika were having a fight and he wasn't bothering to hide his feelings. I kind of sympathised with him, just give us the bottom line already.

Erika glared at him for a second and then straightened her shoulders. "The size of each family varies, so some may be able to offer more than others." She reached for the map and spun it back towards her, her fingers going to each coloured area, while she obviously calculated numbers in her head. After a couple of minutes she sat back with a frown on her face, making her look like a very angry miniature Barbie doll.

"Well?" Michel said impatiently. He and Jett were definitely on the same bandwagon right now, so maybe Jett wasn't throwing a personal hissy fit at Erika after all.

"All up, there's about 620 vampires in the Council of Families, their elite fighting corps makes up about 40% of their numbers, the rest are all either part of the dynasty structure, or out on their own paying tithes to their heads. And of the 40% they would use no more than half of their force for external defensive requirements, even then they would try to skimp on the number, leaving more in their home territories than not. So," - she rounded up, seeing the ever more impatient looks on the male vampires surrounding her - "you're looking at an army of maximum 120-130 elite fighters."

Considering the number of vampires in America alone, that didn't sound nearly as bad as I thought it was going to be. Just a shame Michel and Jett didn't feel the same way.

"*Merde*," offered Michel quietly.

"Fuck," spat Jett a lot louder at the same time.

"Will they come here?" I asked.

Erika looked relieved to offer more intel and get away from the numbers for a moment. "Unlikely, they will expect us to come to them, but for that they will have to entice us."

"Entice us?" I didn't like the sound of that.

"They will take, or already have taken, something of ours and they will ransom it."

Whoa, this sounded familiar. I glanced around the club and quickly spotted all the people who were important to at least me. Amisi, Gregor, Doug at the bar, Shane Smith, his blonde curls bobbing as he laughed at something in the corner. Yep, all present and accounted for.

"What could they take?"

Michel shifted in his seat next to me, but didn't answer my question, instead he directed an order towards Jett. "Account for all of the line and those of our allies."

Jett was gone in an instant, but the orders weren't finished. To Erika he added, "Ensure Lucinda's parents are secured." She nodded and disappeared.

I hadn't even thought of them, and hell yes, I would move Heaven and Earth to get them back if they had been taken. Michel's fingers laced with mine and he pulled me close.

"Now we wait, *ma douce*. It will become obvious who is missing before long."

Before long, didn't mean before sunrise. As dawn approached both Jett and Erika had not returned with any news, so we headed back to St Helier's Bay and the house, our personal guards in tow and settled in to wait for news in the comfort and privacy of our home.

No one was able to sleep though. The guards settled themselves into subtle positions inside the house, every corner covered, Michel and I never entirely out of sight, but not shadowed wherever we went either. They had picked up a few tricks since I had returned and their guarding had become much less obvious than before. I was grateful for the show of space, even if I knew it was only an illusion.

Nothing settles my nerves like coffee, so it was with as much focused attention as I could muster that I went through the motions of preparing the perfect cup of Java. First the beans in the hopper, then set to grind. Let the machine tamp the grinds firmly in the portafilter basket and listen to it force the water through the packed grounds. A few seconds later I was rewarded with thick, rich smelling caffeine permeating the air. The last touch, milk in the frothing jug, another button and the machine did the rest. A perfect cappuccino every time.

Coffee has been my friend for a long time, this new machine was a replacement for one I had spent the better part of a month's salary on, but had it destroyed by a very angry Taniwha making a very loud point. Michel had simply made sure this one was waiting for me when I moved into his home here at St Helier's. God knows how he had managed it on such short notice, but he is a miracle worker at times, there's no denying it.

I turned with my perfect brew and found Michel watching me, the corners of his lips twisting into a smile.

"Miracle worker?" he asked, eyebrows raised.

"You've got to get out of my head, Michel, one day you may not like what you hear."

"*Ma douce*, there is nothing you could think that I wouldn't love to hear. Nothing."

I believe he really meant that, but no one can think nice thoughts all the time, sooner or later I'd screw it up.

He shook his head. "You forget, *ma belle*, I love all of you, every stray thought, every single part." He glided over to where I was resting against the cupboards sipping my coffee. I managed to just get the cup down on the bench before his lips found his new mark on my neck, his mouth making quick work of worshipping the spot, making shots of heat burst through me so quickly and easily I thought he had me under a mind spell. It was a spell, I thought vaguely, losing all sensation below the waist, just one of the heart, not of the mind.

"Mm," he murmured, against my neck. "Every stray thought." His mouth had made it to my ear and he started nibbling in earnest there, knowing damn well the effect that spot had over me.

I was quite happy for him to continue. I couldn't have cared less about the location, or the fact that his vampires had all now moved inside the house, as the shutters were down already. And that two of them were just through the door of the kitchen in the hallway standing guard, hearing every word spoken, every sound made. I didn't care, I just wanted to keep feeling what it was he was making me feel.

So, it was a surprise when he paused and cocked his head to the side.

"What is it?" I asked, recognising his expression, the one he normally took on when communicating over a vast distance with his vampires telepathically. The closer they were, the less concentration required.

"Your parents are safe. Erika has found accommodation for those of the line she has with her nearby and our Day Walkers are guarding them for now. They will not know they exist, Erika has cloaked them." He smiled then, a look of pride coming over his features. "It seems Erika has picked up a few tricks from our Jett, I had not known she could cloak."

I smiled too, remembering how good Jett was at cloaking us, having had to do that once when we were in Wellington. Erika was certainly picking up a few hidden talents from her liaison with Michel's second. I was relieved with the information she had provided too and couldn't help realise that was why Michel had been so amorous, to help me focus on something other than the wait for news.

"Who are Day Walkers?" It was a term I hadn't heard him use before.

"Human servants, in this case trained as guards." I had always known Michel had humans in his employ, I had seen them at *Sensations*, but I hadn't realised he had guards as well.

He pulled back and smiled at me, a lazy amused smile. "I have been forced to take additional precautions, *ma douce*, since your abduction and it seems it was worthwhile."

He was right, I couldn't complain, despite part of me wondering how he kept the humans in line, ensuring they didn't divulge any information about his day sleeping location or anything else inherently vampire. I knew the answer he would give though, *we are vampyre, Lucinda, it is what we are.*

He laughed out loud at my poor imitation of his French accent and mannerisms in my mind. "Do I really sound that bad?"

I smiled, despite the seriousness of our situation, we still hadn't heard back from Jett. "You can be very superior, you know?"

"That is because I am," he added in mock autocratic tones. "And you would be wise to remember."

I just laughed at him and he shook his head in exasperation. "You are impossible." His smile turned genuine, his eyes flashing amethyst and indigo in amongst the blue. "Entirely, impossible." His head had just bent low to cover my mouth with a warm kiss when the front door crashed open and a whole lot of swearing in a thick Egyptian accent could be heard storming closer to the kitchen.

Michel's lips left mine in a sigh and his head rested against my forehead as we waited for the obvious wrath of Egypt to barge in on our little scene.

"I see our Amisi has picked up a few of your more choice language skills, *ma douce*."

Yes, I wasn't too happy about that myself. Amisi had always appeared to be such a lady, a tough, capable, kick-butt lady, but a lady all the same. I may be quite comfortable swearing like a trouper, I am from a farming background, but hearing Amisi cuss the same way was a little embarrassing. Embarrassing that I influenced her in such a bad way. Nero could bring out the perfect warrior in her, I brought out the gutter snipe. Great.

"That fucking no-good, egotistical, self-absorbed, over-confident, arsehole." She really had managed to pick up colloquial English since moving here, hadn't she? "You know," she added as she slid into a bench seat in front of us as though we had been awaiting her arrival and the opportunity for her to vent. "He thinks he can just snap his elegant long manicured fingers and I'll come running. He does not know how Egyptian women have been raised. We are nobody's play toy to command. If he thinks, he can just flirt his way into my good books with those damned sexy moves of his, he has a serious mental deficiency. I ought to have staked him where he stood, then see how he tries to grab my butt."

"He tried to grab your butt?" I couldn't help it, I was dumbfounded Gregor had been so obvious in his pursuit of Amisi, I thought he had more intelligence than that. Amisi was going to need a very gentle hand. As far as she was concerned, he was still evil incarnate.

Michel sighed even louder and pulled away to make himself a coffee, or maybe Amisi one, he was clearly unhappy though that I was entertaining Amisi's little rant and not making a quick escape with him to a more private setting.

"Not just my butt," she said incredulously. "He practically pawed all of me."

Oh hell no, I could not picture that. "Why?" I asked.

"What do you mean why? He wants to bed me of course," she replied angrily, then added with emphasis, "Slut."

I couldn't help it, I laughed and received a furious glare in return. Still, I just didn't get it. "How did he misread the signals, Amisi? Gregor is not thick."

Michel just snorted at that, but kept at his task of coffee making.

Amisi shot Michel a look, but he had his back to us both and then she wouldn't meet my eyes.

"Amisi?"

She squirmed for a second or two in her seat, suddenly all anger vanished from her face, replaced, surprisingly, with a bright red flush, tracking up her neck and consuming all of her lovely dark face.

"I might have kissed him," she whispered. My mouth fell open at her confession, unable to come up with a suitable reply.

But it was Michel's uncontrolled laughter that did it, his shoulders shaking, his hands holding on to the bench to steady himself, as he gave in to the moment and really let loose with delightful peals of laughter.

He glanced over his shoulder at Amisi and tried to say something, only to fall about in laughter all over again.

Finally, I had to put the poor girl out of her misery. "Michel, if you have something to say, then spit it out now."

He wiped his tear streaked face with the sleeve of his expensive suit jacket, not caring about the mess he may be causing to the delicate material and took a deep breath.

"Amisi, my dear. You have bitten off way more than you can chew."

She clenched her fists and glared back at him, a retort no doubt already forming in her mind, but he just raised his own elegant hand to stop her and added, "He has tasted you now, my sweet, the predator has been unleashed."

I didn't think Michel was being overly dramatic, I knew the predator he was referring to, I'd had Gregor's predator after me at one time too and once released, there is no going back. I kind of did feel a little uncomfortable for Amisi then, even *I* thought she would have held out a little longer before kissing him.

To both Michel and my surprise Amisi smiled slowly, a little wickedly I reluctantly admitted.

"Then he has no idea who he hunts, Michel. I am not an easy prey."

That's my girl, I thought patting her on the hand that rested on the bench in between us and then grabbing my kindred's hand and squeezing it before he had a chance to answer.

Never show fear. Never give an inch. Always stay on guard.

I think Michel may have needed a little reminding of that.

20
WAITING

It wasn't until well into the afternoon that Michel heard from Jett. All of our line and Enrique's, Alessandra's and Gregor's were accounted for. No one was missing at all.

"Well that's at least something," I said into the the tense air that had followed Michel's report from Jett. He and I were cuddled up on the couch in the lounge, unable to face bed and sleep until we knew what we were up against. Amisi was sitting in an armchair to the side, a book opened in her lap, although I hadn't seen her turn too many pages in the past hour. And a couple of Michel's guards were lounged along the edges of the room, having ventured inside once I had felt sorry for them skulking out in the hall and insisted they join us.

We'd had the TV on, then resorted to the stereo, then finally just been talking quietly amongst ourselves about anything and nothing in an effort to pass the time. I had been bone weary tired, but unable to sleep, instead just falling into a kind of stupor as Michel stroked my back and talked softly to his men and occasionally Amisi. It had been a while since I had said anything at all, but now with the news report, I was wide awake again.

"Yes," Michel answered, but he hadn't relaxed since he'd passed on the latest from his second. "Although, one must wonder what exactly they *will* use against us. If not any of our line, nor your family, then what?"

Amisi gave up all pretence of reading and shut her book, bookmark firmly inside, placing it on the side table next to her. Her legs were curled up underneath her body in the oversized armchair and she looked a little frail and way more petite than her nearly six foot frame. Amisi was all about illusion, sometimes I marvelled at her shifting appearance, one minute she could seem bigger than any vampire she faced, next she could trick them into believing she wasn't a threat at all. I admit, I occasionally felt jealous of her skills. She may not have been the *Sanguis Vitam Cupitor* and all the rest of the Prophecy as I was, but she was certainly an asset in this war.

"I have also been in touch with Awan and all of my extended family are safe."

God, I felt awful. I had totally overlooked Amisi's family of Nosferatin and Awan Hamadi's vampires back in Egypt. Amisi didn't speak often of her family left behind, she seemed so entrenched in our world I had forgotten entirely she'd had a life before New Zealand. With Nero and Nafrini gone, it almost felt like Egypt no longer existed. Selfish, selfish bitch, I chided myself, only to feel Michel's arm tighten around me and a kiss softly touch my head.

"He mentioned you had been in touch, Michel. I thank you," she added, giving Michel a friendly smile, which only made me feel like more of a pathetic excuse for a friend.

"Your thanks are unwarranted, Amisi. Although I did warn Awan, my contact was purely to enquire of his support." I'm not sure if Michel was admitting this for my benefit, to make me think he hadn't been as noble as it had initially sounded. I wouldn't have thought he would have admitted to such mechanical desires, it would have suited him better to let Amisi think he had shown concern for her family's safety.

Amisi didn't seemed surprised though by his admission, she had been raised around vampires, she would have expected nothing less. Even though she had often said Michel was not a *normal* vampire, I knew she never entirely lowered her guard around him.

"He never let on," she answered. "Did he offer allegiance?"

"Alas, no. He has no cause to support us in this. Should it involve the Prophecy, he may be inclined to lend a hand, but as it stands, this is a domestic issue."

"You don't sound surprised?" I asked, picking up on his tone.

"I would have answered the same, *ma douce*."

Amisi frowned, a look of deep concentration on her face. I wondered what she was thinking, but thought it best to not ask. I could only assume she felt a little abandoned by Awan and the Egyptians, whatever happened to New Zealand affected her, yet Awan had made it obvious that he no longer felt compelled to get involved. Had it been Egypt's old Queen Nafrini, with Nero by her side, the offer of support would have been a given.

Things had changed beyond recognition for Amisi. Going home now obviously not as firm an option as it had once been. I untangled myself from Michel and went across the lounge to perch on the arm of her chair. I wrapped my arm around her shoulders and let her lean into me for support. She didn't say anything, nor show any emotion on her face, unlike me, Amisi rarely cries. I had once been that good at hiding my emotions, but no longer. Too much had happened in my life not to wear them close to the surface now. Some people begin to bury themselves deep when faced with so much trauma, others begin to crack. I guess I'm a cracker and Amisi is made of sterner stuff.

You are not weak, ma douce, just caring. I would have you no other way.

I looked up at Michel watching me as I hugged Amisi close, the look of utter wonderment on his face making me catch my breath.

Your compassion is one of your most finest characteristics. You place others before yourself constantly. Is it no wonder that I feel obliged to protect you?

I'd like to be stronger, I replied in my mind.

He shook his head at me and smiled. *You are perfect as you are.*

Amisi cleared her throat and squeezed my hand. "I think I'll go have a shower and grab some sleep."

"You are right, Amisi. There is little else we can gain today, we all need our rest," Michel answered and also stood at the same time as my Nosferatin sister. The vampire guards immediately on alert as their master prepared to leave the room.

Amisi bid everyone good sleep and left, the guards shifting out into the hall to await our departure.

"I don't know if I can sleep," I admitted to Michel as he took my hand and helped me to my feet. "There's still so much to fear."

"But little we can do about it right now, *ma douce*." He pulled me into an embrace and kissed the top of my head. "I can help you sleep, if needed."

I pulled back and gave him a sceptical look. "Just what sort of help did you have in mind?"

He chuckled against me. "Do you tempt me, *ma petite belle*? I had been referring to a little of my influence, but if you have another suggestion to suitably exhaust you, I am all ears."

How is it that he can make it seem like my mind is the one always in the gutter? He's a bloody vampire, sex is always at the top of his list. He brushed a finger over my cheek where I was sure a slight blush had appeared. "You are incredibly irresistible when embarrassed. I had thought nothing would continue to make you blush, you have seen so much for one so young, yet you hold on to your innocence with such ferocity it makes me breathless. You truly are an angel come to me. An angel full of Light."

His lips brushed against mine and he lifted me in his arms, making me wrap my legs around him. He always managed to manoeuvre me into whatever position suited his desires, well before I had cottoned on to his goal. With me suitably placed he walked us up to our bedroom and shut us in. No guards, no Amisi, just us.

Despite all the worries still circulating through the minefield that was my mind, I allowed him to strip me naked, slowly, with such care and attention to detail. Taking several minutes to remove each piece of clothing and revelling in what was revealed beneath, before moving on to the next. Once he was satisfied with the final result he started layering kiss after kiss across my body. Starting at his new mark, then moving around to his first on the other side of my neck, then slowly, teasingly, bit by bit to his final mark, on my right breast. Dragging it out as long as he could, until I was begging with my body for him to find that final sweet spot, where I knew his kisses would provide me with what I longed for.

He chuckled against my nipple as my back arched off the bed. "Such impatience, my love, we have all day."

"I won't last all day, Michel, get a move on."

"Now, who is in command here, *ma douce*? It seems to me that I have you exactly where I want you, naked on my bed beneath me. I am in charge, not you." His kisses moved around my breast, still not giving me what I wanted.

I tried to turn the tide, put myself in the position of boss, I pushed against him in a smooth and swift move that would have caught most men off guard. Of course, Michel is not most men. He simply grabbed my hands, from where they had attempted to push against his chest in order to flip him over and pulled them out above my head, securing them with one big firm hand. His body straddling mine making it impossible to make another move. Within less than a heartbeat he had me trapped.

"As I was saying, I am in charge, *non?*"

I bit back a retort and shifted against him, trying to rub up against his groin. The angle wasn't quite right, he held himself back just enough to deny me the contact I was seeking. His smile turned wicked.

"I am in charge," he repeated, moving his kisses lower, completely bypassing the spot I had been calling for.

"You can be a bastard, you know that?"

"You do have a tendency to bring out the worst in me, my dear. And the best." His lips came back to my breast and even though I had been begging for it moments ago, I had given up all hope of his touch right there, that it was such a surprise I called out in shock.

Within seconds he had me writhing beneath him, incoherent words spilling from my lips.

"You are beautiful," he breathed against me, shifting to my neglected breast to lavish attention there.

He had me well and truly at his mercy, so I wasn't surprised my Light made an appearance, although normally it was at the moment of climaxing that it made its presence known. Not before, when I was just awash with delicious sensations of heat and lust. I had been moving and shifting beneath him, almost thrashing in need for him to be inside me, but I hadn't been anywhere near orgasming, anywhere near where my Light would have normally wrapped us up in its glow. But, now I slowly realised, through the fog of Michel's touch, it had engulfed the entire room, dancing along the walls and ceiling, filling up every corner and crevice, chasing away the shadows and brightening the space, to an almost blinding cadence of light.

Michel had his eyes closed, so involved in what he was tasting, he hadn't picked up on it immediately, but it must have become obvious, even through closed lids and when he registered what was happening he sat back and stared around in disbelief.

"A little premature, aren't you, *ma douce*? Or am I really that good?"

I had also stopped moving beneath him and was just staring at my glow, beginning to feel a little concerned that it wasn't dimming at all.

"Um, I don't think it's me."

Michel's eyes shifted to my face, concern now replacing the amusement. "What do you mean?"

I didn't know how to answer that, only that I knew for certain I wasn't in control. I haven't always had perfect mastery of my Light, sometimes it has a mind of its own and especially where the *Lux Lucis Tribuo* powers are concerned. But this was different and I couldn't have explained how I knew that, but that I just knew it wasn't my Light.

"Who's Light then?" Michel asked, having heard all of my thoughts.

And that was the question, wasn't it? Who else could have this sort of Light and make me feel it, see it, be surrounded in it?

"Nut," he whispered. Thank God he had his voice, because mine had well and truly failed me.

Nut was inside me, as soon as that conclusion had been reached, I knew it was the truth. I have had Nut inside me before, sometimes I wonder whether she ever really leaves me, but at times it's obvious she is with me, like now. Not always quite as blatant as a room full of Light, sometimes it's just a sensation of well-being, a feeling that she cradles me in her arms, that she guides me in my thoughts and actions, comforts me or bolsters me, depending on my need. She's not always so evident, but I got the feeling that right now she had something important to tell me, something important she wanted me to know and for Nut to make such a massive statement, it must have been very important indeed.

Michel moved back as I tried to sit up, once his weight was off me he helped me to sit upright. I racked my brain for what the message was she was trying to relay. Although a goddess and although I hold a special place in her heart, I don't have a hotline directly to her ear, deciphering what she wanted me to see was not always so straight forward.

"It's important, whatever it is, but I have no idea what she's trying to say. She's not giving me images or sensations, just Light and a feeling that it is grave." That about summed it up all right. It was important and grave. The more I thought about that, the more anxious I became.

Michel started running a hand up and down my arm to try to calm me.

"OK," he said, clearly trying to think through the problem. "Whatever it is must have something to do with the Prophecy."

"Or something to do with Nosferatins." I didn't get the sense it was focused solely on the Prophecy itself, more likely something that could effect the Prophecy in the long run.

"Why would she be worried about Nosferatins?" Michel asked.

I thought about that for a moment, but couldn't come up with an adequate reply. Maybe it wasn't Nosferatins at all, maybe it was something to do with me? But, that didn't feel right either. I took a deep breath in and decided to sink into that nothingness I use to *seek* and Dream Walk and see if I could sense anything else. Initially, I got nothing, just the familiar black nothingness void, then suddenly Nut sent me a cascade of sensations; fear, concern, heartache and despair.

All of which felt familiar. I came out of the nothingness with a gasp, Michel cradling me in his arms. I tend to forget sometimes, that when I enter too far into that void, my soul or essence, or whatever, leaves my body and if I don't have it lying down, then it just collapses to the floor. Michel gets extremely irate when I do that, I can't blame him, watching my body go vacant and fall to the ground can't be a pleasant experience.

"Sorry," I muttered, registering the pain and panic on his face.

He swallowed, twice, then asked, "What did you sense?"

I told him and tried to home in on where I had felt those sensations before. It took a moment and then it clicked. I had felt them when Gregor had told me of Nut's reaction to the massacred Nosferatu before he had been turned. Nut had felt deep fear, concern, heartache and despair. I hadn't realised she had sent me those sensations when Gregor had told me of his pre-vampire life, but they had been there. And they were here now.

Michel looked surprised at the thoughts he was receiving. Part of that was no doubt because of my conclusions and part was no doubt Gregor's history. He hadn't been in my mind when Gregor told me that story, he was probably a little shocked at what Gregor had once been. It had been Michel, after all, who had said a Nosferatin could not be turned into a Nosferatu.

"So," he said, bringing us both back to the present. "She is worried about a loss, but is it a loss of Nosferatu or Nosferatin?"

Good question, I didn't know. But, I thought I might be able to find out.

"Where's your laptop and my satellite phone?" I asked, jumping up and grabbing some clothes from inside the dressing room.

"In the office," he replied, already gliding off the bed, watching me with shrewd eyes as I frantically dressed, an elegant eyebrow raised on his porcelain face.

"I think I need to check on a few acquaintances," I answered, heading out the door, my stomach churning at the task ahead.

I hadn't been on Nero's website since he had died, it had been one of those tasks I had swept under the rug and simply ignored. I had met Nero on that website, it was his baby, his way of reaching out to what was left of the Nosferatins in the world and providing them with a place of refuge and guidance in the Dark storm. Not all of the Nosferatins left were on it, it was highly protected, but if I, a bank teller in New Zealand, could have found it and managed to hack inside, then others had too.

I had a sinking feeling, as I booted up Michel's computer in his plushly decorated office downstairs - the warmth of his presence at my back which unfortunately couldn't quite chase away the chill - that if Jonathan wanted to ransom something important to me, then how much more important would a few of what was left of the Nosferatins in the world, from my network of support, be?

"*Merde,*" Michel whispered, as he heard my quiet thoughts.

21
CALLING ALL NOSFERATINS

There was only one Nosferatin on-line when I finally managed to hack back into the website. It had been a while since I had been there, so I didn't have the latest login password, but was determined not to wake Amisi to ask, before I was certain my fears were founded. One of us panicking was quite enough. In a final act of desperation I typed in N E R O and was rewarded with instant access. Maybe those left behind couldn't quite let go either.

I forced any emotional response to that aside and started up a dialogue box with Citysider. It took a few minutes for him to respond, just because he was logged in, didn't mean he was in front of his computer. Citysider is based in London, I had never met him, but we had certainly conversed in cyberspace and over the satellite phone on many occasions. He had a great Cockney accent and a friendly attitude. I hadn't realised how old he was when I first was introduced, he's not as old as Nero was, but not far off. England may not be the Old Country as far as vampires are concerned, that honour goes to France, but it is certainly one of the first they emigrated to and therefore Nosferatins needed to inhabit as well. Citysider has been around for a while, that was for sure.

How goes the Kiwi? He typed when he obviously returned to his screen to see my hello.

Worried. Have you been in touch with the others recently?

There was a pause, then: *Last full count, minus you of course, was two days ago. We had arranged to meet again on-line this evening at 4am G.M.T.*

4am G.M.T. Was of course, 4 am Greenwich Mean Time, *Citysider's* time. He was obviously the one now in control of the website, having had to take over from Nero's absence.

What do you know? He typed, when I didn't immediately respond.

Better to talk on SP.

OK. Five minutes. He logged out and I retrieved my case from Michel's safe, he had already opened it ready for me to grab my toy, the one Nero had gifted me. The satellite phone provided a secure way to contact other Nosferatins, scrambled and undetectable to our enemies. I also registered my stake case was inside the vault. And to my utter shock, my Svante. I hadn't remembered Michel's beautiful gift to me, but now memories of its intricate dancing dragon design came flooding back in. Funny how I hadn't even known where they were, I was still a little out of it, it would seem.

"I moved them there when you went missing. I wanted to protect them." He didn't need to say anything else, it was written all over his face, in amongst the blame and loss and fear he had obviously felt when I had been taken. I reached up and stroked his cheek, leaving my hand there for a moment, then turned to place the case on his desk.

I wanted it powered up and ready in time for Citysider's call.

Nero had usually given us half an hour to get the satellite phone ready in the past, but nobody had Nero's patience. I kind of liked Citysider's more urgent speed. Especially right now.

The phone chirped at exactly five minutes and I pushed the responding call button and entered in my code.

"Kiwi here."

"Citysider acknowledges Kiwi," came the Cockney accent, I guess some things will always stay the same. Nero had answered me like that on the phone too.

"What's happenin' *Sanguis Vitam Cupitor*? I'm starting to get a creepy feelin' in my back, luv. Spill us the beans, then."

"I've had a little message from Nut, I'm not entirely sure what it means, but my immediate interpretation is my kidnapper has taken some Nosferatins hostage. We received a call to arms from America last night. None of our line or allies are missing."

A low whistle came down the line in response to that news. Of course, all of the Nosferatins on the website had been kept abreast of my month long trip to the States by Amisi, that wasn't what would have surprised him. I was guessing the call to arms was. Like Erika said, it had been a long time since America last called an enemy to arms.

"OK. I'm guessin' the call to arms is due to you escaping Jonathan's clutches, is he in good with the King then?"

"He is the King."

A short intake of breath. "Righ' then. I'll make the rounds with phone calls, regular ones that is, to those missing the meetin'. Until I can ascertain who is out huntin' and who is actually AWOL, we'll just have to hang tight. I'll be back in touch, keep the phone on."

He rang off without further discussion. Clearly Nero had placed good faith in Citysider as his backup on the website for good reason. He didn't muck about when faced with an immediate threat.

Another wait. I switched the phone to standby and gently lowered it to the desk. Michel's arms came around me again, his lips brushing against my head.

"How about a bite to eat?" he offered quietly.

I was so not hungry, I almost answered back something along the lines of *not fucking likely*, but he turned me to him and stared long and hard into the eyes. "You haven't eaten for over twelve hours, *ma douce*. Do not fight me on this."

I smiled, despite myself, he was in charge after all.

"That's my girl," he said, his mouth twitching at the sides.

He wouldn't let me make it. Michel is not a cook, certainly not like Amisi, but he is capable of throwing together a damn good sandwich, usually laden with meat and salad and decadent dressings. He always manages to surprise me with a new flavour combination that works. This time was no different, beef, tangy relish, lettuce and tomatoes, it was a work of art.

"You got an extra one of those?" Amisi said, stepping into the dining room, rubbing sleep from her eyes, dressed in striped pyjamas which somehow managed to look cute on her lithe frame.

"Where did you come from?" I asked, moving the satellite phone aside to make space for my towering sandwich, my mouth already salivating at the thought of biting in. From not being hungry at all, to being unable to share even a bite of my food with Amisi was one hell of a leap. Michel just laughed and started making another for her.

"I woke up with a feeling that something wasn't right. It isn't is it?" she said, staring at the satellite phone on the bench beside me.

I gave her a brief run-down on Nut's message and my conversation with Citysider while she waited for her sandwich. By the time I was finished, she had hers and I was well and truly into mine, the odd sound of delight escaping the back of my throat.

"Well," Amisi managed between mouthfuls. "If this doesn't make it Prophecy related I don't know what would. Awan will have to consider aiding us now."

"I like your reasoning, Amisi. You should have been a politician," Michel murmured from across the kitchen, a slightly surprised look on his face as he watched her.

"Let's just see if any are missing first, before we start wheeling and dealing for support," I interjected.

"True. Still, I would like to bring Alessandra and Enrique up to date, they are aware of several Nosferatin throughout Europe and those that assist the *Iunctio*, Gregor will be able to trace. This, if it does prove to be Nosferatin related, may not just be centred on those Nosferatin you are in contact with. This could prove bigger than we fear." Not words I wanted to hear at all, but he was right. Nut had seemed almost beside herself with fear and even though a couple of lost Nosferatin was bad enough to elicit that type of response, it was almost an explosive feeling of despair, as though all was totally lost.

My stomach sank and my sandwich decided to do an awesome flip landing uncomfortably at the bottom of my belly. I forced a rising tide of nausea down and swallowed several times to get myself under control. Michel came around my side of the bench and kissed me on the forehead.

"Whatever it is, *ma douce*, we will deal with it." He glided out of the kitchen/dining area, obviously on his way back to the office to contact his allies.

Amisi pushed her half eaten sandwich away and looked as pale as me.

"Will Awan let you know if any of your community go astray?" I asked, concerned that the Egyptians may not be free from this threat just yet.

"Yes, he promised to let me know if their situation changed. When we last spoke, he had already put measures in place to protect them. Michel's call had given him ample notice I think, to reinforce security there."

At least that was one thing. Amisi came from the largest community of Nosferatins in the world. There's just not that many of us left alive. When our ancestors decided to deny the Nosferatu our power, they pulled away and hid. In doing so, their first borns, Nosferatin vampire hunters like Amisi and myself, were unable to join with a Nosferatu, so one month past their 25th birthdays, they all died. Over the centuries that they hid, our numbers declined drastically. It has only been in the last century or so, that we have started coming out of the closet.

Nero, however, had kept his community hidden, but not turned his back on the Nosferatu. He and several others had joined and Amisi was slated to join as well. Now of course, she would have to find a Nosferatu here in New Zealand to join with, those in Egypt were no longer an option. Luckily, she had a bit of time, she was only just on 20 years old, five years before her ticking time bomb exploded.

Still, with so few Nosferatin left in the world it was a real fear if a handful went missing. The balance of good versus evil was on a knife edge as it was, we barely managed to hold back the Dark. The Prophecy was only meant to be activated at a time of terrible imbalance. We had all thought that was because right now the Dark was still a little stronger than the Light, our numbers just not enough to hold back the tide of evil that was spreading across the globe. What if that wasn't the case at all? The loss of more Nosferatin would certainly prove a terrible imbalance between Light and Dark, wouldn't it?

Maybe the Prophecy had anticipated this move and started in preparation for its fallout.

"Oh shit," I said with feeling, rubbing my queasy stomach. "This could be bad."

Amisi didn't disagree, she just sat there in silence rigidly still. I was sure she had come to the same conclusion as me, but saying it aloud, just seemed bad. Really bad.

Oh Nut, what now? If we lost more Nosferatins, where would that leave us?

The satellite phone chirping made both Amisi and I jump a foot in the air. After pulling myself back together, I hit the call button and entered my code. Clearing my throat, I announced I was there.

Citysider's voice came down the line, but it felt a universe away, by the time his words reached me.

"I can't raise six of our members. Yankee, Smurf, Islander, Elvis, Braveheart and Marco." The silence that followed that announcement was complete.

I knew four of those Nosferatin fairly well, one I had met in Rome. Marco was an immature Nosferatin, when I Dream Walked to him, Gregor had him by the fang. It was the first time I had met Gregor and back then he'd had a death wish. He had been attempting to feed off Marco, reeking evil like bad cologne, hoping it would attract me. He had heard of my success as Michel's local vampire hunter and he wanted me to bring him the final death.

I didn't. I saved Marco, introduced him to Nero through the website and set about saving Gregor too.

The other three Nosferatin from Citysider's list were all familiars on the website, I had conversed with them on many occasions, traded information, garnered support and guidance. They were all people I would consider friends. Yankee was obviously American, based in New York I think. Smurf was based in Atlanta and Islander was based in Singapore.

"Where are Elvis and Braveheart from?" I asked, trying to get a fix on the global aspect of those missing, maybe there was a pattern.

"Elvis was from Las Vegas and Braveheart was from Edinburgh," came Citysider's accented reply.

So, three from America, which made sense, those would be easy pickings for the Council of Families, but then one from South East Asia, one from Europe and one from Great Britain. It just didn't make sense.

"I can understand the American Nosferatins, but why the others?"

"I don't know. Maybe there is a reason they aren't answering their cells. I'll keep trying and if I get a reply, I'll let you know, but for now we assume they are AWOL and we need to discuss a plan to get them back."

"Michel is still to determine how to respond to the call to arms, he will no doubt be meeting with his allies this evening. I'll let you know what I can, when I know more myself." I suddenly felt a little defeated then, it probably made my voice sound hollow.

There was a sigh on the other end of the phone, then Citysider's surprisingly soft voice came down the line. "Kiwi, you need to consider not going yourself."

What the? "Are you joking? Of course I'll have to go, the call to arms is because of me!"

"I understand the desire to fight, believe me, but I am only saying what Nero would have said if he were still here. You are too important to risk."

"Bullshit!" came my strident reply.

Another sigh. "Kiwi. If we lose these Nosferatin, then we have already made our job damn near impossible. But, if we lose you too, we have lost the war."

I didn't know what to say to that. My heart was shouting no! But, my mind was reeling at his logic. I wanted to believe I was strong enough, capable enough, to fight all the Americans, to get to Jonathan and end this once and for all. But I also knew, I was weaker than I once was and I also knew, reluctantly I might add, that Citysider was right.

Without me the Dark *would* prevail.

"Fuck," I muttered with dawning comprehension. "I'll think about it." I was shaking my head, but my jaw had stubbornly set. I wouldn't go into hiding quietly.

"All right," Citysider replied with a hint of compassion. "We'll talk soon."

He rang off and I just sat there and stared at the phone in my hand.

"I suppose you heard all of that?" I asked into the oppressive silence that had suddenly engulfed the room, knowing damn well that Amisi next to me had heard the entire conversation, her ear practically glued against the other side of the phone, but also knowing Michel, who had stood silently behind us, had heard it all too.

"He has a point, *ma douce,*" he said softly.

I rounded on him, ready to blast his bloody over protection to hell and back, but he just spread his hands and cocked his head to the side, a look of resignation on his face and spoke before I got a chance.

"I will support whatever decision you make, Lucinda, as I know you will make the right one." He didn't wait for a reply, just simply turned from the room and vanished.

Well, that was a novel approach. Michel and I had run the gamut from controlling, to over protection and now it seemed, to open and accepting trust. He'd let me make the decision. I suddenly felt suspicious.

"What's he playing at?" I muttered to Amisi.

She shrugged but said, "He is perhaps afraid that if he tells you what to do, you will rebel, but if he lets you come to the right conclusion by yourself, you will be easier to handle."

"What if my conclusion is not his conclusion?"

"Well, that is the risk, isn't it? But, he is right about one thing, Luce, you will make the right decision. This is more than just Michel or Citysider trying to boss you about, this is about the Prophecy and Dark versus Light."

She quietly stood, threw her uneaten portion of sandwich out and placed her plate in the dishwasher, then exited out the other door of the kitchen towards the hall.

I was left wondering if all my friends and loved-ones were playing me or not.

Shit. I hated to be backed into a corner. This was feeling decidedly like a corner to me.

Ah shit.

22

MAKING MICHEL'S DAY

I sat in the kitchen on my own for a good hour, not moving, not really thinking, just sinking into myself. It's not a healthy place to be, it's depressive and addictive, the longer you allow yourself to wallow, the harder it is to claw your way out of the pit.

The whirring of the shutters rising for the night broke the spell and watching the blurry shadows of Michel's guards moving through the back yard to position themselves around the property sent cognitive thought tumbling back in. This wasn't all about me. It was high time I stopped acting so precious and started putting the Prophecy ahead of my feelings, started acting like a saviour of the world should.

I laughed a little to myself then. I'd always had tremendous trouble accepting the saviour of the world thing. I mean, I was raised on a farm in rural New Zealand, I am a bank teller by profession, an unclaimed Nosferatin who never knew her parents and now I was meant to save the world from the Dark.

I'd met the Queen of Darkness once, she's impressive. It's not like you can honestly believe you can come up against a goddess and win, it takes an enormous leap of faith, or a huge ego. Neither of which I have in abundance. But, I do believe in Nut. Maybe not at first, but having met her, having had her interfere and guide me, having seen the staunch belief in Nero's eyes, I have come to trust that Nut must know more than me. I have come to trust Nut, my goddess.

Nero was the one to introduce me to the story of my goddess. He told me of the fact that we Nosferatin, are the *Children of Nut*. It goes something like this: Thoth, the God of Wisdom and Knowledge once prophesied a child would be born to Nut who would become Pharaoh after Ra. It was told that she had five children, Osiris was the first born and it was proclaimed to the heavens on his birth, 'The Lord of All comes forth into the Light!' We are descended from Osiris, Nut's first born son. We are the *Children of Light*.

It all sounded pretty much hokey nonsense to me when I first heard it, then I met Nut herself. It's hard to disbelieve something when you are presented with them in person.

But, who the Queen of Darkness is, I don't know. I have always just assumed she was another goddess. She looked pretty similar to Nut and part of me wonders now if she is the descendant of another of Nut's children. If Osiris was the Lord of Light, then maybe there was a Lord of Dark too. I'd have to ask Amisi.

All this deep thinking was giving me a headache. I stood stiffly and stretched and went to make a cup of coffee. Nothing like caffeine to scare away a headache before it begins.

So, I was a tool of the Prophecy, something I had long been fighting, denying even, but like Michel said in the front yard of that Church, I am the Prophesied and there's fuck all I can do about it. What I can do, is try my hardest to live up to the faith Nut has placed in me and that means, dammit all to hell, that I can't just rush off and get myself killed in a battle that isn't even the final one. Jonathan may be putting a spanner in the works right now, but he is not the Queen of Darkness, she is still out there and although he seems to be playing into her hands right now, I still have to face her if we have any chance of fighting the Dark and balancing our universe out.

It's not going to be easy, I still don't know what my final power is meant to do, but it, along with the other two, is meant to be enough to bring back the Light and banish the Dark. I would just have to trust that when the time came it would all fall into place.

Hell of a thing to leave to fate.

I would also have to trust something else. I would have to trust that my kindred could avenge my honour and take out Jonathan without me by his side. I almost dropped my coffee when I thought that thought through. Oh God, how do I let him leave me to do this?

I heard Michel come up behind me, softly, he wasn't going for stealth, but he probably had been going for careful. I'd sensed him approach a few minutes ago, he'd probably held back so I could get my thoughts in my head to settle. His arms came around my stomach, his head resting over my shoulder and laying a kiss on his new mark at my neck. I felt the warmth of him through my back, the reassuring feel of him around me and I inhaled deeply his scent, allowing it to calm me even further. It always surprised me how much of a soothing effect he had on my nerves.

"I will kill him, *ma douce*, of this you can be assured." His words were said with such conviction, it was hard to doubt him at all, but I was scared. What we faced was enormous and it wasn't even the last of what was ahead. Why was it that we kept facing these hurdles which in essence had nothing at all to do with the Prophecy itself?

"I'm not sure how to let you go," I admitted, my voice cracking slightly at the end.

He sighed and turned me in his arms to face him, resting his head in his favourite spot. "It will not be easy for me to leave your side either, but it must be done. Jonathan threatens more than just us, *ma douce*, he threatens the balance of Dark and Light." He paused, gathering his thoughts it seemed. "Gregor has confirmed that seven Nosferatin have vanished from Europe; Rome, Lucerne, Copenhagen, Salzburg, Milan, Naples and one in Lubeck."

"The Rome one will be Marco, the others I don't know. Are all the Parisian Nosferatin accounted for?" I was hoping they were, but if they had vanished, we could have relied on the *Iunctio* to get involved.

"Yes. Although, that is to be expected, Jonathan is not unintelligent, taking a Parisian Nosferatin would have had him on the *Iunctio*'s hit list, this way they have no real desire to get involved, despite the imbalance this could cause if they are not recovered. The *Iunctio* has always swayed towards the Dark. For now it would suit their purpose."

Not a pleasant thought.

"So, twelve Nosferatin unaccounted for."

Michel went on. "Enrique has confirmed all of Spain's Nosferatin are safe, but we could assume there may be more we are not able to trace, South America has always been unregulated. Many vampires who congregate there have dropped out of the *Iunctio* for one reason or another, but just because they are not regulated does not mean they could not have their own Nosferatins within their mix."

"Still, we can't know for certain, let's just stick with the dozen we know for sure and if there are more, you'll find them with the others."

It was easy to say the words, but not so easy to believe them. Finding the stolen Nosferatin and successfully rescuing them were two outcomes that were not necessarily set in stone. The enormity of what we faced, once again threatened to overwhelm me.

"*Ma douce,*" Michel said with sadness, picking up on my emotions and thoughts. His hands came to cup my face as his lips tenderly brushed mine.

I allowed myself a moment to sink into the kiss, to savour the taste and feel of him, to float in the warmth and love that he wrapped around us. And then I pulled back and took a deep breath. Time wasn't on our side, we needed to get things in motion, we needed to rescue those Nosferatin before the Queen of Darkness made her next move.

"There is always time, *ma douce,*" Michel said nuzzling my neck, his tongue laying a wet trail along the length of the blue blood vessel there, making my pulse jump out towards him. "Mm. Always time," he added, as his fangs came down and scraped over his favourite spot.

"Michel," I whispered, meaning to admonish him for distracting us, but not nearly delivering the word as forcefully as I had intended. He was now sucking on my pulse point, his hands running all over my back and arms.

"Yes?" he asked in between kisses.

"When are you meeting with Enrique and Alessandra?" I managed to get out before he took away all reasonable thought.

"When I arrive at *Sensations* and not before," he answered before switching to the other side of my neck and starting to lay wet kisses there.

"So you're keeping them waiting?"

"Perhaps, but I have not fed this night, it is only reasonable that I feed before facing such a meeting, is it not?"

Well, when he put it like that, it did make sense. There was no way I wanted him to face Alessandra without my blood inside of him. Not that I thought for a minute that he would be tempted by her, especially not for blood, although vampires can feed off each other, nourishment is only gained from feeding off a human, or Nosferatin. But, I wanted him flushed, warm and alive, because of me. And I wanted her to know it.

He chuckled at my thoughts. "So possessive, *ma douce*. I like it."

"So, get on with it then, have your dinner." It had taken me a long time to be so flippant about feeding. Let's face it, I am born to hunt vampires who prey on the innocent, many of which I catch in the act of biting. I had an awful lot of prejudices to overcome when Michel started drinking my blood as his sole form of energy.

"I would never rush such an intimate moment with you, *ma belle*. Your blood is to be savoured, not guzzled on the run."

Now he had me smiling, Michel never guzzled. It was more of a slow dance, a sensual movement involving all of his body against mine, not just his fangs and tongue. That was part of the reason why it had been easy in the end, to let him feed from me. It in no way reflected what rogue vampires do when they feed off unsuspecting Norms.

Still....

"Michel, we don't have time to turn this into a marathon event, bite me and let's get to *Sensations*."

Of course he ignored me and started kissing down across my collar bone towards my breasts.

"You can't drink through my T-Shirt," I pointed out helpfully, as his face began to nuzzle the material above the dip between my breasts. His response was to raise up my T-Shirt from the bottom and kneel down in front of me, letting his mouth lay a wonderful trail of kisses across my flat stomach. He paused over the ridges of my hips, the bones sticking out a little too prominently even for my liking.

"I need to look after you more, *ma douce*," he observed softly, then kissed along the ridges there, his finger sliding into the top of my yoga pants and pulling them down ever so slightly, to make way for his tongue.

"Michel," I warned. We were in the kitchen, a well used and common part of the house. Amisi could walk in at any second and man, that was not something I ever wanted to experience. I knew Michel had an exhibitionist side to him, but I couldn't freely allow a seduction to occur here.

My guards are keeping us private, he simply said in my mind. The thought that they were outside the two entrance ways to the kitchen and dining area did not make me any more comfortable with where Michel was going with his hands and tongue.

"Please. Michel," I managed, as he removed my yoga pants altogether and lifted one of my legs over his shoulder. My underwear was still on, but I felt extremely naked all the same. Michel's lips just kept trailing a line down the inside of each thigh, ignoring my protests and making it impossible for me to step away.

"What are you doing?" I breathed, as he nuzzled the crease between the top of my thigh and my pelvis.

He pulled back slightly and looked up at me, the most adorable cheeky look on his face. "I desire of a different location for my dinner, *ma douce*. One must have variety in one's diet."

Before I could protest he bit, right above my femoral artery, the blood rushing out of the puncture marks into his mouth making me gasp. One of his hands came around behind my butt and pulled me closer to him, his tongue lapping quickly as my blood filled his mouth.

But of course, he didn't stop there. His fingers on his other hand slid beneath my underwear and started working just as furiously as his tongue, making me gasp again and arch against his touch. With the intense combination of sensations of his mouth on my sensitive skin at the top of my thigh, his emotions flooding back down through the bite filled with deep desire and a hot ardent lust, the pull of my blood leaving my body and entering his, and his fingers making me build to an alarmingly high peak within seconds, I could barely stand. But he held me firm and worked his magic. Filling himself up with my precious life giving blood and making me come in magical waves of unbelievable releases against his fingers again and again and again.

Finally, he pulled his fangs out and gently licked at his bite, his fingers continuing to gently rub as they ever so slowly withdrew, only making me continue to shudder against him in mini orgasms until he eventually released me from his spell.

Still kneeling before me, my body arched back over the bench above the cupboards, his hands now firmly holding me on my hips, he licked his lips and smiled up at me, taking the length of my body in.

"I would have preferred to have you naked before me right now, arching back like that, languishing in the afterglow of my touch. I can almost picture it, *ma douce*, how inviting your body would be. Your perfect breasts peaked and begging for attention, sweat slowly glistening down your stomach waiting for my tongue to lick you clean, your wet, wet folds swelling in anticipation of my entering you, filling you, making you scream for more."

I shuddered against the cupboards making them rattle slightly from the sudden movement. His words almost making me orgasm again, the images he sent to my mind as real as if I was seeing them, feeling them for myself. I don't think he had really intended to make them so vivid, to make me so close to coming again, he was just teasing, playing a game, being Michel, but suddenly I was on fire and the thoughts I sent back towards him had him taking a sharp breath in and his fingers digging into my skin.

"Michel," I managed in a plea to put me out of my misery.

"I know," he husked, as he quickly removed my underwear and undid his trousers, before lifting me off the floor, spreading my legs around his hips and sliding his rock hard length deep inside my folds. "Oh dear God, I know," he exclaimed against my neck as he reached the very end of me, his mind sending the thoughts, *you are mine,* at exactly the same time. The claiming, he was finally giving in to it completely, losing his control. And I relished it. I had missed it. I needed the break, but no more. I welcomed his vampire's need to claim as though it was my very own.

There was nothing for him to push against where we had been standing, just empty space above the cupboard and bench, so he quickly moved me back against the fridge and used that as a wall to thrust against, his hips moving in quick surges as he pulled in and out and in and out, again and again and again.

We were probably making a shit-load of noise, not only both of us crying out in need and hunger, but the fridge slowly rocking back and forward with every thrust. The bottles or jars or whatever inside clinking and rattling and adding to the cacophony of noises we were creating. I forced the thought of all the disturbance that must be floating from the kitchen and us throughout the house and concentrated on the orgasm that was about to engulf me with fire instead.

"Yes," he breathed, as he felt me nearing my release. "God yes, come for me again. Let me hear you call my name."

It's kind of a turn on to be ordered around when you're so near climaxing. His fervent demands only adding to the urgency and making me fight the need to remain ladylike. Giving me an excuse to ignore the obvious, the noise and the fact that we had no doubt woken up the entire house and just give in to the moment because he had commanded it so.

"Say it," he thrust inside me again. "Call my name." Another thrust of his damn sexy hips. "Let them all know I am inside you." Thrust. "Scream it to the world." Thrust. "Oh yes, say it." Thrust.

I'm not usually so easily ordered around, but somehow he had found the right buttons to push tonight, because when I came, the whole neighbourhood would have heard me shout his name.

As soon as I screamed in release his movements faltered, as though he had only just been holding on to the control himself and he came in a rush of uneven thrusts and pounding of groin against groin and a primal cry of surprise at the force of his orgasm filling me up.

"*Mon Dieu!*" he managed, before collapsing us both down the side of the fridge onto the floor. "*Qu'est-ce qu'etait cela?*"

I shook my head, unable to answer straight away and just listened to his heavy breathing as he held me tightly in his lap. His hot breath coming in short sharp stabs against my neck where his face had come to rest. The weight of his head on my shoulder told me how spent he actually was.

"I think you had better stick to the neck from now on," I finally managed to breathe out. It did seem like the safer bet for dinner.

He chuckled against me and shook his head. "Oh no, *ma belle*, that was definitely a meal I intend to enjoy again and again."

I couldn't argue, it was fan-fucking-tastic, but still, the night was only so long and *Sensations* was calling.

"We had better get a move on," I offered, but didn't make a move in any direction at all.

"Give me a minute, *ma douce*. I do not think I can shift from here just yet."

I started laughing at him, but abruptly stopped when Amisi's voice drifted in from the hallway.

"I can send a guard in to help you, Michel. But from the look on their faces they'd only add insult to injury and as I've just had a call from Enrique demanding your presence within the next half hour, I suggest you find the strength and get your over-sexed arse out here and in the bloody car!"

"Ah," Michel said quietly beside me. "She has found her claws at last."

"She never bloody lost them," I muttered, feeling the familiar wash of red up my cheeks.

Michel just laughed softly and traced a finger over my face, following the warmth that had spread there.

"Beautiful," he whispered.

"Clock's ticking!" Amisi yelled from just outside the door.

Oh shit. An angry Amisi was not something you cared to face half naked so I scrambled off Michel to quickly dress.

Michel just laughed harder.

And of course he would, wouldn't he? We'd all just made his day.

23

LETTING GO

Despite Amisi's harsh words Michel was not to be rushed. He casually walked past the steaming Nosferatin and the two straight faced guards in the hall, with my hand in his and walked up the stairs to our bedroom. As soon as the door was shut he pulled me to his chest, wrapping me up in his arms and laying a kiss above his new mark on my neck. I was guessing he was still very much on a high from that latest *Sigillum* and it would be some time before he took it for granted and left it the hell alone.

"You are impossible to walk away from," he murmured against my skin, more kisses making their way up my neck to my jaw.

"Michel, you're just being obstinate because Amisi has told you to hurry and Enrique has demanded your presence."

"Who me?" He pulled back and gave me a mock look of incredulity. His hand began stroking my jaw and then more seriously he added, "I am the Master of this City, Lucinda, no one orders me around."

"Don't be too hard on her, Michel. She's upset about the missing Nosferatins. It's very much a part of who we are, she feels their loss keenly. As much as I do."

His features softened immediately. "And she believes I am stalling and not doing enough to get them back?" He looked me in the eyes for a moment. "Do you believe that?"

I forced a smile on my face, I couldn't be mad at this man even if the accusation was true, which I most definitely did not believe at all. "No, not at all. I think you're just as scared as us and want to hold on to me as tightly as you can."

He looked at me a moment longer before he spoke. "I am still not entirely used to having someone to worry about, *ma douce*. Especially when she is the *raison de mon existence*."

He'd called me his *reason for my existence* before, among other things, such as his *little light*. Even before I came in to my Prophecy powers, Michel made me know how important I was to him. Sometimes I couldn't believe my luck. How many women have a man so devoted to them, who isn't afraid to let them know?

"I'm not going anywhere, Michel. I've already made my mind up to stay behind. I'll be safe, you just work on keeping *you* safe too." I poked a finger in his chest as I said the last.

He nodded slowly and bent down to brush his lips against mine, a soft, slow, perfect union, which ended much too quickly as he stepped away.

"Why don't you take your time coming into *Sensations*, *ma douce*. I can catch you up on my meeting with Alessandra and Enrique when you arrive. I think it best you not join me in the shower." His mouth curved slightly at the edges, his eyes flashing amethyst as they took in the length of my body in a languid glide.

I didn't argue, there was no way he wouldn't get sidetracked if I joined him in that bathroom and besides, I really had very little desire to see Alessandra. I was still pretty pissed of at the Italian vampire and would likely rip her throat out if she said anything remotely inflammatory at all.

Michel chuckled at my thoughts but didn't move towards the bathroom, he seemed rooted to the spot, no doubt wanting to prove to me I had no reason to be jealous. Or maybe me being jealous was a turn on and he was thinking of ways to take advantage of the mood. That actually sounded more like it.

I threw myself on the bed and stretched out, if I wasn't going to shower I might as well make myself comfortable. A low growl came from Michel's throat, but he managed to get himself under control and turned towards the bathroom reluctantly. It was my turn to laugh then.

I listened to the water falling and had almost drifted off to sleep by the time he came out of the bathroom, a towel wrapped around his waist, his deep cream skin practically glowing in the lights of the room, his hair, still slightly damp from the water, hanging over his shoulders. He looked like a god, something so perfect, not of this world. My sleepy state made his appearance seem like a dream. I held onto the moment, not allowing myself to wake fully, just floating in the warmth the vision before me created.

His lips quirked as he took in my body reclined on the bed, lids heavy, mouth slightly parted and then he casually removed his towel, throwing it over a nearby chair. Michel had never had a problem with nudity, he flaunted it with abandon whenever it suited.

"Care to help me dress, *ma douce?*" he asked, voice low.

I forced myself awake and took a deep breath in, shaking my head and closing my eyes in an effort to break the spell. Hell, Michel didn't even need to use his *Sanguis Vitam* on me anymore, I was so completely and utterly undone by this man. I was his.

His smile broadened and he added, "No? Pity. Then I shall have to make do on my own." He turned and went into the dresser, disappearing for an unfortunate moment, then making sure he was visible through the open door while he dressed. Allowing me the full benefit of his fine muscles at work as he slipped his boxers on, then his shirt, trousers and the rest of his outfit, finally stopping at his tie, while he chose which one to wear. This time a lovely pale blue shot with silver, the light in the dresser catching the metallic sheen as he tied it with practised ease.

When he returned to the side of the bed, he was immaculately dressed in Armani perfection. He sat down beside me and swept a strand of hair off my face.

"I will leave some guards at your disposal, they will follow you in. Please do not try to lose them, *ma douce*, they are as much for your protection as my own piece of mind."

I cocked an eyebrow at him. "I'm not stupid, Michel, I know I need the guards."

"I would never think you were stupid, *ma douce*, stubborn yes, maybe even rebellious, but not stupid."

He lithely jumped up and out of the way of the punch I had aimed at his shoulder for that one and blew me a kiss from the door, then he was gone.

I couldn't even begin to decipher all the feelings of loss at his departure. I struggled to tell myself I'd see him again in an hour or so and that there was no immediate danger to us right now, but they persisted and even threatened to consume me. I had rolled over onto my side and curled up in a little ball while I fought not to be a complete and utter useless *Saviour of the World*, when the door softly opened and a short moment later a delicate hand rested on my shoulder as I sensed Amisi sit down beside me.

"Michel sent me in to you," she said softly. "I think he desperately wanted to come back upstairs. Tell me, what is wrong?"

I straightened out next to her and looked up into those almond shaped deep chocolate brown eyes, full of concern and care. "Just the usual," I answered, pulling myself back together with the help of her nearness, her comforting presence. "Scared of losing him, scared of something harming him. Just scared."

Admitting it was harder than I had thought. I'd already acknowledged in my mind that I was a scaredy cat, but saying it aloud to Amisi was another thing entirely. I felt myself take a deep breath in and hold it, while I waited for Amisi to scoff at my obvious lack of courage and strength.

"That would explain the look on his face then," she said contemplatively.

"What look?"

She shook her head, but didn't answer my question. "He will be OK, Luce. He's not only a first level master and Master of a City, he's joined to the most powerful Nosferatin in the world. He is more than capable of looking after himself. What he isn't so sure of, is being able to do that and worry over you as well." She absently stroked my hair down my head and onto my shoulders, a surprisingly comforting movement given she is only a friend and not Michel. But then, I loved Amisi like a sister. She was just giving me some sisterly love in return. It's surprising how strong the bond of a sibling could be. Even a sibling by choice, not by birth.

"I think you have made the right decision. Staying here, not going after Jonathan yourself. I know it must have been hard, to give that away. You're one of the most focused people I have ever met. I can only imagine the desire to seek revenge must have been great and yet you have put the rest of us ahead of your own needs, yet again."

I didn't know what to say to that. She was right, I wanted to be the one to kill Jonathan, to watch the light leave his eyes and see that he knew who it was who brought him the final death. Such Dark thoughts, such horrid desires, but true. I wanted him to pay for not only what he had done to me, but what he had put Michel through as well. But, I had chosen this path for the Prophecy. Finally acting like a *Saviour of the World* should.

I smiled at Amisi with genuine thanks. As far as pep talks went, it had been a pretty good one. The subtle ones always are.

"I'm going to have a shower, Amisi, I think I can face the night now. Thanks."

"No problem," she said lightly, jumping up off the bed. "When you get downstairs I'll have some breakfast ready. We've got time to eat before we face the baddies of the night."

She skipped out of the room, no doubt planning a feast and I headed for the bathroom. Once all clean and dressed in my usual hunter garb of black short skirt, T-Shirt and fitted jacket complete with stakes and silver knife, a pair of comfy black flats on my bare feet, I headed down the stairs.

Waiting at the bottom were the two guards Michel had left for me. I knew these two, they'd been part of Michel's stable since I first came to Auckland. The choice of these particular vampires for my personal guard would have been a conscious decision on Michel's part. Vampires I was familiar with and could trust.

"Hey," I said to Matthias, the first to stand as I made it to the bottom. He rose to his full height, just over six feet, his broad shoulders and chest taking up the hallway we were standing in. Matthias always wore a serious expression on his face, he took his job as guard to heart. Michel hasn't always felt the need to have personal guards around, when I first met him, Matthias was just one of the many fighters in amongst the line. Although when needed, he was always the first to be at Michel's side to offer protection. It made me think that perhaps he had always been a guard and I just didn't realise it.

I took in his bright blue eyes and dark brown hair, long as per usual vampire fashion, tied securely at the back of his neck. He was dressed in the normal Michel line colour, black, this time cargo pants and T-Shirt. He looked the epitome of military chic. I didn't doubt that the bulges under his clothing were weapons. Matthias looked lethal and scary as hell. He didn't scare me though. I flashed him a smile.

His lips quirked, but he just nodded in lieu of a greeting. Man of little words. The other guard I was also well familiar with. Marcus was just as tall and broad as Matthias but whereas Matthias was dark and brooding, Marcus was blonde and cunning. Dressed much the same, he wore his clothes with flare however, well aware of how good they made his body look. Marcus, when he wasn't on guard duty, always had a bevy of human females at his side. A lothario through and through. Together, they made the perfect mixed bag of *M & M's,* one chocolate centre, the other a peanut to the core.

"Hey, Luce. You lucked out. I bet you begged Michel for us as your guards."

"In your dreams, Marcus." I shot back as I slipped past Matthias.

"Wouldn't you love to know what I dream about," he shouted after me, but I'd already made it through the door to the kitchen. I chose not to bother with a reply.

The smell of hotcakes and bacon and maple syrup met me and had me halting in my tracks. Amisi had gone all out, a tower of delicious looking pancakes was already waiting for my attention, stacks of fried bacon, dripping fat, sugary maple syrup ready to pour and full-fat whipped cream for the final topping off to the side.

"Dig in," she ordered, flipping yet more of the golden patties over the stove top.

"Are you trying to give me a coronary?" I asked, but still proceeded to pull the stack of hotcakes towards me, as well as a few cardiac attacking strips of bacon.

She laughed. "I've been given orders to fatten you up."

Oh God. "You are not Michel's servant to boss about, Amisi."

"And doesn't he know it," she replied sarcastically. "I don't mind, Luce, it's not like I'm paying rent or board, I don't even have to buy food or toiletries. The housekeeper keeps my bathroom stocked to the brim and the pantry and fridge over flowing. It's the least I can do. Besides, you've lost way more weight than you can spare. Michel has a point."

I humphed a reply, Michel expected everyone to obey his commands, Amisi was not one of his line. He should have known better. I momentarily forgot what I was thinking as I bit into a delicate, fluffy morsel of pancake, maple syrup dripping down my chin. My God, Amisi could cook.

She slid into a stool next to me at the breakfast bar and proceeded to pile her own tower high with bacon, whipped cream and maple syrup. I watched in amazement as she started in on the mountain before her without a guilty pause. Amisi's appetite is something like mine, little and often, not huge sittings like this.

"He's given you an order to fatten up too, hasn't he?" I asked eyebrows raised at the amount she was just about to shove in her mouth.

She shrugged. "Yeah, his arguments can be quite persuasive." The fork full of hotcakes cutting off anything else she may have added.

I shook my head in disbelief. I never thought Michel would be able to get Amisi to bend to his will, she was just so damn independent. Wonders never cease.

We finished off our enormous breakfast. Despite it being eight at night, we often called the first meal of the evening brekkie. Both Amisi and I had taken to a nocturnal schedule completely now, when I returned to the bank things would change. A small voice in the back of my mind laughed at that thought. *If* I returned to the bank.

Great.

Amisi and I decided to take my car, *M & M* could follow behind my BMW in their own Land Rover. I really did not need them chauffeuring me any more, I was adamant I'd get myself back in the swing of things and my life firmly back under my control. It was fantastic to be in my car again, at the wheel, tearing along Tamaki Drive. I didn't bother to put the roof down, although summer was well and truly here, it was a particularly chilly night. A wind from the South had decided to coat the city in icicles straight off the Antarctic.

We'd made it as far as Mission Bay when we felt it, a thrill running through my body at the thought of the hunt. It felt like a lifetime since I last confronted a vampire and slid my stake home. This was what I was born to do, the absence of it lately may have been unavoidable, but now I was back.

"This one's mine," I told Amisi, she just smiled a knowing smile and nodded in return.

We parked up a block from the pull, just off High Street. The goons managing to find a park not too far away despite the popularity of the area, high end bars and restaurants, in amongst the closed for the day fashion boutiques and hair salons. Matthias was at my side even before I made it out of the vehicle.

"What is it? Why are we here?" he demanded, not even bothering to hide his dislike at this side trip. We had intended to go directly to *Sensations*, this was outside of the plan.

"Ease up, Big Guy, it's just my pull. Hunter business, you know? Just hang back and let Amisi and me deal with it."

I could see him battling with indecision, no doubt his instructions were to get me to *Sensations* safely, this was not what he had in mind for safe transit to the end point.

"Are we going to have a problem here, Matthias? You and me? You know what I am and so does Michel. This is my job. This is what I do."

He looked at me with those startling blue eyes, no emotion showing in their midst, just an empty pool of glass, reflecting a non-existent sunlit sky. Finally he nodded, a swift short motion of his head.

"We will watch from the shadows." And with that they both disappeared into the dark at the sides of the street.

Shit. That was impressive. I looked at Amisi and noted the wide eyes and startled expression. "They're good," she whispered, then palmed her stake.

My heart leapt at the sight of her weapon, silver glinting in the glow of the old style lamps that dotted this part of the CBD.

I slowly took out mine and sent my senses towards the vamp we were hunting. He was on his own and hungry, his blood lust rising at the sight of his victim's rapid pulse.

Just as I said, "Let's do this" another pull yanked us both in the opposite direction.

"Bugger," I muttered. How often did we experience two at once? Hell, it was hard to come by one a night, let alone two at the same time. The second wasn't too far away, towards the bottom of Queen Street, we could just deal with this one and then chase down the next. There was still time.

I was about to suggest this to Amisi when a third and then a fourth pull, both in precisely the opposite direction of the CBD from where we were, slammed into our chests. We both bent double and gasped.

The sudden realisation that more than just an ordinary night on the hunt was unfolding, had me sweating and straining to control my rising panic.

Oh no, this was not good. Not good at all.

24
ON THE HUNT

As the oldest Nosferatin and also the Nosferatin of this city, Amisi naturally deferred to me. She raised her eyebrows in a question, waiting for me to issue the command.

Without hesitating I took the reins she offered and swung towards the shadows watching intently at our sides.

"Marcus take Amisi up Queen Street, she'll tell you where."

He peeled away from the darkness and materialised in front of me.

"My orders are to stay with you. We both stay with you."

Shit. I didn't have time for this. Four evil pieces of crap in my city about to strike. It was only a small miracle that we had a second Nosferatin to call on at all, without Amisi being here, I wasn't so sure I'd be able save every one of the innocents currently under threat.

The two closest felt like the biggest threat, that's why I'd chosen to stay and face them, they had a hint of something other than the normal Darkness that makes vampires stray from the rules. It was familiar, yet also nothing I could put my finger on. I felt a little out of practice and the sooner this current series of confrontations was over and successfully tucked up for the night, the better for my peace of mind. Not to mention my returning confidence.

"Amisi is just as precious to the coming battle as I am. We cannot afford to lose another Nosferatin to Jonathan."

That had him stopping in his tracks. He flicked a glance back towards the shadows, where no doubt Matthias was hiding and then with a short nod he grabbed his keys out of his pocket and motioned to Amisi to follow. They ran off together to the Land Rover and I turned my attention back to the immediate threat.

I felt a fission of tension run down my spine, then with a roll of my shoulders I was off. It didn't take long to find the first vampire, down a small alley between a designer clothes shop and a well known fine arts store. His prey was lying at his feet, undoubtedly glazed into submission or just plain unconscious. I wasn't sure which I preferred. Glazing from a vampire could be complicated and if the vampire was strong and intelligent enough, dangerous. The human no longer a simple victim, but also a threat. If they were just unconscious, I could ignore them until it was all over and then call for an ambulance to help them out.

I took in the crumpled form, but couldn't tell which reason it would be for his current collapsed state. Moving my gaze up to the vampire above him, I did a quick scan of what called me to this spot.

Of medium height, he had shoulder length blonde hair and flat grey eyes, staring out of a slack, unmoving pale face. He was casually dressed, but not messily. There was no dirt or rips and tears on the cream sweater, or over the pale blue denim jeans. His boots only sported a couple of scuffs, nothing to indicate a Rogue, but he wasn't a sophisticated master either, just barely a level five as it was. His own gaze stayed fast on me throughout my assessment, his fists clenched at his sides, no obvious weapons to speak of.

"So," I started with. "What's up?"

His aura fluctuated slightly, giving me a hint of the Dark within, but also of a desperation that enveloped his entire body. I frowned. Either I had forgotten what the normal pull was like, or this was something else altogether new to me

"They said you would help." He had an English accent, middle of the road, fairly pleasant.

"In what way?" I asked fingering my stake.

No two hunts were ever the same. Sometimes, there'd be no conversation, the vamp would spot me and simply go in for the bite. I'd have no choice but to act swiftly and certainly, without hesitation. Stake straight through the heart. Sometimes, they wanted to play, a little sparring, obviously confident they could get the better of the Nosferatin in front of them. And at other times, they'd decide a bite from me was more appetising than the human in their arms and they'd change their target. And then again, sometimes they'd want to talk. I could never predict what way a hunt would go, so I had long ago stopped second guessing and just gone with the flow.

But, on this occasion, something felt decidedly different.

"That you'd stop it."

I tried not to sigh, he just wasn't making sense. I hated twenty questions and I was conscious of pull number two nearing its prey. If I didn't wind this up soon, I'd be too late to help the next Norm, currently being sized up for supper. I was vaguely aware that Amisi had taken out one of her vampires already and was closing in on the the last. I had to catch up. But, no matter what happened now, here in this alley, the outcome would be the same, it always is. We'd either fight, or banter, or I'd simply end his life. Either way, he'd end up with my stake between his ribs. So, why did I bother to entertain anything else whilst on a hunt?

Even vampire hunters despise the act of killing.

Tonight though, I didn't have the luxury of thinking there could be an alternative outcome. I had always approached each hunt as though maybe, this time, they would back down, apologise for what they had done and walk away reformed. It had only ever happened once before. And really, the only reason why I didn't kill that vampire immediately, was because I was unarmed. Gregor had been able to get the better of me in that Dream Walk and I'd had little choice but to let him go.

As it happened, he had been remorseful and had eventually reformed.

But, he was an exception to the rule. No other hunt had ended that way, regardless of any hopes or wishes I harboured.

So, this was going nowhere new. Time to end it just as Amisi had done her first vampire back at the top of town. And the pull further down Queen Street was getting stronger, almost impossible now to ignore.

"Are you going to behave yourself and walk away from this?" I asked as my last act of *giving them a chance*, but I was already stepping closer, my stake rising up in front of my advancing body.

His eyes flashed on the silver and then back to me, with an almost pleading voice he said, "They said you would help."

Maybe, if I hadn't have been under such pressure I would have asked more questions, investigated this strange turn of events more, but just then I felt pull number two strike and I was well and truly out of time.

"Yeah," I answered. "I'll help." The look of relief that washed his face was the last thing I saw before my stake entered his unguarded heart.

"Fuck," I whispered, as the dust began to settle about me. "That was not right."

Matthias was beside me in a second. "Do they always seem so desperate for you to end it?" he asked, surprise written all over his large face.

"No," I muttered, cleaning off the dust on my stake and returning it to my pocket. "And we're not done yet."

I quickly dialled an ambulance while checking the victim on the ground. Probably just fainted, but the paramedics would make sure. After getting the person comfortable and ensuring help was on the way, I turned towards that second pull. It was too close to bother driving, but it was a block or two away, so the run provided an opportunity to reflect on what had just happened. That vampire had wanted something other than the final death, I was sure of it. And he was certain I could have provided it. I tried to settle the churning feeling that had started in my stomach, the sense that I had missed an opportunity was looming like a giant above me. All grisly teeth and snarly eyes, it felt like any second I'd get crushed in a pudgy oversized hand, the giant's voice echoing that, I *was meant to help.*

I knew, with conviction, that I had not helped at all. I had missed something and it made me feel sick. But, there wasn't time to consider my mistake, I had to suck it up and help this next innocent survive.

This vampire was better dressed than the last, although still casually attired in jeans and lightweight shirt, his clothing looked immaculate and expensive. Not Michel or Gregor expensive, but chosen with care. He was a level four master, so climbing the ladder, but not yet impossibly powerful to pose any real threat and was again just medium height, this time blonde long hair, tied back and deeply brown eyes. Not a bad specimen and not my usual hunted Rogue at all.

I skidded to a stop a few metres away. We were hidden from the street and any passing Norms by a billboard advertising *Tip Top Ice Cream*. The picture showing a young attractive girl eating a *Trumpet*, chocolate topping and chopped peanuts popping out of the picture like fireworks on New Years Eve. I walked slowly past the sign and stopped in the shadows to face pull number two.

He was still holding his victim, which I instantly knew had been glazed into a stupor. When the vamp spotted me, he lowered the inert body carefully to the ground. Reason number one to be suspicious. They don't usually take this sort of care with their meals. Again, this vampire reeked evil, the Darkness oozing out of his pores. But again there was a sense of desperation, as though this was his last chance at something. Something he was prepared to die to get.

"You came," he said softly, his face a mask of awe. "I did not think you would." Once again a Brit. I guess there just seems to be a hell of a lot of vampires in Britain. Strange to have two in one night.

"You're not exactly hiding your Darkness there, bud. It's kind of hard to miss," I answered, trying to assess where the strike would come from. His hands were bare and he didn't look to have any concealed weapons on him, but then again, if they were concealed, I wouldn't see them, would I?

He smiled and he actually looked like a normal vampire, not a crazed blood thirsty freak about to eat an innocent victim on the sly. OK, reason number two to think something was definitely hinky here.

To hell with this. "What exactly do you want from me?"

He blinked slowly at my question. "Release of course."

I scratched at my ear in frustration. Release could mean a stake through the heart, but something still held me back.

"How do you suppose I give you that release then?"

He did look surprised then. "I would not know, you are the *Lux Lucis Tribuo*, you should know how to release us from the Dark."

Holy Mary Mother of God. It all came crashing in on me, in a mad rush of comprehension. These were not my usual pulls, the evil-lurks-in-my-city pull, they were part of the Forbidden Drink, called here by my blood, by the Light within my soul. They were seeking the balance the Prophecy could give them, but I had never been confronted with this readily requested desire. Every other vampire who had come to me because of my Light, had been evil through and through and just couldn't help themselves. Like automated robots, they came when called and then just mindlessly did what all vampires at their hearts do when laced with so much Dark, took an innocent and prepared to chow down in front of me.

These guys, the two at least I had faced off against, were conscious of their moves, of why they were here, of what I could offer them. Shit. I had no idea how to help him and if I didn't give him what he wanted, what then? Would the evil inside him take over and strike back?

"What if I can't give you what you want?" I asked unsteadily. This was all such new ground.

He looked genuinely puzzled. "But you are the *Lux Lucis Tribuo*, how could you not?"

Yeah, right. I may be the Giver of Light, but I have no idea how to give that Light, do I?

I ran a hand through my hair. This guy, for all his Dark, seemed pretty normal. I was sure he would be an exception to the rule, surely not all of those seeking my Light would be as communicative, as cooperative, but this chap seemed able to control that Dark, at least for now. How he was holding it at bay, I didn't know, he seemed to be all but Dark within, yet here he stood, openly asking me to help. I got the distinct impression that he would let me do anything I wanted to him right now.

"OK. I've got to admit something. I haven't actually... um... helped a Dark vampire before. Other than to stake them. I don't know if this will work. And, ah... as I kind of don't trust all that Dark seeping out around you, I'm going to ask a friend to come out of the shadows and help me out. Don't freak OK?"

He looked expectantly at me, but didn't seem at all surprised by my crazy ramblings. Maybe he faced off against crazy Nosferatins on a regular basis, with all that Dark I wouldn't have been surprised if Citysider knew him well.

"Matthias," I said softly into the night. "Can you come here, please?"

Matthias appeared at my side and the Dark vampire did take a step back then.

"Who is he?"

"He's my personal guard. I kind of ran into a little trouble recently and I no longer take my safety for granted. He will only do what I ask of him and no more. You need not fear."

I waited for the vampire to nod and then I asked - the first time I had ever asked this question of a Dark vampire I thought I may have to stake before - "What's your name?"

He blinked that slow blink again, as though every action he made was an effort. I could only imagine holding back the Dark and functioning on a normal level was hard work. That thought made me think time was probably not on my side right now and I had better get a move on with whatever the hell it was I was planning to do. Shame I wasn't sure right now what that was.

"Samson."

"OK Samson, I'm Luce."

"I know who you are." That didn't surprise me in the slightest.

I powered on with my half-formed, crazy-assed idea. "I'm going to try something, Samson. It will require me touching you and I have absolutely no idea if it will work, so please don't go bat-shit crazy on me if it fails, OK? I really don't want to stake you or have Matthias break your neck. We understand each other?"

He nodded slowly, then said through gritted teeth, "Hurry."

I didn't need to be told twice, I could see his strength failing, whatever power he was using to hold back his Dark side was waning and I was sure as much as he didn't want to fly off the handle at me right now, in a few more minutes that might all be moot. I took the last step needed to place my hand on the side of his face.

I had no idea why I chose there, for all I knew any skin to skin contact would do, but something told me I needed to touch him for this to work. I needed that direct contact, that pathway to his soul.

Many people have questioned whether vampires indeed have any souls. They are creatures of the night, laden with evil, most believe when they were turned they lost their souls, they lost their right to Heaven. I'm not of that same school of thought. I have felt whatever it is that exists inside vampires before. When Michel had been gravely injured once, near the final death, I felt his presence - his soul for want of a better word - floating nearby. I called, or at least talked, to that presence and guided it back to his body. Since then, I have always considered vampires have their souls.

They are not too dissimilar to me. We once were of the same ilk. Sure we parted ways, them into the Night and us into the Day, but if Nut is in Nosferatin heaven, then Nosferatu could have a place of permanent rest too. They call it *Elysium*, the afterlife for the eternal dead. If it exists, which I believe it does, then they must have souls too.

Somehow, I just knew that in order to reach Samson's soul, I needed to touch his skin.

I had tried to fashion my Light in many different forms before, I have used it successfully as a weapon and as a tool of pleasure, both from afar, but it has always been when I have touched Michel when using my Light, that the strongest, the best results, have occurred. I hadn't tried to bring my Light to a Dark vampire before when touching them. Sometimes it's hard enough to get a stake to their chests, let alone get close enough without compromising myself and place a hand on skin. But, I was being presented here with an unusual opportunity: a compliant Dark vampire. And as though Nut herself was guiding me, I proceeded as if drawn by a pull.

I gathered my Light with the intent of banishing the Dark and when I felt it hum with a musical note of sheer brilliant beauty, I released it from my heart. Down my arm, through my hand and across to Samson's skin. Forcing it past his shattering shields and seeking out the Dark within.

It all seemed so very easy, so very straight forward. Why I had never thought of it before, I did not know. But the moment my Light found its goal I knew it had worked. The Dark expanded in an effort to smother my Light, but I was simply too strong. My Light batted it aside, then tore right through it, as though it was a tangible shape and my Light was a knife.

I felt Samson collapse to his knees and a scream wrench from his mouth. I almost faltered at the sheer pain that scream conveyed, but my Light surged and brought my focus back and I relentlessly pursued the Dark until it all but vanished. I didn't attempt to get rid of the last little bit of Dark, my Light was almost completely in control and it wanted nothing to do with the token Dark that had survived. I had been told once that, *where there was Light there was Dark and where there was Dark there was Light*. I knew without Nut having to say it, that Dark would always have to exist along side the Light.

I slowly pulled my hand away from Samson's sweat soaked cheek and gasped in shock. Not only had his aura completely altered, a bright Light now, instead of the thick Dark black of before, but he had a mark on his face, where I had touched him. Almost like a *Sigillum*, but not quite. It was made up of my bright colourful signature, a geometric design of crossing colours and interweaving swirls. But it held no *Sanguis Vitam*, like my *Sigillum* do, it just marked where I had touched him and returned the Light to his soul.

It was in the shape of star. I smiled at it, you couldn't get more Light than in a luminous sphere of plasma.

I crouched down next to the shaken vampire and reached out a hand to touch his shoulder.

"Samson? Are you OK?"

He didn't say anything immediately, he was too busy catching his breath, which made me consider whether I had accidentally given him a metaphysical orgasm as well, my Light had been known to do that without my consent.

After a few more deep breaths in and out, he reached up a hand to hold on to mine and then repositioned himself in a low bow - which considering he was on his knees, was quite impressive - and then looked up into my face.

"Mistress," he said with more meaning than I cared to acknowledge. "I am your servant forever more."

I had absolutely no idea what that meant, but Matthias seemed to have cottoned on to the significance straight away.

"Holy shit," he muttered, almost to himself. "You've made him part of your line."

Huh?

25

MISTRESS

A couple of things happened then. Amisi came tearing down the road from one direction, Marcus close on her heels, their footfalls a rapid thumping of drums as if on approach to some ancient battle field. And Michel flashed in from the opposite direction, appearing at my side, his hand coming to rest on my shoulder.

"Interesting," he said casually, but I could feel the tension thrumming through his body. "You have broken his blood bond with his master."

"I've what?" I said, jumping up to my feet and staring at him. His hand had slowly lowered to his side when I had moved, as though he was worried any quick movement now would startle me and cause a complete tantrum of exorbitant proportions. I didn't blame him, I was definitely beginning to freak out.

"*Ma douce,*" he said softly. "Please breathe."

I realised my fists were tightly bunched and I had in fact been holding my breath, but I really didn't feel like being molly coddled right now.

"What did you mean, Michel? How could I have broken his bond with his master? I didn't even know that was possible."

He must have recognised my need for direct honesty, because he didn't hold back. "Of course it is possible, my dear. The theft of servants has been a long practised tool in accumulating strength in one's line. However, it is only the most powerful masters who possess enough *Sanguis Vitam* to overcome a blood bond. Blood bonds are the strongest ties in our world. They make a vampyre kin. Obedient when commanded, willing to sacrifice themselves for their master. It is how our world has survived."

I swallowed and took in that breath I had needed well before, but I still felt like I would faint. Oh shit, oh shit, oh shit. I was a master.

"How did this happen?" I asked no one in particular.

"Matthias said you were attempting to use your *Lux Lucis Tribuo* powers, this must be what happens when you banish their Dark. A vampyre gains his power from his master, it would be feasible to believe that they also gain the amount of Light or Dark within, from their master too. In order to make the transfer of Light more permanent, the tie to the old master must be severed. If not, the Dark would simply come pouring back in."

Well, it made sense. It never failed to surprise me how intelligent Michel was. He was always very quick to reason things out, usually correctly. I didn't for a moment think he had misjudged what had happened here. I looked back Samson, still subservient on the ground.

"What now?" I asked, again just into the air. Anyone can answer, I don't mind.

"Well," Michel offered, continuing with that soft, soft voice. "You must provide for him, he is your kin. You get his obedience and service, he gets your protection and care."

I laughed, a little bluntly. "I can't take care of him, I can hardly take care of myself." And then I suddenly thought, "What if I *steal* more Dark vampires each time I use this power? What if I end up with hundreds in my care. Oh shit." I started pacing and wringing my hands, I didn't even notice Michel glide over to me, or realise he was trying to wrap me in his arms, until I felt him pull me against his chest and start to stroke my hair.

"Breathe, *ma douce*. For the love of God, please breathe. You are worrying me. This is not a disaster, this is a miracle. You had thought yourself incapable of having children and now you have been presented with the vampyre version of a child. He is yours to care for, to guide, but he is not uneducated. He is a level four master, he has been around for a while. You will not need to teach him how to survive, you will only need to make him feel welcome. And that is not too hard, is it? We have space at the house, down in the cellar. We can have rooms made available for your kin, if they wish to stay by your side. And if we need to expand, it is do-able. This is all do-able, Lucinda and it is part of who you are. Please do not fear, *ma belle*, it will be all right."

He said all of this in my ear, so only I could hear his soft voice. The warmth of his breath caressing me, the warmth of his voice enveloping me, the warmth of his words calming me. Bloody hell. I had a *child* and I'd probably end up with more. This was so much freakin' news to take in at once it boggled the mind. But, Michel didn't seem in the remotest bit worried. He seemed calm and accepting and encouraging, all of the things I needed to be, but couldn't manage right now.

Let me help you, ma douce. Let me be your strength until you find your way with this.

I nodded against his cheek.

"You need to welcome him into your line," he whispered in my ear. "Tell him you accept his fealty." Then he kissed me on the forehead and stepped away, his eyes flashing amethyst and indigo in the low lights of the street.

I turned nervously towards the waiting vampire, who was looking up at me with a mixture of apprehension and anticipation on his face. He was obviously waiting for me to say something and unsure if I would utter the words he wanted to hear. I could only imagine what the effect would be if I denied him my support. He would be cast aside, no line, no family, masterless, alone. I suddenly felt a strong desire to protect this strange vampire, even though I knew jack-shit about him other than the fact he had once been bad.

I saw Michel smile and his chest rise in a chuckle off to the side, obviously hearing my thoughts and experiencing my emotions. I had no doubt done something he thought was amusing.

"Samson," I said, ignoring the chortling vampire in the shadows. "I accept your fealty."

The relief that washed over his features was astounding. The power of words, I guess. Sometimes, vampires put so much behind simple words, they mean more than their letters could ever convey.

"You can get up now," I muttered when he failed to move from his dirty spot on the pavement. He stood with that easy glide vampires can do, all languid limbs and smooth motions.

I took another moment to get a good look at him, now he wasn't about to bite into an innocent or attack me for my interrupting his meal. He seemed quiet different than before, and I could only guess that was because of the Light that shone around his aura. He had seemed so stark and hard in his face, but now he held emotion and life.

Michel sauntered over to my side again. "You bring life to all you touch, *ma douce*." He took hold of my hand and squeezed it, then turned towards my vampire. "Samson?" Samson nodded. "Welcome to my City, you are granted passage and hospitality here, as long as you are under my kindred's line."

Samson bowed low, his arm across his chest. "Master of the City, I gratefully accept your offer and will abide by all your rules." He rose and flicked a glance at me, seeking approval I think for his response. I just smiled at him and watched the effect my smile had on his face. He positively beamed.

Well, I guess his previous master had been a tyrant then.

"I think we could all do with a stiff drink," Michel announced. "Matthias, would you drive Amisi and Samson to the club while Marcus takes the young human Samson has glazed home, I wish a moment alone with my kindred."

I didn't think for a second that the *M & M* brigade would have left us if Michel didn't have some more of his personal guard scattered about us right now, because they didn't hesitate or baulk at his request, simply nodded and led the others away. Amisi managed a mock awed expression, mouthing *Go Momma!* as she passed.

I just shook my head at her, I really had nothing to say.

When we were left completely in silence, Michel turned to me and gathered me in his arms.

"Are you OK, *ma douce*?" I noticed the raw edge in his voice and realised he had been quite concerned for me. Was it because of my first hunt since returning from America, or was it because of what the hunt had entailed?

"I'm fine, Michel. Just overwhelmed and a little tired."

"You have no idea how hard it was to let you do this without me by your side." Man, it sounded like he was going to break down and cry. "And when Matthias told me you had sensed four pulls and were separating from Amisi, I had to get Jett to contain me in my chamber for fear I would rush to your aid."

Holy shit. "But you didn't, you let me do my job." Thank God, I so would not have appreciated him butting in.

"You do not understand, *ma douce*. I was paralysed with fear. I had to get my line to distract Enrique and Alessandra before they both realised I was incapacitated. Before they could take advantage of my state of distress."

"Michel, what are you saying? Would Enrique and Alessandra have harmed you?" I just couldn't see it, Alessandra might be a double crossing bitch and Enrique was sleeping with her, but they both had an accord with Michel. To attack would be unheard of.

"Things had gotten out of hand during our discussions, it was quite plausible they could have pushed their point with force."

"Well," I said after a considerable pause. "You didn't give in to your fears. You let me do my job. You were strong, Michel and it will get easier. Next time, I bet Jett just has to threaten to send you to your room rather than forcefully hold you there."

I saw him cracking, just a little, a small smile appearing on his lips, his body relaxing slightly.

"And," I went on, feeling the length of him begin to mould further into me, as more and more tension released. I allowed my fingers to play with his hair at the back of his neck, running along the skin there, encouraging more calm in their wake. "I think a show of force may be needed to remind Enrique and Alessandra who's city they are in."

His smile became genuine then. "What did you have in mind, my dear?"

"Well, us turning up at *Sensations* without a care in the world, for starters."

"Mm," I got in response, as his mouth started muzzling my neck.

"And maybe a stake through Alessandra's icy little heart."

"Probably not a good political move, *ma douce*, but we will keep it in reserve." A quick nip of his teeth against my flesh above his new mark.

I gasped and tried to concentrate on how we could put our two closest allies in their place.

"What do they get out of being allied with us?" I asked instead.

"Prestige. Our assistance should they require it in battles. Free access to our lands."

"What would be the most important to them?"

"They have few battles to warrant our assistance at present, both of their cities are well in hand. Visiting our land, is not considered a privilege, but more of a requirement and we need them here for strategic planning. So, prestige would be their main reason for aligning with us. We are powerful, even if they forget how much."

"Then we announce via the *Iunctio* that they are out of favour with us. That we are barely tolerating their assistance. That they have disappointed us in their lack of support."

The *Iunctio* isn't just the Council that runs the vampires, it is also a supernatural network that vampires can hook into and get the latest news, rules and warnings from. It's a formidable gossip line, one every vampire who keeps abreast of the political climates throughout the world visits each day. Michel is often popping into the network and telling me snippets of news.

But, by announcing our displeasure in Enrique and Alessandra's support I hoped to gain more than just embarrassment for them. I hoped to send a message to Jonathan, a false trail of our weakened state. If we were fighting with our allies, then he could assume we weren't as strong and could therefore lower his guard and make a mistake.

"Sneaky, *ma douce*. I did not know you had it in you. There is one problem, however. If Enrique and Alessandra truly believe we are disgruntled with them, we may lose their support entirely."

"That's why I think we should let them know our reasons behind the move. Such as wanting to throw America off guard. The end result will still be the same, shame on their lines for disregarding an accord in the eyes of the rest of the vampires and also evidence of the power we wield, but also provide them with the safety of our friendship - now secretive - and the hope we will correct the *Iunctio* in due course."

Michel started laughing. "I like it. They not only fear the repercussions of the announcement, which has already gone out, but they will desire for its correction, keeping them in line. And to be sure they cannot offer up an argument in favour of not going down this route, I shall announce it now."

He kissed me on the forehead and went deathly still, vampire still. It was always a little creepy when he did that, but I was used to it by now. Communicating on the *Iunctio* took them out of this realm, to another and while they did it, usually so briefly it didn't even warrant concern, they were otherwise not home. Michel relaxed a moment later and kissed me again.

"It is done. Let us go see how our guests appreciate our political ruse."

Michel drove my car and within minutes we were parked in the underground carpark at *Sensations* and walking through the door. The club had been closed off to Norms, with so much resting on battle plans, all of Michel's line were here, waiting on direction and working on tasks to give us as much information as we could muster. We needed the space the club provided for war plans, more than we needed the revenue the club would have earned.

It was immediately obvious that Enrique and Alessandra had received the news through the *Iunctio*, they both stormed over to meet us as soon as we arrived. Michel casually wound his arm over my shoulder, but I could feel his guards circling in closer should the need for their assistance be required.

"What have you done, Michel?" Enrique asked. "We have not broken our accord. This is intolerable."

"Now, now, Enrique. Did you really think I wouldn't have picked up on your subtle threats. I expect such treachery from Alessandra, but not you, my friend. You have a head for politics, surely you understand the message I am sending here."

It was obvious Michel was relying on Enrique's ability to see through the red haze of anger and recognise the benefits of this news reaching Jonathan's ears. He wanted Enrique to figure it out and not have to say it in so many words. The less Michel said, the more ambiguous the threat to the accords they held with him and therefore the more damaging to their psyche it would be. After all, this was payback for threatening him in his own city.

Enrique paused, considering Michel's words carefully, but Alessandra had no qualms letting her displeasure be known.

"You have overstepped the mark, *mio caro*. How can you expect to win the coming war without our aid. You have forced our hand, now we shall have to retaliate."

Michel just smiled calmly back at her, his hand softly stroking my back in an almost absent movement. One he would normally have done if he was at his most relaxed. I knew it was all an act now though, he was wound up tight like a coiled spring.

"Alessandra," Enrique interrupted. "We will not fight Michel. This is only a ruse. Jonathan will hear of it and play into our hands."

Alessandra glared at Enrique with total disbelief. "You are weaker than even *I* thought possible. You believe he will correct this?"

Enrique shot a look at Michel, who simply raised his eyebrows and smiled openly back at him, neither confirming nor denying Enrique's assumption.

"I believe he will. It would be in his best interest."

"Naturally," Michel offered.

"And in the mean time, we are the laughing stock of Europe," Alessandra spat.

Michel leaned forward, practically planting himself in Alessandra's face. "Never forget what I am capable of, *dolce*. Never doubt what lengths I will go to, to prove a point." His *Sanguis Vitam* filled the space around us, making Alessandra's long blonde curls fly off her shoulders and whip around her head, reminiscent of an act of power she had used on me the first time I had ever met her. No doubt she was also receiving the pin pricks of pain all across her body, the same ones she had also forced on me that day. Michel had a very good memory it seemed. She fought not to show any reaction, but it must have been bloody awful, because sweat had started to trickle down her temples and her whole body was vibrating with the effort to remain stock still.

"Very well," she said through gritted teeth. "I would not take for granted our accord and the extension of protection you could provide."

The *Sanguis Vitam* around us slowly dissipated, leaving Alessandra a little worse for wear. Her hair had knotted nicely into clumps of tangled strands. I tried not to smile, but really, the woman had it coming. She had made me look like I'd been rolling in hay. Payback was a bitch.

"I would expect nothing less, my dear," Michel answered. "Now, you are welcome to stay and celebrate with us. Lucinda has successfully used her *Lux Lucis Tribuo* powers this evening and started her own line."

I knew immediately Michel had been planning on dropping that little bit of news once he had proved his point. Not only had he just proven how strong and determined he was, he was backing it up with a blatant show of my powers too. Like he had said earlier, to steal a vampire from another was only possible if you had enormous power yourself. By the looks on both their faces, they registered the significance of his words straight away.

Enrique was the first to speak, offering me a small bow. "Congratulations, Lucinda. I never doubted you would discover your Prophesied powers soon." His eyes, when they came up from the bow, assessed me, taking a leisurely moment to cover my body from head to toe.

Are you mad? I thought. Michel's just threatened to excommunicate you and you're goggling his kindred. Michel just laughed silently beside me and in the next minute I could see why he was so relaxed over Enrique's attention on me. Alessandra rounded on the Spaniard in a fury, grasping his arm and quickly making their excuses while dragging him away from where we stood.

"You knew they'd both do that, didn't you?" I asked in amazement.

"They are like open books. Alessandra may act as though Enrique is nothing more than a convenient lover, but she is besotted. And Enrique has never been able to hide his desire of the female form."

I just shook my head as he spun me towards him and kissed me firmly on the lips. It took a moment for me to catch my breath once he had pulled back.

"You are amazing, *ma douce*, truly outstanding. Not only a stunning beauty, a kind heart and a courageous soul, but you are remarkably astute for one so young. I am fortunate beyond measure to have you by my side. You are my soul mate in everything I do."

His lips met mine again, this time in a slow, soft caress, conveying everything he had just said in those beautiful words that had reached my very soul. I could have drowned in that kiss. I could have lived there for eternity. It filled me up with everything I needed to survive. He gave me life through his lips and I treasured it.

Only to come crashing back down to Earth at a disruption across at the bar.

It took me a few precious seconds to comprehend what I was seeing. The blonde curly hair of Shane Smith in a head lock, his eyes bulging and his arms flailing about him, while he cussed out his captor in a fluid stream of filthy swear words.

And who would his captor be?

Samson.

Oh shit. The joys of heading a line.

26
WHO AM I?

"What the hell is going on?" I asked, hands on hips as I stared down at the newest member of my family about to crush the windpipe of a vampire I considered a good friend.

Samson straightened up, but didn't release his hold on Shane. Being only slightly taller than the curly haired vampire in his grasp, it wasn't much of an advantage, but Shane had never been a powerful vamp and probably never would. I felt Samson's *Sanguis Vitam* swirling around them and knew he was using a little power to hold on to the slightly smaller man beneath his hands. It certainly wasn't all physical strength that held Shane where he was.

"This imbecile insulted you mistress," Samson announced in an even voice.

I could hardly believe that Shane would insult me. One, he lacked the balls and two, he liked me. Or so I thought.

But, I also didn't want to directly dismiss Samson's loyalty. I hardly knew the guy, but I had the feeling that dashing his confidence right off the bat was not going to set us up for any easy get-to-know-you conversations in the near future. If he and I were going to be family, I had to give the guy a chance.

"How did he insult me?"

"He said you lacked the strength to face your kidnapper and his master would do it for you." He spat the words out as though they were poison and tightened his grip on Shane.

OK. Well, he was kind of right, but what the...?

"Shane, is that true?" I asked and then realised he couldn't form any coherent words at all right now. "Let him go, Samson."

Samson hesitated, clearly unhappy to be releasing the fiend, but I was his mistress and all, so he gave up on the urge to argue and slowly released his grip. He didn't stand away though, but towered over Shane as he bent double trying to catch his breath. A strange sight, as vampires don't actually need to breathe.

"Shane, you can cut the theatrics, just tell me your side in all of this." I wasn't in the mood for a show. I was tired, hungry, grumpy and the centre of attention – the whole friggin' bar was watching the little show-down with ill concealed delight – this had better be good.

He straightened, fingering the marks on his neck and shooting a look of disgust at Samson, then looked me in the eyes. "I didn't mean it like that, Luce, ya know I think you're awesome. I just mentioned that Michel was going to America and you were staying here to get strong again."

I knew Shane hadn't really meant any harm and that he genuinely wasn't trying to insult me, but my pride prickled all the same. It was one thing for me to think of Michel as my rock, even I admit, as my protector sometimes. But, it was a whole other thing for these vampires, even vampires I trusted, to think I wasn't strong. *Never show fear. Never give an inch. Always stay on guard.*

I didn't want to make a fuss, I wanted to just laugh it off and make Shane and Samson kiss and make up. But, the truth is, I *was* staying back in New Zealand because of my role in the Prophecy and because I'm not so egotistical to think I am invincible. And getting myself killed chasing after a vendetta was not going to help us win against the Dark. But, I did know - damn straight - that I could take Jonathan if I had to. I knew it deep down inside and my decision to stay behind had absolutely nothing to do with me being weaker than I was before, it was merely strategic. I reluctantly acknowledged however, that most of

Michel's vampires had seen or heard how much of a mess I had been this last week, what sort of an effect my month held captive in America had on me.

I needed to prove a point and as much as I hated using Shane as an example of my returned strength and Nosferatin don't-mess-with-me attitude, I had to take advantage of this episode or run the risk of vampires everywhere trying to make a move because of my supposed weakened state. Vampires pride themselves on strength and on attacking opponents who lack it. If they spot a weakness they will pounce. And as much as I trusted Michel's vampires to behave themselves - he holds them on too short a leash not to - word could get out to others. Alessandra's. Enrique's. Hell, even the Queen of Darkness could hear how damn pathetic I had become. It was time to put myself out there again and scare the living daylights out of my fanged friends.

I had my stake against Shane's chest in a split second, pushing him all the way back against the bar. It would have been a blur to even the supernatural eyes surrounding me, I had pulled on my Nosferatin powers and Light to prove a point. I could tell the whole bar was aglow with a luminous shine and the vampires nearby thrumming with anticipation. They do love a good confrontation.

"Never doubt my abilities, Shane," I said evenly, loud enough for everyone to hear.

I felt a little guilty at the look of outright fear on his face, but even worse at the look of utter shock. He had never expected me to hold a stake to his chest. I almost crumbled, right then and there. Shane had only ever been nice to me. He was the first of Michel's line to welcome me into the family when Michel and I had joined. He had fought alongside Michel against Max, the vampire who had tried to claim me as his own. And against the Taniwhas, when they had tried to kill me. He was not only an ally, but a friend.

I really didn't want to be doing this, but I knew I had to.

"Let me make this perfectly clear." My voice was very low and very threatening. "I am more than capable of staking any vampire who deserves it. Here or abroad. I do not need to be physically present to slide the stake home. Do not forget who I am. Or what I can do."

Shane frantically shook his head from side to side, his eyes bulging as much as they had been when Samson wrung his neck. I felt a little sick at scaring my friend, but this was war and I couldn't allow myself the luxury of being weak.

"Anyone else want to question my strength?" I asked the room, not removing my eyes off Shane.

No one said a word, all the vampires now standing stock still, almost vampire still, waiting for me to proceed. Either release Shane or stake him. I had no intention of staking him and although I wanted to make sure they all knew I was back, I also didn't want to lose sight of who I was.

"OK then," I said, removing the stake from Shane's chest and patting him on the shoulder. "Didn't you tell me you were the liaison for all the new vamps joining Michel's line?"

Shane looked at me as though I was mad. Not hard to imagine why he was going down that path. I just raised my eyebrows at him as I returned my stake to its inside pocket. I think the fact that the silver had disappeared made a bit more of an impression on Shane than my question, he visibly relaxed, but still looked a little freaked.

"Well?" I prompted, picking up a drink Doug had just pushed across the bar behind Shane towards me. Man I needed that drink.

"Um... Yeah. I help them get to know the city and the ropes, you know the rules and stuff."

"Fantastic," I said, trying not to cough at the strength of the drink Doug had poured. "Jesus Doug," I spluttered, tears beginning to stream down my cheeks. "I do like a splash of *Coke* with my *Bacardi*." He just laughed and went on with his next order.

I turned back to Shane who was the epitome of confusion. "So," I said, managing another small sip without gagging. "Samson here is new to the city and as I am considered a part of Michel's line, therefore Samson is too. You, my friend, have just got yourself a new protégé."

Shane just gawked at me, mouth open, eyes wide. Samson, at least, had a voice.

"Ah, mistress, is this necessary? I am a level four master, he is nothing."

OK, so that may be true, power wise, but Shane was not nothing.

Not to me. Just because I had eaten him for breakfast right now, did not mean anyone else could.

"Trust me, Samson, it's necessary. Shane will help you assimilate. I trust him to do a good job and make you feel welcome. And I trust *you*, to take full advantage of this offer."

I followed that up with a little Nosferatin mojo. I guess he got the message, because he bowed low and nodded his head in agreement. I flicked Shane a look, to make sure he had got my understanding too. He was still considered my friend despite what had happened, but I expected him to look after Samson too. He nodded towards me, face serious, maybe planning how best to *guide* Samson into the fold.

"Good, all settled, have fun." I turned and walked away, leaving the two new friends to get to know each other. I was now beyond tired, beyond caring, I'd used up the last of my Nosferatin-hear-me-roar impetus and was sliding down the dangerous slope of exhaustion.

Of course, that was ironic, wasn't it? Having just made sure every vamp and their fangs knew I was still the big bad vampire hunter, I was now threatening to face plant in the centre of the dance floor.

I made it to the private door to Michel's chambers and had just thrown myself prone on his big bed when I felt him come in. I knew he had watched the entire scene, hell everyone had, but he had stayed back and allowed me to find my way. I knew why too, he wanted me to prove not only to the vampires around, but also to myself, that I wasn't weak, that I was capable of holding my own. If he had thought for a moment that I was getting myself into a bad situation he would have stepped in. He's not so hard up for entertainment that he'd watch his kindred make an utter fool of herself, but still, I did kind of wonder if he questioned my methods. Or the result.

I felt the bed dip down next to me as his body lay out beside the length of mine. He propped himself up on his side on one arm and started trailing down my spine with his fingers of the other. Soft little butterfly touches immediately making me relax.

"I think you've made Jett a wealthy man, my dear."

"Mm?" I managed in reply, unable to muster any more energy to form words.

"He was running a bet on how swiftly and what form you would respond to Shane's transgression. Odds on favourite was for a stake through his heart within thirty seconds."

"It didn't go through the heart," I mumbled, as he shifted to start kneading the knots in my shoulders and back with both his hands.

"No. That's why he's rich. He bet you'd flash silver and Light, but would make both Samson and Shane kiss and make up."

I almost laughed, it's exactly what I had wanted to do, but it sure as hell didn't feel like it.

"I forced them to spend time together. Hardly kiss and make-up. One of them is probably going to die."

"Yes, but to Jett that was close enough. Everyone else just thought you'd *send the stake home*." He'd said the last like he was quoting me, I guess he was. It was certainly a term I had used in the past.

I rolled on to my back, to look at Michel. He'd done a fine job of making my shoulders relax, but I needed to see his face for this.

"Do you think I should have staked him?"

He didn't hesitate in answering. "Not at all. But, had you have staked him, I would have backed you completely."

"He didn't deserve it, Michel. He barely deserved the reaction I gave."

"He most certainly deserved the reaction you gave and my line would have expected nothing less. We are not human, *ma douce*. Humane responses are lost on us. Strength. Power. The ability to manipulate a situation in your favour. These are all things we respect." His hand came up and brushed my hair from my face. "You walk a fine line, *ma belle*. Half human, with as much of their sensibilities, but entrenched in our world. You did exactly what you needed to do. I am proud of you."

I wasn't sure I wanted his pride. I knew I'd had to make a point. I've been wallowing in self-pity and hiding behind what happened in America and everyone knew it. I might want to be a normal human, doing normal things, like working in a bank and going to the cinema and lying in the sun at the beach on a Saturday, but that's not who I am. Not any more. I'm the *Sanguis Vitam Cupitor*, the *Prohibitum Bibere*, and the *Lux Lucis Tribuo*. I'm married to a vampire, I have a vampire in my very own line. I kill, I save. I am not who I was, but I miss her.

Shit. I miss her.

"I think... I think I need to go home and see my parents."

It's not very often that I surprise Michel. You know, the sort of surprise that leaves him speechless that is. Sure, every now and then he gets a nice little surprise, but it's welcome and he's quick to let me know how much. But this time, he really did look shocked.

He recovered fairly fast though. "Why?" Ah, but the short sentences let me know he wasn't impressed.

"Can't you read my mind? My emotions?"

"Yes. But I do not understand them," he admitted.

I shuffled up the bed and rested against the headboard to look at him. I wasn't trying to put distance between us, I just needed to get out from under him and meet his gaze on an even level. He'd gone very still though.

"Do you feel threatened, Michel, that I want to go back to the farm?" I couldn't quite put a finger on his expression, but if I had to, it would be anger.

He blinked. And then blinked again. "We are leaving for America tomorrow night, we plan to head out at 5am." I knew what he saying. One day left together before he faced the might of the American Families and I wanted to go back to mummy and daddy. And leave him here alone.

I ran a hand through my hair and flicked a glance around the room in search of inspiration. I didn't want Michel to leave without knowing how important he was to me. Hell, I didn't want to be apart from him at all. He was my life, my very breath came and went because he existed. The thought of him going to face Jonathan without me crushed my heart. But, I was having a little personalty crisis right now and although I knew I should wait until after he left to go back to my folks, I needed my mum right now.

You know how it is, when the world comes crashing down around your ears and you think you've lost your way, you need to go back to your roots, you need to be reminded of who you once were, where you came from. My mum and dad, or in point of fact, my aunt and uncle, would put me right. They could tell me if I was no longer me. They could tell me if who I had become was OK and not some awful mistake I would regret for the rest of my life.

"You plan to tell them everything?" Michel looked a little less angry now, maybe because he'd heard my thoughts, but he was still pretty stiff, sitting there opposite me. Almost a world away already.

I took a deep breath in and let it slowly out. "I don't know who I am anymore, Michel. Sometimes, it's as though I do things that seem so foreign, so not me, but makes sense only because of the Prophecy. Is that all I am now? The Prophesied? What happened to Lucinda Monk? Is she gone forever and is that OK?"

"You know I love you just the way you are, *ma douce*. A vampyre would have harmed Shane for his poor choice of words this evening, possibly even brought him the final death. Your actions were appropriate, but also lenient. Does that not prove you are still you?"

"Would I have placed a stake against a friend's chest for simply saying something taken out of context in the past? It's a hell of a reason to threaten a person's life. Everything feels like it has... I don't know... much more weighing on its outcome, than it did before. You know what went through my mind when I heard what Shane had said? I thought I couldn't let any vampires see me weak. Never show fear. Never give an inch. Always stay on guard." I shook my head slowly. "I don't know who I am anymore, Michel and I know the timing sucks, I know you have to go to America and I have to start preparing for the Queen of Darkness who could appear at any moment, but that's why I have to do this now. If I don't figure out who I am before the shit hits the fan, then it might be too late."

I moved forward on the bed onto my knees to just in front of him, taking both his hands in mine.

"I intend to survive this war. It's not ending when we beat them, life will go on. And I need to know that who I am coming out of all of this is OK. Not something I will regret and pay penance for, for the rest of my life."

He started stroking the back of my hands, such a familiar motion, one he has been doing to me since not long after we first met. "You need to like who you are now and after it's all over." He looked up into my eyes, his so deeply blue and hypnotic. "It's not enough that I like who you are, is it?"

I smiled at him. "Michel. You'd like me if I grew two heads and started drooling like a dog. You'd like me no matter what. You're too far gone not to." He managed a faint smile at that. "But, my mum, she'd love me no matter what, but she'd also let me know when she didn't like me. I need my mum."

He sat there for a moment and then nodded. "Very well, *ma douce*. But I drive, you need to sleep."

He got up off the bed and headed towards the dressing room, grabbing an overnight bag and throwing a few clothes in, his and I noticed, some of mine. Although we didn't stay at *Sensations* much any more, we still made sure we had changes of clothes and all the necessities if we got caught out by daylight and had to overnight there.

I followed him to the door and crossed my arms over my chest. "What do mean, *you drive?*" Me going home had not included a driver in tow.

"*Ma douce,*" he said throwing me a look that said, *what do you think I mean?* "If we leave now, we will make it before sunrise. I can stay with Erika at the day resting place she has secured nearby for your parents' guards, while you visit alone with your mother. And then in the evening I can join you. We'd be back well in time for my departure at five."

When he saw the shocked look on my face, he stopped packing and came over to stand in front of me, a small wicked smile curving the edges of his mouth.

"It is well overdue for your parents to be introduced to your husband, is it not?"

Huh. I got the distinct impression this had all been turned into a very convenient opportunity for my kindred.

Hadn't he just told me that vampires prize *the ability to manipulate a situation in your favour?*

27
TOGETHER

I had intended to take Michel's advice and sleep on the road trip to Cambridge. I was so tired, but also hungry. As time was precious, we stopped at a *McDonald's Drive Thru* for a nutritionally balanced *Kiwi Burger* and *Strawberry Shake* to eat enroute. After that little early morning snack, I was kind of wide awake again and feeling decidedly greasy.

Squashing the after effects of consuming too much fat and sugar, I instead allowed my mind to wander, hypnotised by the flashes of light outside my window. South Auckland was still alive and well even at this time of the night. The lights of cars and houses, as they streamed past the car, danced and twinkled in the black of the deep dark night.

I'd thought I had well and truly come to terms with what I had become. Starting with the revelation that I was a Nosferatin by birth, a descendant from a goddess, sharing DNA with vampires. It's a hell of a heritage to accept, but I had got there. Or so I thought. Now, as my mind tumbled through its myriad of thoughts, I wasn't so sure.

I had always felt a little removed from the others, from Nero and Amisi and those I had met on the website. They all knew what they were from an early age, raised by Nosferatins, educated by a long line of history, experience and skill. I, on the other hand, know how to birth a lamb, I can shear them too if I have to and I certainly know how to grade wool, feed out silage and drive a tractor. Those are things I've done since I could walk. Not hold a stake at the right angle to avoid the ribs, nor speak Latin and cast a ward or two.

Sure, I've picked up a lot in the past two and half years, some of it becoming so normal, so second nature that it's hard to argue the fact that it is what I am meant to do. I don't doubt that I am Nosferatin by birth, that would be ridiculous to deny, evidence is too strong to the contrary, but I do question my ability to be this *Saviour of the World*.

Why would Nut have chosen me? Surely someone like Nero, or even Amisi would have been a more appropriate saviour. I have been on a steep learning curve for too long now and I still don't feel worthy. Amisi would make a fine Prophesied. But no, Nut chose me. And as much as I am trying to trust her judgement on that one, it still baffles me, it still makes me shake my head in wonder and doubt.

Not that I think my parents will have all the answers, how could they? My Aunt and Uncle have raised me since I was a little baby and my biological parents died in a car accident in the South Island. Had my biological father lived, he was the one carrying the Nosferatin gene, I would have had a different upbringing. No farm, that's for sure, maybe a city life, near vampires. Maybe knowing all about them and the world I had been destined to save.

But, then again, maybe not. I met my cousin recently. I didn't even know he existed. I kind of suspected there'd be relatives, but they'd never come to seek me out on the farm. They would have known where I lived, my parents' farm has been in my father's, my uncle's, family for generations. They could have found me. But they didn't, so it was a little of a surprise when Tim turned up on my doorstep and introduced himself as a long lost relative.

He also made it quite clear, just before he tried to kill me, that my father had been of the same opinion as him, that the Nosferatin should deny the Nosferatu their powers no matter what. Meaning, my father had intended to kill me, or at the very least let me die unjoined to a vampire, thereby denying the Nosferatu my power. I'd had trouble believing Tim on that one, but I had nothing at all to base my beliefs on. Tim had said my father tried to kill us all in that car crash; my mum, me and him. Maybe he did. I don't know.

But, I do know my Aunt and Uncle would not have the answers I sought. So, why go back to the farm? I really couldn't answer that, all I knew was I needed my mum. She was a farmer's wife through and through. She was tough and hard, but full of love and smelled like cookies and lamb roast and pickles and conserves. Her kitchen was her haven and my memories were dotted with times spent at the kitchen bench, my mother telling me off for some prank or another I had played on the farm hands. Hauling me over the coals for some acrobatic stunt in the hay shed, or some ill conceived notion that I could get out of my chores. Life wasn't exactly hard on the farm, but it was demanding. And my mum made sure I pulled my weight and did my fair share.

So, as much as I knew she loved me, I also knew she'd have no problems putting me in my place should I need it. And right now, I needed it. Not that I was sure whether I would tell her everything, but I could certainly skirt around the main points and give her the Cliff's Notes version. Either way, she'd tell me if I had become a shallow, self-centred wench, or whether I had become a hardened and uncaring daughter.

I needed to know.

Michel had said nothing to me as the towns sped by and my thoughts sped with them. He no doubt was getting the full force of my emotional turmoil, not to mention my erratic and self flagellating thoughts. He didn't interrupt or offer excuses, or even tell me he loved me just the way I was. I knew he did and he knew I didn't need to hear it. He just let me have the time to sit quietly, to roll through each unanswered question, each doubt and fear, without the impediment of his opinions.

I silently thanked him for that. This was a road I needed to travel alone, just having him beside me was enough. Knowing he had dropped everything to make this happen, ensuring I wasn't alone in the process.

We'd just passed Hamilton when I drifted off to sleep. My mind a numb mass of snarled questions and thoughts and emotions. My body unable to sustain conscious reasoning any longer, but insisting on the sweet release of sleep. Michel must have sensed my impending slumber, because he wrapped his scent around me, a fresh sea breeze and clean cut grass, comforting me, soothing me and making the last bastions of my troubled mind give way to blessed, longed-for and much-needed repose.

I woke to his arms lifting me from the car, but he shushed me back to sleep. I trusted we had arrived at Erika's retreat, somewhere near my parents' farm and let the ties to dreamland pull me back under. I really was exhausted and a little more sleep would not have gone astray. Besides, I had all day tomorrow to catch up with my mum.

When I did finally open my eyes to the day, I was lying in a comfy bed. The smell of coffee and oranges filled the air, the room a softly lit sanctuary, save from the vampire sitting in a chair in the corner reading from his tablet computer. Nice to know Erika had arranged Broadband for their little stay. Can't have the vampires guarding my parents uncomfortable, can we?

I pushed myself up the bed to rest against the head board and something small rolled off my chest and thunked against the wooden floor.

"You're not supposed to throw it away, *ma douce*."

"What is it?" I asked leaning over the side of the bed to try to pick it up. It had rolled underneath, making me stand practically on my head to get close enough to reach the offending wayward article. Michel hadn't moved from his comfy chair to aid me, no doubt enjoying the contortionist movement I was currently trying to execute.

By the time I had retrieved the little bugger and hauled myself upright in the bed, he had a wide grin on his face and the tablet had been discarded on a side table to his left. I turned the little box over in my hand, it was clearly a jewellery box, there's no hiding those.

"What is it?" I asked rather lamely again.

"Open it and see," came his oh so casual reply.

For some reason I was nervous. Michel's aura was aglow with sunlit mauves and striking violets. Something was definitely up. He stood and glided over to the side of the bed, resting beside me. He raised his eyebrow in a question.

"Are you afraid?"

"No, of course not. It's just a box." He just laughed at my poor attempt at lying.

"Open it, *ma douce*. It will not bite." He flashed a little fang at that. Typical.

I sighed, whatever game Michel was playing he wouldn't miraculously drop it. There was nothing for it, I had to open the damn box. I flicked the lid with a twist of my thumb and stared down at a beautiful white gold ring, the metal catching the lights in the room like my stakes do, flashing a prism of colours against the far wall.

I looked up at the deep pools of blue and indigo in front of me. "What is this?" I asked, extremely un-originally I might add.

He reached forward and took the ring out of the box, holding it between two of his long elegant fingers. I could see gems on the inside of the band, covering the entire circumference; pale blue, no doubt blue diamonds, like the eye of my dancing dragon necklace, matching the colour of his eyes, when they dare to outshine the azure of the Mediterranean Sea.

He took hold of my left hand and without allowing me a moment of protest, slid the ring on my wedding finger, then ran a thumb across the plain band. The blue diamonds hidden from sight, only he and I and the jeweller who had fashioned this item, knew they existed at all.

"I may not believe your parents should know everything of our world, *ma douce*, but I insist on them knowing this. You are my wife and I believe as such, you should wear a ring. Is that not how it is done in your parents' world?"

I was speechless. He had called me his wife enough times now for me to feel that I was, plus as far as vampires were concerned, we were joined, Bonded and I wore his *Sigillum*, there wasn't much more I needed to prove to be considered married.

Unless of course you're a human farmer who knows nothing of the creatures of the night.

"We could have just told them you were my boyfriend," I offered, unable to take my gaze off the ring on my outstretched finger.

"But I am not, am I? And this is something I insist, my dear. I will not be considered a transient part of your life by your parents. I am not, therefore they should be aware of this."

Well, I wasn't so sure it was necessary, but he had that tone in his voice. The one that said, *don't push me on this*, the one I rarely tried to argue with, it just wasn't worth the fall-out. Usually, it was something I could readily accept, or at the very least, work around, but this was fairly monumental. One, my parents would have a fit that I had married without letting them know and without throwing a party. And two, well, it just made it that much more real, didn't it? I mean, in my heart I knew I was Michel's, but in my mind I still fought for that last scrap of independence.

Married. Shit. I could already hear my mothers screams from here. And I thought it was going to be bad enough letting her see the mark on my neck, the one that looked suspiciously like a tattoo. My mum and tattoos don't mix. That alone had been an real concern, but now this? Ah shit.

Michel's lips quirked at the edges, his eyes flashing amethyst and violet in amongst the blue. "Wife," he said simply, then slowly lowered his head to brush his lips against mine. "My wife," he murmured against my mouth, then ran a line of kisses down my neck to stop above my newest mark. "Mine," he whispered again, nuzzling my neck and placing a gentle nip above my pulse.

One hand came up behind my neck, the other around the small of my back, pulling me tight against his chest as he continued to lick over my vein, then gently blow against the wet line left behind, making me shudder against him.

He moaned in response, his fangs scraping against my skin. "I need to taste you, *ma douce*," he whispered and immediately bit down. As far as warnings went, it left a lot to be desired, but it did tell me he was on edge, unable to stop the impulse, unable to call on his normal vast amounts of control. I loved that Michel lost it so readily around me, that he wasn't the cool calculating master vampire, but instead a bundle of raging hormones and impulsive responses. I loved that I had that effect on him. And I loved his bite.

I had never felt as close to Michel as I did when he fed from me.

Sex was intimate, don't get me wrong. And fantastic and marvellous and out of this world. But, sharing your blood with a vampire who desires you, who would level the world flat if it meant keeping you safe, who would throw himself into the fires of Hell if it meant one more kiss, one more taste, one more moment with you by his side. Nothing compares to that.

I felt it all, through the bond of the bite. All his desires and cravings and passions and need. It flowed down through his puncture marks, back through the flow of my blood and settled deep within my soul. There was no hiding how you felt, for a vampire, when you bit into your prey. Not always as beautiful as Michel's bite was for me right now, but always true. No chance of denying their basic response to that bite. Sure, they could just glaze you, influence you into believing something other than the truth, but not when that vampire is joined to you. Michel lost that kind of influence over me the moment we became kindred. Now, all I got was the naked truth.

And I loved it.

Normally, he would have let this become more, but for some reason I got the impression he was keeping it as pure as he could, the moment, the feelings, the connection. He withdrew his fangs and slowly licked the marks away.

His voice was husky when he spoke.

"You are hungry, *ma douce*. Our Day Walkers have brought you a care parcel from Cambridge." He turned and reached over to a tray, where the delectable smells of coffee and orange that had permeated through the room when I awoke, had come from. "Nothing as exciting as Amisi's efforts, I'm afraid, but there is coffee and I think, orange and date scones. I hope it will do."

He settled the tray on my lap and slid over my legs to lie beside me. No doubt settling in to watch me eat, one of his favourite pastimes.

"You seem to be behaving yourself, Michel," I said taking a sip from the still warm Latte and then breaking open a scone to lather it with butter.

"It is already well past midday, *ma belle*. Should I give in to my desires right now, I may not let you leave for your parents' farm until well into the night." He sent me a few images of what he had been *desiring* to do to me. I just about choked on my scone.

Okaay. So wanting to go there, but no. He was right. I needed to see my mum.

I polished off the breakfast and sat there taking in my kindred for a few more moments, then tore myself away to shower and dress. He reluctantly let me, or maybe the phone call he received as I hopped off the bed, helped out. By the time I came out of the shower to dress he was in full Michel, Master of the Line, mode. His conversation in depth, authoritative but concise. It was always fascinating to watch Michel work and right now with a trip to America scheduled in the next few hours and a battle against a formidable enemy planned, he was in full command. It was downright sexy.

I watched him for a moment, just taking in his mannerisms and imposing voice, while I dried my hair with a towel and brushed it straight. He had returned to his chair and was tapping away on his tablet computer at the same time as issuing instructions to whomever was on the other end of the line. I reluctantly gave up on being mesmerised and returned my attention to dressing myself. It was only after I had dried off completely and managed to get my knickers and bra on that I realised he had gone silent.

I glanced up, not having heard him end his conversation and noticed his phone was still to his ear but his eyes were all for me. I laughed, I couldn't help it, I could hear the caller on the other end of the phone asking if Michel was still there. In person, he was, but in mind he was long gone.

"See something you like?" I asked, cocking a hip suggestively. He just growled. The caller squawked. I laughed some more and put him out of his misery by slipping on some yoga pants and a tight fitting T-Shirt. My hunter garb was not farm friendly.

He finally smiled ruefully at me and answered the caller before they sent in reinforcements to make sure he wasn't under attack. By the time I was dressed and about to slip past him into the rest of the house, he was back under control. Enough to wrap an arm about me and prevent my escape while casually finishing up his call.

"That was unfair," he said, as he nibbled my ear. "Completely and utterly unfair."

"It wasn't intentional. If you insist on taking business calls while I dress, I cannot be held responsible for the effect on your concentration."

"Mm," he responded, moving to crush my mouth with his. A deep and urgent melding of our lips and tongues along with the press of our bodies, threatening to make us as one.

"Michel," I managed, whilst struggling for breath.

"I know. I know," he answered regretfully, pulling away at last.

"Go see your parents, *ma douce* and expect me on night fall." He kissed my forehead and led the way out into the lounge.

Erika and a few of Michel's line I recognised were all dotted about the space in relaxed positions, some playing cards, others watching TV and others just flipping pages in magazines.

"You guys look bored," I commented, as I picked up the keys to my car from the side table.

"Better bored than challenged, *chica*," Erika offered. I couldn't argue, as long as things remained quiet here, it meant my parents were safe.

"Thanks," I said to the room at large. "For taking care of them."

All the vampires looked up at me and crossed their hand over their hearts as one. A sign of solidarity, respect and their honour to be carrying out such a task, albeit a boring one.

I felt my eyes well up with tears and took a deep breath in to force them back where they had come from. Damn those stupid tears.

Michel gave my shoulders a squeeze and led me to the front door. Somehow, Erika had managed to source a house with a closed vestibule, two doors, the distance between providing the necessary shelter from the sun when I walked out the front door. We stopped in between the two doors and Michel turned me to face him.

"I hope you find what you are seeking, *ma douce*. I truly do. I would take away all your worries if I could. I would make you safe from harm, no matter what form that harm took. But, I know I am unable to fix this for you. I know it is not me you need."

I could hear the anguish in his voice, that fervent desire to be my protector, my knight in shining armour, for me to need no one else but him.

How wrong he was though. I might need to sort a few things out with the help of my mum right now, but I could never survive without him. Even doing this, I needed him nearby, for us to be together. Had I have come here on my own, I would have been a mess, I don't know if I would have made it. He brought me here though, to what I needed. He would always be *my* saviour.

"*Ah, ma douce. Tu remplis mon coeur de la joie.*"

I filled his heart with joy.

28

THE FARM

It had been well over a year since I had returned to my parents' farm last. I had visited it enough in my dreams, the dreams Michel creates. We often met on the hills above the lambs' paddocks in those. They had been Michel's way of making me feel safe, of helping me to lower my guard around him. In those early days, I had held onto my fears with a strength he couldn't fight. It had taken time and persistence on his part, to sway me, to allow me enough trust to let him in.

Michel was nothing if not patient in those early days.

Nothing had changed since my last trip here, well, apart from my mode of transport. I had usually bussed to Cambridge and my father had picked me up from there, so the long driveway, shaded by Oak trees on either side, had been negotiated in a *Holden Ute* not the *BMW Series 1 Convertible* I drove now. Thankfully, my father was meticulous in keeping the driveway intact. No potholes to avoid or overgrown clumps of grass. It was smooth and well maintained, the low body of the sports car brushing the central grass, but not hindered by it.

I could see my mother in the window of the kitchen, no doubt wondering who was coming down the drive in such a spectacular and totally inappropriate-for-farming car. I had considered taking one of the Land Rovers instead, that's the sort of car my parents could relate to, but if I was going to tell them I had married an Armani suit wearing businessman from the city, I might as well let them see my car. The car was me now, I hated to admit. I had fought this bloody car when Michel had first tried to foist it on me, but now, it was definitely all me. If I wanted them to see who I had become, there was no point hiding myself. I wanted their honest assessment, they needed to see the truth. Or at least what I was prepared to tell them.

The big old white house stood out in the afternoon sun like a beacon to the weary traveller, a welcome and familiar vision, conjuring up glorious memories of hours spent in and around its eaves. My mother's colourful garden wrapping around two sides of the porch, providing a strip of paradise, uninhabited by farmyard creatures. I smiled at the memory of The Goat Attack. We'd kept a goat when I was young, in order to keep the grass down on the sides of the driveway. Old Billy was meant to be tethered, allowing free range over a portion of the drive and no more, but the allure of the sweet smelling petals and buds in mum's garden had proven too great and he chewed through his leash and managed to open the gate. The result was disaster and a goat banished to the furthest field on the farm.

It had taken my mother a whole year to get the garden back to where it is now. A whole year of bitching and moaning and cursing goats to Hell and back. I get my swearing from mum, not dad.

I parked up on the return at the front of the house and slowly got out of the car. Now or never. Mum came out and stood at the top of the steps to the porch, her apron on, hands covered in flour. A huge smile gracing her delicate features. My mum is short like me, like my biological mother, her sister. I get my height from that side of the family, my biological father was taller.

"Hi, mum," I managed before she wrapped me in a bear hug, threatening to crack a rib. She's a whole lot stronger than she looks.

"Lucinda! You never said you were visiting. And who's car is that monstrosity? Your bank manager's?"

Why she would think I would be driving my boss's car, I don't know. I guess you always cling to the familiar when you're a little threatened by the truth.

"Ah, no, it's not his. It's..."

"And what on Earth is that on your neck? Why the hell would you get a tattoo?"

"Well, you know, it's..."

"And you have lost weight." She held me at arms length. "What do they feed you in the city? Crap no doubt."

Yeah, that's my mum. Calls a spade a spade.

"Let me get a good look at you." She held my hands, making me stand at arm's length from her, sweeping a look from head to toe, her fingers gently running over my ring. I swear, my mother should have been a police detective. Nothing gets past her. Nothing at all.

She slowly raised my left hand in front of her, the colour draining from her face. Shit. I could have planned this better, I could have slipped the ring in my pocket and put it on just before tea. I could have parked at the bottom of the drive and walked up the mile long strip. I could have worn loose clothing and a scarf at my neck. I could have done all of those things, but she would have known. My mum can read me like a book. I had forgotten how thorough her gaze could be.

"You best come in. We obviously have a lot to catch up on, you and me," she said in a small voice that ripped at my heart and made me long for Michel at my side. He would charm her, hell he could glaze her, anything would be better than this gut wrenching pain at disappointing my mother.

She led the way into the kitchen, a traditional farmhouse kitchen, brass pots and pans hanging from a rack above a huge central island, well worn wood, currently sporting the remnants of my mother's latest baking efforts. A glance at the oven proved them to be cheese scones. I loved my mum's scones.

She started wiping down the residue flour and dregs of batter stuck to the wood.

"So, who is he? The boyfriend Amisi mentioned?" That's right, Amisi had been speaking with my mum on the phone while I had been in America, she at least knew of Michel. That made me feel marginally better. Marginally.

"Yeah. His name is Michel Durand. I've known him as long as I've lived in the city. He's coming by this evening to meet you, he had some business to take care of today."

"Good then we'll have dinner and get to know him." She flashed me a look. "He should have introduced himself before now if he intended to marry you." I knew that look, that was a *if you were young enough I'd send you to your room* look. "I gather that is a wedding ring." I just nodded, there's not much you can say when my mum's on a war path. "When did it happen?"

I closed my eyes, I could fudge it, but she'd see through me and besides, didn't I want her to see the real me? Well as much of it as I could stomach.

"A week before my 25th Birthday."

She stopped wiping the bench and just stilled for a few heartbeats. Crap. This was so not going well.

Finally she spoke, the bench at least clean, even if I felt a little dirty on the other side of it.

"I guess you had your reasons for keeping it from us. I don't understand why, but I trust there was a valid argument for it. So, why tell us now?"

That's it mum, cut to the chase. You were always good at getting through the bullshit.

"I needed to see you. Life's got a bit complicated recently and I just needed to touch base."

She looked at me with total understanding, an understanding that she shouldn't have had at all. "Life and death complicated?" she asked quietly.

I just stared at her for a moment. "How did you know?"

She sat herself down heavily on a stool to the side of the bench, a twin to the one I was perched upon. "I've been expecting you to come to us since you turned 25. I didn't know how long it would take, but Mary had told me it would be then."

Mary was my mum, my biological mum. What the fuck?

"What are you saying, mum?"

"I think it might be better if you hear it from Mary."

My heart stopped beating altogether. Just outright quit on life. No doubt my body would protest when it failed to get the necessary oxygen in due course, but for now my heart didn't give a toss.

Ma douce? Are you all right?

Of course, Michel could feel me, he could probably hear my thoughts if he desired, but I had the impression he was giving me some space, so it was the emotions he had responded to. And weren't they just a bundle of mess?

Fine. Just fine. My heart performed a loud thud and kicked back into gear.

I felt Michel's presence in my mind linger, maybe until he was sure my heart was working adequately again and then he left, sending me his scent, washing me in his love.

My mum hadn't noticed my quandary, she'd just got up from the stool and headed out of the kitchen towards the back of the house. I followed her into her sewing room, a room I never really entered, it was her personal space, her sanctuary. She never forbade entering it, I just didn't want to tread on her toes. She always hummed when she was in there, it seemed an important, but wholly personal place.

She fished around in the cupboard, tipping over stacks of magazines and pushing aside old clothes and shoes, until she found a small box, hidden at the very back, secured by a padlock. She nimbly fitted a key from inside her pocket into the lock and clicked it open. Inside were old photos and letters and cards and scraps of paper, but at the very bottom was a bundle of envelopes tied together with string.

She turned to the small two seater couch and sat down, patting the empty spot beside her for me. I inched forward, my heart at least beating, but still stuck in my throat and sat down gingerly next to her. I had a feeling of what this could be and it scared me beyond measure and also made me shake with unbridled joy.

"I couldn't give these to you sooner, she made me promise to wait until you turned 25 and came to me. She didn't tell me what you would ask, but that you would no doubt seem confused, uncertain and maybe quite different from the daughter I had raised." She glanced up and ran a cool hand across my *Sigillum*, I had no doubt she felt the raised marks of Michel's bite beneath her finger tips, but couldn't have registered what they were. She looked at my face for a while longer, hers showing a sadness and a loss. I wasn't sure if that loss was because I had changed, or she was remembering losing her sister all over again. "I'll let you read them in peace. The scones will be ready soon. I'll get your old stove top espresso maker out so you can make yourself a coffee. I think I've got a fresh pack of beans in the cupboard."

She got up from the sofa and swiftly left the room. I sat there looking at the small bundle of envelopes, registering there was just two inside the string. The sun was slanting in low through the window, dancing across the the brown of the string, making it seem bigger than it actually was, casting shadows on the envelope beneath.

I took a moment to steady my nerves then picked up the bundle and loosened the bow. The first envelope was addressed to me, *My darling daughter Lucinda, from Mummy.* The second, not so many words, just *With love, Daddy xx.*

My hands shook as I ran a finger over their writing, trying to get a sense of what they had been like through the scroll of their penmanship, the curve of the letters, the slant of each one. I couldn't tell, but it made me feel better.

I knew instinctively that it was my mother's letter I wanted to open first, so bolstering myself as best I could, I slipped a finger under the flap and pulled it free. A hand written page fell out. I was momentarily disappointed there wasn't more, that she hadn't written a novel. Surely there should have been too much to say that a single page could have sufficed?

Sucking in a breath and pushing any negative thoughts aside, I began to read.

My precious bundle,

As I write this you are blissfully asleep in your bassinet beside me, sucking your little thumb. You have brought so much joy and happiness to our lives, such utter contentment, we could not have hoped for a more beautiful and peaceful baby. We only wish there was more time.

If you are reading this, then we have failed. I can only hope your father and I gave you time to escape, to live a little before they found you, before you had to grow up.

I have faith that Aunt Maggie and Uncle Mark will look after you, my darling and will guide you through to adulthood and beyond. They are good people we trust, even if we cannot share our secrets with them.

Have faith also in yourself, you are destined for great things and never forget that the blood of your father's family runs through your veins and so you will never truly be lost, but also that the blood of mine is in your soul, so you will always find your way home.

With love, now and forever,

Mummy

For a page it was pretty good, I decided, as the tears streamed down my cheeks. She had loved me, she had known what lay ahead for me, it would seem, she had known more than even I could have imagined she would, but she had also known they wouldn't be there for me. Or perhaps she had just guessed, their time was up. So many questions had been answered, but I still felt there were so many more.

Why did she think they would fail, that I would have to be raised by my aunt and uncle? How did she know I was destined for great things? And as I read and reread the section on their blood running through my veins and in my soul, how did she know I would feel so very lost?

My father's blood would mean I was never truly lost, but my mother's would bring me home. I think that's what had affected me the most.

I brushed the tears aside and opened the last envelope, a slightly longer letter fell out in a slightly less controlled scrawl. Masculine, I think you'd call it, a little harried and abrupt. I couldn't help smiling at it, it was a little like mine. I never seemed to have enough time to write beautifully, unlike Michel, who has penmanship learned centuries ago. Mine's a little like a doctor's; messy, hurried, illegible. A bit like my dad's.

Baby girl,

I am sorry you are reading this, because it means I didn't protect you and your mother well enough. There's so much to tell you and I don't know what you have already learned, but I can only guess you know about them and about us. What we are, what we are born to do, what we must be, in order to carry out our task.

But, just in case there's a little confusion there, I'll give you a heads-up on your immediate family.

Don't trust my remaining brothers, nor I guess their kin. They have chosen a path I cannot condone and now they are after us. They mean you harm, baby girl, they will not stop, I fear you will have to stop them and it breaks my heart not to be the one to teach you how. But I have faith in our goddess, she has told me of your path. I lay my daughter in her hands, a more heart wrenching task a father could surely never face.

I used to believe, as do my brothers, that we could not rejoin our kindreds, that we must deny them all we are. Please forgive me this mistake, it was before you were born, before you were even dreamt of. I was young and naïve, my older brother Jeffrey was still alive and my world was untainted by loss.

Things changed. Jeffrey died one month past his 25th birthday, I met your mother and fell in love and wanted a baby with her so much, we tempted fate. Of course, once I laid eyes on you, there was no going back. And then she came, our goddess, and told me all.

Dear Lucinda, forgive me for bringing you into this world. Forgive me for abandoning you to your fate. I love you more than life itself and can only hope that your mother and I have given you enough of our essence to take you through what lies ahead. I pray we have helped you become the sort of woman I can only imagine you will be. Fierce, strong, caring, committed, but above all else, forgiving – of us and of yourself.

You will have to face far greater hurdles than we have. I can only imagine what they will be and if you are anything like your beautiful mother, it will be hard for you to face them, on more levels than one. Be true to yourself, baby girl, but do absolutely anything you must to succeed and survive.

We will be waiting for you in Elysium and we will be proud of whatever you have become.

Your father, with love and hope for eternity.

I don't know how long I sat there staring at that letter, the words becoming blurry, melding into each other, like one long swirl of ink, a decoration on the page, making no sense nor providing any beauty. My tears had long stopped flowing, not too many having made it to the paper, thankfully not blotting out the meaning behind each hastily written word.

My father had not tried to kill us, as my cousin Tim had made me believe. He had been raised to think the Nosferatu should be denied our powers, but he had come to his own conclusion, irrespective of his family's wishes and he had fled. Well before I had been born. I think this, at first, was the one thing that touched me most. I had truly feared my father was the cause of my mother's death, that he had not wanted me, that he had designed my demise. But, it was not so. He loved me, more than life itself. Oh, how I would treasure those words.

And then there were the words about what I must become, what he pictured me to be: fierce, strong, caring, committed and of course, the most important, well the most important to me right now, forgiving. Forgiving of them and me. They didn't need my forgiveness, there was nothing to forgive at all.

But me?

Yeah, I could do with my forgiveness. I started laughing. I thought my Aunt could help me, because she is so down to earth, so quick to put you in your place, but she hadn't helped me the way I had thought she would. She had just handed me a connection to my parents, having guarded it as per their instructions for the past 25 years. She had done her part, I wouldn't have understood half of my father's letter had she have handed it to me earlier. I had to be ready to ask, it had to be now.

And now that I had read their words and understood who they were, when I had needed them so much, it was... a help. A definite help. I had my Nosferatin blood from my father, which made me *what* I am, but I had my human blood from my mother, which made me *who* I am. I realised then, that there were two parts to me. The hunter, the Prophesied, the Saviour of the World, the side of me that needed to do whatever was necessary to succeed. And then there was the human in me, the compassionate, the caring, the committed and loyal, the side of me that would have to forgive the hunter, that would have to forgive me.

That was it, wasn't it? That was what I was looking for. This is who I am. Is it OK? Could I live with this person?

I thought about that for a moment, noticing the sun was just setting above the implement shed, my father's quad bike coming back up the dirt track towards the house, making dust and debris scatter behind him, catching the very last of the sun's rays for the day. I'd missed the scones and coffee, my mother hadn't disturbed me at all, she'd let me have my moment with my biological parents, she'd let have this time alone.

So, now that I had, was I OK with who I had become?

Yeah. Yeah I think I was.

I folded the letters carefully and placed them back in their respective envelopes, sliding them in my pocket for safe keeping. Dad's bike came to a stop at the front of the house, the silence after he had switched it off making everything else seem so loud.

Especially, the sound of my kindred's greeting, his deep voice matching my father's in pitch, but making me feel so much more than just the sound of someone's voice should ever do.

Like... shit, my dad doesn't even know about him yet, what the hell was he doing here so early?

I jumped off the bed and was running towards the front of the house even before my father's voice came down the hall. A familiar shout, one I had always associated with a right royal telling off.

"Lucinda!"

Oh shit.

29
FATHER-IN-LAW

I came to an abrupt halt on the doorstep, just managing to keep myself in the shadows as I watched the horror scene before me unfold, unable to make my legs carry me any further and have to then join in on the debate.

Michel sensed I was there of course and sent me a harsh thought: *What the hell?!* But he still couldn't see me, I was staying well and truly out of it for now.

"Mark! Calm down. Don't scare the poor man to death."

Funny mum, really funny. Not that she knew how much of a comedienne she was being.

"Are you telling me you knew she was married, Maggie? And that it is OK?" My father shot back. I could see the veins sticking out on the side of his neck. No doubt Michel could too, I dreaded to think what he thought of *them*.

"I found out earlier today, but I didn't make a scene about it."

"I'm not making a scene," Dad answered automatically.

"You are making a scene. You're being entirely too precious, in this day and age, it happens all the time."

Always ahead of her peers, my mum. Go girl!

"Not how we have raised her, Maggie. Not how we have raised her."

He was starting to wind down now, so I ventured out onto the porch. The fireworks had subsided, I might not get singed after all.

"Hey, dad," I said softly.

He glanced my way and for a moment I thought I'd misjudged the finale and the artillery shells were still about to explode, but he took one look at me and his face crumpled. "You OK, pet?" he asked softly, but it was Michel who was beside me in an instant. I don't even think he realised he vamped it there. My parents, thankfully, missed the flash, too busy taking in my puffy face and red rimmed eyes.

"*Ma douce*, what is wrong? Why have you been crying?"

Clearly my dad was impressed with Michel's attention of me, because a small smile had crept into the corners of his mouth.

"I'm OK. I've just been reading some letters from my mum and dad, my... biological mum and dad that is," I answered, accepting Michel's arms around me and his kiss against my forehead.

I chanced a look at my father, the smile had gone, a look of understanding was now on his face. The same look my mum had worn when I arrived and she'd spotted the *Sigillum* and my ring and I'd told her I needed to come home.

"Well," my dad announced, clearly starting to feel uncomfortable at Michel's familiar mannerisms around me. "I'm starved, what's for dinner?"

He walked past us, patting me on the shoulder. He'd normally hug me, but Michel wasn't letting go. That could backfire on him, I thought, but he's a big boy, I'd let him dig his own grave there.

My mum smiled at Michel, I think she was kind of in awe of his good looks. I couldn't blame her, he is bloody handsome and otherworldly.

"Well come on in, Michel, the storm has passed."

I was relieved my mum had made the invitation, I wasn't sure if I could have managed to slip one in undetected. Michel, being a vampire, needed to be invited into a mortal's home. Mum had just covered that nicely.

We ended up in the lounge, like any family home there were knickknacks and treasures dotted here and there, and the obligatory yearly photos of their daughter scattered about the room. Michel immediately took to surveying my childhood photographic history, a small smile playing on his lips.

I was not a cute child, so I knew what that smile meant. He was bloody laughing at me, the bastard.

I am not laughing at you, ma douce, you were adorable.

Yeah right.

I followed mum into the kitchen and let Michel front dad alone. Served him right for laughing at me when I was only five.

My mum glanced up and smiled. "You all right, love? Did it help?"

I sighed. "It was hard, but it helped. Thanks for keeping them."

She came around the bench and wrapped me in her arms. "We love you, Lucinda. So much."

One final squeeze and she was off to check on the roast. Lamb. Yum yum. I had no idea how Michel was going to cover not being able to eat. This should be fun.

"Why don't you go wash your face, I'm sure you don't want Michel to see you in such a state."

I laughed. "Mum, he sees me first thing in the morning, trust me, he's seen worse."

She smiled, a little awkwardly. "If I were you, I wouldn't mention that just yet to your father. Give him some time to get to know the man first, OK?"

She had a point and now I suddenly wanted to make sure Michel was OK in there alone with dad. I mean, I hadn't heard any broken glass or shouting, but there were silent ways to kill.

I quickly washed my face in the laundry off the kitchen, not sparing enough time to go all the way to the back of the house to the bathroom and then hot footed it into the lounge.

Michel and dad were sitting in armchairs drinking whiskey, having a very normal, very civilised conversation. Bloody hell, he'd glazed him, I was sure. Michel flicked me a glance and raised his eyebrows at me. I slowly made my way over to the settee next to his chair and sat down. Trying to determine if dad was under a mind spell or not. He seemed normal, a little cantankerous, but starting to relax. Another whiskey or two and he'd be downright jovial.

He was firing questions at Michel. What did he do for a living? How had he met me? What sort of house had he provided for me? Where was he from? Did he have a criminal record?

"Dad!" I interjected. "He is not a criminal." A blood sucking vampire, but not a criminal.

Michel stifled a laugh at my thoughts.

"No one drives around in the type of cars I spotted out the front and the type of the suit your man is wearing without bending a few financial rules," my father shot back.

Jeez, when did he become Columbo?

"That's ridiculous, dad. Being rich is not a crime."

He just humphed, clearly wanting something to complain about.

"What about grandchildren? Are you going to give us some of those?"

Oh bloody hell. "Um... I don't think..."

"I do hope so, Mr Monk. I would love a mini Lucinda to dote on."

I shot Michel a look, he just smiled all bright eyed and bushy tailed. *At least we could try, ma douce. Every day perhaps? Maybe even twice per day? I can be quite accommodating should you feel the need to try.*

I resisted the urge to roll my eyes and stood up to mix myself a drink. Dad was clearly too distracted to offer.

"How long are you staying then?" Dad was running out of ammo, thank God.

"We can't stay dad, Michel has a plane to catch."

"You go away often then? Leave our girl on her own?" Ah bugger, he'd make a weapon out of anything.

"No dad, we usually travel together. This is different."

"I'd keep an eye on him, Luce. If he starts travelling too much on his own, I'd have him followed. You never know what these Frenchmen get up to."

Oh, for the love of God. "Dad," I admonished, flashing an apologetic look at Michel.

He just looked amused, but didn't bother to reassure my father, I noticed.

Just then mum came in and announced dinner was ready. Saved by the rack of lamb.

Dad led the way, but Michel pulled me back before I made it through the door.

"*Ma douce,*" he whispered in my ear, wrapping his arms around me, his breath hot against my skin, sending a delightful shiver down my body. His own stirred in response. "I cannot partake of the meal, either I make an excuse now and leave, or you allow me to glaze them."

Shit. My parents. Glazed. I was about to say you'll have to leave, I really couldn't stomach invading my parents' minds to that extent, but instead I just whispered, "Do it. Glaze them." I couldn't believe my own ears, but the thought of Michel leaving now without me, was too hard to even contemplate. I needed him, I couldn't let him go just yet, when in a few hours he'd be flying away from me for real.

"I will take great care," he murmured and led me into the dining room.

I don't know if Michel took the liberty of glazing my father into being a more hospitable host, but as the dinner progressed - my parents and me eating succulent roast lamb and vegetables, Michel's plate remaining conspicuously empty, well conspicuously empty to only me - my father started joking with Michel, sharing little stories about my childhood and generally doing all those things parents are so not meant to do and embarrass you in front of your new partner.

Michel, of course, lapped it up, flicking me the odd look of mock shock at certain escapades I had gotten in to when younger and then at times giving me one of his rare smiles. Those smiles he keeps hidden, doesn't let any of his line see, the ones that would make them think he was something other than the big bad Master of the City, something quite lovely and kind and utterly gorgeous. The ones that he brings out only for me.

My mum and dad were sold. With the minimal amount of vampire mojo, Michel had won their hearts. And I had found a modicum of peace before the storm ahead. I'd reconnected with my parents, had a better understanding of where I had come from and what I had meant to them and also how to handle what I had become, without losing sight of me.

And Michel, had the chance to meet my family, gain an inordinate amount of ammunition, with the plethora of stories about my childhood, to last a lifetime and then some of hassling the crap out of me. He was one very happy vampire. And I was pretty happy too.

I even got that hug my father had missed earlier and another from my Mum, before we left. My mum slipped a hug in for Michel too and my dad proffered a hand shake, so all in all, despite the unfortunate start to the evening, it was a success.

And now it was time to leave. Which meant it was that much closer to Michel leaving for the States and for God knows what would happen then.

I followed Michel's Land Rover back to his vampires' safe house nearby, with a heavy heart. The night was passing too quickly and from being so happy in that lounge after dinner, watching my parents accepting my kindred, I was now almost in tears again with the thought of being separated from him so soon.

On entering the house, Michel threw the keys to my car to Erika, who flashed out the door with a wink as she passed.

"Where's Erika going with my car?" I asked.

"She will meet us at the airport, *ma douce*, where you can have your baby back again. Erika will join me in America, her knowledge is too valuable to leave behind."

"But why is she taking my car?" I didn't really like sharing my car, it *was* kind of my baby as he had insinuated and if she was taking my car, then how were we getting back to the city?

He turned towards me, having looked at a few messages left by Erika while answering my question and pulled me into the circle of his arms.

"There are only a handful of hours left before I must leave and I intend to spend them with you in my arms." He nuzzled my ear, adding a little nip at the end of his sentence.

"How will you manage that and get us back to Auckland?" I breathed, already losing myself to his touch.

"Dennis will drive us in one of the Land Rovers and you and I shall be undisturbed in the back." His fangs scraped down my neck, making me collapse into his hold.

"Michel," I managed, with a little dignity too I might add. "I am not having any hanky panky in the back seat of a Land Rover while one of your personal guards sits in the front."

Did he think I was totally friggin' unable to stand up to his advances. Hell, no! I was not going to be the talk of the rest of the line. Well, any more than I already was, anyway.

He just laughed, his chest rising and falling in a lovely rumble against my body.

"He will not watch, nor hear, nor smell, vampyres are capable of switching off all senses and using only those that they require at any one time. He will drive and not be aware of the back seat at all. I have already commanded it so," he promised in a low whisper against my skin.

"I... I can't Michel." I shook my head to emphasise. "I just can't do that."

"Oh, my dear, I think you can. You most definitely can."

I doubted it, I really did, even as we slipped into the back seat of the car and Dennis slid in the front removing the rear vision mirror from the windscreen and starting the vehicle up. No conversation, no glances our way, just an intense focus on the road in front of him.

Just about as focused as Michel was on me right at that second. His lips all over my face, my neck, down to my breasts.

"Michel," I begged. "Stop this, you're embarrassing me."

"He can't hear us, *ma belle*."

I didn't believe him.

"Dennis!" Michel practically shouted over his shoulder. The big vamp in the front didn't even flinch. "Satisfied?" he murmured whipping my T-Shirt off over my head, then swiftly making quick work of my bra and pushing me back against the rear seat, then climbing up my body to lavish attention on my nipples.

Hell no, this was way more exhibitionist than I was prepared to swallow. I fought him, I really did, but it only turned into a game. Every time I tried to cover up, he'd just whip the item away, we went back and forth like that for several minutes, in the end he tossed the offending item in the front seat where there was no way in hell I was reaching over there for it. My yoga pants quickly followed, as did my underwear. The front seat might as well have been a million miles away. I think he was quite pleased with himself for that one.

"What if we get pulled over by a cop?" I asked, getting more and more breathless. Dammit. I was losing and I knew it.

"Dennis would deal with them." Another kiss, another nip, another few minutes of distracting me in the dark that shrouded the back seat.

I finally managed one last ditch effort to claim some of my morals and dignity back. "Michel!" I admonished.

"I do love it when you shout my name, *ma douce*, but I would prefer an altogether different tone." And then he bit, right over the soft skin of my upper thigh, into the large free flowing blood vessel below.

Game over. You lose.

"No fair!" I breathed out, almost in a whimper.

I never play fair when there is something I desperately want.

He let me think about that for a while, as well as the delicious sensations of lust and heat and desire and ownership he sent rushing back down the connection we shared.

Now, how about that different tone, ma douce?

His fingers deftly found their mark, slipping into my already moist core, his thumb easily finding my special nub, rubbing in time to his deep finger penetrations, making me arch off the back seat of the car and forget entirely where I was and who was with us. By the time he'd had his fill of me I was panting and fighting every fibre of my body not to fall off that cliff and give him what he wanted. I would not scream his name.

"Oh, you *are* being difficult," he whispered and replaced his fingers with his tongue.

Oh sweet Lord, how on Earth did I fight this?

30

THE LONG KISS GOOD-BYE

And oh God, I could feel everything. His dark, silky hair splayed out over my naked thigh, his firm fingers digging in to my butt as he raised my rear up to meet him, the leather of the seat against my back, his mouth, his lips, his tongue and his teeth. It felt so damn good and sinful, the dimness in the car, barely any light, save from the occasional passing vehicle, making it feel like a dark little piece out of time. A very naughty, dark little piece out of time.

Michel was determined to make me scream his name and was using every weapon in his arsenal. The speed and precision in which he ravished me; a small lick, then suck, then lick, then oh my god bite, then suck, then lick, was erotic beyond measure. It was driving me insane. The more I refused to scream out, the more intense it became and the more determined he was to make me.

I promised myself I *would* seek revenge.

But there was nothing I could do to stop the orgasm he so faithfully sought out in me. I bucked and shuddered beneath him, swallowed the cry of release, which made me pull back what should have been a mind blowing orgasm into merely a really, really good one, but despite denying him the scream, it was still out of this world and I loved it.

I drifted down from that wonderful high, as he crawled up my body, laying butterfly light kisses across my stomach, up my ribs, over my breasts and into my neck.

"You are so stubborn," he murmured against me, nuzzling into my hair.

Stubborn huh? We'll see.

He had removed his jacket and tie before we got in the car, so some of the work was already done for me. I made short issue of his shirt, swiftly undoing the buttons and running my hands underneath, along the hard plane of his marble-like chest, receiving a satisfying groan from the back of his throat. He'd obviously been way more affected by my arousal and refusal to give in and scream his name, than he had been letting on.

Lifting my head I licked around his dusky nipple, nipping and sucking it to a little peak, then offered the same attention to the rather neglected one across from it. Michel was either proving a point or simply unable to stop himself, because his vocals were a hell of a lot more audible than mine. He made very sure I knew he was enjoying it. I didn't mind in the slightest. I might have had an issue with drawing attention to myself, but I had no such problem with him screaming out *my* name, that was for sure.

Before I even knew what was happening, he had flipped us and now he lay on the bottom against the leather seats and I was draped across the length of him. Manipulation at its best, but I took advantage of it, all the same.

He helped me remove his shirt and after I had kissed my way down his body, I removed his trousers, boxers and shoes and socks. If I was going to be buck naked, he sure as hell was too. All of his clothes got tossed in the front seat, although I was certain he'd have no qualms reaching over and grabbing them when needed.

After disposing of those, I returned my attention to his body, allowing myself a moment to take in the glorious sight of him. He had a slightly amused look on his face as he lay there watching me look down at him, as though this was exactly what he'd had in mind all along and I had fallen directly into his trap. Of course I had.

Damn him.

No going back now though. I could hardly ignore the excellent example of manhood in front of me, now could I? Lowering myself down between his legs, well out of sight of any stray headlight beam through the windows and began my revenge.

Slow licks around the top of his hard, long erection and then light kisses down the length of it, to end up with his sac in my mouth and an immediate writhe of his body along with a wonderful gasp stolen from his mouth.

I stopped and looked up at him, waiting for him to get himself back under control. His eyes were flashing amethyst and violet by the time he opened them again to look at me.

Once I had his attention again, I repeated the action down the other side of his hard sex, receiving the same response and then a pause to watch the after effects.

"You're teasing," he managed, when his head came back up and his eyes latched on to mine.

I shrugged and offered a slow smile, licking my lips and catching his look of desire before taking as much of him deep within my mouth as I could manage and getting a nice shout of surprise as he convulsed in pleasure beneath me. His hands came to my head, wrapping his fingers in my hair, encouraging me to continue. I slowly withdrew his length, allowing my teeth to scrape a little down the sides. His fingers fisted, tugging a bit at the strands of my hair, but I didn't care, I knew I had him completely at my mercy now.

I alternated long and deep with short and quick, mixing them up, making it impossible for him to anticipate what I'd do next, what he'd feel next, unable to ride that wave anywhere he wanted it desperately to go. His breathing had become ragged, he hadn't released my hair and finally I think I had broken him, because he let out a moan and in words I barely heard said, "You're driving me crazy, *ma douce*, I have to be inside you."

I didn't subscribe to that thought, I wanted to see him writhe. So, I doubled my efforts, sucking and nibbling, stroking and fondling, receiving satisfying growls and groans from the back of his throat and the beginnings of slow rolls of his hips. His hand in my hair stayed glued to my head, the other caught in a fist at his side. He was enjoying it, I could tell, but I wanted to see how far he'd let me go.

I was so busy concentrating on getting that final result, I had stopped paying attention to anything else, other than the hard length wrapped in my hand, beneath my tongue and in my mouth. I think I was getting as much pleasure as he was, because although he was still rolling his hips in a way that made me believe he wasn't even aware of what he was doing, I had started writhing above him. Rubbing myself against the length of his leg, grinding him into the seat beneath us.

A low chuckle competed with his moans of pleasure and in a flash of preternatural speed, he had removed his hand from my hair and placed both hands on my hips, guiding me above him and pressing his hard tip against my sweet centre.

"Hey!" I protested, wanting my lips around his sex again. Wanting to see him lose control.

"I want to be inside you, *ma douce*. I want to watch you come as I spill myself deep within." With those soft, huskily spoken words he lowered me down so slowly onto the tip of him.

He watched my reaction closely, waiting for me to respond. I shuddered above him, closed my eyes and bit my bottom lip, and then he pulled me firmly against his hips, sheathing himself completely inside me.

He groaned, I gasped and we started moving. I couldn't help it. I'd gone from wanting to give him pleasure, wanting to see him lose himself because of my lips and tongue and touch. To wanting, needing, craving my own release and to hell with anything else. A small part of me felt selfish, but he only urged me on with murmured words of encouragement as I ground myself against him. Alternating between lifting up and off his body and then rocking, rubbing back and forward against his hard length.

I lowered myself down to his chest, his arms wrapped protectively, lovingly around me as we rubbed up and down against each other, his hard length moving so sensually inside me, stretching me wonderfully in all the right directions, making my body beg for more.

"Yes," he whispered, hot breath against my ear. "Oh God, yes. You are so sexy, *ma douce*. Let me bring you to orgasm, let me make you come."

His words were like fuel to the fire, my body was burning with desire, a need so raw. I worked myself against him, allowed my body to hungrily seek that release and worshipped the man beneath me as he worshipped me.

"Oh, *ma douce*." I could tell he was close too. Even though we moved together in a way that surely did more for me than it did him, he was still only just holding on to his own release. Waiting for me to find mine. Giving me the time I needed to crest that wave. Not allowing himself to seek his own final pleasure until he had fully satisfied me.

I knew in that instant that I loved this man beyond any shadow of doubt. And that he loved me. His arms wrapped so lovingly about my body. His breath feathering against my cheek in such sweet caresses. His closeness, his smell, his entire presence about me, making me feel so loved and wanted and safe.

I came with a gasp and low moan. My body breaching that final, beautiful wave and floating back down the other side. He groaned loud against me, pumping himself deep inside, pulling me tightly against his chest and savouring the drawn out moment of his orgasm as though it was a miracle, something he treasured and letting me know that it was me who had given him this precious gift. This moment out of time.

He cradled me against his body, letting the sweat on our skin meld between us. From somewhere he found a blanket and draped it over the top of me, wrapping us up in a warm cocoon. I lay my head down on his chest, just under his chin and listened to his heartbeat, took in the feel of his warm body moulded to mine and allowed the scent of him and our lovemaking to wash around me in the darkened space.

After a few minutes, with his hand running through my hair and down my back, I managed to find my voice.

"I still didn't scream out your name."

He started laughing and held me tight. "Give me a minute and I can remedy that, *ma douce*."

I bet he bloody well could too. I raised my head to look out the window to get my bearings. We'd only made it as far as Huntly, so there was still an hour before we hit Auckland.

"There is still time, my little one and I intend to use every single second of it appropriately."

I gave up arguing and just snuggled in closer, wrapping my arm and leg over him. I had slid down between him and the back of the seat and felt totally safe and warm and protected.

"How many vampires are going with you?" I asked, taking him by surprise at the change of subject. I don't think he'd wanted to talk about the coming trip to America, but I hadn't been able to stop thinking about it, despite the beautiful distraction he had just provided.

He took a deep breath in and accepted the topic change gracefully. "I have fifty of my line, some already have gone on ahead, some are flying with me. Gregor, Enrique and Alessandra are providing a similar amount and Awan has also sent 30 of the Egyptians to meet us there. We have the numbers and the skills required, *ma douce*. It won't be exactly easy, it never is, but it is more than achievable. I have complete faith in the outcome."

I was relieved at the figures and even more relieved that Awan had joined the battle as well. The Egyptians were formidable warriors and now that it had been proven that Nosferatins were being held hostage and the Prophecy could be affected, he had finally made that commitment to us. A tenuous alliance, unlike what we had experienced with Egypt's former vampire Queen, Nafrini, but a welcome one all the same.

"Where will you land?"

"We are all arriving by smaller private jets, so have managed to secure an isolated landing strip near Denver. Some of those already in position are spreading out and providing intelligence for us. By the time we land, we will have a very good idea of what we face and where he wants us to battle."

"He'll be expecting you and have a location already in mind, won't he?" I couldn't help feeling they were walking into a trap, but what could we do? Jonathan held all the cards, not to mention all of the Nosferatins too.

"Yes, we will only find what he wants us to find, but we are not inexperienced in this type of warfare, *ma belle*, all of us have fought calls to arm before."

"But not fought Jonathan."

"No. Not Jonathan." His hands started roaming over my body again, his face nuzzling into my hair. I knew he was trying to distract me, to make me think of something much more pleasant than the risks ahead, the possible deaths that might occur, the loss of so many.

He'd have to work harder.

He laughed out loud at that thought. "I can work harder, *ma douce*," he murmured, shifting position so he was looking down at me, still to the side, but allowing me more room to lie on my back. There's a surprisingly large amount of space in a Land Rover Discovery 4's back seat.

This time he took it even slower, so very, very slow. As though he was discovering my body for the very first time. Or maybe, the very last.

"Shush. Don't think that," he whispered against my lips, then kissed me, so carefully, so perfectly, so softly.

His hands painted beautiful pictures on my body, his fingers trailing patterns across my skin, his lips lighting a path in their wake. It was wonderful, sublime, splendid and I never wanted it to end.

By the time we joined body to body, in a slow languid movement, his whispered words of *you are mine* floating away into the ether, the world had stopped moving around us, nothing mattered but here and now, him and me, this moment, this sensation, this union of two bodies and hearts and souls. I loved this man with every single part of me, the realisation of how deeply ingrained that was in my soul making tears slowly seep out from my eyes and trail down my cheeks, to be swiftly caught by Michel's lips and tongue and hot, hot breath.

I knew what I wanted to do then, I knew it with a certainty that rocked me to my core. I even let my Light build within me, shaped it, moulded it, held with such care. I let him see my intention, but I held it back at the last second, conscious still, despite the moment, of how very much I wanted him to have more than just me to come home to, more than just survival to consider, but the promise of something he had wanted so fiercely for so very long. My mark. My *Sigillum*.

"Come back to me and it is yours," I whispered against his cheek, then let the Light wash around us, wrapping him in my love and promise and showering us in my desire and passion and need.

He started murmuring words in French, too fast, too hurried for me to translate, too emotional to stop his accent from seeping through. I didn't care, I didn't need to know the exact words or phrases he uttered against me, I felt what he meant through his touch and care and movements. I felt what he meant through the glorious wave of heat he took us up and finally, after such attention and restraint and beautiful, beautiful emotion, over, in a burst of complete and resounding bliss, wrenching a gasp from my lips and a softly whispered, but extremely uneven, "Michel!"

We lay still for several minutes, neither of us able to pull away from the embrace, from the moment. His body still lying so carefully over mine, between my legs, inside me. Our breathing in time with each other, our heartbeats synchronised, our souls truly as one.

Finally, Michel whispered against my neck, in a very masculine sounding voice, full of amusement, happiness and vindication.

"Now *that* is a tone I can accept."

I smiled, thinking how very typical, he hadn't needed a shout or a scream. He hadn't even needed the titillating thought that others may hear me, he just needed me to let go, to give in to the moment, to express in some fashion, what he does to me. The effect he has on my body, heart and mind.

It really wasn't that difficult to give him, was it?

"*Je t'aime, ma douce. Je t'aime si tres, tres beaucoup.*"

I swallowed past the lump in my throat and whispered back, "I love you too."

We stayed wrapped in each others arms, just kissing and cuddling for the remainder of the trip. When the lights of the city began to invade our little sanctuary Michel reluctantly retrieved our clothes from the front of the vehicle and we dressed; silently, slowly, a little sadly. Neither of us wanted this time together to end.

But it had to. And as the bright lights of Auckland International

Airport streamed in through the windows of our car, reality hit and my stomach flipped and my hands started wringing in my lap. Michel reached over silently and took hold of them in his, softly rubbing the back of them, but unable to voice what he was thinking or feeling, just like me.

The car pulled up in front of his private jet and the hangar it was usually tucked up in, the fuel truck rumbling away and the pilots doing their pre-flight external checks. Michel's guard got out of the car and stood by the door, but didn't open it, just stood there taking in the scene before him, watching for threats and no doubt communicating with the rest of Michel's line already on board and standing out around the brightly lit area. I noticed my BMW off to the side - so Erika had made it, although I couldn't see her anywhere to wish her well or goodbye.

"I must go, *ma douce,*" Michel said softly, lifting my hand to his lips for a lingering kiss. "You do not have to wait for the plane to leave, I can walk you to your car and you can just drive away, if it is easier."

It would have been, I think. Still painful, but easier than watching him board that bloody machine and see the doors slam shut, so tightly, so finally and watch that sleek jet taxi out on the runway and then lift off into the sky, defying gravity and all reason. It would have been a hell of a lot easier, but I couldn't. I couldn't be the one to leave.

I shook my head and managed a small smile.

His lips twisted. "My brave, brave girl."

The door opened, no doubt from a telepathic command from Michel to Dennis and he led the way out into the night. His vamps becoming immediately alert, some of them gliding on to the plane, some remaining scattered about for his protection. Marcus and Matthias flashing over to the Land Rover, I was guessing they would be following me home.

I looked a little rumpled, I was sure of it, but Michel just looked like Michel. He reached in and grabbed his jacket and tie from the rear of the car, slipping his arms in the sleeves and hanging the tie around his neck. His shirt not completely buttoned up, some of his glorious cream coloured chest peeking out at the top. He looked well sated and relaxed and extremely sexy.

As much as I was determined to stay and watch him leave, there was no way in hell I could walk him to those stairs. He knew, so just pulled me into one last embrace, one last long, deep kiss and then spun and left without another word. What else was there to say?

They didn't muck around once he was on board, God knows if they had clearance to taxi out yet, but Michel would have commanded the pilots to move regardless, for me, probably even for him. The plane slid smoothly along the tarmac, off into the distance and within less than two minutes had left the ground. I stifled an almost hysterical laugh at the thought that the commercial flights all gave way to the Master of the City and then slowly slid down the side of the Land Rover, to land in an undignified heap on the ground.

My *M & M* buddies didn't say a word, just stood by in formation, backs to me, fronts facing any threats and let me have my moment of utter loss alone.

Five minutes later and I was done. I stood up and brushed myself down - useless, I still looked like a woman who'd had way too much sex in the back of a car - and cleared my throat.

"I'm going for a drive."

They just nodded, Matthias walking beside me to my car, Marcus starting the Land Rover. Then once I slipped in to the familiar seat and brought the engine to life, Matthias flashed away and they followed me out of the airport.

I had no idea where I would head or what distance I would travel, but after making it as far as Orewa, just North of Auckland and realising I still had a couple of vamps faithfully following behind some distance, regardless of the approaching sun, I did an illegal U-Turn and high tailed it home.

It was time to face the music, or at the very least, the impossibly long and painful wait for news.

Oh God, I missed him so much.

31
FAMILY

The house was quiet, really quiet. No Erika. No Michel. Only the two personal guards who flashed in the door behind me, beating the first of the sun's rays. And hopefully somewhere Amisi. Oh, and Samson. I could feel Samson downstairs, not like I sense vamps normally, more of an awareness, a connection I still wasn't quite used to. When I tested that connection, I got a surprising answer back, kind of like an acknowledgement of my tug on the line that spread between me and my vampire. Freaky.

I shook it off and said good night to Marcus and Matthias, who looked like they could do with a breather, the race against the light along Tamaki Drive having frayed the last of their nerves and then I went in search of Amisi. I could certainly do with a friend.

I found her in the office, on-line, using Michel's computer. He wouldn't have minded, it was more of a communal computer anyway, we all tended to use it.

"Hey," I said and threw myself into the chair opposite the desk.

"Hey, yourself. How'd it go?" She sat back and ignored what was on her screen, giving me her full attention. That was Amisi, she always made you feel like you were the most important person in her world, regardless of any interruption you might have caused.

"Mum and dad freaked, then got won over by Michel's superior parent wrangling skills and I found out a bit more about my biological parents and came away feeling pretty centred." I paused, gathering myself. "And now I need a distraction." It was the best I could do. I just couldn't put into words the loss I was feeling having just watched Michel leave - and truth be told, I really thought the best approach was to just ignore it altogether and get on with day to day life. At least until we started getting reports back from America.

"I understand," she said, switching the computer off. "I was just catching Citysider up on what was happening. There's not much he can do from where he is, but his kindred has offered support if it's needed. Michel seemed to think it wasn't."

I agreed, from what Michel had said, he had the numbers, it was just a matter of handling whatever tricks Jonathan threw their way.

Amisi shifted in her seat and suddenly looked a little uncomfortable. I had a bad feeling she was about to drop a bomb. It never rains but it pours, that's for sure.

"OK. Spit it out," I demanded, crossing my arms over my chest in preparation. She really did look uncomfortable.

"Gregor phoned."

"He didn't go to America with the others?" I'd just assumed all the first level masters had gone. Enrique and Alessandra had definitely gone, as had Michel of course.

"No, he stayed behind so there was a Master of the City in New Zealand. A safeguard, I think. He and Michel must have planned it that way."

It made sense, like the American Families, Michel and Gregor wouldn't want to throw everything into the call to arms, leaving a core contingency here for protection of their territories was a prudent move. And it's not like Michel could have stayed behind, the call to arms was directed towards him.

"Yeah, so he's still in Wellington and he's got a bit of a problem. There's been an influx of rogue vamps, three Norms so far have been killed, he fears there's going to be more."

Shit, that wasn't good. Amisi had been going down to Wellington at least once a week, for there to have been that many attacks since her last visit was unheard of. It needed investigation and it needed a Nosferatin.

"You gotta go," I said, making it easier on her. She had no choice, she had to go when Gregor asked, she was officially his city's Nosferatin, despite living with me here in Auckland. Her staying was only a temporary measure, as soon as the Prophecy was fulfilled, she'd be gone for good.

"I'm sorry. I know you need me right now. I wish I didn't have to go."

I held my hand up to stop her. Yeah, I needed a friend, but we also had responsibilities and maybe it was for the best. I'd probably lean on her too much if she was here, now I'll just have to get my mojo on and deal with the separation by myself. The power of one.

"Nah. It's all right, Amisi. You have to go and I'll be fine. When do you leave?"

"I'm heading out to the airport now. Gregor's jet has just returned from dropping off some of his line in America and swung by here to pick me up on the way down the line. It's either hitch a lift with them or go Air New Zealand domestic. I'm kind of strapped for cash right now."

Hell, I hadn't even thought about that. I was no longer pulling a salary from the bank, having taken extended leave, but I did have a little bit tucked away. Amisi, on the other hand, had never had a job and although her parents sent her money, I knew it wasn't much. Both she and I had been living a fair bit off Michel's good grace, not that he would have had it any other way. Still, I think Amisi was of the same mind as me. As soon as this Prophecy shit was over, we were both going out to work.

"You need anything?" I asked, knowing she wouldn't take money, but maybe there was something I could help her with.

"Nah. Gregor's putting me up, I get a free flight, I think I'm set."

"You're staying with Gregor?" Now that would have been entertaining to watch.

She gave me a good hard glare. "Purely professional."

"If you say so," I said, getting up from my chair and dodging the pen she threw at my head just in time. "Hey! I'm just saying."

"Whatever!" She retorted, but I could see the smile. She was amping to get down to Wellington, I could tell.

I let her off lightly though, with just a few taunts before she headed out the door. She'd called a cab before I had made it home, not sure if I was going to make it in time, so refused my offer of a lift. That meant, within half an hour of getting back in the house I was, in essence, alone.

Marcus and Matthias and Samson, all out for the count, or as much as vampires do during daylight hours and I was left to rumble about the house in silence. After a few rounds of pacing, unable to settle enough for a sleep, I opted for a workout in the gym downstairs. No point wasting the day away.

An hour and a half later, covered in sweat and just winding down on the treadmill, Samson walked in.

"Mistress," he acknowledged quietly, standing just inside the doorway, a little uncertain, I think, of how to proceed.

I switched the treadmill off and grabbed my towel to wipe away some sweat.

"You know, you can call me Luce."

He looked at me for a moment and then nodded. I was kind of relieved. I thought he might argue with me on that, vampires tend to like hierarchy and formalities, but at least this meant he had some self respect as well. I *so* did not want a hanger-on with confidence issues. I had enough of those on my own.

"Do you like coffee?" I asked, throwing the towel in the hamper for the house cleaner.

"Yes, I do."

"Follow me then. We have the King of coffee machines upstairs. Let's go have a cuppa."

It was actually not nearly as uncomfortable as I had thought it would be. Samson took half a cup of Long Black a la Lucinda style to unwind and finally we were into a more casual form of communicating. He was still a little formal, but I was guessing that was just all him. He was about 150 years old, meaning he grew up in Victorian London, some things are hard to change. I got the impression that Samson would open doors and rush to the aid of all women at the drop of a hat.

But then again, his previous existence since being turned had not been a bed of roses, nor had he been the gentleman vampire. With all that Dark, I could see why.

"Do you want to go back to London?" I asked, making a second coffee for us both.

"I would like to return one day. I have a debt to pay."

I raised my eyebrows in a question, but he purposely avoided eye contact. Okaay. Personal issue, I could relate.

"Do you need to go back now?" I'd be happy to let him go, it's not like I wanted to be his keeper. We could remain in touch, but he's a big boy. I didn't want him to feel tied to me like a slave.

"I would prefer to stay here and be of assistance."

"You don't have to, you know. You can come and go as you please, as long as you don't get into any mischief that's going to come back and bite me on the arse, I'm happy for you to do whatever pleases."

He watched me finish off the coffees for a moment and when I pushed his second Long Black towards him he nodded, slowly. "That is kind. But for now I will stay."

"Because you think I'm not strong, just like Shane said?" I did not want this vampire to think I couldn't handle myself. He might have been in my line now, but I still didn't know him from Jack. Michel had said that it would be impossible for him to harm me, his sole goal would be to please and protect. I kind of understood what he was saying, but truthfully, I still didn't really get it. It was all bit too mystical and magical to make sense.

"Not at all. I know you are the strongest Nosferatin in the world and I am honoured to have joined your line. I thank you for rescuing me. I stay because I want to." He paused and looked around the room as if seeking divine inspiration or guidance. Finally he must have organised his thoughts enough, because he added, "I feel at peace when I am near you."

All right then. Good to know.

"OK. You are welcome to stay as long as you like, but it's your life, you don't serve me. Obviously you have to answer to me, but only in so much as your actions reflect on me. You are welcome to spend your hours as you please within Michel's guidelines for the city."

"I understand," he replied, still a little formally. "I will seek a role within Michel's business structure. I may have skills that suit his need."

I liked that idea. A vampire who wanted to make himself useful. I also liked how comfortable I was beginning to feel around Samson, even though his language was still stilted, I could see he was completely at ease too. In a short amount of time we had formed, if not a friendship, a bond.

"Sounds good to me. Now I gotta get some sleep." All this talking had finally worn me out. The coffee didn't do it. The exercise didn't do it. But talking to my first vampire *child* wore the shit out of me. Not because it had been hard, but just because it was so new.

I trundled off to the shower in our ensuite bathroom with thoughts of vampire lines and the responsibilities of heads of those families ringing through my mind. No matter which way I looked at it, my life had turned upside down. But, like Michel had said, it wasn't that bad. Sure I was having to open my door and to a certain extent my heart, to these strange vampires – even though there had only been Samson so far, I knew there would be more – but, their connection to me made it seem so much easier. I wanted Samson to be happy and safe and feel welcome and not bound to me like a servant, but content enough to stay for his own reasons.

I knew it would take time to get to know him and any others that came my way, but for some strange reason it didn't seem so hard. Not a mammoth task after all.

I have never been one to have lots of friends around me, I spent my younger years occupying myself on the farm with the lambs for mates. And as a teenager, I had a few girlfriends and later even a couple of boyfriends, but never a bevy of chums surrounding me at any one time. I had thought that was just the way I was, a bit of a loner. But, I'm not so sure now. I have a lot of vampire friends. A lot of Nosferatin friends too. Even a couple of ghouls. And I was once very close to the local Taniwha Hapū. All of which I befriended with ease. I was beginning to see that my lack of friends as a youngster had nothing to do with any inability to connect with another person, but more my natural instinct to avoid Norms at all costs.

With Samson, I understood him. I felt connected to him, not just because we shared a Master/Vampire Bond, but because he was a part of my world. A world that was not normal, nor was it full of normal people. It was different and supernatural and hey, just fine by me.

I had long ago felt like I had come home when I was near Michel. Even before we joined, I felt at ease. Sure, I was still crazy scared of his fangs and his power, but inside, deep down, I was home. Samson, somehow, gave me that sense too.

I crawled under the covers of the bed, pulling Michel's pillow in close to hug and smell. I felt a little sad and lonely, I missed him, like a hole in my heart, but I also felt OK. I could feel Samson downstairs and that connection to someone so a part of me settled my stomach and pulled me back down to Earth. I hadn't expected to be able to draw on Samson so closely. I tried not to analyse it too much and just accept that right now with Michel gone, it was a lifeline I could use.

Surprisingly, or not, it didn't take long for me to drift off to sleep and I'm sure I would have slept the rest of the day away and all of the night, but despite my heavy lids my stomach had other thoughts.

At 7pm, just a half hour before sunset, I woke to a loud grumble. The realisation that Amisi wouldn't be in the kitchen fixing me a delectable treat had me rolling over to try for a few more minutes slumber, but nothing worked to stem the noise. So, washing my face and teeth and quickly dressing in my normal hunter gear, I fled downstairs to whip something up.

It ended up being a sandwich, kind of like the ones Michel makes, piled high with protein and salad and scrummy dressing. I'd made it through most of it when the phone in the kitchen rang. Swallowing the last bite in a mad rush, I picked the handset up before any of the vamps in the house could, expecting Amisi or maybe even Michel, telling me he'd landed and he missed me already.

But it wasn't. It wasn't anyone I had expected at all.

It was him. The one vampire I didn't want to talk to. The one man I never wanted to entertain in any way, shape, or form again.

Jonathan.

And he wasn't on an international call.

32
I JUST CALLED, TO SAY

"**S**weetheart. Did you miss me? I missed you."

I couldn't answer. I couldn't think. Panic washed through me like a tsunami, slamming into my chest and paralysing my body. The phone shook against the side of my head and I could feel my palm, where it held the receiver tightly, become moist and wet with sweat. I knew my breathing had hitched and that, no doubt, Jonathan could hear it. I was playing into his hands to perfection and there wasn't a damn thing I could do about it at all.

"I like your city, sweetheart. So many lovely hidden spots for my men to find entertainment. They are looking forward to becoming more familiar with the local sights this evening. I hope you don't mind, but they intend to have some fun. As do I."

The threat to innocents in my city helped settle my confused and frantic mind, I squashed the almost unbearable sense of panic and sucked in a deep breath. He already knew I was off guard, I didn't care that he heard me trying to rally myself, it was more important to just get some semblance of logical thought processing through my head. I needed to think this through. Where was he? What did he want? What could I do to prevent it?

And most importantly. If he was here, what did that mean for Michel?

"This is a strange way to battle a call to arms, Jonathan. Leaving it to the other Families left in America to honour your reputation?"

He hissed down the line in response. If he had thought I was going to be that drugged out weakling he had held captive for a month, he had another thought coming. I was on familiar territory and I was a Nosferatin by birth. I had already headed into Michel's home office and unlocked the safe, bringing out my stake box and grabbing a couple of extra silver knives and my Svante sword. I hadn't been wearing it lately, just two stakes and one knife inside my jacket, but now I held the phone to my ear with my shoulder and strapped on the extra daggers in thigh sheaths on both sides and began to get into the back sheath that would hold my Svante out of sight. If he wanted a battle, he would get one.

Jonathan pulled himself together quickly and managed a laconic reply. "Sweetheart. I am King, they do what I command."

"So, how many did you leave behind? How many did you think would be sufficient to hold Michel?" If I could get him to divulge some tactical information, it could prove helpful to either Michel or me. Either way, I wanted to keep him talking. I had already left the office and gone back upstairs to the bedroom to retrieve my cell phone from beside the bed. I needed to let everyone know what was happening and quickly. A mass text would do the trick.

He laughed in response. "Never fear, my love. There are more than enough of my kin to occupy your kindred. He shall be well involved before we even conclude this conversation. What were you thinking sending him away? You know how weak you are when separated."

That had me stopping short of the bedside table, my hand outstretched, ready to pick the cellphone up, but now hovering in the space between, a small tremor running through it back up toward my shoulder. The longer I was away from Michel, the weaker I would definitely become, but as soon as he knew Jonathan was here, the quicker he would return to me. He wouldn't stay in America, he would leave that task to Enrique and Alessandra and his men and he would come straight back to me. It would mean only a couple of days apart, that wouldn't have too adverse an effect on our strength. Any longer though and that could be quite different.

I picked the cellphone up and started tapping in a message to send, but answered Jonathan at the same time.

"We have strength to burn, Jonathan. We have spent every second together in each other's arms since my escape from you."

I knew the effect that statement would have on him and I wasn't disappointed. A low, loud growl rumbled down the line, sending a shiver down my spine I couldn't stop. An automatic reaction to all that anger that accompanied the sound, prickling along my skin and wrapping around my throat, the knowledge that he could use his *Sanguis Vitam* on me over the phone, making me have to fight that panic all over again. This vampire was strong and I wasn't sure if I could face him on my own. I needed help.

"You shall pay for your transgressions, Lucinda. You are no one else's, but mine."

I swallowed past the restriction in my throat, not a lump of fear, but the angry prickle of his power slowly constricting my wind pipe.

"I will never be yours," I managed in what sounded decidedly like a squeak. Not exactly the inflection I had been going for.

Just hang up. Just hang up. Just hang up. It was all I could think to end the connection, but my hand couldn't move the phone from my ear in order to hit the end button. It was glued in place with concrete.

"Now, sweetheart, let's not fight. I would like our reunion to be a happy one. I have such plans for our reconnection."

I did manage a shiver at that thought, a genuine reaction of revulsion, not *Sanguis Vitam* induced in the slightest. I knew exactly what Jonathan's idea of *reconnection* would entail and it would not be nice.

My thumb was hovering over the send button on my cell, I had already typed the short message out. Simple, to the point: *Jonathan here in Auckland*. I hit send before he could distract me further. It was done, the cavalry would be on its way. The text was programmed to reach not only Michel's cell phone, but Erika's, Jett's, Gregor's, Amisi's and my two personal guards downstairs. I hadn't yet managed to put Samson's number in my address book, but he wasn't far away. I could just shout.

"So, my love, why don't you come out and play?"

I had no intention of playing with Jonathan, kill maybe, but not play. But I needed to be prepared, there were still too many variables in this little party he had planned, I needed to narrow down specifics.

"What did you have in mind, Jonathan?"

"Mm. I do love it when you cooperate, sweetheart, it swells my heart."

I did not want to think of any part of his body swelling, but I also didn't want to give too much away. If he had no idea anyone else was aware of him being here, so much the better.

"So?" I prompted, as he had gone silent on the other end of the phone. "What did..."

"You have been very naughty, my dear," he abruptly interrupted. "Did you think I wouldn't know you'd call for help?"

As the meaning of his words sunk in, Marcus and Matthias appeared in the doorway to my room, Samson behind them, all of them looking decidedly ready to fight. I held a hand up to stop them talking and returned my attention to the phone.

"What do you mean?" How could he know I had sent texts out? Did he have some way of intercepting my cell?

"You know, Lucinda. You are not playing by the rules and rule breakers must be punished. It pains me, but I will have to set an example and as I have no wish to mar that gorgeous perfect skin of yours again just yet, one of Michel's vampires will have to do. Who shall I pick?"

What the fuck? This was all wrong. He knew too much and he couldn't possibly have one of Michel's vampires already. What the hell was happening here?

"Maybe the big burly one behind the bar. You there! What's your name?" He sounded like he had lowered his phone and was shouting at someone near him. I couldn't hear the answer, but then I don't think I really needed to. The sun had set here in Auckland, all of Michel's vampires left behind would be in his club and the only one near the bar would be Doug. "Doug," Jonathan confirmed that same second. "How unoriginal. So, Lucinda, shall it be Doug or perhaps one of the nine other vampires Michel left behind for your protection? Not many, is it? He really doesn't value your safety, my sweet. I would have ensured you were surrounded by at least 100, in fact, I intend to make sure you always are from now on. You shall never escape again."

The words were out before I even considered the ramifications. "You don't have me yet, Jonathan."

He just laughed, a cocky, self assured, I-hold-all-the-cards laugh. "Don't I?" Then I heard the scream. I couldn't tell who it belonged to, because it was so raw with pain, so high pitched and yet guttural, full of agony and fear. "Doug does make a lot of noise, doesn't he, sweetheart?"

I had lowered myself to the edge of the bed, unaware of what I was doing. The thought of Doug being hurt, tortured, was unbearable. I wanted to run to *Sensations,* to blast through those doors and to stake every offending vampire in that club right now. I felt Samson's hand come down on my shoulder. He could either sense my distress, or more likely, hear what was happening down the phone line and see the effect it had on my face. His presence centred me, allowed me to breathe and made me focus on what was important.

If I was to rescue Doug and Michel's vampires, I needed a plan and a level head.

"So. I think my point is made."

Yes. It had been, hadn't it? But, I don't crumple that easily. Doug was a powerful and old vampire, he could last a little longer I was sure. Where this hard and mechanical thought process had come from, I didn't know, but I did know I needed to be like this to get through what lay ahead.

Just then my cellphone chirped. I glanced down and read the text. It was from Gregor. Short and to the point, just like me. *I'm on my way. Amisi to stay here.* I breathed a sigh of relief. All I needed now was to hear from was Michel or Erika or Jett and I could unclench my heart and actually let it beat.

"Now, I'm sure you can understand the situation, Lucinda. I have all those at *Sensations* imprisoned and will kill them one by one for each hour you delay in getting to me. It's simple, them for you. Are you strong enough to sacrifice these vampires, my love?"

He didn't wait for my reply, but simply ended the call. I listened to the dial tone for a moment and then when the phone went dead dropped it to the floor.

Matthias appeared before me. "We can't reach Michel." I didn't want to hear that. I looked up at him and just stared. "He is shielded somehow, we have no connection and he has not answered your text, has he?" No, he hadn't. "I think we are on our own."

"Gregor is on the way here now." At least that was something. I allowed myself a moment to search for Michel down the Bond we shared and received static in reply. I'm guessing, that's what Marcus and Matthias had got as well. Nothing. No emotions, no sense of well-being or fear or pain or distress. Just white noise nothing.

My cellphone interrupted my downward spiral with a buzz, this time a call, not a text. I fumbled for it off the floor and answered without looking at the number.

"Yes," I demanded, thinking it was Jonathan.

"We're surrounded, it's been well planned," Gregor's voice informed me. "He's cut us off from helping you. Have you heard from Michel?"

My mind was a swirling mass of torment, questions spinning like a tornado through grey matter, slicing at any calm I had left in me and churning up panic and fear in its wake.

"No," I managed.

"Who do you have with you?" He didn't sound surprised or fazed in the slightest, straight into assessment and regroup and no doubt, plan and attack would quickly follow. I wished I had his concentrated reserve.

"My guards, Marcus and Matthias and my vampire Samson," I replied mechanically.

"That's all? Where are the vampires Michel left behind?"

"Jonathan has them."

"Shit!" No more concentrated reserve. "Shit!" he said again to emphasise. I couldn't have agreed more.

"I can't help you, Luce. We are barely holding them off as it is. I'm going to have to help my men soon, we've retreated as far as we can. I'm so sorry." And he meant it, I could tell. There was so much unsaid in his voice, but that didn't mean it wasn't still all there.

"We'll manage," I answered with far more strength than I actually felt. "Take care of yourselves."

I hit end before he could answer. He needed to concentrate on his problems, not on me.

"We're on our own," I told the vampires before me. "If you've got weapons to secure, I suggest you arm yourselves now."

"What do you plan?" Matthias asked, while the other two headed out to saddle up. "You know Michel would want you to protect yourself no matter what cost."

He would. He would rue the loss of so many of his line, but he would be furious at me for trying to rescue them and getting myself caught. Ten vampires at *Sensations* was not a price I was prepared to pay however. I shook my head at him and he just crouched down before me, to look me in the eye.

"What about the Prophecy? With you gone there is nothing to stop the Dark."

"Playing Devil's advocate, Matthias?" I asked, feeling a sense of numbness start to invade my body, hardening my resolve and stealing me from distractions. My father had said it in that letter. I had to do *anything I must* in order to survive, but that I also had to remain *true to myself*. I could not let ten vampires meet the final death because of me, Prophecy or not.

"I don't plan to die, Matthias. And he doesn't plan on killing me. But, he will kill them."

He ran a frustrated hand through his long hair. "So, you're just going to give yourself up to him in exchange for their lives? Then what?"

"I am not without abilities, I will think of something."

"This isn't exactly a plan, Luce. This is suicide." He stood up though and didn't add anything else, just headed out the door to grab his weapons. He was right, I didn't have a plan and I needed one. Three vampires and a Nosferatin against an untold number of Jonathan's men. We may be familiar with the territory, but we sure as hell didn't have the upper hand. I needed an ace up my sleeve.

I grabbed my jacket from a nearby chair, pocketed my cell next to one of the two stakes already in situ inside and headed down the stairs and out towards the Land Rover parked in the drive. Samson and Marcus were already waiting, Matthias followed me out not long afterwards. All of the vampires were heavily armed, not just hidden beneath their clothes, concealed and tucked away, but strapped across their broad bodies and displayed with pride and no doubt, a little threat. Hell, if they weren't sworn to protect me, then I would have felt bloody threatened myself.

"Where to?" Marcus asked from the driver's seat. I'd grabbed the front passenger seat and Samson and Matthias had slipped in the rear.

"Newmarket," I answered. He swung me a puzzled glance but started the vehicle anyway.

"What's in Newmarket?" Matthias asked from the rear.

Hopefully a friend, I thought quietly, but instead said aloud, "A bar. I need a drink."

All three vampires looked at me as though I was mental, as though I had totally lost the plot.

I just smiled and tried to hold the laugh in, getting hysterical right now was not an option. But, I couldn't help thinking, *wait 'till you meet my friend.*

Vampires and ghouls do not play well together. I was hoping Pete would make an exception, if the price was right.

I was also hoping, I had something worthy of payment.

Ghouls did not come cheap.

33
PAYBACK

The trip to *Guts and Glory* was relatively quick, although a fair bit of traffic on the road for a Thursday night, Marcus had the usual vampire driving skills; not only lightning quick reflexes and a heavy foot, but an uncanny ability to avoid traffic snarls and red lights. Dodging down side streets, taking the teeniest, tiniest gaps when presented and generally not having to stop once. It was impressive, if not a little uncomfortable from the front seat.

The entire time I watched wide eyed and nervously spun my wedding ring around my finger, as though the speed I turned the metal could counteract the speed in which we travelled. It didn't. Go figure.

We parked within walking distance of the bar. Newmarket, as usual, being busy but not clogged like the CBD near *Sensations*. It certainly had a whole different feel to it, although only a few kilometres from Queen Street, it was like a completely other world. I had never been a Newmarket groupie. The shopping was good, not just the boutique style shops, but also a nice selection of chain stores to offer an enticement to a wide variety of clientèle. And after dark, bars, bars and more bars.

Guts and Glory is a sports bar. I would have preferred an English Pub or even one of those flash Wine Bars, I know very little about sports. The obligatory plasma TV always displays the most recent All Blacks rugby game, or sometimes a cricket match and on ladies night, the Silver Ferns playing netball. All of which are just games to me, nothing more. But to the patrons of *Guts and Glory* they are Mecca. This was a popular bar, but not just because of the the huge TV and not overly priced beer, but also because it was spotless, pristine, shiny like a brand new toy. Pete did not like a mess in his bar. In fact, if you were caught making a mess, you were lucky to just get evicted. Ghouls took punishment of misdemeanours to a whole new level.

Not that the average Joe knew Pete was a ghoul. Ghouls look like you and me, just well built, strong and quick to anger. Oh, and they like their meat raw, really raw, like practically running raw. Not that they tend to attack too many humans any more, they may not be vampires, but they firmly fall under the *Iunctio*'s rules and therefore under the Master of the City's rules. Ghouls are not allowed to attract attention to our world, so that means dead raw meat and no hunting.

They might grumble and bitch about the restrictions, but the flip side is they can blend in better this way and every ghoul likes to feel useful. A ghoul without purpose is a loose cannon waiting to go off. And my friend Pete here, is the employer of almost every ghoul in the city. Sure they all have day jobs, but Pete is their boss, they answer to him first and Michel second.

I've known Pete pretty much since I moved here. Not that he sought me out, like Michel did, I was just drawn to him. Similar to how I found Rick, my old Taniwha friend. I simply followed my nose and turned up on their doorsteps within days of shifting house. And although they didn't know what I was immediately, they both felt it; the difference, the supernatural thing that is me. And both of them, bless their souls, took me under their wings. Unfortunately Rick turned out to be a bad apple, but Pete has never let me down.

That may be because I'm a good bet. I pay well and I play by the rules. Pete's rules. Ghoul's rules. You see, ghouls are the information highway of a supernatural city. They are the eyes and ears of what's happening at any given time and every decent vampire hunter needs a good source of information. Pete is my man. It's just that his price can sometimes be high and ghouls don't accept hard cold cash. No, their currency is knowledge. And they definitely work on a you scratch my back and I'll scratch yours philosophy.

So, it was with a little bit of trepidation that I led the way into *Guts and Glory*, three vampires at my back. Not only was I not sure if Pete would step outside his information exchange network for me, but I really didn't know how he'd take my companions. As I said, ghouls and vampires don't mix. But, I wasn't leaving them in the car. Protection, protection, protection.

The atmosphere in the bar shifted as soon as we entered, not that there were too many ghouls in the room, maybe about four or five, that I could sense, but enough to change the whole feel of the environment, to tip it out of whack. The Norms would have only felt a slight ominous shift in the attitudes of those around them, not enough to be alarmed by, but enough to make you want to maybe finish your beer and try out the new Irish Pub down the street. Vampires were bad for ghoul business, but only because the ghouls couldn't help reacting to their presence.

I approached the bar carefully, but purposefully. No point beating around the bush. Pete was behind the bar, his favourite spot, the other ghouls dotted here and there. I knew exactly where and how far away and I was betting the vampires behind me did too. I slipped onto a bar stool, my *M & M* guards standing either side behind me, backs to me and fronts to the bar, Samson looming over my shoulder, eyes on Pete. Jeez, Marcus and Matthias had recruited Samson, no longer just a tag team of two, this had progressed to a trio. I shook my head and suppressed the urge to say *down boys*.

Pete didn't waste time finishing with his current customer and sauntered over to me, not a care in the world. Maybe because he has an unprecedented accord with the Master of the City and no longer has to fear any of Michel's vampires controlling his ghouls. Vampires have the ability to command ghouls to do their bidding. Naturally this is a cause for concern for all ghouls, but because of me, Michel showed his softer side and gave Pete and the local ghouls freedom from such manipulation and control. No other ghoul in history has had that kind of exemption to the supernatural rules.

Pete really did still owe me for that one, but I was guessing he'd think the debt had been paid. Any new help would cost me.

"Hey, Pete," I offered with a smile.

"Luce." Pete's a man of little words. What's with all the barmen in my life, they so do not fit the normal bartender persona.

"Can I have a beer?"

"Your usual?" he asked, already pulling on the tap and filling up a crystal clear schooner. I just nodded.

He pushed the cold beverage across to me on a paper coaster and leaned nonchalantly on his elbow atop the bar.

"So, what's up, Hunter?"

Yeah, I kind of deserved that one. I tend to only visit if I am after something, but that's our relationship, there's no point denying it.

"The usual. I'm in trouble and could do with some help."

Pete's eyes did a slow scan over the bodies of my entourage. "Hence the guards. Last time you were here, you just had one."

I raised my eyebrows at him. "Michel is not a guard."

"Yeah, but he'd die protecting you," he replied and I didn't correct him. Michel would actually do everything in his power to stay alive, not out of any self preservation instinct, but because his death would mean mine. It wouldn't bother me too much, except for two reasons; one, I wasn't sure whether his life after death would be in the same location as mine and two, if I die, the Dark prevails. Either option not good enough to shake off this mortal (or in our case semi-immortal) coil. "So where is he?"

Right. Information exchange number one. "Are we on the books?" I asked. It always pays to get your cards out on the table when you start sharing knowledge with a ghoul. There's no point offering up information for free. They wouldn't hesitate to take it, but they'd think you pretty dumb for giving away something that may be precious. Ghouls liked dealing with savvy opponents, not pushovers.

He smiled appreciatively at me. "If you say."

Good enough for me. "America, responding to a call to arms."

Pete blinked slowly, just once and then stilled. "This is not common knowledge, Luce." Michel had obviously kept that quiet. Pete would be wondering why his network of informants hadn't picked up a tasty bit of gossip such as this. I didn't for a second think that Pete wasn't aware that Michel was out of town, but the call to arms was my coup de grace. A bit earlier in the game than I had intended, but sometimes a shock and awe approach does wonders. And really, time was not on my side. My first hour was almost up and Jonathan would be getting testy.

"It's a recent development, in response to my kidnapping."

"Jonathan," he replied. His knowledge of my kidnapper did not surprise me at all. I nodded.

"Not a lot I can do for you in America, Luce. It's a closed shop. My boys are not welcome in amongst that riff-raff." I guessed he was talking about the local ghouls. I didn't need clarification, America wasn't why I was here. I'd had to push the problem, or more to the point, the gnawing fear, of America, aside. I was trusting Michel to handle his end, my worrying would only make what I faced an impossible hurdle to climb.

"I'm more concerned with Auckland right now and that's where I'm hoping you'll fit in." He shifted slightly, into a more comfortable position it looked like, but I didn't miss the inference, it was a clear, *I'm all ears, do tell* kind of move. "Jonathan is here, not in America facing off the call to arms."

"The son of a bitch," Pete muttered. "Cowardly bastard." I whole heartedly agreed, but I knew Jonathan not manning up to his challenge was more of a disgraceful act to a ghoul. They may be bottom feeders on the supernatural ladder, but they were honourable ones.

"Where do we fit in?" Well, that was a promising question, the fact that Pete wasn't hedging any more meant I may have him on board already. No telling though, until I spilled the beans.

"He's got ten of Michel's vampires hostage at *Sensations* and he'll kill one an hour until I give myself up."

Pete just looked at me for a good twenty seconds, then scratched at his short trimmed beard. He flashed his hand open, in a quick sign, something equivalent to a shrug. "Why would this be a concern for me? You wouldn't exchange yourself for ten vamps, Michel would not accept that."

"I'm not Michel and these are good vampires. I will not let them die because of me."

Pete took a deep breath in and blew it out long and slow. "You court danger, you do, Luce. Danger and mess and a whole shit-load of don't-want-to-know. But, I do owe you and I always pay my debts." His big brown eyes caught mine, a flash of something else hidden in those deep sepia pools. "This will leave us even, Hunter." I nodded, I hadn't expected to have had enough news to warrant his help, I had always known the price for his involvement in this would be bigger than any titbit of gossip I could provide. I was just relieved Pete felt obliged to pay back on the accord I had set up. I wasn't entirely sure if his involvement in the battle against Max had covered that debt or not. I guess it hadn't, or maybe he thought the ghouls aiding Michel was not really aiding me. This was a more honourable way to pay back that debt, something important to only me.

"How do you want to play this?" he asked.

"Distraction. Outside the bar, after I go in." Matthias turned on that one, but before he could enter the argument, I gave him *the* look, the back-off-if-you-know-what's-good-for-you look and proceeded to give them all a run down on what I expected.

Once the details had been driven home, we took our leave. Time was almost up and although it would take Pete at least another 30 minutes to gather his ghouls and possibly another 30 to get them all to *Sensations*, I couldn't wait. A vampire, possibly one very close to me, was about to meet the final death. I was officially shit out of luck.

We headed towards Karangahape Road and *Sensations* in silence. I'd made it clear that only Samson and I would go in and the *M & M's* would remain hidden outside. I was betting on Jonathan not being aware of my personal guards, but Samson he would know of, so there was no point hiding him for now. He'd be my escort and Matthias and Marcus would be waiting for the ghouls and acting on the distraction when it was made. Them storming in from the outside may just provide enough chaos for Samson and me to perform a miraculous act of God knows what, to free those vampires and if not stake Jonathan, then at least, get the hell out of there.

We had no intention of parking at *Sensations*, so we stowed the Land Rover a block away and proceeded on foot. Within twenty metres of the premises I pulled up short. Not out of any concern of detection, nor because I desired to suddenly change the plan, but because I felt the pull. That blasted, inconvenient, why-friggin'-now, evil-lurks-in-my-city pull. What was with these arsehole rogues and chomping down right when I was already neck deep in the smelly stuff? An innocent needed help, potentially they could be killed. It is what I am, a saviour of the innocent from the deranged habits of the rogue vampire on the hunt. I couldn't ignore it, it would just get stronger and stronger and harder and harder to concentrate on what I was doing, but a quick glance at my watch told me I didn't have time. Five minutes and Jonathan would be calling my number. So. Innocent versus vampire. Who do you save?

My instincts told me the human. Hell, my inner monologue screamed it at me. But, my heart just couldn't believe a vampire was not as important as a Norm. Just because they are the undead evil creatures of the night, did not mean they didn't deserve to live. Not all of them were Dark and certainly not the vampires currently being held by Jonathan. Doug, Shane Smith, the others whose names I no doubt knew, but couldn't quite remember right now. None of them deserved to die either. So, what the fuck did I do?

I stomped my foot in frustration. A real tantrum throwing move, but I didn't really care, frustration didn't even cover where I was currently at. I let my senses roam and picked up the exact location of the rogue, down Queen Street, near the Town Hall, in the vicinity of the Aotea Square. The closer I got the more accurate I would become, but that was a fairly narrow area and for a vampire hunting another vampire, it might just be enough.

I turned to Marcus. "Aotea Square, one rogue about to eat an innocent. Take care of it and meet Matthias back outside the club when you're done." It was the only solution possible. No one else could barter for the lives of the vampires held by Jonathan, but reluctantly, I had to admit, that someone else could take care of the rogue. It went against every natural instinct I had. The Nosferatin in me wailing a lament at my decision not to hunt. I forcefully pushed that part of me aside. I couldn't be everything to everyone at once. I just couldn't.

Marcus hadn't moved. "What are you waiting for? He's about to be dinner and I'm picking this rogue lacks table manners." They all did, this one would be no different, so time was of the essence.

"I am not leaving you to face Jonathan on your own. The Master would not want this."

Oh shit. Calling Michel the *Master* was pulling the big guns, but I had big guns too.

"One. I will not be on my own." I pointed a finger at Samson and then at Matthias. "And two. Michel is out of the city, which means as his kindred Nosferatin I am in charge of the line. I say do this, this is my command, you will obey." I followed it up with a little Light, a little Nosferatin mojo and watched the expression on his face change from grim determination and defiance, to simple acquiescence and acceptance of my demand. Gotta love vampires and their stupid rules. Not to mention supernatural mojo.

He nodded once and flashed away towards Queen Street, where Aotea Square was located. I didn't wait for the pull to disappear, I simply did not have time. I took a quick look at Matthias, who nodded and seeped into the shadows out of sight and then Samson and I walked the final few metres to *Sensations* and banged on the locked door.

Show time.

34
SHOW TIME

A quick feel with my senses let me know no other vampires were out and about nearby, but there were some thirty inside the bar. One in particular, sent a shiver down my spine and an uncontrolled roll of my stomach. I swallowed past the fear and nausea and straightened my shoulders and lifted my chin.

The door opened all of its own accord and Samson and I walked in. A swift glance about the main clubroom floor let me know Michel's vampires were all on the ground beside the bar, all ten, chained by silver. Doug looking a little worse for wear, but alive and also staring very angrily at me right now, no doubt of the same opinion as *M & M* - I shouldn't be here at all. The rest of Jonathan's men were not all in the same room. Some I sensed down in the cellar, Michel's vampires' accommodation wing and also towards Michel's chamber, in his office and down the hall. I sensed one or two in the garage, maybe waiting for our approach through there, but otherwise, there were still at least a dozen in this room alone. Too many to take on, even for me.

I couldn't see Jonathan, but I sure as hell could feel him.

Samson and I walked into the centre of the dance floor and stood still, waiting. I itched to palm some silver, the Svante sword feeling heavy at my back. I wanted to take heads and hearts and I wanted to do it now. From sheer force of will alone, I held off.

A whole minute passed and nobody said a thing, nor approached us, nor disarmed us either. The room was still, laced with a heavy dose of anticipation and if I wasn't mistaken, a little fear. I sniffed the air to home in on that fear and felt my lips curl when I realised it was Jonathan's men. They'd only ever been around me when I was drugged and even then I had escaped their master's clutches. Now, I was the big bad vampire hunter, the *Sanguis Vitam Cupitor* and all the rest. I was guessing, I was a baby vampire's nightmare, the sort of thing a master threatens their newly turned with if they misbehave. Don't drip blood when you feed or the *Prohibitum Bibere* will call you to them. Watch your manners or the *Lux Lucis Tribuo* will steal your Dark soul.

I started laughing, I couldn't help it.

"What is so amusing, sweetheart? I hardly think it the time to make a joke."

I just laughed harder. Eventually, having to bend over and wrap an arm about my stomach, great big rib cracking guffaws making me have to wipe at my eyes and slap my thigh to try to get it under control. I could feel the uncertainty rise, not only from Jonathan's men, but also Michel's and Samson at my back. *It's all right boys and girls, I haven't totally gone bonkers yet. Just a brief side trip to the loony bin. That's all. Nothing too drastic.*

Finally, I got myself back under control and took a deep breath in and stood up straight. "Shit, that was cathartic!" I exclaimed to the room at large. Then looked Jonathan in the eyes for the very first time.

We just stared at each other for a while and I think he got it. I wasn't scared. I wasn't terrified of the man who had held me captive for a month. Who had drugged me and deceived me and attacked me. I was looking at him with a steely gaze. He was my prey, nothing more. He shifted a little uncomfortably, then tried to hide it with a straightening of his suit jacket and tie. At least he'd dressed for the occasion.

I smiled at his reaction. *You are so mine, meathead.*

"You are late," he said, voice even and well under control.

"And you're a sneaky, lying, good-for-nothing, bloodsucking bastard. We have to make do with what we got."

"You think this is all a game?" His *Sanguis Vitam* filled the room, making bottles behind the bar shatter and the lights sizzle above our heads in response. The buzzing of electricity, combining with the hum of power, coating everything in a hair raising fission of energy threatening to explode at any second.

I let him have his moment, it was all a show and hardly touched me at all, then I filled the room with my calming Light and simply washed his powers aside. As though they were nothing more than a pesky insect, flitting around my head and annoyingly buzzing in my ears.

"You want to play whose is bigger, I got all night, but I'm telling you here and now, I *will* win." I probably said that a little bit more forcefully than I actually believed, but I didn't question my choice of words, I kind of felt a little removed from it all right now and was just along for the ride.

"My, my, Lucinda. You have grown teeth since you left." He flashed me a smile with a whole lot of fang. I didn't move an inch. "You know," he went on conversationally. "It only makes me want to taste your blood again. It was tainted before, not at its best, but I am picking it would be divine now."

I tried not shudder at his words, I knew what he was doing, trying to make me remember all the *good* times we had shared. I knew it was all a ploy, but tell that to my body. I couldn't help the wave of nausea that rolled through me, even as I battled to not let it show.

He spotted it though. He's a predator at the top of the food chain, he didn't miss a thing. It almost felt like my little act of nonchalance and bravado on entering the room had all been dashed to hell. I took a deep breath to settle my nerves and levelled my gaze at him.

He just smiled a knowing smile and didn't that make the anger come rushing back in. Every single friggin' vampire I had ever crossed, including Michel, had that same knowing smile, as though their centuries of living couldn't possibly be beaten by my mere 25 years on Earth. My anger helped centre me and I instinctively let my Light swell within, opening a connection to Nut and drawing on her ancient strength and knowledge. It momentarily surprised me, but then I felt her brush against my shields and wrap me up in her glow. I relaxed into the sensation and weight of all that time, that length of her existence and then let it flow out across the room and smash against Jonathan's internal walls.

"Do you still want a bite?" I asked a little breathlessly, watching the shock and indecision flood his features.

"What are you?" he asked in awe.

OK. *So*, not expecting that question. He knew damn well what I was, who I was, why I was even on this Earth. How could he not? Every vampire knew my destiny. They may not have approved of it, hell, a lot of them wanted to deny me it, but they all knew. Including him.

"I'm guessing that's a rhetorical question. You know damn well what I am."

He pulled himself back together, brushing aside my answer with a flick of his hand and walked over to the bar, managing to find an unbroken bottle and glass and pouring himself a stiff drink. Very civilised, very normal. Huh.

"Would you like one?" he asked, offering me the glass.

I ignored his question. Alcohol wouldn't have been a good idea right now, my brain was already functioning on so many different levels it wasn't funny, throw alcohol into the mix and you'd have a cocktail of disastrous proportions. I could feel the pull down in Aotea Square, Marcus had still not taken out the rogue. I was constantly testing my connection to Michel and getting back zip for all the effort it took. And then there was my connection to Samson, my sense of all the vampires good and bad in the room and a slow realisation that I was feeling more.

My *Prohibitum Bibere* powers were humming in the background, as though they sensed an imminent threat and attack. *Please Nut, not now.*

I rolled my shoulders to shift the feeling of dread, while Jonathan returned his attention to the drink in front of him.

"You and I have business to discuss, Lucinda. These vampires for your return to me. I gather, by your presence, that is an acceptable exchange."

Not hardly. A stake through your rotten heart and the release of the vampires seemed far more appropriate, but beggars can't be choosers.

"You leave me little choice," was all I actually said.

"Yes. That was the plan. Still, it is not a bad thing, is it? Being with me? I did take care of you."

I was beginning to think Jonathan was mad. Stark raving, certifiable, loony bin, kind of mad. Did he really live in a dream world where he and I could be together, happily ever after? You had to wonder, he never gave up on the charade.

"At the risk of stating the obvious. You drugged me. You held me against my will. You attacked me. How is that taking care of me?"

"Lucinda," he mock pleaded and then took a few steps toward me. I stiffened in response. "I had no choice. It was either that or let her kill you. I didn't want you to come to me against your will, that defeats the purpose of my revenge, I needed you to come willingly, before I crushed your soul. But my hands were tied." I realised then just what Jonathan was playing at. This was where it all started, right here in *Sensations*, where I had turned him down and treated him with contempt. He was exacting his revenge for my spurning him. This was personal, but not intimate. This would hurt.

And then he said something, that considering everything else bizarre that had spilled from his mouth, took me utterly by surprise. "I saved you, sweetheart. You should be thankful for my help."

"You are mad," I said matter of factly. "Completely and utterly bonkers."

He looked a little aggrieved then. "It is for your own good, my love. She is not to be taken lightly, her powers are phenomenal. You would not stand a chance and I cannot lose you now." He placed his drink carefully on a table to the side and then reached in his pocket and withdrew a syringe. My heart did a flip-flop, my stomach wasn't nearly as delicate in its tumble and churn. I knew that syringe would hold the very same drug he had used on me before. I felt sweat break out all over me and a fine shiver start to invade my muscles, making me clench my fists in a pathetic attempt to still the shaking from consuming me.

If it wasn't for Samson's warm, soft hand touching my shoulder, I would have collapsed on the floor. I took a precious few seconds to draw on his strength, down the connection we shared and then did the only thing I could think of to stall for time. I started rambling.

"What about our deal? The vampires for me. Let them go first, Jonathan. Then I'll do whatever you want without a fight. That would be better, wouldn't it? No hassles, just you and me, the way you want it."

He took another step closer, both Samson and I took one back. But a quick glance over my shoulder told me we only had another one, maybe two, of those retreating steps available to us, before we ended up in the clutches of Jonathan's men.

"They would continue to provide a threat until we leave. I will release them, sweetheart, you have my word. You did come when asked after all and I am a reasonable vampire. But, they won't be released until I can guarantee our safe exit."

I scrambled my thoughts as quickly as I could, before Jonathan took that next step closer. This was simply a dance and sooner or later, I would run out of moves to use. But, I couldn't give in just yet. A few more minutes and Pete would be in place, but if those drugs were already on board, I would be as good as useless. Memories forgotten, lost in a sea of don't know.

"What about Michel and the others in America? You haven't told me what's happening there. If you want my full cooperation once we leave here, you have to promise they will be safe from harm."

He laughed dangerously and cocked his head. "Sweetheart, you won't even remember your kindred when we leave here." He lifted the syringe and wiggled it between his fingers in a blatant taunt. "Besides, I have plans for Michel, that do not include his release, nor his safety from harm."

"What... what do you mean?" I wasn't thinking nearly as clearly as I should have been, the pressure of the moment, the threat of that horrid memory stealing drug, the pull and the buzz and the hum of whatever the hell my powers were numbly trying to tell me, were making me a jumbled bag of nerves. From standing my ground so solidly when we arrived, I was barely keeping my head above the water now.

Jonathan stepped closer, but Samson held me still. Obviously

Jonathan's men had moved in from behind, we had no more room for retreat.

"Do you not remember, Lucinda? How sick you became without your kindred near? I will not make that mistake again. His nearness, when needed, will keep you healthy and that will keep you strong enough for my revenge."

Oh. Not good. Not good at all.

"You won't hold him. He's too powerful, he's surrounded by warriors who would die for their master before they let you capture him." I couldn't believe that Jett or Erika would allow anything such as this horrible outcome to occur. They would simply throw themselves on silver stakes in a effort to let him escape. And unlike me, he would take it, their sacrifice for him. It's not that he's unfeeling, but he is Nosferatu. Survival at all costs.

Jonathan smiled, a sad smile. Why? I didn't really know, but I kind of got the impression, I wouldn't want to know either. Shame he didn't feel the same way as me.

"My darling, Lucinda. Do you think I haven't planned for all contingencies? Do you really think, the King of the American Families would not have an ace up his sleeve? Or more appropriately, a spy. This has not been a flight of fancy. This has been a passion of mine since the moment I met you on this very dance floor so long ago. Fitting, that it ends here. This is where it all began, after all."

One more step closer, one less beat from my dying heart.

"Who is the spy?" I asked numbly. Running out of time. Running out of options. Running out of courage.

"She has been very useful, if not demanding, but I fear disclosing her identity right now would be a little rash. She may still have some tricks of her own. I don't entirely trust her. She has proven slippery in the past."

I couldn't think who he was referring to. He'd mentioned a female before, one who had insisted on me being drugged, who would have killed me if he hadn't have complied. I had no idea if this was all a ruse, or a trick of his own, but if not, then I could only assume the female he referred to as the spy and the female who had threatened my life, were one and the same. But who? Alessandra? It would make sense, she was more than capable of such treachery, but that didn't help me right now. Jonathan had taken the last step and stood right before me, an arm's reach away.

Samson stepped in front of my body as a shield, but Jonathan only laughed.

"Do you wish me to kill your child, sweetheart?"

"Stand down, Samson," I heard myself say. He didn't move. I lifted my hand to pull on his sleeve and found myself on my knees on the floor.

What the fuck?

It took a moment for me to sort out the sensations; the pain, the fear, the dread, the surprise. The realisation of the truth.

Samson knelt down next to me, as did Jonathan. The latter being close enough to strike with that needle he still held firmly in his grasp, but he didn't. At the same time as Samson asked if I was OK, Jonathan did too.

"What is it, Lucinda? What is wrong?"

I swallowed twice before attempting to answer, my breath a ragged gasp in my chest, my heart frantically trying to escape out of the pulse at the side of my neck. I curled my body against the onslaught, my shields shattering, my mind invaded and threatening to explode. My hands came up to the sides of my head and I screamed and screamed and screamed. I couldn't fight this, I couldn't possibly win. I wasn't strong enough and she was too much for me.

"Lucinda!" Jonathan shouted, dropping the syringe to the floor and using both hands to hold me by the shoulders and shake.

It helped, a little, the pain of his grip and the disorientation of my head lolling back and forward as he shook, managed, somehow, to loosen her hold. I felt an unusually powerful presence in my mind then, frantically building my metaphysical walls. I knew this signature, I had felt it in my head before, but I simply couldn't place it. Not right now, not when so much was happening all around me.

As my shields were hastily erected and I felt that new presence casting her out of my mind and slamming the door behind her, I heard a male voice say, *It is all I can do for now, child. Use the time I have given to gain your strength, she is near and you must face her now, or all is lost.*

Who are you? I asked inside my head. Friend or foe? Good or bad? Dark versus Light?

You know me, we once fought side by side. My promise to your mother has been kept, now keep yours and hold the Dark dear.

With that he was gone, but not before he washed my body with his own Light, so bright, so strong, so much more than even mine. As big as Nut, as powerful as the strongest vampire, as warm and loving as a father to their child.

One name rang out in his absence. *Ambrosia*. He was the Ambrosia. A member of the *Iunctio's* council, an ancient vampire who had once stood beside me as we battled an attack on the Champion's life, the leader of the *Iunctio's* council.

He had been in my head at that time too, that's why he felt familiar. And he had spoken to Nut through me. Shit. I'd forgotten the old vampire, but I couldn't forget the Light that shined in him. He was brighter than some Nosferatins I know. Nut had called him father and that is exactly what he felt like right now. A protective parent, looking out for his child.

I didn't waste time gathering myself, he'd given me a reprieve, I wasn't going to throw it away and let Jonathan use it. I quickly rolled over and picked up the syringe pushing the plunger all the way down and making the drug spill out onto the polished concrete floor. Jonathan's frantic movements to stop me, told me everything I needed to know. He didn't have another immediately on him, no doubt he could get more given time, but now, as they say, his time was up.

With the force of 100 tonnes of TNT the back half of *Sensations* crumbled to the ground in a hail of bricks and mortar, dust and debris. Coughing through the carnage, my hand firmly in Samson's as he led me across the dance floor, somehow managing to find Michel's vampires despite the lack of vision, I knew Pete had gone for bust.

As far as distractions go, he wasn't pulling any punches.

Chaos reigned, ghouls stormed in and vampires good and bad, began to fight.

And all I could feel was her presence, near the rogue and Marcus, down in Aotea Square, calling, beckoning, teasing.

The Queen of Darkness had come for me and she wanted to play.

35
ESCAPE

Locating Michel's vampires in amongst the mayhem of falling masonry and attacking vampires was one thing, releasing them from their chains of silver, a whole other. It took precious minutes to unbind each vamp and even when one was free, his recovery from the effects of silver was too steep to aid in releasing the others. Samson and I were on our own, the ghouls holding off Jonathan's men and Matthias AWOL. I couldn't even sense him and I had the feeling something bad may have, in fact, transpired.

Bad. Ha! That was a laugh. Right now bad would have been OK, what we had could definitely be classed as up shit creek without a paddle.

I'd just managed to undo the last vampire in the row, Samson was still working on his final prisoner, having a little more of a challenge with silver than I, when the vampire in front of me squawked. His eyes went wide, saucer wide and before he had a chance to shout a warning, I was pulled back into the swirling dust cover by a hand in my hair.

Bloody hell it hurt. My hands instinctively went up to try to grab my hair back, or at least get a grip between my scalp and the fist that had a hold of most of my hair. A barrier to ease the pain, but whoever it was, was holding on tight and dragging me from the scene at high speed.

I struggled and kicked and when I realised I couldn't get a hand in my hair to ease the stinging pain of having it almost wrenched out, I started whacking at the body over my shoulder, in a flurry of flailing arms and slapping palms. He didn't stop, nor even attempt to shield himself from my blows, he ignored everything I did to him as though possessed and on a mission from God. I changed tactics - a fighter has to adapt to challenging situations - and started trying to grab hold of tables and chairs and door jams to halt our retreat.

That slowed us down, but didn't stop our increasing distance from the battle that raged in the bar. And instead of going out the front of the building, the path of least resistance, but undoubtedly the one swarming with ghouls and now Michel's freed vampires, we were heading out the back, across fallen walls and ceilings and rubble the size of Mt Cook.

God dammit. Not only was my head screaming for release, but now I was covered in the criss cross of scrapes and bruises from jagged concrete and the odd reinforcing bar. And still I couldn't stop our retreat.

Finally, we emerged in the garage, or what was left of it. The vampire holding on paused, no doubt considering his next move, so I took advantage and elbowed him hard in the stomach, twisting in his grip and ignoring the several strands of hair that came out during the motion and prepared to whack him across the face.

"Hold still, sweetheart. I've got to find us a car."

"I am not your sweetheart!" I countered. I'd known it was Jonathan as soon as he'd grabbed my hair, but I'd refused to allow myself to acknowledge it. The longer I believed my assailant to be anonymous, the stronger I was able to be. No such luck now, the creep had opened his mouth and removed all shadow of doubt.

He ignored me and with his arm now wrapped around my waist, hauled me off the ground and ran across the car tossed space, to the very end where one of Michel's Land Rovers had miraculously survived the ghoul attack. Reaching into his jacket pocket, I had moment of abject fear - thinking a syringe would be revealed - and was unbelievably relieved to see only handcuffs, which is why I was too slow lashing out with my fist before he managed to handcuff both my hands to the hand rail inside the passenger side door.

In a second he was around the driver's side and starting the vehicle with a simple hand motion over the ignition. Vampires would make great car thieves, no need for any tools.

"Where are you taking me?" I demanded over my shoulder, trying to glare at him, but the position of the hand rail and both my arms, making it damn near impossible to face him straight on.

"Away from here. She is close and I will not have her kill you."

OK. I sympathised with the notion, but...

"Who the fuck is she?" I'd had enough of guessing. I wanted answers.

"She rules the Dark, Lucinda. She wants us all. Every Nosferatu, every Nosferatin, she wants us all cloaked in Dark."

"The Queen of Darkness," I breathed, feeling that pull, that enticing attraction to where she waited at Aotea Square.

"I don't know if she is a Queen, but she is the strongest vampire I have ever encountered. And the Darkest."

"Who is she then?" I couldn't believe I was having a somewhat civilised conversation with Jonathan, but then he was driving me away from the evil Darkness that was spreading out through Auckland CBD, like a fog on an early autumn morning, swallowing up all the scenery in its path.

"I don't know her name, I'm not even sure if the woman I met is her true identity. She was cloaked in more than just *Sanguis Vitam* when we met. And she also... wasn't exactly there."

"Well, that's helpful, Jonathan. Really descriptive. And you think we can just out run this uber-powerful vampire?"

"I'm willing to give it a go, for now. Until I can get another dose of the drug into you, it's the best shot we have."

That fucking drug. "Good luck with that," I muttered, then uselessly rattled on the handcuffs holding me tight.

He laughed and ran a shudder-worthy hand over my thigh, thankfully removing it to negotiate a difficult intersection.

"I told you, you are mine and I always take care of what is mine.

With the drug on board, you are separated from your Prophesied powers, she can no longer sense you, nor find you. Nor do you provide a threat to her goals. She will give up hunting you, just as she did when you were drugged before. As I said, sweetheart, I have no choice. It has to be this way."

"There are always choices," I said absently, trying frantically to think of a way to get out of the damn cuffs and sliding my stake into his broad chest.

"Yes. There are. But, the drugs have the added bonus of making you forget your previous existence and fall into the present. I am your present. The only reason it failed before was the loss of connection to your kindred and I have him now. So things will go according to plan."

He sounded so sure, so positive, that Michel was his and I didn't want to believe him, I so didn't want it to be the case at all, but I couldn't sense Michel and that would only mean one thing. He was shielded to me, most likely by a combination of silver and drugs. I closed my eyes and tried to push the pain of that thought away. How the hell did he get Michel? Michel, a level one master vampire, Master of a City, joined to the most powerful Nosferatin in the world. How the hell, did Jonathan get the upper hand?

I concentrated on my Light, on my Nosferatin powers and on the powers of our Bond. If it was likely I was going to be drugged soon - and although I intended to make that as difficult as possible for Jonathan to achieve, I wasn't so cocky to believe it wasn't a viable outcome - then I would use the time I had left to send what I could to my kindred. If he had a boost in powers, maybe it would be just enough to get himself free.

I let the Light build inside me until I felt it bursting at the edges of my skin, I vaguely heard Jonathan exclaim something next to me, his firm grip on my shoulder, a shout in my ear, but I was too wrapped up in my Light to really notice and when I could hold it no longer, I let it out, down that connection, that Bond to Michel. And before I knew it, I was hurtling down that Bond myself and slamming into a wall. My body ached from head to toe, as though I had been literally thrown against a brick building, the full force of the impact rattling in my bones. My head throbbed, my back felt like it had been split in two, my chest was bursting with a frantic need to breathe and my stomach gave an almighty heave, but thankfully held its contents. And then the wall shattered.

And I fell on the ground at Michel's feet.

Despite the aches and pains throughout my body, I was up and crouching, a silver stake already in my hand. My gaze took in the scene around me immediately. Michel, chained by silver, hanging against a plastered wall. Welts around his wrists, where the chain securely held him, his arms above his head, stretched out on either side. More chains and welts around his neck and again at his ankles, spreading his legs to form a star fish against the wall. He was naked and had marks and cuts and deep gashes all over his skin. The blood slowly dripping down his body and into a pool on the floor.

So much blood.

I shook my head to clear the frozen image of a bedroom full of blood, a mattress floating in a sea of red and forced myself to continue to take in the rest of the environment around me. We were alone, in a small, unfurnished room. I sent my senses out and could feel vampires all around us. Some of them ours and some of them clearly not. We were outnumbered and out gunned. I could feel all of Michel's vampires in a similar situation as him. Chained, silvered, compromised.

Except one.

Erika.

I couldn't understand why she was free, but I didn't have time to think about it right now. I glanced down at my body, it looked normal, corporeal, me, but I had a feeling I was kind of Dream Walking, although I had never Dream Walked down the Bond connection to Michel before, so this was all very much new territory. I couldn't rely on my usual Dream Walking skills; invisibility, no smell, or sound, or the ability for vamps to sense me. I hoped it was like a Dream Walk, but I couldn't be sure, so time was of the essence.

I stood up and returned my attention to Michel. He looked unconscious, maybe even retreated into that place vampires can go to when threatened, when trying to conserve their energy, or appear non-threatening to an enemy. He wasn't breathing, there was no pulse, he was supernatural still. But I could feel him in front of me, despite not being able to feel him when back in my body, here I could feel it all. He wasn't drugged, so maybe the room itself was the shield. It didn't matter, the relief of him not being drugged was enough to make me smile like an idiot, regardless of how much shit we were still neck deep in.

I didn't know how much time this latest Dream Walk-like moment would give me, so I rushed over to the chains and began frantically trying to undo them. Before I'd fumbled for less than a minute, I knew I couldn't free him without a tool. They were padlocked and beyond finger manipulation. I groaned in frustration and bit my lip.

"Use the Bond, *ma douce*," came Michel's weakened voice, as though he was talking from so very far, far away.

"Michel?"

"Use the Bond, it will overcome any obstacle to get to me."

I had forgotten that the Bond could do that. It allowed us to stay connected over distance, to overcome any hurdle to get to our kindred despite how far away they might be or how trapped they could be kept. I closed my eyes, with my hand over one of the locks and tried to home in on the Bond, or whatever it was that connected us. Nothing happened, not even a tingle. Maybe I wasn't trying hard enough? Maybe I needed to think of a magic word? Open Sesame. Abracadabra. Kazam. Nothing. Zip. Not a thing.

"Breathe, *ma belle*." Michel actually laughed. Damn him, silvered and chained, he still managed to laugh at me. "Just relax and breathe, it will do the rest."

I took a deep breath in and when I released it, the padlock clicked open and the silver chain unravelled releasing his arm. He groaned as the silver slid against his raw skin and his arm moved stiffly down to rest against his chest. I made quick work of the rest of the locks and when he was finally free, he stumbled forward into my arms, both of us collapsing to the floor.

"I am weak. I need blood." I knew he could feed from me when Dream Walking, although he couldn't really see me, once a vampire had me in their arms, they had no problem finding a vein and biting deep. I could be drained, killed, while Dream Walking. It had its advantages, but it wasn't completely safe. Not that I thought Michel would drain me, no, I was just more grateful he could actually feed from me right now at all.

I took hold of his head and directed his mouth to the curve of my neck. His tongue came out and lapped against my pulse, locating the precious blood beneath the skin and then with a moan he slid his fangs in. Wrapping his arms around my body and pulling me into his lap. He pulled deeply on my blood, a soft purr coming from the back of his throat. It took no more than a minute, longer than he would usually feed, but not long enough to have too adverse an effect on me once I returned to my body. And he didn't make it anything else other than a warm and loving sensation, a sharing of power and strength, his gratitude mixed with his promise, that he would return to me, no matter what.

When he withdrew his fangs and licked the marks, he rested his forehead against mine for a moment and inhaled deeply.

"Are you safe?" he asked softly, after a moment of enjoying being near.

"For now," I lied, only to have him pull back and look at me deeply in the eyes, or whatever it is he sees when I'm Dream Walking. I hadn't fooled him though, he could probably read my mind even though I wasn't really here.

"Do you know where he is taking you?"

I shook my head. "We were heading west, out of the CBD. He just wanted to get me away from the Queen of Darkness. For now he wants me alive, but he will drug me as soon as he can."

"Does he have the drug on him?"

"No. For now I am safe." Or as safe as I can be.

Michel nodded and then sighed. "I have been a fool, *ma douce*." He didn't elaborate, just looked around the barren cell, as though taking his environment in for the very first time. "You need to return to your body, conserve your energy and make a move when you can. If he drugs you, I will still find you. Do whatever you need to do to stay alive. I *will* find you."

He kissed me hard and long, with a passion that said more than his words could ever convey. His tongue making a possessive sweep of my mouth, his arms crushing me to his chest.

"Now go," he whispered huskily as he pulled me to my feet. "I am recovered and I will soon have my men free and be on my way back to you." One last kiss and then he turned his attention to the door, his *Sanguis Vitam* building, pressing against my body, stealing the breath from my lungs. "Go, *ma douce*! Go now!"

I let my mind sink back down the connection, through a similar black nothingness void I usually travel when Dream Walking and woke up in the front seat of the Land Rover, Jonathan all up and in my face.

"What the hell happened?" he demanded, his fingers digging into my upper arms.

"Fainted," I stammered, the first excuse that came to my mind. I did not want Jonathan to know Michel was breaking free of his vampires right now and that I had helped him.

He looked at me, a whole lot of *yeah ri-ight* written on his face, but didn't argue the point. Just turned back to the front of the vehicle and starting pulling us back onto the road. I noticed we had been parked up on the kerb. I couldn't quite tell where we were, but I was picking Mt Albert and I was pretty sure, given a few more kilometres we'd be hitting the South-Western Motorway, on a direct path to Auckland International Airport.

I could not let that happen.

I gave myself a mental check. Body intact, not too dizzy from Michel's feed, Light within touching distance, all systems go. I wanted to time this right and the fact that I wasn't wearing a seatbelt was also a little of a concern, but I'm not human, not by a long shot and what could prove fatal for a Norm, would just be a pain in the butt for me. Still, no one likes to intentionally hurt themselves, do they?

I waited until we were on a section of road without too many potential hazards, no other vehicles ahead, no late night pedestrians on the pavement and a stretch of road that had meant our speed had increased to above the legal limit. Perfect. Letting my Light build again inside me, I worked through the knowledge that I wasn't feeling entirely 100% and concentrated on the end goal. I wanted to fashion it into a weapon, to cause maximum pain, but the drain on my body from Michel's feed was greater than I had expected and my body was still recovering from the trip down Bond-Connection Lane, so I settled, reluctantly, on my natural fall-back position and let my Light build to a blinding cadence then slammed it against Jonathan in the driver's seat.

He hadn't even seen it coming, I'd obviously got good enough to contain it all within, not letting a beam escape around my body. The only warning he got, was a sudden blinding flash filling the cabin of the car, right before he shouted out in ecstasy, as my Light washed all over him, giving him, unfortunately, the best orgasm he would ever likely experience in his undead life. And making him lose complete concentration on the road. Why my natural born Light instinct has to be one of erotic pleasure and not bad ass pain, I do not know, but I took the opportunity it had provided, to lash out with my legs, twisting my body around in the seat, my hands still fastened above and behind me on the hand rail and kicked him hard in the head.

The vehicle swerved, uncontrollably, lurching over the centre island, taking out a road sign, narrowly avoiding a rock feature and then tipping over sideways, unable to stop the momentum carrying the top heavy bulk of the Land Rover over on its side. And then tumbling, over and over and over and over in a mad crash of shattering glass and wrenching and screeching metal and bangs and booms and a cacophony of noises that shrieked through my ears threatening to explode my ear drums and turn my brain to mush.

I felt the wrench and pull, my body lurching in a multitude of directions all at once, my head banging against the side beam of the vehicle's main cab, the smell of a stringent chemical as the air bags released around me - not really cushioning me, as so much as suffocating me - and then things got too crazy to take it all in. But I did know my hands had come free and were uselessly flailing around my head and body as the world tumbled by in a colourful frenzy accompanied by so much sound.

And then, nothing, but silence.

Complete and utter stillness. Not even a rolling hub cap, or steaming head gasket, just a void of noise that made my ears ring.

36

BAD LUCK

I don't know how long it took me to get my bearings, but eventually noise began to filter back in, as did cognitive thought. We were upside down, the engine was still running and Jonathan was out cold at my side.

Yippee fucking ki-yay!

I scrambled out the side window that was no more and landed in a pile of shattered glass and tiny scraps of twisted metal beside the car. I could hear Norms approaching, someone saying they had called an ambulance, someone else trying to wrap a blanket around me. I knew I couldn't stay. I'd escaped, but I wasn't yet free. Jonathan would come round all too quickly and if I didn't get away now, it would be too late.

I took a shattering deep breath in, feeling the pull of torn muscles and no doubt a couple of fractured ribs, but before I could allow my body to focus on the aches and pains, I staggered to my feet. A person next to me tried to push me back down into a sitting position, telling me to *take it easy, help was on the way*, but I'm stronger than the average 25 year old female and he didn't stand a chance. After the world stopped spinning, I patted him on the shoulder and said, a little unevenly, "The car is stolen. The driver is on drugs." And ran.

Shouts and a few pounding feet followed me, but I kicked it into Nosferatin gear, dug deeper than I have ever had to dig before and just zoned out the chasers and concentrated on putting one foot in front of the other at maximum velocity. I knew I wasn't at my top performance level, but even now, hurt and drained of energy, I would have been little less than a flash to those houses I passed and people I skirted around to avoid.

After running at top speed for ten minutes, I allowed myself a slower pace, using some of the freed up Nosferatin powers to scan my environments for threats. No vampires, no ghouls, no Taniwhas, nothing untoward. I slowed to a walking pace and tried to figure out where the hell I was.

After a few heart pounding seconds I came up on a round-a-bout, the busiest in Auckland City, although not so busy at this time of night. Royal Oak. I took Campbell Road at the intersection and picked up my pace before my body had a chance to collapse. I needed shelter, but I didn't have the strength to make it back to the CBD. Breaking and entering is not my kind of thing, so natural shelter was the best I could hope for.

I entered Cornwall Park at the main entrance and weaved my way across the grass and carpark and playground, towards the trees in the centre. I'd had a memorable practice session with Nero in these trees. I knew them well. Sliding down a large trunk, my back to the bark, a stake already out and settled in my hand, I let my body crumple and I slowly assessed my injuries.

Head hurt. Back. Neck. Chest, no doubt ribs. Hip on the right side. Right knee. And both wrists. I looked at the hand cuffs still attached, the chain broken somewhere in between and rubbed gingerly underneath the metal. My skin had been gouged raw on both sides, the metal practically cutting through to the bone. Thank God I didn't remember the actual moment the chain busted and my hands came free, the aftershock was bad enough.

At least I was conscious, breathing and alive. And as I let my senses flow out about me, alone. I wasn't sure if Jonathan could track me, he'd have to have come to and got away from the Norms. Not a hard task, but hopefully someone had called the cops after my little disclosure about car theft and drugs, and a Taser or two could hold him in his place. For now, I was marginally safe, but it wouldn't last.

I allowed myself a moment to check on Michel. I could feel him strong and sure down the Bond connection now, not even muted in the slightest. I had a feeling he was holding himself open to me, maybe sending me some of his power, maybe using some of mine. I couldn't tell, but I did know he was focused and healthy and extremely irate. Whatever had got him angry was now receiving the full blast of a level one joined Master Vampire. I could only imagine he was still fighting Jonathan's men, his battle wasn't over, even though I got the feeling he had everything well under control. That reassurance allowed me some modicum of peace, so I withdrew and concentrated on my own little battle at hand.

Still no sign of approaching threats, so what now? I could rest a while, then try to move on. But, where to? I couldn't go back to *Sensations* and I wasn't strong enough to face the Queen of Darkness, whom I hadn't even attempted to locate out of fear of giving myself away. I had battened down the hatches, all metaphysical doors inside my mind bolted and padlocked shut. The only pathway open was directly to my kindred, I wasn't risking a *Prohibitum Bibere* episode, that was for sure. I'd feel the evil-lurks-in-my-city pull, if one happened to come along, but even though it would pain me, I could ignore it, fight it, resist it. So, where to? I had no human friends I could turn to outside of the CBD and really, I wouldn't have wanted to get them involved. And the longer I sat here, the more it became apparent that I was shattered, beaten and in no state to move at all.

Shit. This was not good. A crop of trees was hardly protection and even though there was probably only two hours of darkness left, even the sun could not guarantee my safety. Jonathan or the Queen could use humans, hell Jonathan had used them already on me when I had been taken that first time.

I shook my head in frustration, letting my mind wander to those vampires I left behind in *Sensations*, wondering if Doug was all right. And Shane Smith. Whether Pete and the ghouls had made it out OK. A sudden thought occurred to me, if Pete was free he could come to me. I fished inside my jacket for my cellphone, only to find its screen shattered and the thing as dead as a dodo. It had obviously come between a stake in my jacket and my chest, in the helter skelter that had been the Land Rover equivalent of a spin dryer set on high. I blew out a breath almost admitting defeat, then remembered Samson. My vampire. My line.

If Michel could telepathically talk to his vampires, could I? I wasn't a vampire, but in theory I was a master. I hadn't felt the urge to try it before now and Samson certainly hadn't given it a whirl, but it was about my only possible chance left of getting myself out of this sparse wooded area and somewhere a little more secure. I calmed myself down with a little Nosferatin meditation, homing in on the black nothingness that usually took me Dream Walking, but not allowing myself to get that far. I'd already supposedly Dream Walked once tonight, all I needed was to be comatose in Cornwall Park for three whole days after a second Dream Walk. And then I sent my senses out to Samson.

I felt him immediately, as though he was standing at the end of a taut line, pulling back against my tug, responding to my poke. I tried to talk to him, to call his name, to ask a question, to shout inside my head. I even spoke aloud, but got nothing back to indicate he had heard me, or understood a damn word I had said. But, I did keep getting that pull, that tug against the line and although I had no idea what it meant it was a kind of reassurance, so I settled back to rest and recuperate and just held on to the end of that connection, letting the random tugs from Samson settle my nerves and provide a false sense of safety.

After about half an hour I felt stronger and even a little rested, but more surprisingly, the tugs were more frequent and a hell of a lot more powerful. I started paying attention to them and could actually sense them get faster, more vigorous, more forceful, until I was sure it was becoming one long tug and not just a series of them anymore. My heart had started beating harder and with a sudden jolt of panic, I shot my senses out and felt him nearby. He was alone and approaching cautiously. I'd been so wrapped up in concentrating on Samson's connection, I had stopped paying attention to my surroundings at all. Idiot.

I rolled my stake around in my palm, not quite ready to jump to my feet, but waiting until he showed himself and I could be absolutely certain. Finally, after what felt like an eternity, but was probably nothing more than a minute or two, he stepped out of the trees opposite me. Eyes darting left and right, nose sniffing the air for threats, fists held in a loose but ready position for attack.

"Mistress. You are alone?"

I smiled and let a breath out that I had been holding. "I told you to call me Luce. And yes, I am alone."

"Well done," he said with a smile. "Did you stake him?"

I shook my head and painfully got to my feet. God everything ached. Samson was beside me in a flash, lending his arm for support and steadying my shoddy balance. "Unfortunately, no, but he's going to have a bitch of a headache."

"Excellent," he replied and swept me up in his arms. "I think it best I carry you, we will need to move quickly, if we are to cover our tracks."

He was running in an instant, the trees just blurs as they flashed by in the dim light of the overhead moon.

"Where are we going?" I asked, battling against fatigue.

"Pete has a safe house, Michel's men are all there. I will take the long route, to be sure you have not been tracked. Sleep," he paused, then added softly, "Luce. I will not let anything happen to you, I swear."

I took his advice and let the blanket of sleep envelope me. When I awoke, it was to an unfamiliar room, in an unfamiliar house, surrounded by very familiar vampires. I slowly sat up on the couch I had been lying on, hoping the stench of beer and beef jerky hadn't yet seeped into my skin. The place was a pigsty, so definitely not Pete's home, but it had the distinct whiff of ghoul to it, so no doubt an associate at least.

Rubbish spewed out of a bin in the corner, filthy dishes were piled high in the sink next to the bin, the table in front of that was covered in wrappers and bottles and various other consumed and discarded paraphernalia. And the rest of the place wasn't much better. The sun's light outside, at least, well hidden behind shutters, but the curtains in front all tattered and torn. The couch I was on wasn't the only one to have been perfumed either, looking at the state of the mismatched armchairs and settees that dotted the rest of the place. But whereas the kitchen hadn't been touched, the seats and couches were clear of junk and just laden with buff and alert vampires. All of which had showered and looked ready to face an army of Jonathan's men.

"Where are we?" I croaked and then had to clear my voice.

"Eden Terrace. One of Pete's extended family's shit hole of a house," Marcus offered and received a huge smile of relief from me when I spotted him in the corner, scrunched between Matthias - thank God he was back - and Shane Smith.

"You're alive?" was all I could manage. I had really thought the Queen of Darkness had had her evil way with Marcus, considering how close he had come to her at Aotea Square.

"Of course I'm bloody alive. I do have skills you know."

"And he knows when to run like a Nancy from a bigger threat than a rogue," Matthias added, dodging the fist that went straight for his head.

"Oh. I get it. You saw the Queen and skedaddled," I said.

"Skedaddled?" Marcus asked, eyebrows raised. "Who uses skedaddled?"

"Give me a break," I muttered. "I'm hungry, sore, tired and a little bit pissed off. I can use whatever god-damned language I like."

"True," he simply answered.

"We don't have any food for you, sorry, Luce." This was from Doug, who I was also extremely pleased to see and also note that he looked fully recovered. Somewhere from *Sensations* to here, he had fed. I didn't really want to figure out how he managed that one, some things are better left unsaid. "Considering this is a ghoul's house," he went on, "it's surprising, but I think it has been uninhabited for some time. So, no edible food."

Bugger. I was starving. "Is there at least water?" I asked resting my head in my hands. Someone thrust a cleanish glass in my hand with what had to be tap water. I gratefully accepted it and thanked my lucky stars I lived in a country where tap water was drinkable if not always palatable. I felt inordinately better after downing that.

"So, what's the plan?" I finally asked, knowing damn well we weren't out of the woods just yet.

"Michel is on his way, with most of our line, he should be here on night fall," Doug answered.

Oh thank God. I hadn't tested the Bond connection again since nearly collapsing at Cornwall Park when Samson found me and I wasn't sure I could do it in front of all of Michel's men. It just seemed a little personal and I was way too close to the edge right now not to make a scene.

"OK, that's good. What else do we know?"

Doug seemed to be the one in charge, which didn't surprise me actually. Although he had always been the quiet one behind the bar at the club, he was also the one who knew the most of what was happening at any given time. I had never seen Michel give him any more attention than any of the others, but the way Michel conversed with Doug, always made me think there was more between them than meets the eye. I was thinking now, that perhaps Doug was Michel's secret weapon. A quiet, observant, friendly face, watching from the sidelines, but more than capable of taking up the reins when the need arose.

"Jonathan is an unknown. Samson said, when he arrived with you, that you had injured him. How badly?"

"Not nearly enough to slow him down. I should think he would be free by now and planning his next attack."

"OK, we can assume he has *Sensations* under surveillance and that his own lair would be nearby, in the CBD. He would expect you to return there to face the Queen, who we believe has commandeered the Town Hall."

"How do you know this?" I asked.

"Pete's men have been running reconnaissance for us, all communications come directly through him and no one else."

That made sense, he would probably see the advantage of continuing to help us. Jonathan and the Queen were both unknown threats, vampires capable of controlling his ghouls. Outside of Michel's line, the ghouls were still susceptible to vampire influence. He would prefer

Michel to remain in control of the city for the freedom of his community.

"Are we safe here?" I asked the obvious. Just because Michel's vampires couldn't influence the ghouls, didn't mean that the visitors could not. Were we safe? Could they divulge our location to the enemy?

"It is a concern. But this house is unknown to any of Pete's ghouls currently in the city. Jonathan or the Queen would have to influence Pete himself, in order to find us. But, in saying that, we must remain on guard. It is a possibility."

I blew a breath out, knowing with my current run of luck, we would be attacked, I wasn't sure if I had the energy for that.

"For now, let's just rest and conserve energy. We may need it before the day is through," Doug concluded.

My stomach rumbled, I felt like shit, but there was nothing else for it. Shane showed me to the bathroom, simply removing my hand cuffs with a flick of his wrist. I guess even Shane has some Nosferatu mojo, even though he's far from master material. The vampires had all had enough time to shower and freshen up while I had been asleep, so now it was thankfully my turn. Luckily, the vamps had been kind and not bothered with too much heat in their showers. Leaving some in the cylinder, allowing me to have a hot soak under a slightly pathetic spray, but it was bliss. It was also heaven when Michel finally reached my thoughts.

Ma douce, are you OK?

I lost my grip on the soap I had been lathering up with when his voice popped into my head. Although we can talk to each other over distance, it requires an awful lot of power and neither of us had any to spare. The fact that he was able to reach me again, meant he was close. If not already landed, definitely not far from our shores.

I'm in the shower, I answered, still battling to pick up the soap, it was the only thing that came to mind.

Really? came his languid reply. *Alone, I hope?*

I smiled. *Yep. Just me and a bar of soap.*

Mm. A pleasant thought. There was silence as he sent me a series of suggestions via technicolour images as to what I should be doing with that bar of soap.

Michel. I'm going to run out of hot water before you even get through with those. I heard his laughter in my mind, filling me up with happiness and wrapping me in warmth.

I will keep you hot, ma douce.

I shook my head and finished rinsing the soap off, then turning the taps closed, stepped out to dry and dress. It might have been nice to spend a half hour sharing thoughts and images with Michel in my head, but I was not entirely safe and being attacked while naked and wet, was not my idea of fun. I am a Nosferatin first and foremost, I was still definitely in battle mode, even if the temptation was huge.

How far away are you? I asked, slipping into my dirty and crumpled clothing again.

We are about to land. You are in Eden Terrace? He'd obviously been in touch with Doug and the others.

Yes, but we'll no doubt move on as soon as the sun sets, I don't feel safe here.

I agree. I will find you, stay hidden. We will be together again before you know it.

He had no idea how much that meant to me right now. I was so exhausted and battered and needed my kindred even more than I needed a hamburger and fries right now. And that was saying something, my stomach was in full-on grumble mode.

Ah, ma douce. Your thoughts are sweet music in my mind.

You can hear me, are you that close?

Oui. And they are beautiful. Je t'aime. And before I could reply, he was gone.

I threw the damp towel in the corner of the bathroom with the handful that already rested there and stepped back out into the room. A dozen eyes swung towards me, all blazing a little eerily red.

"What's with the glow, dudes?" I asked, wondering if we were under attack or not.

"The master is having trouble shielding his thoughts from us," Doug offered, lowering his head so he couldn't look me in the eye.

"What does that mean?" I asked slowly, really, *really*, hoping it didn't mean what I thought it would.

No one answered me at first, all of them trying to look anywhere else but at my face. It wasn't helping the sense of oh-my-God I had going on, that was for sure. Of course, it was Marcus who had the balls to speak up.

"I didn't realise you could do that with a bar of soap," he said innocently and flicked me a none-to-subtle red glowing gaze.

"Fuck you!" I managed, reaching for an empty bottle to throw at his enormously satisfied face. The crash of the glass against the wall was way louder than it should have been, I mean it was just a *Steinlager* bottle, no more than 300 odd millilitres in size. But the noise it created, made us all stand stock still.

Until we realised, it wasn't just the bottle.

It was a horde of influenced ghouls bashing down the front door and crawling through the now shattered windows.

No. My luck couldn't possibly be changing.

37

THE SHED

Michel's vampires were in battle mode immediately. A shout from Doug to protect me, had me throwing him a scowl over my shoulder while I was palming a slim silver knife in one hand and a short silver dagger in the other. I could take care of myself, thank you very much.

Marcus and Matthias were beside me in an instant, Samson somewhere behind and we all fell into a routine, if you will, of slashing and guarding, attacking and retreating. A deadly dance with lethal repercussions against ghouls that should have been on our side.

As much as I would have liked to tell the vampires around me to *not* shoot to kill, it was impossible not to land a few deadly blows. We were fighting in a confined space against crazed and blood thirsty ghouls. Even if I knew they belonged to Pete, I was not offering myself up for dinner. Ghouls fight rough, no rules, all strength and brute force, their only goal, to bite and chew and then quickly follow that up with a swallow.

I hadn't even realised what Matthias and Marcus were doing until it was too late. We'd carved a path through the ghouls in the lounge and kitchen and ended up by the back door. Before I had a chance to protest, Marcus had thrown himself through the still closed door and

Matthias was pushing me after him. We'd made it out of the building, but not out of the battle. Just as many ghouls surrounded the house as those inside keeping Doug and the rest of the vamps busy. The only difference here, was that the sun - although low in the sky and shielded behind a scattering of clouds, was still shining - and the vamps at my side had started to slowly fry.

I wondered briefly if that would put the ghouls off, they do like their meals raw and a barbecued vampire wasn't exactly a fresh temptation. But then that only made me feel like the prime rib on the plate, the one they all would fight over, so pushed that thought aside and concentrated on getting us out of this mess.

Unfortunately, my Light does squat to ghouls, its only purpose is to bring vampires back from the Dark, so that left silver, or now that we had a bit more space to manoeuvre, my Svante sword. I sheathed the dagger and pulled out the sword in one swift motion, slicing the head off a ghoul as it tried to take advantage of my weapons change and came a little too close.

"Nice," I heard Marcus shout beside me, before punching a ghoul in the side of the temple and sending him flying.

M & M sensed I needed a little more room to swing my Svante than I had for my dagger, so slowly moved further away. Samson had made it outside now and took up guard at the rear, also giving me space and then it was game on. As if we'd fought together a million times before, all three vampires set the ghouls up, like a volleyball team, one vamp swatting a ghoul towards my reach, so then I could finish it off with a clean swipe of the sword. Each vampire timing it, so only one ghoul advanced at a time into my spider's web.

Within ten minutes, we had cleared the back garden enough to see the fence and although I was determined to stay and fight every single one of them, ensuring the vampires still trapped in the house could break free, Marcus and Matthias had other thoughts. And when a gap appeared and the ghouls were immobilised for the time being, they simply picked me up under each armpit and ran across the backyard, vaulting the fence in unison and flashing away from the scene.

"What the fuck?" I shouted as we careened down the side streets of Eden Terrace, Samson coming up the rear. "Put me down, you idiots!"

"Doug has it in hand," Matthias calmly told me, neither vamp releasing their grip nor slowing their pace.

I gave up struggling five minutes later, just simply running out of juice. My intent to continue to give the two vampires at my side a thrashing was still well and truly there, but the body's willpower to carry out my commands was gone. I was beyond exhausted. Hungry. In pain. Tired. The thought that we would have to hide and probably continue to run for some time yet, simply sapping the last of my anger and resolve.

When they sensed my capitulation, they stopped briefly for Matthias to take me in his arms and then all three picked up speed and the world was again a blur. I vaguely recognised a few landmarks, a *McDonald's* coming into focus, then more blurs, then at last they must have determined we were far enough away and our tracks well enough covered, for us to stop and take shelter. The form of which was a storage shed behind the Auckland Museum in the Domain.

The sun had set some time ago, I had no idea when, but the Museum was closed for the day and the storage shed quiet and empty of Norms. Matthias propped me down on a padded seat in the corner and then collapsed against the wall. He could have kept running all night, but we'd been running in sunlight. All three vamps looked a little worse for wear. Samson shuffled across the dusty floor and plopped a *McDonald's* bag full of the sweet smell of burger and fries into my lap. Then he simply slid to his knees at my feet and rested his head against my shins.

Shit. They'd pushed themselves to the limit to protect me.

I glanced over at Marcus, who had the door slightly ajar and was resting on the floor, looking equally as shot as his mates, but determined to keep a look out on the darkening expanse of the park outside.

For all the exhaustion and aches and pains I was feeling, the sensation of affection for these vampires with me now, outweighed all of that. For a moment I couldn't think or move, just let the deep seated feeling of respect and warmth towards the three of them engulf me, and then my stomach rumbled and I hungrily opened the bag to stodgy fast-food heaven. The burger lasted all of 20 seconds, the fries a little longer and finally I was done. A greasy, sated, fat-filled joy washing over me.

"What about you guys? You need to feed?" I asked into the dimmed silence.

"You offering a vein?" Marcus replied, Samson growled in response, stiffening at my feet.

"We're fine, Luce. We'll feed when reinforcements arrive," Matthias interrupted what was undoubtedly going to become a pissing contest between my guard at the door and my vampire at my feet.

"How long? You all look like shit."

"Not long now," Matthias answered. "Michel is close."

I felt him then, almost as though he was responding to Matthias' statement of how close he was. He was already in the Domain and cautiously approaching. I felt a tingle run through my body at the nearness of him and had to consciously pull my Light back in, as it threatened to blind us all in the shed.

"Whoa," Marcus remarked, casting a quick glance over his shoulder at me. "I'd love to see how bright you get when he's right on top of you."

I was about to answer with a sharp witted retort, when Michel appeared at the door and swept him off the floor, his hand at his throat as he stepped over the threshold into the shed.

"A sight I am sure you will not live to see."

"Master," he croaked in reply, trying to look contrite, but unable to lower his head enough to get away with it.

Matthias was on his feet immediately, standing respectfully still, Samson just shifted to my side and stood slowly. A measure of respect in his stance, but still a protective position next to me.

"Michel," I whispered, not to get him to stop, not to tell him to behave, but simply because I couldn't help myself from saying his name out loud.

He lowered Marcus to the ground and looked him directly in the eye. "You may go feed," he stated simply, a command to all three of the vampires in the room. None of them hesitated, not even Samson and within seconds we were alone. Michel slowly shut the door behind him, no doubt his own guards surrounding the shed and keeping a watchful eye. And then he turned towards me, letting a wash of amethyst, violet, indigo and then magenta flash through his eyes.

"*Ma douce,*" he husked, then flashed to my side. His hands coming up to touch my face, almost shaking as he reached for me, then slowly covering my body from head to toe. His *Sanguis Vitam* filling the air, my shields lowering automatically to let him in and his healing power touching all of the aches and pains, scrapes and bruises, cuts and gouges, and smoothing them away.

He sat at my feet for a moment, just looking at me, both of us stuck fast in a moment we couldn't have broken free of, even if we had wanted to. Just taking each other in, soaking up every feature, memorising every plane, unable to pull away.

"*Mon Dieu,*" he whispered. "You are beautiful."

I smiled down at him. "You seem surprised."

"Not surprised, *ma belle*, in wonder, in awe, that you should be mine."

"If I'm yours, then why haven't you kissed me yet?" I breathed in reply.

His lips quirked a little at that. "Perhaps I wish to take things slowly."

"We don't have time for slow."

His smile widened and he flashed a hint of amethyst in the deepened blue that had returned to his eyes. "As always, *ma douce*, you are correct." He rose up and wrapped me in his arms, his lips smoothly finding mine, softly brushing against my mouth and then quickly deepening when my own lips parted, letting him in.

He softly groaned against my mouth and pulled me off the padded seat I had been perched upon and into his lap, regardless of the less than clean floor he was kneeling on. His hand running up my back into my hair and wrapping around the strands, anchoring himself there, the other smoothly stroking over my hip and stomach and coming up to find my breast and nipple under my T-Shirt.

His lips began spraying my face with feather-light kisses, across my cheeks, over my jaw and then down to his new mark at the base of my neck. His face nuzzling in against the colourful *Sigillum* there, his voice muffled as he spoke.

"I want you so badly, *ma douce*, but we simply do not have time. I promise I will make it up to you when this night is through. But, for now we must regroup and attack before they realise we have returned."

Logically, I couldn't argue with him, even if my body screamed out in protest against his hard, broad chest. I wanted him so badly, I didn't give a toss we were in some old mucky shed in the middle of the city within spitting distance of evil and the threat of the Dark. I even resented a little, the fact that Michel was a master tactician, a warrior at heart, that even with me in his arms he was thinking of the battle, survival at all costs. It was unfair of me, Michel would devour me in an instant, if it were safe for us to entertain such pastimes, but it was not. I should have been grateful that at least one of us was thinking with their head and not some other part of their body, but I wasn't. I'd nearly died while he was gone, he'd nearly died while he was gone, I wanted to feel alive and I wanted to feel it with him.

"Oh, *ma douce*, you are breaking my heart."

There was a knock on the door, before I could even formulate an answer to that statement. I wasn't sure if Michel had planned it, telepathically ordered a vampire to interrupt. Maybe he didn't have the strength to deny me on his own and needed a little help to pull away. Either way, it worked. I stiffened, he pulled back and the door opened to reveal Jett.

"Master. We need to discuss plans. The night is progressing and we may not remain safe here for much longer."

"Of course," Michel answered helping me to my feet and brushing a kiss over my forehead. "Bring the others in."

Jett turned away and Michel lifted my face up to his with a tilt of my chin. "I will make it up to you, *ma douce*," he whispered, low enough for only me to hear.

"Promise?" I asked, letting a small smile play on my lips. I couldn't stay mad at Michel for long.

"Cross my heart," he said with a wink and even did the action over his chest, as five of his top vampires piled into the little shed. I could still sense twenty more out in the night and knew he probably had more further afield as well.

Michel spun towards the others as Jett closed the door behind him and someone flicked the light switch in the corner of the room. The vampires spread out and made themselves comfortable around the room, all of them looking in top condition. You'd have no idea they had recently fought a battle in America, but then they'd had a flight on a luxury jet to recover since then.

Michel sat down in the padded seat I had been on, the only real chair in the room and pulled me back into his lap, his arms coming around my waist protectively. He may not have allowed our passions to take over, but he wasn't prepared to let me out of his touch.

I glanced around the room taking in the vampires, the ones he usually had at his side when business called, be it his run of mill every day operations, or in times of crises, like now.

One of them was Doug. No surprises there. He was the highest ranking vampire in Michel's line left behind, the one in touch with what had been happening in Auckland in his absence. I absently thought Erika was usually at these meetings, but then maybe she had been left behind in America, to clean up the mess there. I'd get a chance to ask after her in due course, for now, Michel's men had started giving their reports.

"Latest report from Enrique, is the Nosferatins have been released and attended to. They will be sent to their respective homes in due course," a vampire by the name of Arturo offered from the corner, his big bulk squashed between a work bench and a packing crate.

"Another twenty of our line are to land within the next two hours. The final amount will depart America when Enrique has secured Denver to his satisfaction," Jerric, a blonde Scandinavian looking vampire added.

Michel nodded in reply to each update, then turned to look at Doug. "Tell me," he commanded the bartender. "What happened?"

Doug flashed me a look that spoke volumes, his anger at my approaching *Sensations* still not entirely disappeared, then squared his shoulders and held Michel's gaze.

"Jonathan has some twenty men with him, all level one or two. We were simply out gunned and then Lucinda..." He paused, trying to pick his words I think.

"Rode to the rescue," Michel offered. I tried to glare at him but he just kept his attention on Doug, a small twist in his lips the only indication he had sensed my outrage at all.

"Yes." One word, full of anger. I blew a breath out in a loud sigh to make my point. *Move along boys, move along.*

Michel huffed a small laugh, then repositioned me in his lap.

Doug continued as though nothing had happened. "She did bring the ghouls with her and that tipped the scale in our favour. At least long enough for us to be released, her to be kidnapped again by Jonathan and then for us to escape and start to track them." He said all of this quickly, no doubt hoping it wouldn't hurt so much if said in a rush, but Michel, who had undoubtedly already ascertained most of this information before, still managed to growl at him anyway. A sure sign of his disapproval at the events that had unfolded.

Doug hurriedly went on. "She escaped him, Samson found her, then we took refuge in one of Pete's safe houses, only to have either Jonathan or the Queen use the ghouls against us. We all escaped and here we are."

Silence followed the last of the summary.

"Where is Jonathan now?"

"We're quite sure he is near *Sensations*, no doubt hoping for our return and the Queen is in the Town Hall, down by Aotea Square at last report."

Michel ran a hand through his hair, then returned it to my waist, absently stroking my hands in my lap.

"Well. We need to take care of Jonathan before we face the Queen. I don't want him jumping out of the woodwork while we are distracted by the Dark."

"Jonathan and the Queen are connected," I finally provided a bit of Intel to add to the reports.

"How?" Michel shifted to look up at me.

"I'm not sure, but he has met her and somehow managed to convince her I wouldn't be a threat if he had me drugged."

Michel's low growl reverberated around the room. There was no hiding his anger at what Jonathan had done. Right now I was picking Michel's emotions were very much near the surface, hiding them, like shielding his thoughts earlier from his line, was damn near impossible. His vampires bristled in response to his anger and pin pricks of fire started dancing across my skin, targeting me from every corner of the room. The *Sanguis Vitam* escalated, as though one vampire's response to Michel, triggered off the next and soon I was gasping for breath and squirming around in Michel's lap trying to get away from the onslaught of power that washed against me with relentless intent.

"Michel," I managed to get out between gritted teeth.

Immediately his power swept all the others aside in the room and his hands came up to cup my face. "*Ma douce, ma douce*, I am so sorry." He kissed me briefly on the lips, then slid me off his lap into the seat and began to pace the small space in the middle of the room.

I've seen Michel pace before, it doesn't happen often, only when he is on the thin edge of a cliff, about to teeter off. I took a steadying breath in and when Michel didn't say anything to his men all waiting patiently, I stood up and cleared my throat.

"Can you give us a moment?" I said to the room at large, but not removing my eyes from Michel. The vampires dutifully slid out of the room, the door shutting quietly at their backs.

I watched Michel continue to pace for a while longer then stepped in front of his path.

"What is it? What has got you so upset?" It seemed like a stupid question. I mean, we'd had a call to arms from the American Families, Michel had left me behind to face the threat, thinking I would be safe, only to have the American King trick him and come directly here to me, capture me, almost have me killed by ghouls. And now the Queen of Darkness, a presence we have long known we would have to face, is now tied up with Jonathan. What wasn't there to be upset about? But I knew this was more.

"Jonathan," he replied simply and for a moment I didn't think he would elaborate further. The name pretty much summed it all up, but still I got the sense that there was more.

Michel finally stopped pacing and turned to look at me, his face a mask of determined aggression.

"He had a spy, Lucinda." His voice was surprisingly quiet, considering the rage that fluttered across his face. "From the moment he first met you, he has planned it all and played me like a fool. I thought now, at least, I had finally out guessed him. The spy has been dealt with, his Families are in disarray, the only threat remaining is him and I will soon have him dead. But, then he manages to surprise me again. In league with the Queen of Dark." He laughed a little bitterly. "And even though he poses such a threat, he actually managed to protect you from her. Something I have not been able to do, despite my fervent desire to do just that."

Oh. It made sense. He felt he had failed and Jonathan had succeeded where he had not.

"I don't want his protection, Michel. I would rather have to face her, than live like that. It wasn't a safe place, it was a lie and the only way I will ever be free is if she is dead." I stepped closer when he didn't say anything, until I was directly against his chest and having to look up into his face. "I need you, Michel, I can't do this without you by side."

Finally, his face softened, his eyes allowing a little of the deep blue to seep back in. He reached up and ran the back of his fingers down my cheek. "Then I shall never leave your side again."

Thatta boy, I thought, seeing a flash of amusement cross his face.

"So, let's go deal to the little creep and then slaughter the hell out of Darkness," I added, taking a step towards the door.

He reached out before I could touch the handle and spun me back against his chest, planting a bone melting kiss against my lips. When he had me sufficiently panting, he moved away, offered a mock bow and opened the door, to allow me to head through.

"So, who was the spy?" I asked, ignoring the chivalry and not in the least expecting it to be a vamp I knew.

He stopped in his tracks and my heart sunk. Why the hell did I have to ask a stupid question like that right now?

I almost said *it doesn't matter, tell me later,* but it was too late.

"Erika," he said, a look of infinite sadness crossing his face.

I couldn't even comprehend the depth of betrayal he felt. I felt numb with shock and disbelief myself. Erika was a friend, she shared my house, she taught me how to wield a sword, she was a shoulder to cry on when things got too hard. Shit. My friend. Michel's *little one*. A spy.

I tried not to think the thought, but it was already tumbling through my head before I could block it from him.

"No," he said in answer to my silent question *had he killed her?* I felt a moment of confused peace. She was alive, maybe it was a mistake and she wasn't all bad. And then he ruined it with his next words.

"Jett killed her, not me."

38
TOGETHER

Jett must have sensed we were talking about him, because he glanced our way as we exited the shed. One look at whatever emotion was playing over my face must have told him all he needed to know and a look of what I could only call a survivor, covered his stark features. Someone who was still waging a war with their demons and determined to win.

There was no time to offer condolences, or a comforting word of support, we would have time enough to grieve later, now my destiny was due. Corny, but true.

God this sucked! How many friends would I lose to this battle? How much more would I give up to fight the Dark? I wasn't sure I had the strength to face that answer, but I couldn't stop it swilling around inside my head. Michel had gone to speak to a few of his men, last minute plans and instructions, revisions of what they knew and what to expect. I was just stuck in a mental loop of self pity. Despising myself, all the while unable to shake the doom and gloom.

Eventually it was time to move out, first stop *Sensations* and I used what little mental fortitude I had left to banish the dark thoughts and ready myself for what was to come. I knew in my heart I wasn't ready for this, in a perfect world I'd get a bit of sleep, a little more food and then tackle the monster. Hell, in a perfect world, Darkness wouldn't threaten to steal your soul. This was not a perfect world and I did not have the luxury of a spa treatment to recover my strength. So I sucked it up, like all good vampire hunters do and palmed my stake, letting the weight of it settle my nerves and chase away the last of my fears.

By the time Michel reached my side, no doubt a well planned circuitous route, giving me time to pull my shit together, I had myself under control. I was on the hunt, my senses open and alert. Objective one. Dispose of Jonathan. Objective two. Face the Dark.

Easy peasy.

Yeah right.

We flowed through the darkened streets of Auckland, quickly approaching Karangahape Road and the club. All the while my senses flowed out in front of me, around me, behind me, checking on potential threats, assessing the number of vampires nearby, acknowledging they weren't all ours. It was quickly becoming obvious we were walking into a trap, but what could we do? Jonathan was in control of the CBD and the Queen of Darkness wasn't budging an inch until I showed.

Perhaps we could have stalled for more time, somehow lured them from the central city, but the end would have been the same, we would have to face them both and why not keep it on territory we were familiar with? I knew every alley, every shadowed spot, every possible location for an ambush and still I walked willingly into a trap.

Enough was enough. I had lost people I cared about, I would not lose my city too. That was it, I was done. I was tired of running from this Prophecy. I had denied it, argued with it, doubted it and hidden from it, but no more.

A calmness I had no right to feel, settled in my soul. I stopped in the middle of the intersection of Queen Street and K Road, and let the unnatural stillness of the night wrap around me. No Norms out on the streets clubbing, no taxis or buses crowding the lanes, even the fire trucks and ambulances on nearby Pitt Street were all tucked up in bed. Auckland City knew the fate of the world rested on tonight. It held its breath, a bit like us.

"What is it, *ma douce?*" Michel whispered next to me, all of the vampires around me coming to a halt when I did. Unable to sense exactly what I sensed, or feel exactly what I felt, or know exactly what I knew.

"Jonathan is in the club waiting, he has twenty vampires around him, some upstairs in the offices, two across the street from the door."

"I sense this too." I heard the unasked question in his voice, *what else?*

"If I go with you she will win," I said simply, unsure where exactly that knowledge came from, but knowing with every fibre in my body that it was so. "She will destroy this street and everything on it, we would not stand a chance."

"So, we face her first," Michel offered quietly, a small amount of tension evident in his tone.

"No," I said adamantly. "I must go alone." There is no way in hell I wanted to face her alone, but I felt the urge to face her now too strong to deny and like Michel said, Jonathan would take advantage of our distraction and attack. It was too great a risk to leave him now.

Michel was in front of me in an instant. "*Non!*" He spat the French word with unyielding force. "We will not be parted again."

I took a deep breath in readying myself to argue. Finally I looked up into his face, fully prepared to make my point, but when I looked at him, I couldn't do it. My heart missed a beat, my throat went dry and my breath caught in my mouth. He took full advantage of my silence.

"We will face whatever happens together. If Jonathan wishes to join in the fun, so much the better. We will be together to face it. You, me, our men."

I blinked slowly, trying to see if Nut would offer a small glimpse of what she wanted me to do. All I knew was, I had to face the Queen now, tonight, before it was too late and that nothing could get in my way from achieving this. If it was Nut telling me this little gem of knowledge, I couldn't tell, but it was strong and deep within me.

It ends here.

I nodded up at Michel, the look of utter relief washing his face making him seem so much more handsome than usual, brilliant yet vulnerable, strong yet close to the edge. A humanity to his features which was becoming more and more a part of who he is. I couldn't see the vampire I first met when I came to Auckland, the one who ruled his city with an iron fist. Who summoned me to his office when he simply wanted to play with the little vampire hunter, who commanded my obedience whilst trying to fight the attraction we shared. Who held on to his control until it shattered about him and made him who he now was. Humane. Vampire. Mine.

"Together," I said, reaching up to brush my lips against his.

"Together," he murmured against my mouth.

With the silence gained from our genetics, we melted into our surroundings and fled away from the club and towards the Dark that called to me, like an old friend. I had no idea if we would see another sunrise, I had absolutely little belief that I was stronge enough to do this, but I had faith. In Nut. In Nero, who had guided me to this point. I had faith and that would have to be enough.

I sensed Jonathan's men moving immediately, following us as one. I felt the prickle of power in front of me, the sensation of Michel gathering his own *Sanguis Vitam* around him. And then we were there.

She didn't come out running to meet me, she stayed hidden, like she had before and let her minions attack as soon as we set foot in Aotea Square.

They fought like well trained soldiers, close formation, skilled, harsh and alert. They were armed with shiny swords, so sleek and long and sharp. Michel's men weren't unprepared and the clang on clang of metal rang out in the night, like the bells of distant churches pealing, pleading, for all to hear.

My Svante slashed through the numbers, unable to land a killing blow, but holding my own, keeping them at bay. My thoughts briefly touching on Erika, all she had taught me, all the times she had taunted me, how close she had pushed me to the edge. At the time I had thought it was to help me perfect my skills, to master the sword, but as I felt myself become one with the weapon in front of me, as though I'd held it centuries before, as though it was an old remembered weapon from battles fought before I was even born, I knew I hadn't needed those harsh lessons she had forced upon me. And that she had recognised it too. Her only goal was to watch me suffer, to see if I would crack. Had she been a friend at all?

I pushed those thoughts aside and concentrated on the here and now. We'd been battling for a good ten minutes, neither side giving an inch, nor gaining an inch either. This could go on all night. Something had to give.

No sooner had I thought that, when Jonathan appeared before me. Where the fuck he had come from, I did not know. One minute I was fighting, what I had come to realise was most definitely an *Iunctio* guard and the next the American was two feet in front, his own sword clashing against mine.

"Sweetheart, you are a beauty to behold. I had not realised your skill with the sword was so advanced. I shall take great delight in watching you fight my men." And no doubt, delight in my being slashed by their swords as well.

"You don't have the balls to fight me yourself, Jonathan?" I countered, performing a perfect spin and landing behind him, to make him lose his balance and respond to my move.

He grunted as he fended off my strike, then righted himself and prepared for the next thrust of my sword. We settled into a rhythm. I wasn't feeling the urgency to finish him off anymore, I had a few a questions of my own.

"I am fighting you now, am I not?" he finally answered.

Barely, I thought, but said instead, "So, how did you convince Erika to join your band of merry fuck knuckles?"

He flashed an angry smile at me, a hint of fang behind his lips. "Many women have found it difficult to resist my charms."

"Oh, you have got to be kidding," I said, slicing a gash down the front of his shirt, but not able to connect with flesh.

He recovered and circled around me. "Is it so hard to believe I am attractive to the opposite sex, sweetheart? I had you all but convinced at one stage, I do believe."

I felt Michel's rage at that comment from where we stood and I knew he was some distance away, on the other side of the square, facing off against three *Iunctio* guards at once. Unable to come to my aid and wishing so strongly that he could just slice his sword though Jonathan's heart right now.

Easy. I sent the thought towards him. *He's not worth losing your concentration over.*

I sensed him pulling back some of the fire that had engulfed his mind and settle back into a rhythm with the guards. I returned my full attention to the upstart before me.

"So, she fell into your bed and disowned all she stood for. Just like that."

"Oh, she wasn't easy to turn, believe me. Her warped sense of loyalty to her previous master was strong, even after I stole her."

My stride faltered and Jonathan managed to land a knick in my arm, the blood hot and wet as it slid down towards my elbow and pooled in my jacket.

"You broke her blood bond to Michel?" I asked incredulously, ignoring the pain at the gash.

"Of course. And managed to hide it from even him. I do have certain skills beyond the bedroom, sweetheart. I would be happy to show you some time."

I couldn't believe he had succeeded in duping Michel. Erika had seemed so tightly bound to him, so loyal, so true. And all along it had been a charade, an act, her loyalty was to America, a place she claimed to despise. I guess we should have picked up on that, she was always so quick to mention her relief at returning to New Zealand, to be by Michel's side. The lady doth protest too much, methinks.

Damn Erika. I had trusted her too. I had let her in, like I had Rick and both times I had been let down disastrously. A girl could get a complex over this.

I straightened my shoulders and decided I'd about had enough of all the news I could handle in one day. Time to end this. I know Michel wanted to be the one to slice out Jonathan's heart, but that honour looked like it was all mine.

I centred myself, allowing all other distractions to fall away and renewed my efforts in earnest. He picked up on the change of pace, the glint of steel in my eyes and easily countered my every move as though he had expected exactly that.

"I don't want to kill you, sweetheart, but I will harm you enough to get that damn drug on board and then she will let us go," he said a little breathlessly, the speed in which we were now parrying and meeting each blow of our swords, only a blur to a Norm's eye.

"Not if I can help it," I gritted between clenched teeth.

I was ready for that final strike, he wasn't exactly making it easy, but I knew I had him. I was better at this than him, I was more determined and had a hell of a lot more to lose, but I hadn't counted on the Dark.

Jonathan had always had a large amount of Dark in him, not completely, but enough to know it was there. The Light within sometimes prevailed, but his underlying essence was all Dark. And with her so nearby, I should have expected it. She would call to his Dark, she would make it stronger, make it surpass the Light. She could all but control him if she wanted, but what she wanted was for me to falter and fall.

The Dark rushed through him, my natural *Sanguis Vitam Cupitor* powers responding to the blackness that grew within. For a moment I was literally blinded by the sight of all that Dark in front of me, my mind closing down the environment around me and retreating to the map I held inside. The one that showed me where all the Dark was at any given time, how much of it prevailed, where the vampires were who sported it, how much lived inside their souls. All I could see was that map with its blinking red lights, the brightest, the biggest, in Auckland and of course right before my eyes.

I lost my footing and collapsed to my knees. Jonathan didn't pause, the syringe came out of his pocket, his sword dropped to the ground at his side. I heard Michel scream a warning in my head, loud enough to clear the map and bring me back to the moment, in time to raise my hand and gather my Light. I had to banish the Dark. If nothing else, I had to do to Jonathan what I had done to Samson several nights before. As Jonathan struggled to hold me still, the syringe with its long, sharp needle inching closer, I built the Light up and moulded it, ready to banish that Dark.

So close.

So close.

So close.

Just as I felt the sting of the needle on the side of my neck, I let my Light go. And all hell broke loose.

The square was shrouded in a thick black blanket of Darkness, her presence a tangible weight on our chests, even Jonathan faltered and fell back. His arms leaving my shoulders, the needle, having not been depressed, hanging loosely from the puncture mark at my neck and my own hand losing contact with his skin. It was too late to stop my Light, it spread from me to Jonathan, as though along a stretchy cord between us, the cord getting longer and longer and longer, and then he fell backwards from me and I fell backwards from him, the crushing weight on our chests getting ever heavier, but despite the growing distance the cord held true. It didn't break, it remained strong and my Light blasted down the length of it and slammed right into Jonathan's chest.

I struggled to breathe against the Dark that had blossomed around us. I couldn't think of a thing to do to battle it, to make it go away, but I was immediately conscious of the connection between Jonathan and me. No longer the cord that had stretched and held true, but a line just the same, similar to what I had with Samson, but not as strong, not as intimate, not as close.

This was more of a sense of awareness, as though I would always know where he was. Not necessarily what he was feeling, he didn't belong to me, but that he was connected to me in some way. Not like Samson. Not like Michel. But, still connected, still drawing on me, although it was difficult to ascertain why.

It frightened me. When something strange and unknown pops up in your face, it's hard to stop yourself from running away. Some people poke at it, prod it, test it, to see what it is, others hide and flee and cover their heads in sand. Me? I just sat there and felt it all and shook from head to toe in fear.

I knew beyond a doubt that Jonathan was connected to me. Forever.

And didn't that just suck?

39
LIGHT GIVER

Precious seconds passed as the Dark got heavier and closer and my breathing all but non-existent. This was it. How could we fight such an entity, such a power? It was so black, so dense, so thick and so strong. Darkness everywhere. Was this what would become of the world? An evil stench reeking through the ether, wrapping around our throats, constricting our breathing and controlling our movements.

I tried to roll over, to move a limb, to grasp my sword and prepare to defend myself against the coming death, that slowly stalked me, like a hungry tiger through the underbrush of an empty urban wasteland. There was no sound, I couldn't hear Michel, but I could still feel him, down the Bond. She couldn't take that from us. So, even in death we would be connected. I could feel his fear, his pain, similar to mine. And his despair. All of it laced with a love so blinding, it was brighter than light. Brighter than the sun.

I tested my other connections. To Samson, who was there, also fighting a losing battle, also scared, but determined to struggle, like us, until the end. Then, because there really wasn't anything else to do, while I waited for her to finish playing with us, tormenting us, I tested the new connection to Jonathan. As expected, I could feel him, not like Michel or Samson, I couldn't tell if he was fighting, or scared, or had expected this and just rolled over to die, but I could feel the Dark in him and for a moment, I didn't comprehend what it was that I actually felt. That it was different from before. That it had changed.

Given more time, I probably would have figured out the difference, but I had other things on my mind, like the heaviness that was cracking my ribs, the fact that I hadn't drawn a breath for at least two minutes. And the knowledge that this was soon to end.

I felt so useless. So much for being the Saviour of the World. Where was my noble steed? Where was my shout of victory? We were losing and it was all my fault.

Although encased in a black nothingness, a Darkness so all consuming, I began to see spots of white light before me eyes. I knew it wasn't a stray moon beam, or the flash of a street light, this was the onset of unconsciousness, the last bastion of a brain firing randomly, electrical impulses flaring spasmodically, as one by one, everything shuts down.

This was it and man, it sure as hell happened a lot quicker than I had thought it would. I had at least expected to face off against her, woman to goddess, Nosferatin to Queen. I thought at least I'd get the chance to look her in the eye. But, no such luck, we had never stood a chance, she was always going to be stronger, faster, Darker, than us. My fate, my destination along that path through life, was always going to end here.

Why had Nut even bothered to give us hope, if this was the end point all along?

Strange. I thought her incapable of playing games, but if this was how it was supposed to end, then what had Nut been doing, other than playing a wicked game?

Sometimes I wonder, really, whether I am worthy of Nut's faith, because I seem to be so ready to accept her failings. And right when I think all is lost and I'm pondering the most horrible and awful thoughts about my goddess, she appears, like all good deities should. I felt her in my mind, a brightness that brought relief. I took the first breath in I had managed in some time and felt the dancing spots of white shimmer a little, fade a little. I even felt my hand shift at my side.

I thought she might talk to me, scold me, urge me to fight. At the very least, I thought she'd bathe me in Light. But nothing as obvious as that happened, it was more of a *hey, I am here with you, now what are you going to do?* kind of thing. Not that she said it in so many words, it was all really just me. My mind wandering, repairing, fighting. Maybe she wasn't here at all, who knows what the mind manifests when bordering on extinction.

What *was* I going to do? Not lie here and become fodder for the Darkness, that was for sure. I couldn't move properly, I could still hardly breathe, but I could call my Light. It was still strong inside me, unaffected, untouched by the Dark. I did feel a little stupid then, I mean, why hadn't I called on it before? I brushed that admonishment aside and pulled my Light together. No time for something pretty, just a collection of all that power, that brightness, that Light and then one great big explosion from inside me, to wash away the Dark.

At first it just blinded us, the whole square became bright white light, then a sonic boom followed, shattering windows around the periphery, making bench seats come unhinged from the pavers and tumble backwards and away. All the leaves on the nearby trees, providing Norms a little shade in the heat of the day, lost their grip and scattered in the wind, a flurry of greens and browns. And then the branches creaked with movement, as the Light blasted past. Even good can be destructive when it has to, even Light can cause a shit-load of mess.

I sprang to my feet in a crouch and took in my surroundings. The vampires around me groaned in pain, writhing on the ground and I'm not entirely sure, but maybe in a little pleasure too. I didn't want to look too closely at that response and anyway, I was too busy trying to find her. She had retreated, but not vanished, just licking her wounds and no doubt, preparing for a counter attack. I hadn't scared the evil bitch off, I'd only bought us a reprieve.

Michel was beside me in the next second, flushed, eyes shining and bright. He grabbed me in a rough embrace, his lips claiming mine as my body crushed against his chest. His hands all over me, in possessive motions, his tongue making a quick path to the back of my throat and if he had his way, I was sure, his body would follow, he seemed intent on climbing right inside.

"Michel," I squeaked, as he lifted me off the ground, wrapping my legs around his hips, his excitement obvious at having survived the attack, or maybe just the Light I had blasted him with. Or even the fact that he had denied himself when we had been in the shed, all catching up with him, so that now, he seemed crazed and horny and completely unable to control himself.

"Cut it out!" I managed as I pushed against his chest.

He laughed in delight at my response and slowly lowered me to the ground, but didn't let go, just held me loosely in his arms and looked down with such love and wonder. So, some control still left there then. Good to know.

We stood still amongst the recovering vampires for a moment and just when I sensed some form of rational thought returning, the flash of realisation that we weren't out of danger just yet, he stilled. Pain washed over his face, so raw and urgent and he thrust me away from his body as the tip of a sword protruded from his chest, right above his heart. He collapsed to his knees, a look of shock now mingling with the pain across his face.

I screamed and reached for him, but Jonathan just pushed him out of the way. I watched, in slow motion, as Michel's body tumbled to the side, the sword still lodged right through him, not killing him, but immobilising him and racking him in pain. I couldn't tell if he was still conscious, I couldn't believe you would stay awake for such an ordeal and then I had my hands full fighting off a rabid vampire with nothing more than my fists.

Somewhere along the way, I had lost my Svante and although I had stakes and silver knives and daggers on my person, Jonathan was relentless in his attack. His fangs were down and his snarl filled the now still air. I had no idea what Michel's vampires were doing, I could only presume they were fighting Jonathan's men, but all I could think was *we don't have time for this, we don't have time for this, we don't have time for this,* over and over and over again.

I blocked out all thought of Michel and how injured he was. He was alive and for now that had to do. I just worked on fending off those fangs. Maybe Jonathan had had enough of trying to drug me and just wanted to drain me dry, it certainly looked like that was the sole purpose left in his undead life. His jaw snapped like a Taniwha at my neck, his fingers clawed at the skin on my arms, he moved with supernatural speed which I barely had the energy to avoid and still I knew this was a waste of time. She would return and all of this fighting was irrelevant, ridiculous, a waste of friggin' time.

"Stop it!" I shouted between dodging a blow to the side of my head and rolling over debris from my Light blast. I could feel something sharp and hard break the skin at my shoulder and dig right in as I rolled over the top of it. It felt like it had sunk right down to bone, but when I pulled it way, it came straight out, just leaving a gaping hole for blood to ooze out of and drip down my back. My arm immediately lost all feeling and hung limply at my side.

"Stop what?" Jonathan growled in response and leapt towards my weaker side, grabbing my arm and spinning me around in a circle, then letting me fly free through the air to crash against a rubbish bin. The bin went flying, surprising it was still there after my Light blast and I lost all breath from my lungs.

I struggled to get up and managed a half hearted movement, only to collapse back down on the ground. Jonathan walked over slowly and loomed above my prone body, his fangs glinting in the light from a street lamp nearby. I looked up at him and thought, what the fuck? This is not how it is meant to end. Where's the Dark I'm meant to be battling? Jonathan had as much Light in him as Dark, he was evenly balanced, he shouldn't even be getting this aggressive. What the fuck?

What the fuck? I did a double take of Jonathan's aura, used my *Sanguis Vitam Cupitor* powers to assess what Dark there was. He crouched down next to me and reached out a hand. I cringed automatically, but when he ran his fingers over my cheek, it was so soft, so gentle, so caring – so different from the feral fangs and supernatural tossing of before.

"Are you all right, sweetheart?"

I just stared at him, at his Light, at his Dark. At the balance that now lived within. He was neither good nor bad, Dark nor Light, he just was. Any choice to act one way or the other was an intelligent one, not a decision based on the amount of evil or virtue within.

"You're not all Dark," I said, rather lamely.

He shook his head at me, clearly not understanding what the hell I was going on about. I was having a hard time figuring it out too. Somehow Jonathan had changed and the only thing I could put it down to, was my Light. The Light I had sent out with the intent of banishing the Dark. I hadn't been able to keep skin contact, but I had fashioned it and cast it as though I had, so it had been different from every other time I had tried to use my *Lux Lucis Tribuo* powers in the past. It had been more.

I let a short breath out in astonishment. I didn't need to touch each Dark vampire that crossed my path, I didn't need to bring each one into my line. I just needed to act as though I was, to believe in what I was doing, no going back, commit to the moment, as though I had my palm upon their flesh. And in return, they got balance and a choice.

Choose to use the Light. Or choose to use the Dark.

It seemed too good to be true, too easy. Wouldn't the Dark come back in? If their master was all Dark, wouldn't they just keep getting more and more from them?

Jonathan reached for my hand and began to help me to sit up.

"We need to get you out of here, she will return before too long."

He didn't mention the drug, he seemed more interested in getting me away from the danger, but I couldn't help feeling that the drug would make another appearance.

I let him pull me upright, but I had no intention of going anywhere with him. I was just racking my brain for what my next miraculous move would be, when from out of nowhere, a flash of shiny silver caught my eye. I didn't even have enough time to shout a warning, I really don't know if I would have, the words weren't exactly on my lips, but it didn't matter, it was too quick. Master of the City quick.

The sword sliced through his neck and came cleanly out the other side.

"Shit," I said, swallowing back a little bile, but unable to turn away from the sight of Jonathan's head separating from his body and the inevitable dust cloud that exploded when his *Sanguis Vitam* seeped out into the air.

"I am so sick of that bastard touching my kindred!" Michel exclaimed loudly and with much venom.

"Where did you come from?" I gasped, looking at the bloody hole in his shirt left by Jonathan's sword. "How did you remove that sword?"

"Jett," he replied, eyes fixed on me.

For a moment he just stood there and looked at me. I'm not sure what he saw on my face. Shock, probably. Regret, possibly. Sadness, maybe. Relief, definitely. And then I felt it. The connection that I'd had to Jonathan, springing back to me. All the Light I had given him, washing back inside and the Dark, that I hadn't even known I had been holding, spread out in the air and simply disappearing. I couldn't *sense* it anymore. It simply had left this world.

I think I grunted, or gasped, because Michel was kneeling down next to me smoothing back my hair and stroking my arms and saying something over and over again in French, which I didn't understand.

"English," I whispered, when the world stopped threatening to spin away.

He said a few more words in French and then abruptly changed language. "What was that?"

"I don't know," was all I could answer, still reeling from the feeling of all that Dark seeping out of *me* into the night.

"It was Dark. It was in you."

"Yeah. I know," I shot back with force, feeling a little dirty and a hell of a lot unsure.

He started to rub my arms again, having stopped all movement when he spoke of the Dark that had been inside me. I could tell he was covering up how he was feeling. He was so tightly shielded, I don't even think he would have been able to break through. I think he was shielding from himself as well as me.

Great. I'm a fucking freak of nature. I'm meant to be all Light, but that was a hell of a lot of Dark that seeped out of me. Maybe I was broken, a defect. Shit.

For want of something to say to fill the awkward silence between us, I muttered, "Jonathan was balanced, he had as much Light as Dark, after I blasted him like I did Samson. But I couldn't keep my hand on him, so we weren't connected like Samson and I were, so it was the same, but the outcome was different. I guess."

Michel didn't say anything for a while and quite frankly I thought that was OK, because I really didn't want him to confirm what I was feeling. *Lucinda, I'm afraid you are a freak.* Nah. That was something I really, *really* didn't want to hear at all.

But I should have had faith in him. I guess my faith has been tested on so many different levels lately, that it was fracturing at every turn.

"You gave him Light, with your *Lux Lucis Tribuo* powers, but rather than banish it and bind him to you, like you did Samson, you instead held onto his Dark. When he died, the Dark disappeared." He looked contemplative, that thoughtful look he gets when he's puzzling something through.

"I also felt connected to him, not like Samson, but as though there was still a line between him and me."

"That would make sense," he said absently. I just thought; it would?

"Yes." He answered my thought. "The Prophecy."

OK. So, I admit I have had trouble understanding my role in the Prophecy from the get-go and I still have not made progress on that one.

"What about the Prophecy?"

"*The Light will capture the Dark and will hold it dear.*" He looked directly at me. "You didn't banish his Dark, because you simply replaced it and held what Dark he had yourself. You held it *dear*. Then when he was brought the final death, the Dark you held *dear*, was simply released and became no more."

Whoa. I knew I was frowning, my brain functioning at top speed. I felt Michel run a finger across my forehead, trying to smooth out the lines that had appeared and then his thumb traced my mouth, which was no doubt in a thin line. I couldn't even begin to process this new turn of events. How many times have I thought I had it all sussed, only for the bloody Prophecy to mean or do something else.

I was just about voice my complete and utter annoyance at the friggin' Prophecy when she returned. Aotea Square went pitch black, no lights, no vision, just a blank nothingness, a complete blackness, that wrapped around us all.

I could feel Michel's hand on my arm as he pulled me against him. She hadn't released any pain yet, she wasn't trying to crush our chests, she was toying with us, letting us know that any second now we would be dead.

Michel's whisper against my ear felt so distant, so far away, but he must have projected his thoughts at the same time as he spoke them, because they reverberated through my head.

Do what you did to Jonathan to her.

I didn't waste any time thinking about it, second guessing Michel's suggestion. If I did, it would be too late, or I would doubt. She is so strong, so powerful. But instead I just gathered my Light, held it as long as I dared and then envisaged touching her skin, placing my hand on her bare arm and set out to banish her Dark.

It was harder than with Jonathan, much harder than with Samson. It took longer and the Dark I chased fought back stronger, but the more I concentrated, the more I felt my Light. And the more I heard Nut singing in my mind.

A sweet musical note of happiness, a long tone that hit just right key. It reverberated through my mind, my body and my soul, like a hundred song birds on a hot summer's night, like the perfect chimes of a thousand church bells ringing through the city, or the sound of a million children laughing, floating on a breeze.

By the time the last note vanished, the square was again awash with light and the Queen of Darkness stood before me.

My breath was caught in my throat. I knew her all right. I had thought she looked like Nut, she did, a little, but not enough to be kin, just a few similarities; long black hair, young perfect china doll skin, big eyes, but not almond shaped pools of gold, just round and blue, bright azure blue. She was beautiful and petite and now completely balanced with Light and Dark.

The first time I had met the Pandora was in Paris at the *Iunctio*'s *Palais*. She had been all Dark, unlike her mate, the Ambrosia, who was awash with Light. I had been surprised at the depth of her Darkness, but the Champion had thought it perfectly normal. I knew differently.

Where there is Light there is always Dark and where there is Dark there is always Light. The Pandora was neither of those.

We stared at each other for a moment, I felt that connection settle between us, but couldn't feel the Dark I had supposedly taken from her to hold dear. If I had, it wasn't affecting me, as though my Light kept it somehow separate. But through that connection I could tell my Light would stay in touch with her, maybe even making sure the Dark didn't seep back in. It was all a bit mind boggling, but a sense of rightness seemed to back up those thoughts. Nut, no doubt. I could only hope, oh and have a little faith.

The Pandora slowly raised her hand and I thought maybe she was about to offer to shake, let's be friends, sorry for trying to kill you, water under the bridge, but within a foot of my body a flash of metal appeared. I felt Michel stiffen, prepared to jump between us, but I have been a vampire hunter for over two years now, and this... being, in front of me, was nothing more than that. A vampire. Not a goddess. A vampire, nothing more.

My stake was in my hand and thrust deep against her chest before her dagger found its mark.

As she burst into dust before me, her Darkness I held *dear* seeping back into the air around us forever lost, my hand still firmly holding the stake where it had come to rest, it all made sense.

I may give them balance, evening out the Light and the Dark within, but they would always have a choice.

To choose good.

Or to choose evil.

The Queen of Darkness, just chose the wrong path.

EPILOGUE

It took a few days to figure it all out and the clean up was a bit of a mess. The last of Pandora's and Jonathan's vampires were dispatched, not all of them given the final death, but after a blast of my *Lux Lucis Tribuo* powers, it was pretty obvious straight away which choice they would make. Those that seemed contrite were sent home, those that tried to kill me, were staked. I make it a fairly firm rule to only stake those vampires who pose a threat to me or mine. Mine includes my vampires, Samson and those of Michel's line, my friends and any of the innocents within my city. If they mean me no harm, then I forgive and forget, and send them on their way.

The thought that I didn't have to make each one a part of my line was more of a relief than I realised it would be. Samson was of course the guinea pig and although a model *child* I really wasn't up to adding to the brood just yet. No doubt, there'd come a time when skin on skin contact during a *Lux Lucis Tribuo* incident couldn't be avoided, but for now, I was just inordinately pleased to blast from afar.

With the Pandora gone, the Light and Dark seemed more aligned throughout the world. There was still a hell of a lot of Dark vampires out there, I could sense them and *seek* them through my *Sanguis Vitam Cupitor* powers, but Nosferatins were on the climb. And those who didn't respond to my *Prohibitum Bibere* powers, could be handled by the local vampire hunter in their city. There would always be Dark vampires, just as there would always be vampire hunters. Of course, many of the Dark ones would still come my way and when they did, I felt confident I could handle them.

I finally felt like I fitted my oversized Prophecy shoes.

Amisi's response to it all was unexpected. She was angry at herself for not having correctly interpreted the Prophecy from the start. But hell, even Nero, the Herald of the Prophecy had got it wrong.

The Light will capture the Dark and will hold it dear.

We had all assumed the Light would just banish the Dark. How were we to know that me being the representative of the Light would actually physically hold the Dark dear? Prophesies are not meant to be literal. I spent a good deal of my time reminding Amisi of that.

Finally, after a couple of weeks of winding down from all the trauma, all of us still remaining on high alert, unable to believe that the battle was over and the good times now reigned, Amisi decided to move out. My God, I didn't know it would be that hard to say goodbye. She was only moving to Wellington, to take on her role as Gregor's Nosferatin, but it wrenched at my heart and left me feeling so very, very sad.

Amisi promised to visit and Michel gave me carte blanche to use his jet when the need arose for a day trip, but still, my Nosferatin sister would be over an hour away by plane and just a voice on the other end of the line.

The times they were a changing.

Summer was in full swing and although *Sensations* was quickly refurbished and remodelled and reopened, Michel was taking a slight back seat. Still keeping abreast of all his businesses, only a small portion at the start of each evening was dedicated to that, the rest of the day to day running was left to Jett.

Poor Jett. He needed to be busy and I think as much as Michel was enjoying monopolising my time, he was also acutely aware of Jett's need to be useful and occupied. I didn't think for a minute that Michel wasn't aware of absolutely everything that went on in his line, but he was grooming Jett, taking him under his wing and at the same time, letting him fly.

Jett was not alone in his loss. We mourned Erika too. Just as I mourned Nero and Bruno and Rick. So many friends lost in the battle, so many souls no longer here. I still didn't know where exactly we would end up after our time on this Earth. The vampires had *Elysium* and Nut waited in the child filled playground in the sky. Nero was with her and I was sure my Dad was too. I hoped my mum, being a human, a Norm, was nearby and could visit, but I really wasn't too certain about the Nosferatu.

Not that I planned on dying any time soon, hell the thought of what would happen to all that Dark that I held so dear once I vanished from this plane, was a little of a concern. But more so for me, was whether Michel would be there waiting when I arrived, or whether in the afterlife, we could no longer be kindred. It worried me. Stupid, really, I should just work with what I've got, but it was a puzzle that rattled around in my head and just wouldn't go away.

I was sitting on our balcony, watching the lights of the ships sailing out of the harbour towards the Hauraki Gulf, when Michel found me. He'd been catching up on his early evening correspondence with Jett and the others in his line. A routine we had established at the start of each night. I'd been reading my father's letter, something I found myself doing more and more.

The folds of the paper were wearing so thin, that I had been forced to reinforce it with tape, before it fell completely apart in my hands. One part in particular had caught my wandering mind's attention this evening. He had written it, as though it was a given, but I couldn't tell if it had in fact been a mistake.

We will be waiting for you in Elysium and we will be proud of whatever you have become.

I had been reading and rereading that sentence in my head when Michel silently sat down next to me on the two seater swing. His strong, warm arm wrapping around my shoulders, his lips brushing over his new mark with a light kiss.

"Why are you thinking of the afterlife, *ma douce?*" he asked quietly, whilst setting the swing slowing going, his feet still firmly on the balcony, mine a few inches short and dangling in the breeze. "The battle has been won."

I snuggled in a little closer to his body, not that it was cold, but because I can and handed him the letter. He read it silently beside me and then folded it carefully and handed it back.

"Perhaps your father is right," he offered, kissing the top of my head. "Perhaps we end up again as one."

He sensed my disbelief, maybe I shook my head slightly at what he had said. I know I wasn't thinking anything coherent, so he couldn't have heard my thoughts, but my emotions were a jumble, it wouldn't have been hard to guess the confusion I was feeling from them.

"Why not?" he asked gently. "We were once of the same ilk. I have never thought too closely on it before. We vampyre have long ago given up all thought of our god." He stopped then, but I knew he had more to say, so I just sat quietly enjoying the swing of the seat, the warmth of his body and the smell of fresh sea breezes and clean cut grass. "Perhaps *Elysium* is where we once again become one. Your father believed it. You have had many unbelievable things happen in your life, why can you not have faith in this?"

It was true, I had come a long way from when I first moved to the city. Hell, vampires were from story books, horror movies screened late at night, the things that go bump in dark, but when I came here, my world changed. I have accepted the undead, I have accepted ghouls and Taniwhas, magic and spells, I have accepted me.

There is Light and there is Dark and there always will be. And I have faith that the Light will prevail and that the Dark will be held dear.

And so, why not have faith in this?

I tucked the letter inside my skirt pocket and took in a deep breath of the clean, night air.

Michel must have known I wasn't going to answer, to voice my acceptance or my faith. I have a stubborn streak, but I don't think that was it, he just knows not to push me, I'll come to my own decisions all in my own time. It probably frustrates him, it's proof positive he can't completely control me. I may be his, but I'll make him work for it.

He chuckled against me and began nuzzling my neck.

"How hard do you want me to work for it, *ma douce?*" he whispered against my skin and followed it up with a wet lick over my pulse.

A beautiful hot shiver ran down my spine and made me moan out loud.

"Harder?" he husked and shifted so he could kiss across my chin and down my neckline. His hands beginning to explore beneath my T-Shirt, so softly, so slowly, so hot against my flesh.

He looked beautiful beside me, the low glow coming from inside the house, blanketing us with light, making his golden cream coloured skin sparkle as though it was lit from within. His dark, dark hair falling over my breasts as he nuzzled and kissed and nipped his way between them. My body arched automatically, inviting him, enticing him further, my own hands moving to run through all that glorious hair. I loved his hair, it was so smooth and shiny and totally addictive. I would cry if he ever cut it.

Without warning he lifted me on to his lap, so I was facing him, my legs either side of his, kneeling above him, but settled against his hard length. I shifted, rubbing myself along the length of him and watched him shut his eyes and throw back his head as a wave of heat washed over him. His face a beautiful mask of bliss. When his eyes opened they were ablaze with violets and amethysts, so dazzling, mesmerizing, so him.

"You have stolen my heart, my body, my soul, *ma douce*. I am yours."

He hadn't talked again of my *Sigillum* since I had offered it before he left for America. Maybe he thought I had changed my mind, maybe he thought I had promised it in the heat of the moment, I couldn't tell, he never said. If that was the case, he was wrong. I had just been waiting for the right moment.

Right here, in the dead of the night, at the home we shared, in the city we both loved, I couldn't think of a better place in time to give it. I didn't hesitate as I felt him stiffen against me, aware no doubt of where my thoughts had gone. I didn't pause with doubt, or indecision, this man was my life, I loved him more than the air I breathed, more than life itself.

I was his, as he was mine.

The Light built blindingly fast inside me, as though it too knew what was about to happen and had been waiting far too long for the moment to arrive. With a knowledge that this was so very right, so very special, but also so very true, I let the Light flow from me, my mouth claiming his in a passionate kiss, letting him feel everything I felt for him. My love, my hunger, my warmth, my respect, everything all at once and then when it met no resistance at his shields, just his welcome acceptance of my mark, my heart burst with a love so strong and pure, and the darkness of the night turned to day, my Light exploding around us and washing us with its warmth.

It took a good few minutes to dissipate. God only knows what the neighbours thought had happened. And then I pulled back to see what mad colourful creation I had designed.

I had expected to see something obvious, like on his face, around his eyes, like Gregor wore, but it wasn't, it was subtle, still visible, but perfectly placed. Michel watched my face for a hint of what I saw, a small smile of intrigue playing on the edges of his lips.

When I started undoing the button of his shirt he laughed a little surprised, no doubt thinking I was about to devour him, not far from the truth, but my actual goal was following where my *Sigillum* went.

The top part of it protruded above the collar of his shirt, up his neck, over his pulse, the point he usually fed from on me. It was colourful and intricate, I was quite certain from what little of it I could see, that it would also be magnificent. As I pulled the shirt back I wasn't disappointed.

A beautiful colourful dancing dragon, the head of which covered his pulse point on his neck, with the dancing body finishing right over his heart. It was large, but only a small portion would be noticeable in his normal attire, but for me, when we were alone and naked, it would shine.

"It's amazing," I said with utter awe.

Michel finally looked down at his bare chest and I heard a slight intake of breath. "What have you done, *ma douce*?" But his face was alight with happiness.

"I think you need to see this," I said slipping off his knees before he could reach for me and taking hold of his hand. In a movement similar to how he had led me to the mirror in his chambers at *Sensa-*

tions to see my new mark, I took him to the nearest mirror in our house, above the fireplace in the lounge.

Turning him away from me so he could look in the mirror, I stepped to the side to catch his expression and held my breath.

"*Mon Dieu, c'est tres beau.*" He looked at it for a moment, his fingers tracing the outline of his dragon, the icon of his family crest. The dragon he had gifted me and now I returned with all my love.

"You are mine, Michel Durand," I said with feeling, as he turned to take me in his arms.

He looked down at me with complete faith. No more questions. No more sadness tingeing the love in his eyes. Just a knowledge that I was right. That this was true. When he spoke it was full of requited love.

"And you are also mine, Lucinda Monk."

And then he kissed me.

MICHEL'S POV

Giver Of Light: Chapter 2

READ ON FOR A SNEAK PEEK AT MICHEL'S VIEW...

My mind is not on the conversation before me. I manage to provide the correct responses when required, but my heart is not in it. My heart is aching. I half-heartedly listen to Erika's report, while I play over this morning's events. Another nightmare. When will they stop?

I had never thought this would continue for so long, but I cannot condemn her for the response. I feel it with her. I have no choice in the matter, we are too connected now for me to switch off that part of *us*. I only wish I could help her through this, to make the dreams, the nightmares, go away.

For a moment there, I think I did help, but she still does not reach for me. She still holds a part of herself back. I crave that last contact. I crave her. I am selfish in this regard. I cannot help it, but I long for her touch, her attention, her care. Anything she can give me I will ravish with delight. Anything at all.

"Michel, are you even listening?" Erika's disgruntled voice interrupts my musings, perhaps I have not been responding as well as I thought. "Did you hear a single word I said?" she demands. She's been very demanding lately, I have been too busy with my own problems to offer my little one comfort and support.

"Yes, I am listening, little one. What has got you so riled tonight?"

"What do you mean? I'm not riled." An automatic female response.

"Erika, I have known you for close to two centuries, I know when you are unhappy." I may not always acknowledge it, but I do care for this petite blonde warrior. I care greatly.

She hesitates, it's almost as though I can see the cogs turning in her head. I smile, amused at her response. When has Erika ever thought before she has spoken before?

"Jett and I are fighting," she offers with a demure flick of her blue eyes.

I don't know what to say. I am no Agony Aunt. I feel a little uncomfortable. Erika is like a sister to me, a little sister I do not see in any way being sexual. The thought of having to discuss her personal life with her makes me cringe.

I man up. "Well... that... ah... is unfortunate."

She puts me out of my misery. "I don't want to talk about it, OK?"

Thank the merciful gods. I nod and pull the piece of paper she has been waving in front of my eyes for the past ten minutes towards me. It's a copy of an email message from one of the American Families. I have been avoiding dealing with this issue, but no time like the present. Erika and I both need a distraction.

"Manuel has taken to placing his demands in writing, it would seem. Why the sudden change of tactics?"

Erika visibly relaxes. Unusual. This is not a topic I would have thought would engender relaxation, but she seems relieved to discuss it. I mentally shrug my shoulders, Erika has never been *usual*.

"He is escalating the battle."

"The battle? I did not know we are at war," I say, intrigued at her choice of words.

She shakes her head. "It is always a battle as far as the Families are concerned. Any correspondence between them is considered a precursor to more."

I consider her words for a moment. "What would Manuel want

other than a piece of my pie?" I ask the question more of myself, but Erika answers.

"You have grown strong, Michel. Something to either covet or fear. Manuel and Tomas fear very little, so what they want is you. Or at the very least, to have you as part of their entourage."

"They are delusional. I will not be *part of* anyone's *entourage*."

"Why not?" she asks, making me pause in my movements to crush the piece of paper before me. "An alliance with an American Family could prove beneficial."

"In what way, Erika? There is nothing in America I desire. I have all I want here."

"You can't tell me that you have grown complacent with life, Michel. You were the one who taught me the more we seek, the more we will enjoy our extended lives. To become complacent is to take the first step towards the final death."

I bristle at her answer. I am not complacent. Merely content. Being happy with what one has achieved cannot be construed as being conceited or unconcerned.

"You misjudge contentment for complacency, little one." I brush her concerns aside.

But she will not drop this. "You have grown tired, Michel. You have lost your charisma and purpose in life. You used to be fun."

The paper gets crushed. Better that than her neck.

Still she forges on like a blind bull in a china shop. The rattle of broken porcelain can be heard in amongst each word.

"What would be so wrong with meeting Manuel? At least opening a dialogue with the American Families."

"I thought you were pleased to be rid of them," I say quietly.

"Oh, I am pleased not be living there, but I'm not naive enough to assume there are no benefits in having a connection to them. They are vast and plentiful, and becoming more and more of a force to be reckoned with in the world. To ignore an opportunity now would be tantamount to political suicide."

That's it, this discussion has gone on long enough. I have been indulging her insolence. She has been out of sorts since returning to my side, I thought a little more length in the leash would enamour her to her new found role in the line. Clearly she has taken too much.

"Perhaps it is time you returned to your duties as my spy." She stiffens in her seat. "I could use an extra pair of eyes and ears in Paris." She pales. Has she forgotten I know her so well? "Alain would happily accept another female in his ranks. You would fit in well."

"Of course," she says hastily, with a crooked smile, "getting into bed with America would cause additional problems. They do like to be top dog and no matter what they say, they would consider themselves superior to you." She cocks her head and looks at me through her long blonde lashes. "You really have become a bit of a grump, Michel." Then laughs.

It takes me a moment to relax, listening to her laughter, one cannot be unaffected. Erika always did have the most infectious laugh. It is almost as though the sun shines when she smiles. To be basking in her attention has caused many a male vampire to fall. I do not think I will fall. I haven't in the nearly two hundred years since I turned her. But, it is good to see her smile. And I reluctantly admit, she is right. I have been... grumpy. My reaction to her suggestions is merely a build up of sleepless nights and overly heightened concern for my kindred. Under normal circumstances, I would banter with Erika much better than I have today.

"My apologies, little one, I fear my dislike of the American Families' bullying tactics has spilled over into my decision making. I will consider his offer." I don't think consideration will make me change my mind, but Erika does not need to know this. I have neglected her lately, I wish to make amends. "In the meantime, why don't we have a drink and you can tell me how you are finding your new home." I begin pouring two glasses of my favourite New Zealand *Pinot Noir*.

She accepts hers and takes a sip, but before she has a chance to divulge her opinion on life in Auckland I feel Lucinda and become instantly distracted by her nearness. She doesn't open a link, purposely leaving me to my business meeting, but her nearness soothes my soul. I relax back in my seat and savour the wine before me, returning my attention to Erika.

"The weather's not too bad," Erika is saying. "And the scenery is nice."

I smile knowingly at her. "Yes, the scenery."

She blushes slightly, it reminds me of Lucinda. On Erika, a blush is striking. On Lucinda it is enticing.

"Well, you have added to the line since I last returned, that was a very pleasant surprise," she adds.

"I'm glad you approve," I tease, taking another sip of wine and enjoying the close proximity of my kindred in the next room. I wonder if she is talking with any of my vampyres. I am tempted to send a thought to Doug to find out, but I do not wish to appear desperate. Only *I* need know of how far gone I actually am.

"How many of the line do you have in Auckland right now, anyway?" she asks, taking another casual sip of her wine.

Lucinda's heart rate has increased. I am distracted again. I cannot get a handle on her emotion, she is shutting me out for some reason. I get an image from Doug, a courtesy. A blonde human chatting my girl up. I am tempted to intervene, my vampyre-within all but snarls in a possessive reaction, but I know Lucinda needs some normality in her life. A human showing some interest in front of my vampyres cannot be of alarm. I quietly acknowledge the bartender's advisement and retreat from his mind. The message will be clear: I am not concerned.

"Are most of them here now?" Erika's question brings me back to the office and the topic of conversation.

I answer without thought. "There are only sixty or so in the country right now."

She nods, seemingly satisfied with my answer.

"Do you feel settled here, little one?"

She looks uncomfortable for a moment, maybe she thinks her answer will displease me.

"I am becoming settled, Michel. I have always felt more settled when closer to you, Master."

I laugh. The intended response, I should think. Erika never calls me *Master* unless she wishes to ruffle my feathers. I laugh a little more.

And then I feel Lucinda leaving.

I immediately stand upright and start rubbing my chest right above my heart.

"Michel?" Erika asks, also standing.

"Lucinda is leaving the building." I haven't even said hello yet.

"A hunt?" Erika offers and I relax slightly. Lucinda could do with a hunt and if my guess is right, Amisi is with her.

I send a thought out to Doug and receive a muffled answer in response. Yes, Amisi is with Lucinda, but I'm not sure whether he believes Lucinda has left the club. Maybe he missed her exit.

I stand still for a moment longer, indecision waging with a need to not intrude. Lucinda has always prided herself on her ability to hunt without assistance. She has Amisi with her, how bad could it be? My chest aches, my hand absently rubs above my heart, my mind is in turmoil.

"Michel, Lucinda is an accomplished Hunter, there is no need to fret."

I glance at Erika, she smiles encouragingly. I force myself to return to my seat. Within a second, Erika has also retaken her own. She takes another sip of wine, but I cannot enjoy the flavour now. All my concentration is on keeping my vampyre-within quiet and not rubbing my chest again.

"You know, I haven't met all of the new vampires that have joined the line," I hear Erika's voice, but the words make little sense. I don't know why I am feeling this, but something is wrong. "It would be nice to throw a party, get them all together. Make sure everyone is introduced to each other."

"Hmm," I reply. "Good idea."

"Shall I organise one? What do you think? Should we make it a theme party? I know Halloween has just passed, but maybe we could make it vampire kitsch. That's always a laugh."

I have no idea what Erika is talking about, but she doesn't seem to want to shut up.

"It would be a good morale booster. I have heard several of the new additions have found it difficult to feel included. I think a party to welcome them wouldn't go astray. What do you think, Michel?"

I think I need to check on what Doug knows. His muffled mind-reply has me concerned. It is not like him to be inaccurate.

I stand up again.

Erika pauses mid drink.

"I'd like to check on the club," I say, in way of answer.

"I can do it, if you like," Erika offers, interrupting my thoughts of concern.

I flick my gaze at her, but I am already half way across the room to the door. I don't have time to argue my intentions with anyone, let alone a recently returned vampyre of my line.

"Come," I say. Sometimes commands make life so much more easier.

As soon as we enter the main clubroom floor I am aware something is not right. I pause at the door to my private area, take in the number of Norms in the bar and then the number of my line. There are several vampyres in the corner over by the bar, being corralled by Doug. He is using force.

But that, although worrisome, is not what makes me pause. Amisi is sitting at the bar. Without Lucinda. A human at her side, his arm around her stiff shoulders. Her stance unfriendly, on guard. A low growl escapes my lips. I send my thoughts out to Lucinda, I attempt to connect with her down our Bond. She is on Queen Street, her mind shut off to me, but the Bond does not comply so easily to her sense of independence. For now, at least, I know she is near.

"Get Amisi away from that human and find out why she has let Lucinda leave on her own," I don't realise I send the request to Erika laced in *Sanguis Vitam*. It was not my intention to command, but my vampyre has risen to the surface. He is ill at ease. In the next instant I am at Doug's side.

"What is going on?" I ask, forcing a level of calm into my voice I do not feel.

Before Doug can answer, Shane manages to send me a look. For a moment I am stunned at the emotion on display: sorrow, fear, regret, shame. I delve into his mind without consideration and what I find makes me stagger back a step. Doug is using his talent to control their thoughts, their communication with me. Not many know Doug has this talent. It is an ace up both our sleeves. But right now, he has prevented my vampyres from communicating with me. I can still read their minds, but it must be initiated by me. I hadn't thought to communicate with anyone other than Doug this evening. I had only conversed telepathically with him, as he can be trusted to a certain degree, to be discreet.

I sift through the memories in the minds of those vampyres being held by Doug and force myself to stay on my feet. In less than a minute I am aware of what has happened. My mind flicks to Doug's and I feel her there. Lucinda has glazed him to believe she is OK and to ensure that none of my line follow her from the premises.

She is not OK. I know this now and I force myself to act, to break free of the grip fear has placed on my body.

I spin and look directly at Erika. I ram into her mind, meeting shield after shield that momentarily stuns me, then in an instant images of what has transpired flash across my eyes. I forget about her mental fortifications and concentrate on what she has uncovered. The human Doug had shown me has forcefully taken Lucinda from my bar.

I let my vampyre float to the surface and roar like a caged tiger. I absently counter-command Doug's mind manipulation over my vampyres. I cannot override Lucinda's glaze, she is too strong even for me, but I can get my vampyre's minds free from my bartender. They will now just have to battle his physical detention only. As I flash across the clubroom floor, stunning the Norms in attendance with my preternatural speed, I send a command to Erika to detain the human, ensure Amisi is safe and tidy up the mess I leave in my wake. She will glaze the Norms, keep my secret from getting out.

Within seconds I am on Queen Street. The Bond tells me Lucinda is still there, I cannot believe my luck. My vampyre urges me on, *faster, faster, faster*. We must get to her before she is harmed. I make it as far as the Town Hall, but then stumble. Lucinda is gone. I struggle to decipher what I am feeling, sensing. Or better said, not feeling, not sensing. I am not feeling her down the Bond connection. I do not sense her at all.

My vampyre threatens to take over completely. He is enraged. But I am Lucinda's kindred, as much as he. I will not let him turn me into a mindless killing machine. She is as much mine to save as his. I pick up speed, I am barely a blur. Not even a flash of colours anymore, I simply wink out of sight with such incredible speed, that to the naked human eye I have disappeared.

I only stop when I reach Lucinda's place of work. Numbly, I bend down and with a shaking hand pick up her Svante sword and dancing dragon necklace. I stare at them for a moment, not fully comprehending what this could mean. The sword disappears at my side with a small smattering of *Sanguis Vitam*. The necklace to my inside jacket pocket, followed by the two silver stakes still lying discarded on the ground. I feel the silver through the thin material of my shirt. It burns slightly, but not as painfully as the wrenching ache in my heart.

I know I have stopped breathing, my heart may ache, but no longer beats. I let my vampyre come closer to the surface, I fear I may falter without him to keep me on course. I lift my head and inhale, trying to decipher the remaining scents. I smell Lucinda and another. I catalogue his scent. I do not recognise it. I follow the scents to the kerb. It is obvious they have driven away in a vehicle. I cannot track a vehicle, but the Bond is still there. I may not be able to sense Lucinda down it, but the Bond will always be there. I let that thought calm me and I set out to follow that unbreakable connection to my kindred.

I will find her. I will rescue her. *She* is *mine*.

I don't know how much time has passed since I left Queen Street. All I know is the hunger in my soul to reach my kindred. I move faster than I have moved for any length of time before. I feel my *Sanguis Vitam* flowing like a life force through me. I have enough to spare, but this is taking its toll. I reach Mount Albert, I know I am getting close. The Bond is stronger than before. I am gaining on her abductors. I will win this race against time.

I force myself to ignore the worry of what they may be doing to her precious body. I will not entertain such thoughts yet. She will be all right. I will save her. She will be in my arms again.

I dodge late night traffic. I weave in and out of unsuspecting vehicles on the road. I take the footpath when a bottle neck appears at the New North Road intersection. I leap across the divide, landing on both feet and running again before even a second has passed. The pound of my feet on the pavement is met with the roar from my vampyre-within. With each step I take I know I am closer to her. I search the vehicles ahead, I try to determine which one she is being held captive in. But none appear any different from the other. The Bond does not co-operate as it should.

As though that thought is a trigger, I feel the Bond slipping from my grasp. Then with a final, resounding crack, it is gone.

I know I am frantic. I feel the wetness of tears on my cheek. The Bond cannot be lost. It is unbreakable. It is fail-safe. It just is. Once a joined kindred Bond is established, it cannot be denied. It may suffer from neglect and maltreatment, if not protected and nurtured and guarded with our hearts. But, it will always exist. Always. Once a Bond has been made, it is for eternity.

I continue on the path I am on, in the hopes of picking up a familiar scent. Of spotting long shining brown hair, hazel eyes, golden cream skin. Of something. *Anything*, that will bring me to my kindred.

No Bond, my vampyre cries in dismay. *No kindred*, he whispers and I growl.

I search and search and search, but it becomes obvious I have lost her. I have no leads. I am roaming blindly. I am desperate. I am a void full of sorrow.

It is some time later that Jett finds me. I have walked every street within a ten kilometre radius. I have even made it as far as the airport, my desperation bringing me to the conclusion I had refused to believe. She is gone. From my mind. From the Bond. Maybe even from the city. The country.

But she will never be gone from my heart.

"Michel," Jett says, his voice soft and laden with concern. "It will be dawn soon."

I continue walking, my *Sanguis Vitam* all but depleted in the search. Jett matches my stride. It can't be hard, I have slowed to human speeds.

"Master," he says, beseechingly. "The sun comes."

I shake my head, but do not answer. What has the sun ever meant to me?

For several minutes we walk in silence, my heart an empty cage, the gnawing hole so big, so large, it threatens to consume me. My vampyre paces within. He is bereft, angry, hungry for blood. I feel nothing but a sense of pure loss.

Gone.

She is gone.

And I didn't protect her.

I stop and fall to my knees, a guttural howl escaping my lips. I recognise Jett's masking, his *Sanguis Vitam* sweeping out to hide us from prying eyes and ears. I let myself go. I give in to the need to release my anguish, my fear, my loss and heartache.

I give in to my vampyre's desire to rage.

Jett lets me, he says nothing, but simply masks me from the world.

I don't know how we make it home, but there are voices around me. Jett's, Erika's, Doug's. I hear my guards being commanded to protect the house. I hear Jett ordering Erika to start investigating the American Families, I don't have the will to decide if he is right or wrong.

Amisi is nearby, she rests a hand on my shoulder. She says something I do not hear. She leaves when I don't answer. Sometime later she returns, but she is not alone. She has a human donor with her. I refuse to feed.

I know I should be stronger. I know I should be doing what I need to do to find Lucinda. But I can't. I just can't. I am in shock. I am numb. I cannot wake from this stupor and yet I know I must. For Lucinda. For us both.

I have failed her. I did not protect my kindred from harm.

Amisi is back. Another donor. Another refusal to feed. She escorts the donor out and I feel... relief. But, it is short lived. The Egyptian returns and kneels before my seat. She takes my hands in her own delicate, bronzed fingers and squeezes, making me lift my gaze to hers.

"You need to feed, Michel."

I just look at her, without answering. Will she take Lucinda's place? Become Auckland's Nosferatin? Will time pass and memories of my kindred, myself, be forgotten? Replaced with only memories of this capable Nosferatin and whomever would replace me as Master of the City. She is a good hunter, Nafrini told me so. But she is not Lucinda.

"Three days," I hear her say. I do not know if she has said something else, I am unsure if I have heard all of her words, but they come to me now. "In three days it will be more than just lack of blood that will weaken you. In three days your window of opportunity will be lost."

I have not heard Amisi talk like this before, something about it intrigues me enough to listen further.

"You are vampyre, Michel Durand. You must survive at all cost."

It is as though her words are spoken from the lips of a goddess. A Light shines around Amisi's head. It is dazzling, captivating, alluring. It is so different from Lucinda's I do not baulk.

"First you must feed," Amisi's goddess voice intones. "Then you must attempt to find her before the first three days of separation have passed." She waits for me to acknowledge I have understood. How can I not? She commands like a goddess. I do not have a goddess, but in this moment I wish my goddess to be her.

I nod in acquiescence.

"Good," she says, her voice still not her own. Then she stands and disappears and the emptiness returns. Only to be replaced by hunger when a donor is brought back in the room.

I blink in surprise. I do not wish to feel hunger, I wish to wallow in my heartache.

Amisi guides the donor to the side of my chair and raises the donor's wrist to my lips.

"Feed," she demands and I do. I bite before I can find the willpower to deny her command.

The first taste makes me choke. It is not Lucinda. This blood is full of life, but not Light. It is not Dark either, it just is not Lucinda's. I have become accustomed to a fine, exclusive wine and Amisi attempts to give me a *house red*.

"Survive at all costs, Michel." It is Amisi's voice I hear, not a goddess, but she is right.

I drink the donor's blood without further pause, lick the wounds closed, thank him for his gift and release him from my glaze. My eyes flick up to Amisi's. She is watching me from the other side of the room. There is no more Light around her head, but for me, she will always shine.

"Thank you," I say simply, she smiles and leaves the room.

Within seconds I have called my most trusted vampyres to me. I am on the phone when they walk in the room. None show surprise on their faces, but I feel it.

I am the Master of this City and my kindred Nosferatin has been stolen from my care.

I will seek vengeance. I will have her back.

"Alain," I say into the mouthpiece of the phone as those present make themselves at home around the room. "Ready your team, this will be your only priority from here on in. I want everything you have on the American Families." I notice Erika stiffen to the side. She's had her chance and she has failed to see this outcome. I fear Jett is right, America is involved. "Who have we got on the ground there?"

"It will take me a few moments to gather what you require, Michel," comes his familiar and calming voice down the line. "I'll have it sent to your phone within the next ten minutes. Anything in particular I should be looking for?"

I take a breath in to fortify my resolve, saying this aloud takes more courage than I anticipated. "They may have my kindred. I want her back."

I don't hear his reply, I don't need to know how he will dedicate himself to the task. He has been by my side for three centuries. His role in Europe is invaluable to me and his abilities to ferret out information unprecedented. I will no longer trust just one source, I will use everything in my power to resolve this issue.

To bring my kindred home.

Three days before the joining will begin to suffer. I pray my heart will stay strong enough to survive. I pray Lucinda will stay strong enough until I reach her.

Three days.

The clock is already ticking.

Printed in Great Britain
by Amazon